Kingmaker
Divided Souls

Praise for the *Kingmaker* series

'It is the most enthralling kind of historical fiction, and the most honest, condescending neither to the past nor to its reader; its mix of the savage and the tender, the wistful and the pragmatic allows full humanity to its characters. The past, here, is imagined with energy, with ferocity, with hunger to engage. Toby Clements' intensive research and comprehensive understanding are absorbed into the flow of a powerful adventure story that fully inhabits the world of the late Middle Ages: its texture, its scents, its taste, its patterns of piety, its bleak acknowledgement of sudden and premature death.' **Hilary Mantel**

'Toby Clements is an exceptionally good writer. His debut was a tour de force. His second novel outdoes that, bringing new depth to his characters, and continuing his vivid, blood-soaked insight into the real, grim, ghastly, and occasionally glorious human cost of the Wars of the Roses. This is history in the raw: powerful, potent stuff, always real, but always gloriously unpredictable. This is a gem of a book, one of my must-reads for this year.' **Manda Scott**

'This is a miserable, vicious world vividly recreated by Clements. Immersive historical fiction at its best.' ***The Times***

'It is Clements' ability to excite both tender emotions and a capacity for bloodthirstiness that has allowed him to achieve what Shakespeare couldn't manage, and spin a consistently enthralling story out of the Wars of the Roses.' ***Daily Telegraph***

'The narrative is quick-paced, direct, and written in the vivid present ... the repression, anger and bloodshed of the Wars of the Roses was itself frequently beyond belief. Clements' pages are aflutter with that conflict's every emotion.' ***Spectator***

'Fans of Tudor history in search of a post-Mantel fix will be intrigued ... Clements' storytelling is evocative and direct.' ***Independent***

'Magnificent. An historical tour de force, revealing Clements to be a novelist every bit as good as Cornwell, Gregory or Iggulden. *Kingmaker: Winter Pilgrims* is the best book I've read this year by some margin.' **Ben Kane**

'Toby Clements captures the grimness, grit and grime of 15th-century life, but with compassion and humanity, as seen through the eyes of common people . . . its period detail is wonderfully accurate as are the set-piece skirmishes and bloodbath at Towton.' *Daily Mail*

'I loved this from the first page, and if you ask me, this is what it's all about. There's an immediacy, an accessibility to Clements' writing that makes the story leap from the page in all its vivid, vibrant glory. In fact this story reads like a film script, which shows that here is a writer who knows his business. Atmosphere, drama, great characters and a brilliantly imagined medieval world . . . Storytelling doesn't get much better than this.' **Giles Kristian**

'If you like books that grip you from the very start, that are fast-paced with fascinating characters, then this is the book for you. Beautifully written, with an exciting plot, this book kept me engaged on every page.' *Historical Novel Review*

Also by Toby Clements

Kingmaker: Winter Pilgrims
Kingmaker: Broken Faith

Kingmaker
DividedSouls

TOBY CLEMENTS

CENTURY

3 5 7 9 10 8 6 4

Century
20 Vauxhall Bridge Road
London SW1V 2SA

Century is part of the Penguin Random House group
of companies whose addresses can be found
at global.penguinrandomhouse.com

Penguin
Random House
UK

Copyright © Toby Clements 2016
Map © Darren Bennett

Toby Clements has asserted his right to be identified as the author
of this Work in accordance with the Copyright,
Designs and Patents Act 1988.

First published by Century in 2016

www.penguin.co.uk

A CIP catalogue record for this book is
available from the British Library.

ISBN 9781780894652 (hardback)
ISBN 9781473535534 (eBook)

Typeset in Fournier MT in India by Thomson Digital Pvt Ltd, Noida, Delhi
Printed and bound in Great Britain by Clays Ltd, St Ives plc

Penguin Random House is committed to a sustainable future
for our business, our readers and our planet. This book is made
from Forest Stewardship Council® certified paper.

MIX
Paper from
responsible sources
FSC® C018179

For Anna Clements, my mum, and a very fine person,
(all three one and the same, btw) with much love, from TC.

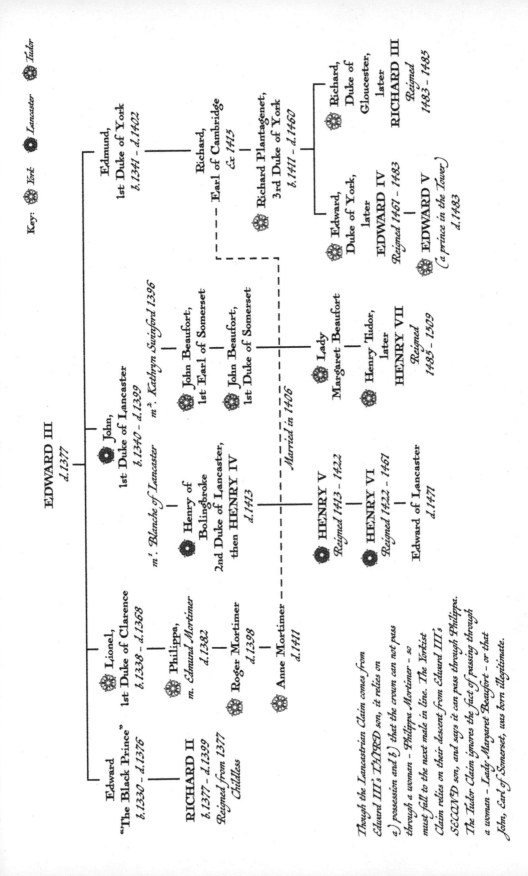

Key: ❁ York   ❁ Lancaster   ❁ Tudor

EDWARD III
d.1377

Lionel,
1st Duke of Clarence
b.1338 – d.1368

Edward
"The Black Prince"
b.1330 – d.1376

❁ Philippa,
m. Edmund Mortimer
d.1382

❁ RICHARD II
b.1377 – d.1399
Reigned from 1377
Childless

❁ Roger Mortimer
d.1398

❁ Anne Mortimer
d.1411

John,
1st Duke of Lancaster
b.1340 – d.1399

m¹. Blanche of Lancaster   m². Kathryn Swinford 1396

❁ Henry of
Bolingbroke
2nd Duke of Lancaster,
then HENRY IV
d.1413

Married in 1406

❁ HENRY V
Reigned 1413 – 1422

❁ HENRY VI
Reigned 1422 – 1461

Edward of Lancaster
d.1471

❁ John Beaufort,
1st Earl of Somerset

❁ John Beaufort,
1st Duke of Somerset

❁ Lady
Margaret Beaufort

❁ Henry Tudor,
later
HENRY VII
Reigned
1485 – 1509

Edmund,
1st Duke of York
b.1341 – d.1402

Richard,
Earl of Cambridge
Ex 1415

❁ Richard Plantagenet,
3rd Duke of York
b.1411 – d.1460

❁ Edward,
Duke of York,
later
EDWARD IV
Reigned 1461 – 1483

❁ EDWARD V
(a prince in the Tower)
d.1483

❁ Richard,
Duke of
Gloucester,
later
RICHARD III
Reigned
1483 – 1485

*Though the Lancastrian Claim comes from
Edward III's THIRD son, it relies on
a) possession and b) that the crown can not pass
through a woman - Philippa Mortimer - so
must fall to the next male in line. The Yorkist
Claim relies on their descent from Edward III's
SECOND son, and says it can pass through Philippa.
The Tudor Claim ignores the fact of passing through
a woman - Lady Margaret Beaufort - or that
John, Earl of Somerset, was born illegitimate.*

Cast of historical figures Easter, 1469

KING EDWARD IV:

The victor of the battle of Towton, crowned king in 1461, been on throne for eight years, but yet to achieve real peace or fulfil his promises.

GEORGE, DUKE OF CLARENCE:

King Edward's younger brother, willingly used as a pawn by those seeking an alternative king.

RICHARD, DUKE OF GLOUCESTER:

King Edward's youngest brother. As staunch, loyal and honest as the day is long – for the moment.

RICHARD NEVILLE, EARL OF WARWICK:

Architect of the first Yorkist victory, later known as the Kingmaker, now not happy with his lot and happy to make use of Duke of Clarence to unseat his former protégé, the King.

WILLIAM HERBERT, EARL OF PEMBROKE:

Chief beneficiary of the King's policy in Wales. Fiery-tempered. Much disliked by the Earl of Warwick.

EARL OF DEVON:

Another of the King's favourites.

EARL OF NORTHUMBERLAND:

Younger brother of the Earl of Warwick, used to be Lord Montagu, promoted for services to the House of York. Strangely inactive in 1469.

WILLIAM HASTINGS:

Ennobled after Towton and still King Edward's chamberlain and procurer, now with a substantial power base of his own.

BARON WILLOUGHBY:

Minor lord, chancer who comes out in favour of the Earl of Warwick, the owner of Tattershall castle.

EARL RIVERS:

The Queen's father, of whom the King was fond, but the Earl of Warwick less so.

JOHN WOODVILLE:

The Queen's brother, again liked by King Edward, and disliked by the Earl of Warwick.

ROBIN OF REDESDALE:

Mysterious figure put up, perhaps, by the Earl of Warwick to press King Edward into yielding to his – Warwick's – demands. He was almost too successful, which led to King Edward's capture.

GEORGE NEVILLE:

Another of the Earl of Warwick's brothers, who was Archbishop of York and Chancellor of England, and was responsible for capturing King Edward at Olney.

More or less everyone else in *Divided Souls* is fictitious and not intended, with the exception perhaps of John Stumps, to represent anyone.

Kingmaker
Divided Souls

Prologue

In July of the year 1465 – scarce twelvemonth after the great castle at Bamburgh had fallen to his Yorkist enemies – King Henry VI was captured hiding in some woods in Yorkshire and taken to the Tower in London, and with this it was widely supposed that any remaining hopes left to the House of Lancaster were lost forever.

But in the moment of his triumph, the Yorkist King Edward IV revealed within himself a simple, fatal, human flaw: a weakness for a pretty face. For in the very same year, on his way north to see for himself the disposition of his people, he met and married – in strained and secretive circumstances – a woman named Elizabeth Grey, a commoner, a mother of two, and the widow of a knight who had been killed in service to the old King.

It was not only that with this marriage King Edward had undone years of diplomatic negotiation conducted with the French King on his behalf by his chief ally, the Earl of Warwick – to whom many believed he owed his throne in the first instance – it was that this Elizabeth, née Woodville, was from a large family of ambitious siblings, and their need for posts at court, and for suitable marriage partners, would bring them – and their new brother-in-law, King Edward – into conflict with the self-same Earl of Warwick, and the high ambitions he held for his own dynasty.

And so now, four years later, while to one another's faces King Edward and the Earl are all smiles, rumours abound that their household men speak a different kind of language, and no man comes to court alone or unarmed. Letters have flown to the arch-meddlers from overseas, the King of France and the Duke of Burgundy, to advise them that the sun no longer shines on the House of York quite as brightly as once it did, and that conversely the prospects for the House of Lancaster are not so occluded as had seemed, and that there might, indeed, after all, be a chance for King Henry and his strong-willed queen, who waits, plotting, across the sea in France . . .

PART ONE

After Easter, 1469

1

In the week after Easter, in the middle of a spell of unseasonably mild weather, Thomas Everingham, John Stump and Jack Bradford began building a chimney in the hall of Sir John Fakenham's property at Marton, in the County of Lincoln. They made it with blocks of pale stone that Sir John had bought the year before from a quarryman in Ancaster, and it took them a week to build, from hearth to cap, complete with a cross of St Andrew that Thomas carved into the chimney's breast as a hex against witches flying down its flue, and in all that time, it did not rain once.

'You see?' Jack said. 'Told you we were blessed.'

But in the week that followed, Sir John Fakenham took to his bed, and in the week after that, he died, and so they came to rue his words.

'By Our Lady, you are a bloody fool, Jack,' John Stump told him.

Sir John gave up his soul as he would have wished, though, as they all might wish: lying in his own bed, a lit taper in his hands to guide his soul from body, a whispering priest at his head. He had his wife on one side, his friends on the other and by his feet, and a newly given Talbot puppy, which was, until the moment of his master's passing, happy with a length of deer horn.

The dog stopped its gnawing when Sir John went and it started to howl, and so they chucked it out of the room, and then down the steps, and the rest of the household came up and stood around the bed like a curtain of living flesh to shield the old man's body from the fenland draughts, and they remained like that all night, praying for his soul with tears in their eyes; and at his funeral, a few days later, the church bell tolled from dawn to dusk, and so many candles were lit within that when it was over the priest had to remove the frames of the windows to let the smell of tallow clear.

'Well,' John Stump says on the way back from the church. 'That's that. We'd best gather our things and be on our way.'

There is a moment of puzzled silence, broken only by the sound of the bell still tolling in the church tower behind and their steps on the damp, dark earth of the track.

'What do you mean?' Thomas asks.

'Well, we can't stay here, can we?' John says, gesturing with his half-arm at the fields around. 'Not now Sir John's gone. Isabella'll need a new husband, won't she? Someone to keep her. Someone who'll not want us around.'

'She might not need to marry,' Jack says. 'Her sons. They might stay?'

John Stump spits.

'No,' he says. 'They'll not linger. They're here to fix a price for the place – you'll see. And anyway, even if they did, would you want their goodlordship? Would you *trust* it?'

Jack is hesitant.

'Well—' he begins.

'No,' John interrupts. 'So there we are. We've had our span. Five years. It's all a man can hope for before some twat with a title comes to send him where he'd never thought of going for hisself.'

Thomas and Jack exchange a glance. John Stump has become a brackish little man, as if he no longer enjoys the extra span of years bought at the expense of his left arm, but today, with all this going on, his words send a creeping chill through Thomas, because perhaps, after all, he is right? Perhaps five years' peace is all a man may reasonably expect?

They walk on in ruminative silence and Thomas cannot help but look up and around at what John says they will soon be forced to leave: at the furlongs alive with a pale green furze of pea seedlings; at the stock ponds in which fat brown trout stir slow-spreading circles; at the sties wherein banks of ruddy-backed piglets suckle at their mothers' teats; at the two pairs of nut-brown oxen bending their powerful necks to graze the lush winter grass underhoof; and then beyond, to the solid bulk of the hall ahead, with its grey stone chimney now letting slip a scarf of pale smoke into the sky, like some lord's battle banner.

And beyond that, nestling among the poplars, is his own house, made over these last three years, piece by piece, gathered and shaped to fit together, the floor packed hard with clay and sour milk, a stone hearth in the middle of the room, stools he's bodged to stand around it, a board he split himself and on which he eats with his wife and his child.

And with every step Thomas feels the thick slice of cured leather under his sole, the soft cling of the fine-spun russet woollen hose warming his legs, and the snug compass of his felted pourpoint. He is conscious of the heft of his thick jacket with its purse-weighted belt around his waist, and of his worsted cap lined with fine linen, and he thinks of how it was before that, what they were doing, and how they did it, and he knows he will do anything – *anything* – to avoid a return to that.

Eventually Jack breaks the silence with a question.

'What do you mean, send us somewhere we'd have no thought to go ourselves?'

'Up north, I bet. That's where it all starts.'

'What starts?'

'The fighting,' John says, miming the drawing of a bow and the loosing of an arrow as best he can with his half-arm.

'But all that's over,' Thomas tells him. 'King Henry's in the Tower, isn't he? Safe at prayer under lock and key, and Christ above!

Aren't his adherents all dead? We saw most of them killed with our own eyes.'

'There's his son, isn't there?' John counters. 'What about him? He's still alive.'

'But barely,' Thomas says. 'And he's in France with his mother, with no two bits to rub the one against the other.'

John snorts.

'You heard what that old needle merchant said,' he tells them. 'How everyone across the realm is up in arms about something or other, with every lord mustering men and passing out helmets and bills and what have you? Why is that?'

Thomas sighs.

'Christ, I don't know,' he says. 'I thought he was telling stories so you'd pour him more ale. And anyway, even if they are, what of it? What's it to do with us? We've no cause to join them.'

John stops and looks at him.

'What about Edmund Riven?' he asks. 'He's still alive, too, isn't he? And wasn't he the reason you were caught up with the fighting in the first place? To dislodge him and – and his father – from – from that castle? From Cornford?'

Thomas stares at John Stump in silence. He would never have dared mention Edmund Riven's name while Sir John was alive. The name went unsaid, like that of a dead child, never quite forgotten, however bright the day, but never, ever mentioned. Hearing it now, bandied about like this, it makes Thomas's chest lurch, and he looks around as if some refectory rule is being transgressed.

'Don't talk of him, John,' Thomas says. 'There's no profit in thinking about him or Cornford, and besides . . .'

He tails off. Besides what? He does not know, only that he remembers killing Edmund Riven's father and he feels perhaps he has done enough to settle his own score with that family.

'So what then, John?' Jack persists. 'What do you suggest?'

John has obviously been giving this some private thought.

'We should go to France,' he proposes. 'Across the Narrow Sea. We could join the Duke of Burgundy. He has need of bowmen, it's said. Proper English bowmen. Pays a shilling a day. Imagine that.'

Jack laughs.

'John,' he says. 'You can scarcely manage a crossbow.'

'I'm a better shot with one hand than you'll ever be with two,' John tells him.

Thomas interrupts.

'But, John,' he says. 'You want to go to *France?* You want to go to France and *fight?*'

'For a shilling a fucking day? I'd go anywhere and fight any man.'

'Have you forgotten what fighting is like?' Thomas asks. 'By Christ! Look at us!'

He gestures to the side of his head, where his hair has grown white over an old divot caused by some blow that – by the mercy of God – he is unable to recall. He gestures at John Stump's missing arm which Katherine was forced to amputate to prevent the black rot spreading after he was wounded in a fight, and then at Jack's leg, which even now still drags at an angle from an arrow that nearly killed him on Hedgeley Moor.

'You're proud, Thomas,' John says, as if this has nothing to do with it. 'And rightly so. Look at this place. You've made it through your hard work. You've made a life here, a home, but it is not yours, is it? It doesn't belong to you. It belongs to someone else and now they want it back. So it is over, our time here, your time here, and now you – me – him – *her* even – we must all shift for ourselves.'

Thomas shakes his head. He refuses to believe what he is hearing.

'No,' he says, but Jack has turned and is walking on in hard, silent thought, as if he has remembered he has things that need doing, and John is looking at Thomas as if to say 'you'll see', and now Thomas does not want to be with him any more, so he stops to let him follow Jack up the track to the hall, and he turns, and he must shield his eyes against the low spring sun so that he can watch the others come up between the green verges of the track from the church, walking at the pace of the slowest in the party.

First comes Isabella, Sir John's widow, still beautiful despite her milky eyes, her down-softened face made fragile by sorrow, her skin like old paper which has been thinned by the rub of so many thumbs that the sunlight seems almost to pass through it, and when she can finally see him, she smiles to find him waiting there with his dog, a comforting reminder of recent happiness, perhaps, and Thomas stands aside and nods as she passes, and his lurcher seems to dip his head as well, and Isabella smiles at that, too.

He tries to read her expression, to divine from it a crumb of optimism, but there is nothing there. It is too early for her to be thinking of such things. There are no tearstains on her cheeks, and Thomas is reminded that Sir John is — what? The third — fourth — husband she has buried? So perhaps, he thinks, she should be used to it by now? But then again, perhaps it does not work quite like that? Perhaps such sorrows are cumulative, and they build up, over time, like the strokes of a whip?

Next comes her sister, a widow also, though only twice over, of similar build to Isabella — though she walks the earth with heavy, splayed feet — who was sent for when it was obvious there was nothing Katherine could do for Sir John, and he had but little time left in this life. She walks with her two maids; likewise sisters perhaps, with corn-yellow hair under their caps, each as broad as a heifer. Jack says they are from Viking stock, and Thomas believes him.

Behind them come three more girls, distant relations to Isabella. Thomas is not quite sure of their relative positions. They are well-dressed women, he can see that, in silks, and on high pattens, and each is married or betrothed to a husband too busy to be here for Sir John's funeral, but who will come for his Month's Mind, perhaps, especially as it is known the King's Chamberlain is likely to attend, and each woman is trailed by two maids of her own, and as they pass in a group, the ladies study Thomas from under lowered lashes, and he finds himself warming under the examination.

After them come Isabella's personal maids, three girls who work within, including Nettie, who is married to Jack, and who bears her swollen belly before her like the bow of a merchantman's cog. She is a pretty girl, by far the prettiest of the three, and Jack is lucky to have her, Thomas thinks, for she is capable, and quick, with a smile never too far from her eyes and lips, though it is distant today, and her eyes are smudged with tears for the dead man.

Behind them, at a discreet distance, come Isabella's two sons, walking with their eyes fixed on the backsides of the girls in front. They have been keeping themselves apart, these two, both tall, straight-backed, boys really, not yet twenty, dressed in velvets and silks with marten trims, and one of them has small vents cut in the purple broadcloth of his jacket sleeves through which scarlet can be glimpsed. Both have dark curling hair, each cut in a bowl as if they were on campaign in Gascony or some such, but while one has a gauzy beard on his chin, with his cheeks clean-shaven, the other is wholly clean-shaven, showing a cleft in his pink chin. Beard and Non-beard. Both wear swords. Thomas wonders who wears a sword to a funeral. Everyone who can, he supposes.

They ignore Thomas, glance at his dog, and they walk past now with their sleek heads tipped towards one another, talking in low voices, and for a moment it looks as if they are still speculating on the shapes of the girls under their dresses, but then one – Beard – points out the windmill that sits on a rise above the river to the west, built two years previously, and he murmurs something appreciative, and the other grunts something less so. Thomas feels a let-down, and understands then that John is probably right about these two, and that they are not here at their stepfather's funeral for their mother's sake, or to look at serving girls, but for another, more obvious, age-old reason.

11

They are from the real world, these two, Thomas sees, from the world those at Marton Hall have tried to exclude these last years. They are harbingers of harsh reality – like crows or rooks – and he knows John Stump is not out of his wits, as he might have hoped, but that he is probably right, and that all this last five years' peaceful certainty: it is come to an end.

Behind Isabella's sons, though, lingering further back still, come those for whom Thomas is really waiting, and those who might yet have the power to cheer him: his wife, Katherine, in dark blue, with a dark headdress, a red belt around her narrow middle, a purse and her knife sheathed in the same leather. No rosary. She is still thin, but no longer painfully so, and in the last two or three years she has lost that haunted look, and her face, once as sharp as a beak, has softened, and she is, to all eyes, not just his own, a beautiful woman.

She is holding the upstretched hand of a small boy, also in a blue gown of the same material, with russet hose and baggy brown boots that Thomas made himself. He is their son, named John after his godfather, and after Sir John, and also after any number of Johns whom they have met in the years past, but everyone calls him Rufus for the wayward plug of wavy russet hair that crowns his head, its colour inherited from his father, yet somehow enhanced and exaggerated, as vivid as a conker, and so springy it cannot be kept down by his linen cap, however tight they tie the strings under his chin.

Thomas stands watching, saying nothing, just relieved to see them come. They stop for a moment with Rufus distracted by two plump doves bending the slim wands of the hawthorn above his head. He is a solemn little boy at the best of times, preferring the company of his mother rather than his father, and he is more often diverted by the behaviour of birds and animals than by humans, but there are times when he will stop and reach for Thomas as if he needs him in the same way he might a drink, and he will let himself be taken up and placed on his father's shoulders, and this moment is one of them. The boy is still easy enough to lift, being not quite five, and after he has been swung up there and settled, Thomas walks listening to the boy's strained breathing, feeling his delicate little fingers exploring the dent in the side of his father's head.

They all know the story of how Thomas had been hit by something, perhaps on Towton Field, nearly ten years ago now, but no one knows with what.

'Did you cry?' the boy asks again.

And Thomas laughs again.

'A bit,' he admits, though he does not know this for sure, and he feels the boy's hand, slightly sticky, stroke his ear to try to comfort him, and he cannot help but be consoled, and he smiles down at Katherine; but she is looking away, distracted, and he wonders if she has spoken to John Stump. However, she says nothing, and so they carry on up the track behind the others, walking in silence, until Thomas puts his arm out and rests his palm on her shoulder and she comes a little closer and lets out a long sigh.

'It might be all right,' he says.

But she says nothing in reply.

And he thinks, Oh Christ, it isn't going to be all right.

It is the week following St George's Day in the year 1469, the eighth in the reign of King Edward IV.

2

Isabella's sister leaves Marton Hall after the funeral, but her sons stay. Thomas and Katherine and the others wait for them to go, and for things to settle, but they do not. While Isabella remains cloistered with her confessor, the two boys take their horses out every day, and they tramp every inch of the estate, noting things that have been done well, noting things that need be done better, noting things that are yet to be done at all. And they go through everything. Every room, every cupboard, every coffer. They weigh lengths of material in their hands, count cups, bowls, pins, an axe head. They check the horses' tack, the blade of a plough, each chicken.

'Taking an inventory,' John says. 'Totting it up. Noting it down. Then they'll be off to London with an asking price against which to borrow, so they can live like earls till they've pissed it all away.'

But later a wagon arrives with things sent up from London: the boys' hawks and a man to look after them, and a pack of three squat alaunt hounds, with short white coats and drooling jaws strong enough to drag a bear to its death. The two sons seem to love these dogs, however ugly they are to Thomas's eye, and there is a man to look after them, too, who even looks and smells like a bear, and is just as incompetent, and who throws up his fat arms when the hounds run wild and laughs as if they are as harmless as rabbits. The hounds send Thomas's lurcher whimpering away with his tail curled under him, and they remind Katherine of the dogs the steward Eelby kept in the castle at Cornford.

'They'll kill one of us, I know it,' she says.

In the week before Ascension Isabella lets it be known she has made her decision as to their futures. She gathers them all – every man, woman and child who works on the estate, from Thomas down to the boy who collects twigs and mushrooms when they are in season – to the hall first to kneel with her in prayer and then to stand while she steps up on to the raised dais that has been installed for the coming ceremony of Sir John's Month's Mind, and alongside her stand her two boys, dressed more modestly today, and in a voice that rises and shakes with emotion, she breaks the news.

Her intention, she says, is not to take a husband, for how could she allow the blessed memory of Sir John, whom she loved most in all the world – even more, it seems, than her own sons' father – to be dimmed? Nor will she sell or lease the estate, either. She is instead to become an avowess. She will take a solemn vow before the priest and she will withdraw from the world, accepting no man's proposal of marriage, intending to live out the rest of her life in quiet prayer, the life of a nun, though uncloistered, and free to enjoy the comforts of her own estate.

When they hear the news, her household – men and women and even children, who have scant grip on what it might mean – first gasp and then clap with relief and pleasure. Hugs are exchanged. Feet are stamped. Thomas is exalted. He feels relieved of a great weight. He finds tears in his eyes. He thinks life will go on for the foreseeable future much as it has up to now, and he will be able to provide the same roof for Katherine and Rufus that he has for these last five years, and all the stuff that John Stump said, well, he was wrong. Around him the crowd of servants are smiling and nodding at one another, and even the mushroom boy has a girl in russet in his arms.

So Thomas turns to Katherine and Rufus, and he wants to gather each up in his arms and hug them to him and murmur sweet blessed relief, but Rufus is bemused and Katherine says nothing. She does not smile, and her stare is fixed on Isabella and her sons, who flank their mother; and when Thomas turns to look at them, too, he sees each is standing with a smile fixed in place and their dark eyes moving so fast they seem to be glittering, registering the reaction their mother's words have brought, but taking no pleasure in it; in fact, disliking it.

That is when Isabella calls for silence, and admits how pleased she is that everyone is so happy, and then she tells them that her boys – William and Robert – are to live with her and to manage the estate.

And the noise dies down, and the pleasure dissipates like steam vapour.

Isabella tells them that the next day she intends to go on pilgrimage, to Fotheringhay, to give thanks to the Lord on the day of his Ascension. She will take Jack, as a guard, and two of the girls, though not pregnant Nettie, and both her boys, and their servants of the body, and they will be gone a week, perhaps, until it is time to return to Marton to oversee the final preparations for the service for Sir John's Month's Mind.

Afterwards, as the household returns to its work, Thomas has time to say something to Katherine.

'The boys,' he says. 'They will not be too bad? They will – let us go on as before? They are not interested in – in making fences? Draining orchards? Building hovels? You've seen them! With their shoes piked? They are not farmers.'

'No,' she agrees. 'They are not farmers.'

Later that afternoon, while the others are called to help prepare for the pilgrimage, Thomas avoids the company of John Stump, knowing he will only feel the worse for hearing his views on what has happened, and he sits in the small yard of his own house, feeding his lurcher some scrapes of dark meat from the shinbone of a deer that has been hanging since before Sir John died. He is a good dog, the lurcher, dark grey, marked with white here and there about the forepaws, with long hair like soft wire, and, until he sees something to kill, his big round black eyes make him appear eager to oblige, though of course he is not, or not especially, and he is often to be found other than where he should be, but after these incidences, he looks so guilty it is impossible not to laugh at him, and forgive him almost anything.

Thomas is watching his dog absently as it now gnaws on the shinbone and the dog watches him back, an eyebrow raised, apparently perplexed that Thomas does not wish to join him in his feast, when one of Isabella's sons — William, it is, with the beard — comes into the yard, carrying on his fist a great grey goshawk in her decorated leather hood. Thomas has always hated such birds. They are worse than foxes in their appetite for killing things.

Thomas greets him. William ignores him, and looks at Lurcher with his shinbone.

'Your dog has been in the wood again,' he says.

Thomas nods in agreement, though he is unsure if it has anything to do with William where Lurcher has or has not been.

'He has brought down another deer?' William goes on.

'He has, yes, of course,' Thomas says.

'But those are not your deer to hunt.'

Thomas is nonplussed.

'But we've always hunted them,' he says, but now he can see where this is going, and he wishes he were standing up.

'You will no longer,' William says. 'If we find your dog out there, we will set the alaunts on it, and if we see it has brought down anything else we will have the houndsman clip his foreclaws.'

Thomas cannot help but glance down at the dog's white paws that are stretched forward, either side of the bone. Clipping his foreclaws would cripple him.

'You cannot do that,' he says.

'No? And why not? This is our mother's land you are on. We'd have a right to do much more than that.'

'But Isabella—' Thomas starts.

'She is not Isabella to you. She is Lady Fakenham. Sir John Fakenham was out of his wits the way he let you talk to her — to him — like that. He was too lax. Too lax with you. Too lax with everything.'

Thomas cannot think of anything to say to that, and he looks down at Lurcher, who is watching the exchange as if he understands some hope is being dashed. After a moment William nods, satisfied with his work, and turns back to his hawk, still perched there on his gloved fist, whose head turns in short sharp movements, blindly searching for something. Weight gathers in William's lips, as if he is about to kiss the bird, but he does not.

'We are not unreasonable men,' William says. 'We only wish to see things done properly. With regard to – to proper ways.'

When he has gone, Thomas rubs Lurcher's bony skull and wonders how any of them will bear it.

When the family leave on their pilgrimage, those remaining at the hall form two distinct factions, and they turn away from one another, and both sides know this is how it will be from now on. The houndsman – Borthwick – brings his alaunts into the hall in the evenings, and Thomas's terrified lurcher presses himself against Thomas's legs, his black eyes huge and round and glistening and his shaggy grey ribs quivering. The alaunts lie watching everything through their blank pink eyes, panting horribly with tongues like raw meat, and there is something demonic about their stupidity.

'It will all be over when Isabella returns,' Thomas tells Katherine the next morning as they sit together in the yard, washing Rufus by the well.

'One way or the other,' she agrees.

The next morning Borthwick makes some remark to Nettie, or offers her something that is thought inappropriate, and, since Jack is away, it is John Stump whom Thomas must stop trying to kill the man. Borthwick laughs as if he is used to such threats, and Thomas can easily imagine Borthwick killing John with the dagger he carries in his belt, or the one he's probably got hidden elsewhere on his person. Nettie weeps for the rest of the day, her hand splayed over her belly, and will not tell them what was said, but from then on Borthwick – whom Sir John would never have allowed on to his lands, let alone sleep in his hall – makes a curious slopping sound with his tongue whenever he looks at her.

'Make that noise once more,' Katherine tells him, 'and I will gut you myself, from bollocks to chops.'

Borthwick laughs again.

'A chit of a thing,' he says, waving his fat, dirty little fingers.

Oh Christ, you fool, Thomas thinks, because he knows she means it.

Nothing happens until the next evening, at the time that Sir John used to call the balance of the day, when the bell has sounded compline, but it is not time to cover the fire, and they are gathered in the hall and the first rush lamp is lit, and in the past Sir John might have called for a song, and laughed when it was not forthcoming, and then there would have been ale or wine, and a game of chess until another lamp needed to be lit, and it would be if Sir John was winning, but not if he was not, and then there would have been some discussion of the outside world, or perhaps a story from his days in captivity in France. But now there is no Sir John, and Borthwick is sprawled in the settle where Sir John used to sit in his last days, and his legs are spread, his codpiece rising greasy and grotesque, and those hounds of his lie scattered around like pale barrels of fat and fur, looking around the room so dimwittedly that Thomas has come to hate them. Lurcher is pressed to his ankles, as is now become usual, paws either side of his lowered head; he is staring up, frowning slightly, his black eyes, each lit by a single white fleck, fathomless in the gloom.

Katherine sits across from Thomas, stiff on a stool with Rufus sitting beside her, in her shadow, away from the dogs, two corn dolls in his hands. He is whispering something, a game, and is seemingly content, but Katherine is unsettled, on edge, and Thomas supposes she likes what has happened here even less than any of them, because this is the only home she has ever known. Yet there must be

19

something else bothering her, for she is the very picture of frozen watchfulness.

Thomas wonders what they can possibly do. If they cannot live here, then where? He thinks about his brother's farm, in the hills to the west of Sheffield. Could they live there with his brother's widow? He has not thought of her for five years, since he heard his brother had died, and he can only hope that she has not thought of him for the same, since her thoughts . . . well, they are probably not Christian. And Jack, of course, would never be permitted back, for the last time he was there he sent an arrow through the daub and killed Thomas's nephew. Unintended – he was aiming at Thomas at the time – but nonetheless.

What about Katherine's family? Where are they? He tries to imagine who they might be, to have sent their daughter away as a four- or five-year-old into a priory such as St Mary's at Haverhurst. No ordinary family would now do such a thing, surely? And that dream Katherine sometimes has – or once had, at any rate – of a fire in a stone chimneybreast suggests something more besides. She will not return to the priory, of course, for reasons even one of Borthwick's hounds might understand, but even if she did, to ask that Prioress about her family, there is not a chance the Prioress would oblige her.

Nettie comes back in from the buttery, drying her hands on her apron, and Thomas sees Borthwick has been waiting for just this; Nettie stops a moment as if she expected no one to be in the room, and she makes the mistake of looking over at him, and he makes that sound again, the sucking noise.

Thomas knows exactly what will happen next.

He is right. Katherine surges to her feet, her shadow flaring across the beams of the ceiling. Borthwick sees her coming. He flings his cup aside and rises to meet her, pulling his great meaty fist back to punch her, but before he can, Thomas stands, and Borthwick, his fist drawn back, hesitates, and his gaze flicks to Thomas just as Thomas sees Katherine has drawn her blade from her waist.

'No!' Thomas shouts.

But she throws herself at Borthwick and he falls back into the settle, elbow cocked, and she presses the blade against his chins and she hisses something in his face. Instantly the alaunt hounds are up, their claws scuffling in the rushes, and they are shoulder to shoulder, deep growls rumbling in their throats, fat ridges of fur stiff on their backs, great yellow teeth bared.

No one moves. Katherine holds the blade at the greasy baffles of Borthwick's chins, but she's heard the dogs and now it is her turn to hesitate, and at this Borthwick swallows, his face creases into a knowing smile and Katherine becomes unsure. Her blade, dull in the orange light, presses less hard.

'Call your dogs off,' she tells him.

But Borthwick's leering gaze slides from her and across to Thomas.

'Call *your* bitch off,' Borthwick tells him.

And then he stiffens as Katherine's knife dimples the fatty swags of his chins.

'Katherine,' Thomas cautions. He still thinks this can end without bloodshed. He holds out his hand and takes a step. And then there is a quick change in the pitch of the dogs' growls, and he knows he cannot do it, and that this is the moment, brief as a heartbeat, before the dogs attack.

But now Lurcher is on his feet. He barks sharply at the three hounds, and they are on him in the instant. One of them has Lurcher's muzzle between his jaws before Lurcher can pull back. Another sinks a bite into his shoulder, to bring him down that way, while the third attacks his hindquarters.

There is nothing Thomas can do unless he is to kill all three hounds.

So he draws his own knife and slashes at the nearest one. His blade tugs through the flaps of loose skin and the thick pelt, and he is disgusted by it, by the warmth of the blood over his wrists, but the dog dies with a choking, splashy yelp. John Stump is in quickly, too, with his knife, cutting at the third dog, but the second is crushing Lurcher's pointed muzzle in those powerful jaws and the noise is hideous and Lurcher's whines are piteous enough to stir stone. Thomas stabs and stabs at the broad-faced alaunt, but it will not let go, and he kicks at it until his foot is half-broken, but the dog seems only to intensify its grip in its death throes.

And now Borthwick has shoved Katherine aside, sending her staggering with a blow, and he is coming at Thomas with his own knife drawn and it is hard to see any other way that this will end other than one of them lying dead.

Thomas catches Borthwick's wrist. Borthwick may have used a bow in the past, but not recently, and he has no strength in his arms compared to Thomas, who can still bend a bow to loose a heavy arrow over three hundred paces, and Thomas turns the man's knife away with his right hand and punches him in the throat with his left fist. Borthwick's knife goes spinning and his legs give out and his stocky body crashes to the floor among the toppled stools and the bodies and blood of the dead and dying dogs.

And now Rufus, who has been too shocked to move, begins to shriek.

Katherine drags herself up from the floor and over to him. A bruise is forming on her cheek and her hands are covered in soot and blood, and seeing her Rufus screams all the louder, but she pushes his hands away and gathers his small body to hers; she buries his head against her breast and hurries him outside into the darkness away from the sight of the blood and the three dead alaunts and Lurcher's whimpering death throes.

When it is over they stand looking at one another, Thomas and John Stump.

'Christ,' Thomas says. He has blood all over his hands, all over his clothes. It is all over John Stump, too, and the dogs.

Thomas kneels next to Lurcher. The hounds have torn him apart, but he raises his eyes one last time to look up at Thomas, and Thomas reads apology in those eyes, and then he does what he must.

When it is over, and the dog is quiet, John says:

'Christ above, Thomas, what in God's name are we to do now?'

3

Mass for Sir John's Month's Mind falls in the week after Pentecost, and is a solemn, and crowded, affair. By the time the bell has stopped its summons, the little church is crowded beyond overflowing, with men and women pressed shoulder to shoulder against the fresh plastered walls, and there are many more outside. Lord Hastings has come, stopping on his way north with a retinue of over 150 men, all of them carrying polearms, even the archers, including the man who had been there to save Katherine's life after she had been dragged only half-alive from under the rubble of Bamburgh Castle's eastward gatehouse.

'So this is him, eh?' he'd said when he first saw Rufus. 'Reckon the shock of his birth must keep his hair on end like that.'

The man – his name is John Brunt – stood as Rufus's godfather when the boy was born, and today – now – he has brought with him a gift for his godson: a small longbow of butter-yellow yew and a linen bag of twelve tiny arrows with blunts for heads. They are for a boy of ten perhaps and when Rufus is given it, he grounds one end of the bow and holds it at arm's length, and it is nearly twice his height, and he studies it in solemn silence.

'You'll grow into it,' John Brunt supposes.

Thomas thanks him, and Katherine manages a faint, awkward smile. Rufus says nothing. There is silence, with all four standing in a small knot in the thin spring sunshine, and Katherine does not know what to say.

After a while John Brunt says: 'Doesn't say much, does he?'

Thomas shakes his head and mumbles some vague apology.

Rufus has not spoken since the night those dogs were killed. When it had happened Katherine had taken him in her arms and bundled him out of the hall into the dark, towards their own home, all the while feeling his whole hot little body struggling against her, his palms pushing and his little feet in their leather shoes kicking at her. He had been rigid with terror and his limbs did not soften until long after she lit a second rush lamp from the dot of the first's dying ember, when finally his little bones melted with fatigue, and he allowed her to hold him, and was still. But he would not sleep. He lay awake, staring at her wide-eyed in the rush's dim light, his sombre gaze never leaving her, not for an instant.

'All is well, Rufus,' she murmured. 'Look. There is nothing here. Nothing to fear.'

But as she spoke, she could feel tears well in her eyes, and she knew that she had brought the violence with her, that she was to blame.

And when at last Thomas came, smelling of blood and ash and turned earth, the boy whimpered and pushed her away again, and since then he has said not one word, only watched them both with eyes that are almost violet in colour, smudged and ringed with exhaustion, and every time she meets his gaze, she feels herself falling.

When Rufus was born, in a welter of blood in a tent beyond the walls of Bamburgh Castle, it turned out he was the second in a pair of twins. The midwife whom Thomas and Jack had found among the camp followers had come with honey and rose water, and other unguents that Sir John Fakenham paid for, and she had delivered the first of the twins – a girl – stillborn, and they had thought that was that, and miserable tears were shed, but Katherine continued bleeding after the birth, and when the midwife tried to staunch the flow, she discovered there was another child within.

This was Rufus, who had been born moments later, very slack, very small, and there was a gasp of laughter when they saw how red his hair was. He was given no chance of life, of course, and nor was Katherine, and because the priest was there already, the boy was swiftly baptised with John Brunt standing as godfather, and then when he was still alive that evening, a wet nurse was found who was not a prostitute and who would take the red-haired child to her, and so while Katherine lay more dead than alive on Sir John's sheepskins, with Matthew Mayhew spoon-feeding her strong-tasting liquids, Rufus had suckled on the girl's breast and together, miraculously, at the end of that first week, they were both still alive.

When eventually they had brought her Rufus, she too was shocked to see the red hair poking from around his linens. He had filled out a little by then, and was pink, and full, and loosely swaddled. They'd placed him on her, and she'd held her breath, so anxious and afraid, but then he'd wriggled, and she'd grabbed him in case he fell, and then she'd kept her hands around him, expecting she knew not what, and had looked down at him, and then he'd opened those dark violet eyes and for a long moment they'd gazed at one another, and she'd felt something give in her, something soften and subside, and she'd felt her limbs glow and then melt and she'd thought this was how it would be forever. Rufus had seemed to burrow into her, to nestle, not just physically but mentally, spiritually, and she'd looked up at them, at Thomas, at Mayhew, and at the midwife and the wet nurse standing there, looming over her, and she'd been unable to stop the tears that broke from within her without restraint, as if from a spring, and she had felt her chin wobbling, and her mouth falling open, and for a long while she was physically helpless with love for this parcel of hot, odd-smelling, linen-wrapped flesh that was her son.

So now she holds him tight, while Thomas thanks John Brunt on Rufus's behalf again, and John Brunt looks from Thomas to Katherine and then back to Rufus. He senses something is awry and so does not box the boy's ears, as he ordinarily might, for his lack of manners.

'Well,' he says awkwardly, and he moves to pat Rufus on the head with a meaty palm, but Rufus cowers and his eyes have become wide again and Katherine bends to him and gathers him to her, and she murmurs vaguely soothing words to the boy while Thomas takes John Brunt by the arm and turns him, and leads him away, mumbling more apology, saying something in praise of the bow, and Katherine is left with Rufus and his bow and his glistening eyes and she feels bilious with guilt.

After the ceremony for Sir John's Month's Mind, there is to be a meal served in the hall. Forty are to sit, and be served on boards hired from Lincoln. There will be cinnamon soup, and then roasted lamb, duckling and spring chickens all served on one dish. Then there is to be crane and peacock roasted in a pepper sauce, then crayfish in a jelly of pounded eel, followed by a sweet pudding of ground almonds, eggs and milk.

Lord Hastings sits on the raised table, and next to him Isabella, and on either side one of her sons. Neither Katherine nor Thomas is invited to sit. They lost that opportunity the night Thomas killed Isabella's sons' hounds. But they are invited within to stand and watch the meal being eaten. And so they do, with Rufus puzzled between, watching in silence while the cloths (hired) are laid by the stewards (hired) and the bread is cut by two young men of Lord Hastings's household, and the dishes (hired) are brought in by more servants (also hired) and laid out on the boards among Sir John's two prized salt cellars and hired goblets and the beeswax candles that are lit though it is bright daylight without, and a steward passes out spoons, and while two of Isabella's nephews who have been hurriedly taught how to carve set to on the roasted meats, Isabella, in midnight velvets, watches nervously, hopefully, while her sons are tetchy and impatient, trying to make it clear to all, and especially King Edward's Chamberlain, that they are used to better things than this.

Lord Hastings meanwhile, sits and watches neutrally, leaning back to let the servants do their work, and it is as if he has no opinion on the proceedings one way or the other, and is only grateful to be fed.

He is modestly dressed, in a dark coat, with blue hose and moderately piked shoes, and though his hat is of damask, or some other expensive cloth, it is restrained enough in design, and he wears only three rings on his fingers, and he does not seem to have changed very much since Katherine last saw him after the siege of Bamburgh Castle. He is a little better padded, she supposes, and there is a hint of grey at the temples, but he remains bright-eyed, and his gaze roves the room, settling on such pretty faces as there are, and of course he looks at her, and he flits past; then he stops, and returns, and stares, and she can see his mind at work. It takes him a moment to recognise her, but even then, it is not absolutely clear exactly whom he thinks he is looking at.

Is it Lady Margaret Cornford he thinks he sees? The woman whom he helped in Hereford all those years ago? But she is surely dead, no? In that case it can only be – can only sensibly be – Katherine Everingham, whom he saw briefly, and in very different circumstances, after the fall of Bamburgh nearly five years ago, the wife of Thomas Everingham, a relatively humble archer whom he once employed as a vintenar to lead his archers at Towton, but who has the habit of appearing at opportune moments, and who has, for one reason or another, come to assume a distant, odd, talismanic importance not only to him, but also to King Edward. Or is she someone else? Another of the many women Hastings is rumoured to have – as Jack would say – ploughed?

She watches his gaze flick to those around her, seeking some context and finding Thomas, and now he knows exactly where to place her, and he raises his finger, as if he has just remembered something, and instantly a floppy-haired boy is at his shoulder; Hastings turns to him and the boy bends his head and Hastings whispers something, and after a moment the boy nods and looks up and over at either Thomas or her, she cannot be sure which, and then Hastings is interrupted by a polite question from Isabella and he turns to her and answers and the boy takes a step back and that, for the moment, is that.

The meal passes slowly. Though wine is poured, and the servants are quick and efficient, and though it is understood everyone is gathered to celebrate Sir John's life as one that was well lived, if touched by tragedy, no one is yet in the temper for jollity, and despite the efforts and preparations that have been made, the atmosphere remains tentative, as if all are waiting to see what will happen next.

When Isabella returned from Fotheringhay with her two sons and Jack, Jack had been incredulous.

'You did what?' he asked. 'You *killed* them? You killed those hounds? No! Each one was worth more than you, Thomas, and twice your value, John. By Christ. What will William say? He will have you hanged. Both of you.'

Had Thomas been another man, Isabella's two sons might well have tried to have him hanged, or to have killed him there and then where he stood, but they are not fools. He is a big man, handy with all sorts of tools that might be turned into weapons, and they know he has a pollaxe and a mighty great bow resting on pegs hammered into one of the beams of his house, and so, Katherine supposes, they may count themselves lucky that Isabella has stayed their hands, and they have not been forced to try to exact revenge yet.

But it is a 'yet' and while Thomas has tried to apologise and explain, even to pay some sort of recompense (though he can ill afford it), Isabella has told him he must not seek her sons' company, and she has instructed them not to seek his, and she has said that it will be she, and she alone, with the help of God, who will decide what is to be done, and when it is to be done. She will communicate her decision, she has said, once Sir John's Month's Mind is out of the way.

But for Katherine the truth is obvious. They cannot stay. They must be on their way. She has been salting things away – both literally and metaphorically – for the journey to come, just as she has done in uncertain times past: a joint of pork in a barrel of grey salt, two dozen tenterhooks in a kidskin pouch that will do as a purse, a half-dozen needles, two lengths of still-green oak, a few yards of good thick linen with one rolled edge. A spare shoe. It is pathetic. She knows that. But it is all she can do, for she cannot even begin to imagine *where* this journey will take them.

When the meal is cleared there are wafers sweetened with honey for the guests and jugs of hippocras are brought in and poured and there are three hired men to play a tune that begins mournfully but changes to something more cheerful as it proceeds, and by now cheeks are at last becoming rosy with drink, and the buzz of conversation rises with the noise of the rebec and pipes and a drum that has small cymbals attached so that when it is hit, the air seems to shimmer. The musicians' leader sings a song about St George and then one about the arrival of summer and those standing in the hall start clapping in time, and then stamping, and soon the garlands and greenery they have hung to decorate the room are unsteady with the rhythm, too, and the footfall of the crowd releases the scent of meadowsweet and violets that have been strewn among the rushes.

It is late afternoon when dinner ends. Then the priest says grace and after it they all shuffle out of the hall and emerge blinking into the courtyard in the sunlight to find Hastings's men ready and waiting to take to the road, among them John Brunt, waiting to say goodbye to his godson.

'Why are you travelling with so many men?' Katherine wonders aloud.

They are all mounted, mostly old soldiers in Hastings's colours, with the black bull badge, all well padded and well armed, with steel helmets, bows nocked and arrow bags loosely tied.

'There has been more trouble,' John Brunt says. 'Up north. And hereabouts, too.'

Katherine looks at him.

'What sort of trouble?'

He rolls his eyes, but looks grim.

'Of the old sort,' he says. 'But so far it is all rumours and no one is sure what's true and what's falsely reported. Old King Henry's retainers in Wales are said to be gathering for some fresh assault, and it is said the Earl of Warwick is in Yorkshire, raising his army to come and winkle out King Edward's queen's brother, whom he has come to hate for some slight. So now King Edward does not ride out without a guard of two hundred or more, and Lord Hastings the same.'

'Say that again?' Katherine asks. 'The Earl of Warwick is raising an army against the Queen's *brother*?'

John Brunt cannot help but smile.

'You are as if cloistered up here, aren't you? You hear of nothing.'

'But the Earl of *Warwick*?' Thomas says. 'He is King Edward's right-hand man.'

'He *was* King Edward's right-hand man,' Brunt agrees. 'But not now. They've fallen foul of one another on divers matters. You know what they are like, these gentles. They spend such moments they are not out hunting or practising in the tilt yard squabbling over lands in distant parts of the country, or fighting over who their sons and daughters will marry. The energy they have! It is all the sugar, and the spiced wine. It makes them hot.'

At that moment the floppy-haired boy appears, sent from Lord Hastings. He bears a family resemblance to Hastings, and shares some of his mannerisms, too. He tells Thomas that Hastings would like to have a word with him, were he to have time to spare, before they make their leave. It is as if he has a choice.

Thomas looks to Katherine.

'What does he want, I wonder?' he asks.

Katherine says nothing. She feels a strange creeping warmth spreading through her, a strange sort of thrill, as if something is happening, and she wonders if this is one of those moments she'll look back on and think that was it: the moment after which nothing was ever the same again.

'My wife will come as well,' Thomas says, making up his mind, as if he too recognises the moment, and the boy shrugs. Nettie arrives to take Rufus to see if there is something he might like to eat among the leftovers, and he takes her hand and leaves with a long sombre look over his shoulder, as if trying to fix his mother in his mind's eye, so that he remembers her exactly like this.

Hastings is standing a slight step back from Isabella's two sons, both of whom are talking and languidly gesturing, the feathers in their caps swaying in time. One of the boys is wearing thin chains on his legs to hold the points of his shoes in place, curled halfway up his shin. Hastings has changed back into riding boots, and he cuts a more modest figure, though on his saddle rests a pale fur-lined travelling cloak. All three turn to look at Katherine and Thomas as they approach, each with different expressions.

'My lord,' Thomas says. 'May God give you good day.'

'And you too, Master Everingham.' Hastings smiles. 'You too, Mistress Everingham. It has been some time since we last met!'

It is the first time either has been addressed so respectfully, and by such a man as Lord Hastings; it makes the two brothers – bearded and beardless – flinch, and their suspicions are made worse when Hastings asks them if they will step back and let him have a moment with his old friend and brother-in-arms, with whom he has shared an adventure or two, and his wife, whom he describes as trusty and right well beloved. The two brothers have no option, but remain resenting and watchful.

'Walk with me, Thomas, please, and you too, Mistress Everingham,' Hastings says. 'Lunch was filling, and I do not wish to sit astride a horse with a belly full of meat, however delicious it was on the first time of passing. Please, if you have a moment, show me the estate.'

He paces slowly, a tall man, almost as tall as Thomas, and nearly as broad, though without the archer's heft, and he remains always elegant as he saunters, hands behind back, through the long shadows thrown by the hornbeams, noting with interest the improvements Isabella and Sir John have undertaken to the estate, delighting in the little details: the chimneystack with its straight lines and clean stones; a new hovel in which green ash logs season; Thomas and Katherine's house with its low eaves.

'I have an idea for a home of my own,' Hastings says. 'New built and not of stone, but of brick, such as they use in Flanders.'

'Flanders!' Thomas says.

Katherine wonders what kind of house Hastings has in mind that might in any way resemble their own, built over the last three years by Thomas with help from whoever, with whatever he has found, whenever there has been time.

After that they talk of the weather, and the prospect of the rain that is perhaps to come later that day, and the best road to Doncaster, where Hastings is hoping to spend the night, and Thomas is gruff but helpful while they circle the point. Katherine has forgotten how charming Hastings can be. His face is very mobile and his teeth oddly white: they flash when he smiles; he bends his head as all tall men do when they listen to small women, and his eyes flit with pleasure from one thing to the next. He is immaculately shaved, too, with indoor skin, and he wears a dark velvet collar, emblazoned with a flaming white rose built up in gold and silver thread with a pearl as its heart, fat as a thumbnail. After a while he engineers a moment's awkward silence, then breaks it.

'So, Thomas,' he says. 'As you know I have many more miles of road today, and so I will be brief.'

Thomas grunts his assent.

'Lady Fakenham,' Hastings starts. 'She is in a difficult position. As you must know her sons have been pressing her to have you all turfed off her land, which she says she has resisted out of goodwill towards yourselves, as well as love and loyalty to the memory of Sir John, but since you killed their hounds, those boys have been pressing her harder yet, and want proper justice – as they see it – and so putting you off the land is now the very least of the punishments they are urging, and she feels she cannot further resist their demands.'

The shock is not unexpected, of course, but even so it comes like a punch. Or something more solid: like the swing of one of the oxen's heads perhaps, catching you in the guts while you are trying to place a harness over its neck. Katherine feels a familiar slick of fear, dank and almost odorous, and, despite the sunshine, despite the songs of the linnets and the yellowhammers in the branches and the distant bleat of a newborn lamb in search of its dam, she clutches her cloak and pulls it tight around her, for she is remembering what it is like to be out on the road at dusk, with one shoe, little food, and no prospect of shelter for the nights to come.

Thomas too is aghast: his face pale, his cheekbones somehow sunk, his eyes very round.

'She cannot,' he says, his voice more breath than sound.

Hastings dismisses that objection with a wave, the rough sympathy of someone who has had to endure similar setbacks, and he walks on, down the track towards the church, leaving them to follow. Katherine sees little point in it now, and wonders if their time might be best spent packing up their scant belongings as John Stump has always said they'd have to one day anyway, before making their way wherever it is they might.

Instead, though, they walk on to rejoin Hastings in silence, appearing at each shoulder, not knowing where to start.

'When was the last time I saw you, Thomas?' Hastings asks after a moment, just as if this has anything to do with it.

Thomas has to drag his thoughts back from the dark.

'It was after Bamburgh fell,' he says.

'And before that?'

Thomas turns his mouth down at the edges.

'Towton Field,' he admits.

Hastings nods.

'Yes,' he says. 'You were leading men, then, weren't you?'

Thomas shrugs. He does not give a damn about that now, Katherine can see.

'And didn't that feel good?' Hastings goes on.

Thomas looks at Hastings as if he is insane.

'May God have mercy,' he says. 'No. Had it not been so cold it could have been hell itself.'

Hastings is taken aback.

'Well, it was not precisely a pleasure, Towton Field, I grant,' he says. 'But look, Thomas, that day, we saved the kingdom, didn't we? Do you remember? We were there, and we did what we did, and we saved the kingdom. And we did it – we succeeded – only because of good men, men such as you.'

'I could not do it again,' Thomas says.

Hastings frowns.

'Well,' he says, 'I suppose no one would, if they did not have to. But no one is asking you to do quite that again.'

There is a moment.

'Then what are you asking of us?' Katherine cannot help interjecting.

Hastings turns to her, and smiles.

'You were always sharp, mistress,' he says.

And now she blushes, distracted by not quite knowing how he would know this about her.

'The truth is,' Hastings continues, all falsely confiding now, as if he has been caught out hiding some truth about which he will now be frank. 'The truth is that we – King Edward, that is, is uneasy. You will have heard the rumours. Even here. By Christ, what am I saying? They are not rumours. They are facts. There have been riots. Up north, and in Kent, too. And the west. In Wales. Everywhere, I suppose.

'Just this last year five hundred men turned up outside my lord of Warwick's great fortress in Middleham, accoutred for war and ready to ride down to London to unseat King Edward, if only Warwick would lead them, which by the mercy of God, and for whatever other reasons of his own, he would not do. But he might have, you see? He might have. And then, Christ—'

'But how is it King Edward and the Earl of Warwick are become enemies?' Thomas asks.

Hastings sighs as if at the beginning of a long story, and tells them of King Edward marrying his queen against the Earl of Warwick's wishes.

'Sir John was right pleased to hear King Edward had married an Englishwoman,' Thomas says.

'Yes,' Hastings says vaguely, as if this has nothing to do with it. They are passing the sty where the red rough-backed little piglets are just now squealing and tussling.

'Ha!' Hastings says, pointing at them. 'Look at them! They are just like us! That one: that is the Earl of Warwick. That muddy one is the Earl of Pembroke, and that one – very fine – he is Anthony Woodville, the Queen's brother. Look at him! Sly boots!'

'But what has King Edward's marriage to do with the Earl of Warwick?' Katherine asks.

Hastings turns to her again, and she can see him wondering how much to tell her, how much he needs to explain.

'My lord of Warwick hoped to use King Edward's marriage to seal an alliance with France,' he starts. 'King Edward, however, shares a dislike of France with the mass of his subjects, but did not remind my lord of Warwick of this, and instead of just telling him he was not interested, he played along, at first to keep him quiet, I suppose, and to please him, only then he married Elizabeth, Elizabeth Grey, old John Woodville's daughter, who is now much elevated of course, and he only told Warwick after it was blessed and consummated.'

Why is he telling us this? Katherine wonders. But Hastings goes on.

'Well,' he shrugs. 'It was an unwise thing to do, perhaps. It left Warwick feeling the fool, and he is not a man to enjoy such a sensation, especially before foreign princes, but Edward is Edward, just as Warwick is Warwick. Edward is the King, isn't he? Nothing like the

boy he was when Warwick first took him on. And as for the Queen –
well, you have not met her yet perhaps, but she is no weak-willed
thing either, and it seems to Warwick that she has spent the interven-
ing months working to undermine him at every stage, putting her
people – her brothers, sisters, mother, father – where he should have
his, and though, when all is said and done, all she has been doing is
what anyone would do, the fact remains that her people have sup-
planted his own.'

Katherine sees Hastings is flattering them. Why, though? Why
bother? What can he want from them? What can he want from
Thomas? Surely he is no different from a thousand other men on
whom King Edward's Chamberlain might call?

They are in the village now. The church is on the left, and further
on the butter cross and the bake oven, and gathered around are all the
cruck-built village houses from the eaves of which smoke gently sifts
into the afternoon sky. Birds are loud in the trees, and somewhere a
dog is barking.

'No,' Hastings says, as if they are in some conversation, 'the truth
is that things have not gone smoothly since Bamburgh fell. Back
then – do you remember? – King Edward promised to live on his
own income, and to take back Normandy, and whatever else was ours
in France. As yet of course he has managed neither, and so people are
naturally disappointed. But they have been so quick – too quick – to
show it and now the land is just as lawless as ever it was in the old
King's reign. Worse perhaps, since old King Henry's adherents are
using people's grudges – a silly tax levied by an almshouse in York,
for the love of Jesus – to take to harness and ride as if they mean to
rid the kingdom of its king.'

Hastings is now pretending to be talking more to himself than to
her or Thomas, Katherine sees as they stroll on, and he tells them
about Lord Montagu, Warwick's brother, who has been made the
Earl of Northumberland, and is charged with keeping the peace in
the north, and has so far done so.

'But he is Warwick's brother,' Hastings repeats. 'You understand? And now, with this schism between King Edward and Warwick, which way will he jump? If push comes to shove? He has such power up there that it is not too much to say that the fate of the kingdom turns on him and his decision. Tcha!'

He bangs a frustrated fist on the churchyard gate, and then they enter, and walk between the stones through long green grass. Sir John lies here, in the crypt. They enter the church, where the priest is overseeing the collecting of the candles – beeswax this time, and expensive – and they stop on the worn oxblood tiles before the painting of St Christopher that Sir John commissioned, and came to see most days, even when his eyesight failed him.

All this while Hastings talks, telling them of King Edward's other brother, the Duke of Clarence, until it is too much even for a man with Thomas's patience.

'Is there some way – I cannot imagine how – in which we can help?' he asks.

And Hastings turns from the St Christopher.

'Well,' he says. 'It is more a way in which I might be able to help you.'

They wait.

'Yes,' Hastings goes on. 'I have been gifted a small property, up in Ryedale, to the north of York. Called Senning. A small manor. Not – not unlike this one.'

He gestures in the direction of the unseen hall.

'At least, I believe it is so, though in truth I have never laid eyes on it. It belongs – belonged – to a man named John Appleby, who served Lord Hungerford. After Hexham he was attainted, and so lost all claim to the property. His son – also John Appleby – has been contesting the attainder but this last month was finally confirmed as unsuccessful.'

Hastings looks slightly ashamed of himself.

'And King Edward, in his generosity, has awarded the property to me. I'm told it is well set up, with its own hall, and a mill, and stables.

There is a tanner, a smith, a priest and a brewer. All the essentials. Its demesne is large, mostly upland grazing, and there is some spectacular hunting to be had up there, and last year the reeve – Evans, a Welshman, though why he is there I do not know – sold eight sarplers of best-grade wool at Scarborough for thirty marks apiece.'

Thomas, who knows about these things, murmurs appreciatively.

'Crucially, though,' Hastings continues, 'there is an inn, with horses to hire, run by a tenant of the manor, who pays his rent on time, and it is set on the road that runs from the port of Scarborough in the east, all the way over to the town of Thirsk in the west, and after that: parts beyond.'

There is some significance to this last piece of information that Katherine does not yet understand.

'What are you saying?' Thomas asks.

'I need someone to occupy the place,' Hastings says. 'To keep the buildings sound. Shear the sheep. Collect up and then pay its rents.'

'Us?' Katherine asks.

Hastings eyes her.

'Why not?' he asks.

'Because . . . Because . . .' Thomas begins. But it is clear that he can think of no good reason why not, and Katherine can see the smile blooming to fill his cheeks, irresistibly pulling his mouth up and out. His eyes shine with a hesitant, hopeful pleasure.

Hastings nods once at the St Christopher and then, watched by the priest and his boy, places a coin in a sconce, and turns and leads them back out of the church into the sinking sun.

'What must we do in return?' Katherine asks as they fall into step beside him.

And Hastings arches his eyebrow at her and feigns shock.

'Mistress Everingham! There is no *quid pro quo*. I am a devoted friend of your husband here, who has done me many favours in the past, and when I find him down on his luck, through no fault of his own, and I find I can help, I do. That is all.'

But he is smirking.

'Then why tell us all this about Lord Montagu? About the Duke of Clarence? Is that of any use if we are farming sheep and collecting rents?'

Hastings actually snickers with pleasure.

'You are too sharp, Mistress Everingham!' he says again. 'Too sharp! And that is why you are so perfect for what I have in mind. I have gone on too long, too indiscreetly, about such things as need not concern you, and yet knowing them might help if you were ... if you were prepared to take over this manor and, in addition to the usual duties, if you were to act as my ears and eyes on the land? From this distance it is hard to gauge the temper of the Northern Parts, to know what weight to accord the rumours we hear. If I had someone there, someone whom I could trust to guide me – informally, as it were, someone who was not in the pay of the Earl of Warwick, well ... You can see the help that might be.'

'So we are to be spies?' Katherine asks.

Hastings drops the pretence.

'It is hardly that,' he says. 'Merely keeping an eye out. Setting a boy in the inn to summon you should – should anyone of interest appear. Asking the keeper to ask a few questions of your own device, though none more probing than appropriate. Is that such a hardship, when you consider the alternative?'

He gestures again towards the hall as they approach it, and there ahead are gathered Isabella and her two sons, and even from this distance it is possible to see the unhappy tension in Isabella's face and the satisfaction in those of the two men.

'But what are we to look for?' Thomas asks. 'How will we know if they are of interest, as you say?'

Hastings stops.

'I am interested in any sign,' he says. 'Anything not of the ordinary: men with too much baggage and no business being on the road; or any wagonload of goose feathers being taken north.'

'North?'

Hastings looks discomfited.

'To Lord Montagu,' he says. 'My lord of Warwick's brother. We need to know which way he will go, when next he is tempted by his brother's siren call.'

There is a long pause. It does not sound too difficult, this task, but there is still something else, she thinks, something Hastings is not yet telling them.

'So what do you say?' Hastings asks.

'Well, what can we say?' Thomas says. 'But yes and thank you for this chance?'

Hastings looks at them and smiles. He is a good man after all is said and done, Katherine thinks, and really, Thomas is right: what choice do they have? But still some vague suspicion, some reservation lodges itself in the back of her mind: that is not *all* he wants them to do.

'Well,' Hastings says, 'that will be a weight off Lady Fakenham's mind. And my own, too, of course. I will be in touch. Look for my messenger.'

He shakes Thomas's hand, and he kisses Katherine's cheeks, each one twice, as if she were a kinswoman, and he is just turning away when he stops, and does that thing, just as if he has just thought of something, and Katherine cannot help but arch her own eyebrow, because, of course, just as she thought, he is not quite done yet.

'Ah yes,' he says, as if he has just remembered something. 'There is one other matter.'

41

PART TWO

*After Trinity, Early
Summer, 1469*

4

When they leave Marton, two weeks later, they leave quickly, with hobbled, awkward farewells, and for that first morning they ride mostly in silence, north again, old heads bent, Thomas with his cap pulled low, Katherine with her cloak's hood up around her ears, each wrapped in their own thoughts. At Doncaster, they join up with an anxious merchant from the brine wells at Droitwich who is bringing his blocks of salt up to the herring fishermen on the east coast, but he has only three men with him to act as guard, and Thomas sees they are of the sort that specialise in low-level pushing and shoving, the sort who will run at the first sight of any real trouble, and the salt merchant knows it, too, and so once he is sure of Thomas and Jack, and half-reassured by John, he is pleased to have them travelling alongside.

'It is getting just as bad as it ever was,' he moans. 'So that a man cannot make an honest penny for fear of having it prised from his purse on the way home. And it is not just in the Northern Parts, oh no: the same ungodly strife has taken root everywhere in the land. In every town and village. It is the same everywhere. Everywhere you go. Everywhere you look.'

And he is right. Despite the sunshine and the light breeze at their backs, there is grit in the air. Something is going on, and as they pass through the towns and villages of the Midlands, busy men and women and children are quick to look up from what they are doing to watch them go, and for an instant everything is still and silent, and everyone is assessing everyone else, and wondering which way this will go, and then it is up to Thomas to show they mean no harm; and once reassured, the men and women and children go back to their work, but they remain wary, and Thomas has the sense they know trouble is coming, and they are hurrying to finish whatever it is they're doing, just as they might do under the threat from rainclouds.

They roll northwards with the salt merchant always talking, Jack and John taking turns on the wagon horse, with Nettie and Rufus in the bed of the wagon, wherein they sit on three coffers filled with clothes, dishes, shoes, spoons, bedding, a small block of hard black Castilian soap as a present from Isabella, and a double-wrapped sack of dried peas they will scatter in Senning to get them going. Thomas is pleased to see that as they go, they seem to be going back in season, to spring, when the elm buds are not yet out, and it will not be too late to scatter the peas. Wrapped in oiled cloth are their bows – including Rufus's, and John Stump's crossbow – and the pollaxe, with a bag of its own over that fearsome head, so as not to frighten anyone who sees it passing.

'Cold,' Rufus says.

'It is that,' Nettie agrees.

Nettie has become uncomfortably pregnant and is unhappy to be moving away from Marton Hall and all she has ever known, but Jack has resigned her to it, and she is reassured by Katherine's presence, who she believes will be able to deliver her baby when the time comes. Katherine has not the heart to tell her what happened the last time she tried to deliver a baby.

Jack and John take turns imagining how Senning will be. They have imagined a paradise: a paradise with a beautiful, plump brewster for John, all dimples and dark eyes.

John smirks.

'I am imagining straining laces.'

'I hope for your sake she is not too fussy,' Jack says.

Sometimes Rufus sits alongside them on the wagon, and other times he rides perched on Thomas's saddle. It is not comfortable, but Thomas likes the weight of the boy against him, and Rufus has started talking again, if only in a whisper so far, and so Thomas is pleased to be distracted by Rufus's excitement whenever he sees a windmill with its sails in flight, or when they meet a party of mummers who are accompanied by an obliging juggler.

It never takes long though, for Thomas's thoughts to return – tongue-tip to tooth socket – to the thing that preoccupies him above all else: the ledger. It is back, resurrected in a single word from William Hastings, and at its mention, on the day of Sir John's Month's Mind, Thomas had felt the sweat prickle his forehead and the gorge rise to stop his breathing. Oh Christ, he'd thought, not again. Not still.

The ledger has been interred for four years, bound in oiled cloth, buried – but never forgotten – beneath the hearthstone of his home, almost as if Thomas built the house as a mausoleum for it. It has not been mentioned since it was laid there, though he has sometimes stood over the flames as they have died down at the end of day, with the clay bell of the fire's cover in his hand, and he has stared down at the rough hearthstone as if he could look through it and see the ledger below, with the hole in its pages left by a pollaxe pick, the grubby stitches puncturing its hard leather spine, its stiffened, rough-edged pages crackling with flaking gall-oak ink. He can almost see those names, long lists of men and the towns they'd garrisoned in France, and his eye is drawn to those pages on which a younger version of himself had drawn perfect marginal additions, such as Abraham reaching through the letter O to harvest plump damsons that would have been grapes had he ever seen any growing, with a sickle that would be gold had he ever had the money for gold leaf. Katherine once told him this version of Abraham is modelled on the man who left them the ledger, a man who died long ago, to whom they owe their lives.

Thomas cannot remember any details of this man, but Katherine has told him he was a pardoner who'd saved them from starving or freezing to death on the first day of their apostasy by letting them share his fire in some woods, and then fed them, bought them clothing and took them with him – as Thomas had hoped – to Canterbury, to appeal to the Prior of All their order to prove they were not apostates. She'd told him about the men who murdered the pardoner at sea on the way there, about how they'd thrown him overboard to drown, and then about how their lives were altered forever by the intervention of Sir John Fakenham and his men, who seized the boat and took it – and them – not to Canterbury, but to Calais.

When they'd landed in France, they found all that was left behind on board of the pardoner's possessions was this book, a ledger of names and places, which he'd earlier claimed was worth a fortune to the right men, though he'd never said why it was so valuable, or who these right men might be. It had taken them five years to divine its secret and when they did, they'd crossed themselves and prayed to God, for just knowing this secret was treasonous enough to place a man in mortal danger of an excruciating death; in there, buried among the details of the many and various toings and froings of the English garrisons in France in the 1440s, was a detail to show that in the month his mother conceived him, King Edward's father, Richard, Duke of York, was in a small town called Pontours, in the south-west of France, while she – his mother – was in Rouen, in Normandy, more than two weeks' travel apart. The ledger proves that King Edward is not his father's son, but is a bastard, with no right to the throne of England. Even to consider whether this might be true or not is to commit treason, and Sir John Fakenham had been vivid in his description of the fate of men found guilty of such a crime.

They'd believed they'd hidden it safely. He'd thought he had, but then had come William Hastings, holding up his hand to stay his men and taking Thomas and Katherine back aside one last time to explain an extra errand they might do for him: find this same, goddamned ledger.

'Sir Ralph Grey knew of it,' Hastings had told them. 'Before the axeman got him after the fall of Bamburgh, he told his priest about a bound record that had come into his hands, detailing the movements of the army in France at the time Richard, Duke of York, was Lieutenant over there.'

'That does not sound – valuable?' Katherine had said and Thomas had wondered at her, but then saw it would have looked peculiar not to have even asked. Hastings had, of course, then become deliberately opaque. He did not – *could not* – say what was so important about this book, or why he wanted it, only that he wanted it very badly.

'And where do we even start?' Katherine had asked. 'The road is easy enough to watch, I suppose, but to find a book in a – a whole country? And in a place we do not know?'

'Well, we have at least a scent to follow,' Hastings had said. 'After Bamburgh fell and he was captured, Sir Ralph Grey told his confessor about the record, about its importance, and his priest – being Warwick's man, of course, and careless of his vows – went straight to Warwick with it. When Warwick heard about it, you can imagine: he came running.

'But then Grey told him he had lost the ledger! To begin with I believe Warwick thought Grey was playing for something grander than a mere pardon, but you know what Warwick is like: no one says no to him. So Grey lost his head. Thinking on it now, though, I don't think Grey was playing at all. I think he had, genuinely, lost it, this ledger, otherwise . . . well. Surely, when you're on the block, you know? You give up your secrets, don't you? I know I would.'

He'd stretched his neck out then, as if on the block himself, and mimed creeping his hands forward to signal to the headsman that he was ready for the blow. Then he'd snatched them back.

'That does not seem a very strong scent for us to follow,' Katherine had said.

'Sir Ralph Grey lost the record when Bamburgh fell,' Hastings had gone on. 'So if it still exists, it will have been gathered up by someone who was in the castle at the time, wouldn't it?'

Katherine had agreed.

'But if it is as undistinguished as you say, whoever took it, well, would they not have used it to light fires?'

Hastings had had to admit that was possible.

'But we must be sure,' he'd said. 'We can't leave this to chance.'

'So we must find out who was with Grey when the castle fell?' Katherine had asked.

It had taken all Thomas's strength not to look at her then. He could feel a noose tightening.

'But it was chaos,' he had said.

Hastings had agreed.

'The men within were understandably quick to lay down their arms and slip away,' he'd said, 'but they were mostly the rump of Lords Roos and Hungerford's retinue, weren't they? Men who'd fled the field at Hexham and had made their way back there.'

And then Katherine had barked a short laugh, and Hastings had smirked at her, because she had seen it, seen Hastings's design, and a moment later Thomas had seen it, too.

'And this manor,' he'd begun, 'this Senning – our new home – once belonged to a man who followed Lord Hungerford?'

Hastings had had the decency to look abashed, but he was pleased with the scheme, and he was pleased they had divined it before it needed explaining.

'Why yes it did,' he'd said. 'Yes. Indeed.'

'And is it that he drew his men from the surrounding area?'

'I believe that is the case, yes.'

'And so we would be ideally placed to watch the road for Warwick's messengers, to watch the country for any sign of tumult among the populace, to keep a weather eye on the temper of Lord Montagu, who is now made the Earl of Northumberland, *and* we are to search among them for any sign of this – this record?'

'And pay your rent,' Hastings had added.

And so that was it. It was ingenious, even Katherine had had to admit.

'What should we do if we find this record of yours?' Thomas had asked.

Hastings had paused and then said: 'Nothing. Just send word. Whoever has this record, they must be taken. Completely. Do you understand? As you might a – a dandelion: whole, with no trace of root or seed left behind. We need to know how they came by it, and what they know of it. We need to know everything about them. We need to know everything – and everyone – they know. We need to know everything – and everyone – everyone they know knows, too. Do you see? It is that important.'

The easy manners had dropped away, and Hastings had become more skull than skin, more iron than flesh, and Thomas had seen then how he could have become King Edward's Chamberlain, how he could have fought alongside King Edward at Towton.

But then he had gone on, intending perhaps to reassure them, but in practice doing the exact opposite, making something they thought could hardly have been worse far more so, as he revealed the all-encompassing extent of their bind.

'But you are not setting about this alone,' he had said. 'I have another working for me, a friar who can speak eight languages. He is in France, trying to find out how the ledger came to be stolen after Rouen fell, where it went and which serpentine paths brought it to Grey's attention. He has sent a message to say he is on the trail of a dealer who specialised in – in such things – but who resists discovery just as if he has vanished under the water. But my man is good. He is like a bloodhound, you know? He will winkle him out, and then we shall see.'

Thomas had not been able to help glancing at Katherine then. He'd seen her swallow as she realised what this meant: soon someone would find the pardoner. Soon someone would find them. It was the worst possible news.

Yet Hastings still had one last blow to deliver.

'So don't despair,' he'd gone on. 'If the record is not there, then it is somewhere else; and, as God is my witness, I shall find it before that bastard Warwick makes use of it.'

'What do you mean, "make use of it"?' Katherine had asked, and Hastings had looked caught out again, guiltily laying one more obligation on their shoulders.

'I should have said before,' he'd admitted. 'Warwick already has a man up there. He is asking all sorts of questions, and has a reputation for uncovering what was once covered through the most pitiless means.'

'Pitiless?'

Hastings had shrugged.

'I don't know,' he'd said. 'You hear things, don't you? He is much feared, at any rate.'

Hastings had let out a long, dispirited sigh, and then he'd looked up at the sky. It was bruising over and, despite the visit to the painting of St Christopher, it did not seem he and his party would make it dry-shod to Doncaster.

'So we are agreed?' he'd said.

And they'd nodded, for what else could they do?

And he'd been pleased.

'When can you start out?' he'd asked.

And they'd looked at one another, and then at the vista of Isabella's two sons, waiting with ill-concealed dislike, and Thomas had said: 'Soon?'

And with that, Hastings had climbed up into his saddle and looked down at them and said: 'Good. Soonest is best, for if this record, this ledger, falls into my lord of Warwick's hands, then we will *all* be queuing for the headsman's block come Michaelmas.'

5

'We should have destroyed it when we had the chance,' Thomas tells Katherine and she agrees, again, for this is the fifth or sixth time they have had this conversation since they set out from Marton.

'We should have burned it,' he cannot stop himself going on, 'or thrown it into the sea. Anything.'

'But that would still not save us,' Katherine repeats. 'Once Hastings knows we know what is in it, even what *was* in it, we are dead.'

'We should have told Hastings we had it,' he says, ignoring her. 'Straight away, in all innocence, to show him we had no knowledge of its significance, or admitted that we knew of it, but we'd used it for splints, ignorant of its value.'

'Yes,' Katherine supposes, tiring of this conversation. 'That would have been best.'

'But we can't say anything now, can we? It just—' Thomas stops and blows out through pursed lips. 'By God. It is never easy, is it?'

She laughs dryly.

'You've heard John,' she says, nodding at the cart where he sits with his crossbow across his knees. 'We've had five good years. And we have Rufus. Perhaps that is all the happiness you can expect in one lifetime?'

Thomas can only grunt. Christ, he wonders, is that it?

'Senning will be all we hope for,' he tells her. 'I am sure of it.'

'I remember riding to Cornford with Richard, sharing the same hopes,' she says. She does not need to finish the sentence. He knows how that turned out.

'It will be better this time,' he says. 'You heard Hastings. There will be a house waiting us, with everything we could need. A smith! A carpenter! A brewster! A pea crop to plant! And sheep. And hills,' he said. 'I missed the hills when we were in Marton. It was so flat.'

'Yes,' she says, and that is that.

They part ways with the salt merchant outside York, after which the journey becomes fraught with disaster. The cart breaks a wheel. A horse goes lame. Nettie is plagued with agues and shakes and Katherine says they must stop at a friary, which presents its own problems, since she will not cross the threshold for some misplaced fear of discovery, despite being much changed from the girl who absconded from the Priory at Haverhurst nearly ten years ago. So Jack must present Nettie to the friars, and offer them money to take her into their hospital while the rest of them take rooms in a roadside inn, a rough-made place scarcely a day's walk from York that is overwhelmed with huge but docile dogs. John and Thomas take turns staying up each night with an eye on the contents of the cart they feel every man in the county will want to steal.

When Nettie is deemed recovered enough to travel the friars tell Jack that she is lucky to be alive, and that all through her delirium she called out for a woman named Katherine, and that he would have been better to find this Katherine than to leave his wife with them, especially if he intends to travel along this road, for the next hospital that he will find along the road's length is for the treatment of lepers.

Hearing this Nettie goes into a decline, and they must stay longer.

But now here they are, having ridden past the leper hospital in silence, enjoying warmer, longer days, rolling north again, and having crossed some low hills they are come down on to broad flatlands where the wind is less sharp and the way dotted with numerous monasteries and villages where they are able to ask directions. Few know of Senning exactly. They ride on. Ahead is a crest of dark hills, and above it boil piles of thick white clouds with broad blue bases, and so even if the rooks were not circling above, they would know it is about to rain.

'How much further?' John Stump shouts from the cart again.

They arrive in Senning three hours later in a heavy, blinding downpour loud enough to muffle your hearing, and William Hastings is right: the inn – another White Hart – is well placed on the road, next to a stone bridge under which seethes brown water running off the hillside behind. On the other side of the river a small herd of cows stand steaming, gazing up from under shaggy fringes, watched over by a child in a coat and hood the colour of turned earth. He sits under the scant shelter of a budding apple tree, unmoving.

'Is he dead?' Jack asks, and John calls to him, and the boy raises his head to look at them but not his hand in answer to their wave.

'Cheerful little fucker, isn't he?' John says.

In the yard, the inn's ostler is quick to come, and the place is as Thomas had hoped: the walls whitewashed, the roofs sound and clean-thatched and the floor swept and dry. The ostler's two boys come running bare-footed through the bouncing rain to take the horses for rubbing down and drying off while another draws the cart under cover, and then another man comes in a long coat of oilcloth and a cone of the same material on his head, and he shouts for someone to come and help, and three girls in clean aprons appear at the doorway and make themselves useful while bags are passed to them, and one takes to Rufus, and he to her, and she shows him she has the same coloured hair as he, and Thomas cannot help but smile with the blooming gleamings of delight. They will do well here, he thinks. They will do well. It will be all right.

In the hall there is a well-fed fire warming perhaps twenty souls, who sit on benches around boards, and the smell is familiar and comforting: unwashed bodies, singeing wool, mutton fat, and there is a black and white shepherd's dog curled yet watchful by the fire. The thrum of conversation sinks when Thomas leads his party in, and faces turn his way, but once greetings are exchanged and blessings offered, the noise picks up again and now the innkeeper appears to show them to a long board from which he cheerfully evicts a dozing friar.

'We expected you weeks ago!' he tells them.

'It has been a long old journey,' Thomas admits.

'You are here now,' the man says. 'Come, rest yourselves by the fire.'

He is Campbell: a wizened little man with dark, glossy eyes that never settle and gingerish hair that lies clapped to his narrow head.

Jack laughs.

'Like an otter in a hat.'

They sit for a moment and let the water drip from their clothes on to the rippled flagstones below and Thomas looks at the others in the room, hoping for — what? He does not know. They are merchants, mostly, with their servants and guards; there are two friars, one grey, the other brown, and three pilgrims on their way somewhere — York perhaps? There is no one, as far as he can see, who seems to offer any threat of being anything other than absolutely ordinary. There is no one to question. No one to arouse suspicion.

It is no time before the aproned girls are back — one is very pretty — with jugs of ale, bowls of soup, broad trenchers of rye bread. The ale is sweet and powerful, the bread mostly free of grit, and the soup is thick, salty, and spiced with something, and there are chunks of good fatty pork in it, too.

'God in heaven,' Jack says. 'This is perfect.'

Even John Stump smiles.

'Not bad,' he says. 'Not bad.'

Campbell returns and sits with them a moment, glad to take the weight off his feet.

'You will rest here tonight?' he asks. 'The house has been empty since Candlemas, and needs fettling, I dare say, and warming. You might light a fire tomorrow and air the place.'

Thomas asks about the estate.

'We are two hundred-odd souls,' Campbell tells him. 'And we thank God for his blessings.'

At curfew Campbell leads them with a rush lamp held aloft up the steps to their rooms in the roof where the rafters cut through the space at waist height. The beds are dry, the sheets are clean, and they need only share the space with one other, who is already asleep in a whorl of blankets on his own mattress, and a black cat with a white chin, there to keep the mice at bay, who when Rufus approaches slinks further into her kingdom of shadows where the roof sinks to meet the floor.

Thomas lies next to Rufus and is lulled into a deep sleep by the sound of the rain on the thatch, and at cockcrow the church bell wakes him. He lies for a moment, getting used to the dark, listening to the birdsong now that the rain has stopped, enjoying the warmth of the soft woollen blankets. Rufus lies on his back, mouth open, snoring gently, his nightcap lost. Katherine lies on her side, frowning in her sleep. He lifts his head. Jack and Nettie are beyond, and John too, though he has rolled clear of the blankets, and he is waggling the pink stump of his arm in the air as if to scratch some itch that he'll never reach.

Thomas lies happy for a long moment, consciously not thinking about Isabella's two sons, or about Lurcher, but then, when he is on his feet, tying his points, he thinks: Has someone been through this bag? It seems rummaged, probed. He feels for the purse of coins that Hastings's messenger brought them for the journey and any necessary expenses, and there it is: unstolen.

He supposes it was dark the night before, and so anything might have happened while they found their beds and so on, and he regrets his suspicion.

In the hall there is ale and warm bread, and much movement of men, and banging of doors as they come and go. Thomas and the others reclaim their board and watch as the merchants rouse themselves and their servants, settle their bills and leave with blessings upon Campbell and his girls. When the rush has died down Campbell comes over and tells them that Evans the reeve will meet them at their new house whenever they are ready.

When they leave the inn it is a bright, northern morning, with a pinch in the air and quick-moving clouds overhead. The boy is still there, under his tree, across the rushing river.

'Definitely dead this time,' Jack says.

'He's not the same one as yesterday,' Katherine says. 'That one had a brown coat.'

At Jack's shout, the boy's head swivels to watch them again, and this time he raises his hand in return.

'That's better,' John says.

But Thomas watches him a moment longer. He could almost be a friar at prayer, sitting hunched under his tree, but there is something odd about him, Thomas thinks. No one else sees anything unusual though, so, after a moment, they move on, following the river up towards the grey stub of the church tower, and Thomas forgets the cowherd when they hear the rhythmic tink of the smith at work, and they smell his work's sharp fumes, and they walk up past his yard, and hear the whoof of his bellows, and then they are met by angry geese being driven down the track by a wide-eyed girl with yellow hair, wielding a long switch and shouting cheerful, godless obscenities at her charges. She is mortified to be caught at it. Then there are pigs and goats: some loose, nurdling among the tufts of grass at the wayside; others penned in, devil-eyed, behind hazel hurdles. Underfoot the soil is dark and rich, and everything is verdant and promising, and soon they come to the river's bank where, again, they hear the women before they see them: the smack of the washing beetle, the burble of conversation that flares into a moment's raucous laughter. There are five of them: three in the water, skirts rolled up, thick legs mottled with the water's cold, beetles hefted in powerful arms; two on the bank, one wringing her linen on the trunk of a willow where the bark has been smoothed by generations of women doing exactly that, the other pinning clothes on the spikes of the hawthorns. The conversation ceases as Thomas and the others approach.

Cautious greetings are exchanged.

'Where are your husbands, goodwives?' John asks. His question is understood as being not without motive, and the women laugh and John is reduced to blushing and blustering then one points a hefty arm up and behind, to where the sun shines on many sheep scattered grazing over the hillside's soft undulations. The sight stirs such a pleasant sensation in Thomas that he nearly walks on up through the village, past the house and the church and the furlongs that he has really come to see, just to be up there, on the hills, with them himself.

Jack laughs.

'Look at you,' he says. But he too is beaming with pleasure at all this, their new home, and for a moment Thomas feels like the prophet who led his people from the wilderness into the Promised Land, the New Jerusalem; he turns to Katherine, who walks with Rufus – their son is absorbed in the mallards on the river – and in the cool clear light her skin is pale, and in her blue dress and pale linen headdress she looks ethereal, and for a moment he catches his breath, and he feels he should not be looking at her like this, that to do so is somehow sacrilege, but then she turns on him, and she smiles at him, for him, and the light catches in her eyes and he feels almost dizzy with love for her, dizzy with happiness. He has done it. They have done it. Together.

They walk on, light-stepped, past rows of low, well-thatched, stone-built houses, their yards already a riot of freshening greenery, pale smoke wafting from holes in the eaves. Everywhere are dogs, cats, goats, pigs, children. The village is teeming with life, boisterous and rude, and he can smell it, just as it should be: fresh and dirty and green.

And when they reach the house, it is even better: a copy of Marton Hall but in stone, and there is even, already, a chimney from which now swirls a column of white smoke. Bees flit in the low sun through the shoots in the garden and swallows wheel above. They stand before the house, on the track's side of a low stone wall, and each can see that this place, it exceeds any wild hope.

'We will live here?' Nettie asks, incredulous.

Jack puts an arm around her.

'Our boy will be born here,' he says.

Even John wipes a tear from his eye.

The door – new oak planks – opens and a man as broad as deep emerges, wearing an old russet jacket that reaches down to his knees, and a suspicious look that only vanishes when greetings are exchanged. This is Evans, the reeve. He carries a staff as if of office, they think, and he has much to say as he points out the buttery, the pantry, the cupboards, the storerooms, the fire dogs, the steps up to the two bedrooms where the strings in the bed frames are still taut. He is bemused by their pleasure in all that he shows them, since he has lived with this all his life. Then he takes them out and shows them the outbuildings, the wood stack, the privy, built near the stream.

'Above the village?'

He laughs.

'Better than below it.'

Evans has a small dog that yaps, tied it to a post that marks some boundary.

'You'll want to see the church,' he says, and they do, sort of.

The priest is of the muscular sort, up a ladder, doing something with a delicate hammer to the broad stretch of leaded windowpanes. When he climbs down he proffers a hand as big as a plate, as thick as a trencher of bread, and even Jack winces from his squeeze. When he looks at Katherine, and then at Nettie, he becomes confused, tongue-tied, and he crosses himself twice and mutters something about the Lord above. He dusts himself down and leads them into the church where they kneel and pray, and Thomas takes a moment to look at the mural that portrays Adam and Eve's departure from Eden, with the figures writhing and leaping across the rendered, whitewashed walls, and they seem fresh and almost alive.

Thomas squeezes his eyes shut. He gives thanks to the Lord so heartfelt he feels he may faint.

When it is over the priest waves them on their way, and returns up his ladder.

'Jacob's,' he says with a laugh.

And they walk back down through the village the other way, to find the bake oven, where they buy bread from a girl in a blue dress and bare feet, and then the brewster, where they each buy a mug of ale that is so fresh it tastes of almost nothing, and then they meet an old man who sells them apples with skins as wrinkled as his own that he has overwintered in his loft, and then they walk up the dale, with Rufus on Thomas's shoulders again, up into the high pasture where the wind blows slightly chilly and level and the sheep — brown-faced things with curled horns and dense wool — are wonderfully numerous. They hear the whistles of the shepherds and meet a boy with a crook aiming deadly accurate stones at the trunk of a wind-stunted hawthorn. They sit on a pile of stones and eat and drink and study the village below and Thomas laughs when he thinks of it as his new kingdom.

'Got everything,' John has to admit.

Thomas's eye follows the line of the river, past the hall, through the village and on to the inn on the road. He can see the cowherd's field, and it is only now, from up here, that he sees what was odd about him.

'Where are the cows?' he asks.

And it is true: they are not there now, nor were they this morning. Why is the boy still there?

They come down off the hill, merely puzzled at this stage, and Thomas wonders if he will be there still; and sure enough he is: keeping watch over an empty stretch of pasture.

Thomas and Katherine leave the others at the inn, and they cross the bridge to talk to him. The boy is about ten, squatting there, unmoving as they approach. He clutches his withy with one bare, bony fist, and they see his rough woven coat is sodden, as if he has been out in all weathers for some time, and as they come he hardly glances their way, and it is only when they stand between him and the road that he looks at them properly again.

'Christ,' Thomas says.

His waxy skin is the colour of wet linen, and there is a dark smudge under each dark eye.

'I've not taken my eyes off it,' he blurts before either Thomas or Katherine can say more. 'Not all week. And there's been nothing save that soap merchant what I sent John to tell him about. And now you. And I sent John for that too. And there's been nothing new since. No one new. Honest to God. Nothing. No one has come past. Not a one. I've not taken me eyes off it. Like he said. Not for one blink. Ask my father. He will tell you. Honest, as I swear in God's name.'

Thomas and Katherine exchange a glance. Thomas moves to stand behind the boy: to see what he sees. The boy does not even flinch. He is so tired that if Thomas were to cuff him, he would not bother to fight back. He's watching the road, nothing else, a hundred paces away. He has a good view of it, from the east to the west, possibly three or four miles in either direction.

'Who set you to watch?' Katherine asks.

The boy hesitates, now seeing he has mistaken them for someone else.

'Himself,' the boy says. 'Himself, of course. No one else. Who would it be?'

They look at the boy for a moment. He is so terrified of being seen to disobey 'himself' that he is bending around them to look at the road, so he cannot be accused of not doing so. Whoever himself is, he has instilled a fear as great as that of God into the boy.

'Who is himself?' Katherine asks.

Now the boy does chance another glance up at them. He shakes his head as if to say the name might be bad luck.

'Go on, son,' Thomas says. 'We just want to know. We are not here to hurt you. We'll fetch you bread if you want? Pottage? Some ale?'

The boy's eyes change shape, soften.

'Well?' Thomas asks.

Still he hesitates, but then he lets go of his jacket, lets it fall open, and with his one long, thin bony finger touches the cheek under his right eye, and he murmurs a name neither hears.

'Again?'

'It is Riven,' he whispers. 'Edmund Riven.'

6

Edmund Riven.

It is a name from a nightmare, the very last they wish to hear spoken. Katherine is suddenly cold, and the sun is no longer enough to warm her bones. Next to her, Thomas looks gut-struck and pale. He has removed his cap, and she can see his hair is glossy with sweat. It is like hearing the plague has come.

'Christ,' is all he says. 'Christ.'

They get no more from the boy, and so leave him and struggle back to the inn.

Edmund Riven is here in the north.

'Why?' Thomas keeps repeating. 'Why?'

The inn is busy. Campbell is seeing to a horse merchant who is buying rather than selling and wants to look in the stables, the aproned girls bring bowls and trenchers to a host of merchantmen on their ways here and there. The fire is lit and men are already drinking. Jack sits in the hall at their by now usual board. Jack is teaching Rufus a dice game.

'No, no.' Jack laughs. 'You must *not* tell the truth.' Then he sees their faces. 'What's wrong?'

Thomas takes a long drink of ale before he replies.

'Edmund Riven,' he says. 'He's here.'

There is an intake of breath.

'Here?'

'In the county.'

'Why? Why is he here?' Jack asks.

It is a good question. What is Riven doing here? And why has he set that boy to watch the road?

One of the aproned girls comes with more ale.

They are silent while she pours.

'Very quiet today?' she says.

Katherine asks if she knows Edmund Riven.

The stream of ale wavers, spilling over the mazer's edge. The girl looks around as if they are like to be overheard and then back at Katherine.

'Why do you ask?' she asks, her lips barely moving, her voice hardly audible. She mops the ale with her apron.

'He's an old friend,' Katherine tells her.

The girl's eyes flatten.

'Edmund Riven is a *friend* of yours?'

She makes it sound as if they are companions of the devil.

Just then Campbell comes, looking anxious.

'Mary?' he asks the girl, and she gives them a significant look before she turns to slip away behind the screen to the buttery. Campbell is suspicious.

'Can't have you upsetting my girls,' he says.

'We asked her about Edmund Riven,' Thomas tells him.

Campbell starts and sucks his teeth.

'What about him?'

'Why has he set a boy to watch the road?'

Campbell looks down at Thomas, and Katherine can see it cross his mind to place him as just a big lunk with strong arms but little brain. She has seen men underestimate him like that before. Lucky for Campbell he does not.

'He wants to know who comes. Who goes. Their names. Their business.'

'Why?'

'Why? It is his position, of course,' Campbell says.

Thomas keeps on:

'But *what* is this position?'

'Oh,' he says. 'He tells us he is my lord of Warwick's Bearer of the Dog Whipper's Rod, but that is his joke. He is more a – questioner, perhaps?'

Katherine feels the skin on her cheeks crawl, her hair prickle. She turns to Thomas.

'Riven is in the household of the Earl of Warwick,' she tells him. 'He is *his* man.' Now Thomas sees it too.

'He is Warwick's man?' he blurts. 'The one Hastings was talking about?'

They stare at one another.

Campbell seems surprised at the strength of their reactions.

'Of course he is,' Campbell says. 'As are most in these parts, one way or another, now that Lord Hungerford is dead and his family attainted.'

'Does he know we're here?' she asks.

Campbell opens his mouth, hesitates, and perhaps wishes he had not spoken up, but he's caught, and after a moment he nods.

'You sent someone?' she presses.

'The lad's brother,' he admits, rising on to his toes and lifting his eyebrows in the direction of the unseen cowherd. 'If I hadn't, Riven would've found out anyway, and then blamed the boy and—'

Campbell makes the sound everyone recognises as that of a neck being wrung to breaking point. Can he mean it literally? Surely not. But now Campbell seems ashamed of his betrayal, the dereliction of his duty as a host, and he is becoming nervous, speaking quickly and shifting from foot to foot, because, after all, Thomas and Jack, and even John, they are formidable, and not the sort to anger unnecessarily.

'Can I get you anything else? More ale?' he asks.

Katherine ignores him.

'Will Riven come himself?' she continues, and Campbell sees he cannot wriggle free.

'He may do,' he supposes. 'He is unpredictable, Sir Edmund.'

'How long until he gets here?' Thomas asks. Campbell shrugs, and opens his mouth to speak; but then there is a sudden sharpening in his gaze, as if a thought has occurred to him, and he says something else.

'Look,' he says. 'He may not even be in the county for all I know.'

'But if he is?

'Well, if he is at Middleham, which is where I sent the boy, then – then perhaps the day after the morrow? Yes. It is a day's ride, and so – yes – then. The day *after* the morrow. Ah. And now I can smell your dinner burning.'

He turns and makes for the screen. But Thomas leans forward, catches his arm.

'Are there many men such as Riven out asking questions on the Earl of Warwick's behalf?' he asks.

Campbell thinks for a quick moment and then agrees that this is possible, though he knows of none for sure, and with a sweep of his free arm he indicates the impossibility of certainty in the breadth of the outside world, and then the urgency of saving their dinner.

'What kind of questions does he ask?' Thomas demands.

'Hold fast.' Campbell tries to laugh, his gaze sliding to the hand on his wrist. 'Now you sound just like him.'

'But what kind of questions?' Thomas presses.

'Just – just – questions,' he stammers. 'Who's been where, and why, and so on. Ordinary questions, in the main. Can I go now? Your dinner, it is—?'

He hopes he is done, but Thomas has one last question.

'And was it on his behalf you went through our bags last night?'

And here Campbell is skewered. He denies it happened, but the denial is so lame, it comes as an admission.

'What were you looking for?' Thomas goes on.

'Nothing,' Campbell says. 'Nothing. In particular.'

'Not a book?'

Campbell opens and closes his mouth.

'Your dinner,' he blurts. 'It is burning.'

And with all pretence at normality gone, he wrenches his arm free, turns and runs and is gone. Katherine sits back and tries to think, but just then Rufus climbs into her lap; she takes him and presses her nose to his linen cap and inhales his sweet, slightly-in-need-of-a-wash odour and she tries to think about the ledger, and if Campbell was looking for it in their bags, and if so whether he did this with all his guests, but she cannot.

Edmund Riven. She has not heard his name said aloud for two or three years now, because whenever it was mentioned, Sir John would surge into an overheated rage that only Isabella could soothe with long hours of low murmurings and perhaps a gallon of spiced wine, but it has never been far from her thoughts. Edmund Riven. She thinks back to the first time she saw him, or he her, in the rye field the lay brothers had reclaimed from the wetlands before the sisters' beggars' gate of the Priory of St Mary at Haver-hurst. She had been coming back from the privy with Sister Alice – may God keep her soul – when a party of horsemen had come off the road, yelling as if hunting after boar. She has since wondered what their intentions were, since for God's sake, they cannot really have meant to rape them, can they? Not there and then. But they were the first men she had ever seen, and in her fright, she, Kath-erine, a sister of the Gilbertine Order, had thrown the bucket she was then carrying in the face of the first rider, knocking him off his horse, taking his eye out, and in that irrevocable moment, she had changed the course of all their lives.

She'd seen him again in Wales, coming back from Kidwelly, when she had been harrowed with guilt and sorrow at the death of Margaret Cornford, at the deaths of Walter, of Dafydd and of Owen, and she had wanted to kill him then, for he was responsible for them all, in one way or another, but she was powerless, of course, and it was only by the grace of God – and the help of William Hastings – that she, and Thomas, had lived to escape him.

Sir Edmund and his father. They were like buboes, erupting with implacable, dismaying malice: to blind Richard Fakenham; to kill Liz Popham; to pack a jury and have her accused of murder; and then finally, that day in Bamburgh, to cause the death of Rufus's twin sister, when Giles Riven had kicked her in her belly as she lay on the ground, forcing her to miscarry the girl child whom she had never held in her hands, whom she had been too sick to mourn. Thomas had killed him, then, with his own pollaxe, and when she had heard of this, later, when she was still in her childbed, she had felt a deep sense of release, as if she were being lifted up from under a press of weight. But now, it seems, his son is back.

All this time Jack and John Stump have been watching, not really understanding. They know of Edmund Riven, of course, and they know a little of the ledger, but neither understand yet that the former is now seeking the latter. Thomas tells them in a quick whisper.

When he hears, Jack is aghast. He sends the dice skittling down the board and over the end into the rushes.

'Not the bloody ledger again? I thought you burned it or something. You said you would, Thomas, remember?'

Thomas nods again. A flicker of guilt.

'It wouldn't have helped,' Katherine tells him. 'It would still be known that we once had it, and that we once knew its secret. Just knowing it existed, and what it proves – that is enough.'

John sits back.

'I told you,' he says. 'Five years. That is all you get.'

Rufus leaves Katherine and goes to join Nettie where she sits at the other end of the board, eating bread. He loves Nettie; he is fascinated by her swelling belly, wherein he believes a playmate is plotting to emerge.

'Edmund Riven must have been with Warwick since Bamburgh fell,' she supposes. 'He was with him while his father was with old King Henry, remember, so that the family would not lose, whichever side won.'

'Will he recognise us? If he comes?' Jack asks.

That is a good question.

'It would not take him a moment to know who we are,' Katherine supposes. 'And where we've come from. And once he discovers that . . . Well. There is no telling what he may do. You see how scared he has made everyone up here? They go in mortal dread of him.'

The second aproned sister appears, the ugliest of the three according to John Stump. She is furtive, anxious someone – her father? – will see her.

'You know Edmund Riven?' she asks.

'From a long time ago,' Katherine tells her.

'You have reasons to fear him?'

They all look at one another before agreeing.

'Then you must go,' she tells them. She is furiously urgent, snapping out her warning. 'Ignore my father. He wishes to keep you here for – for him. For Riven.'

Her anxious gaze slides to Rufus. It is possible to see her imagining him being burned.

'You must go!' she repeats. 'He is the devil. Or made by the devil. He always takes two. He tells us so. Boasts of it. A husband and wife. Or mother and son.'

'Why?'

'To burn one, right in front of the other. He takes a glowing coal and lays it on the skin of the first, and the second spills his secrets out of love for the first, or out of fear of being burned hisself.'

'Jane!'

It is Campbell at the screen. The conversation in the hall lulls. Jane turns with an entreating look and is gone. Campbell scowls as if it is they who have done the wrong; then he turns and follows her behind the screen. Conversation in the hall resumes.

'Bloody Riven,' Jack says. He can see that this is not where his son will be born after all.

'Does he know you killed his old man with that axe of yours, Thomas?' John asks.

Thomas shakes his head.

'He'd've come for me at Marton if he knew that. Surely?'

There is a long thoughtful silence.

Then Jack asks if Riven knows they have it.

'I mean, you've not – you have not *brought it with you*, have you?'

Thomas shakes his head again.

Katherine thinks of it, buried safe under the hearth in their house in Marton.

'Well, thank fuck for that at least,' John mutters. 'But for the love of God, Thomas, why'd'you bring us here? Of all places? We thought you were like that Jew bringing us out of the fucking wilderness to the Holy Land, but you're not. You're bloody Daniel, aren't you? Leading us into the lions' den!'

It is, perhaps, intended as a bleak joke.

'It was not my choice,' Thomas tells him. 'Lord Hastings wants us to look for the ledger too.'

'But you know where it is!' John says, banging a fist.

'Hastings doesn't know that!' Thomas says. 'And we can't tell him, because then he'd know we knew of the ledger, and if he knew we knew . . .'

Thomas tails off with a repeat of Campbell's neck-breaking noise. John takes a drink.

'Why does Hastings want it?' he asks when he's put the mug down.

'He wants to stop Warwick getting it.'

'Warwick wants it?' Jack asks. 'Oh Christ. Of course he does.'

Now they understand. John rubs his stump.

'God's bollocks, Thomas,' he says. 'You are caught, aren't you? Caught between those two? The devil and the sea? A rock and a hard place? Dear God! That does not even begin to cover it. You are – we are – fucked.'

After a moment, Thomas nods.

'Jesus,' John goes on. 'Isn't it always the way? Always. We are caught between two fuckers with more time and money than sense, with the power to order us about, to send other fuckers after us, to chase us from pillar to fucking post. It is always the fucking same.'

There is a truth in what he's saying, but it does not help in the immediate term.

'So what can we do?' Jack asks. 'Wait for him to come?'

Katherine thinks on what the second aproned girl said. Riven takes two. A husband and wife. Or a mother and a son. She will not be taken, nor will she let Rufus be taken.

'No,' she says. 'He must not find us.'

Thomas looks at her levelly. No. He agrees.

And Katherine's spirits sink. She looks around her at the hall of the inn, and she thinks of the village up the hill and of the house in which she hoped Rufus would grow, would be protected from men exactly such as Riven, and now here he is. The worst possible person. Worse than the snake in the Garden of Eden. Riven. Here.

'Lucky we did not unpack, I suppose,' Jack says.

They look at one another and Thomas hangs his head. He too had pinned his hopes on this place, Katherine knows, and now the road is all that awaits them. She stretches a hand to touch the back of his.

'It will be all right,' she says.

He looks up at her.

'In the morning, yes? At dawn?'

They each nod.

Campbell returns and looms over them, watching, suspicious, knowing.

'You are not leaving?'

'We must,' Thomas tells him.

'My daughters,' he says, waving towards the kitchen and buttery where they are at work, 'they exaggerate. Edmund Riven – he is not a bad man. He is nothing like they say.'

Thomas shakes his head.

'We have a history with Edmund Riven,' he tells Campbell.

'A history? You are old friends!'

73

'Not quite,' Thomas says.

'Oh, I am sure you have nothing to fear from him,' Campbell tells them.

'It is not just him,' Jack says. 'It's the half-dozen men with whom he'll arrive.'

It will be more like two dozen, now, Katherine thinks, and once Campbell tells Riven more about them, and the existence of a connection, it will be more like five dozen.

'Well, if you must,' Campbell says. 'I will make sure you have a fine last day at any rate. I have some pork that has been pickling since last year.'

'We will leave at first light tomorrow,' Thomas says.

'First light? No, no, no. There is no need for that, surely? Riven cannot be here until late afternoon even if he rides all night.'

'We have a long journey ahead of us,' Thomas says.

'But there is a haze over the moon, did you see?' Campbell tries. 'It will be raining through the morning.'

Katherine knows there is no haze. When they came in, the sky was clear, with the stars around a bitten sliver of the moon like headscurf on blue velvet shoulders. If anything there will be a frost.

'And one of the horses, the gelding, is lame,' Campbell goes on, now with a kind of comic desperation. 'I can see to that in the morning. We have oil for it. The smith can make a new shoe. And wherever will you go? Back south? To Lincoln?'

'North,' Thomas lies. 'We have well-willers in the Northern Parts. Near Newcastle.'

Campbell nods. He is thinking fast. His eyes move fast, and he is chewing his lips.

'Newcastle, eh?' he says. 'Then you must take the east road. It is the safer way.'

'Safer?'

'Yes. There are rumours of trouble up north. Along the western road.'

'What sort of trouble?' Thomas asks.

'Someone is mustering men under the banner of King Henry. King Henry as was, that is.'

Thomas glances at Katherine. This is the sort of thing Hastings wishes to know.

'Who is he? This someone?'

'He calls himself Robin of Redesdale,' Campbell tells them, pleased to have something to delay their departure, even by a moment or two. 'And there's a rumour – only a rumour mind – that he's related to none other than the Earl of Warwick himself.'

There is a moment's silence, but then Katherine says:

'Everyone is related to the Earl of Warwick.'

'Not everyone,' Campbell counters. 'Robin of Holderness wasn't, was he? He raised his banner too, last year, just like Redesdale, but because he wasn't related to Warwick, he didn't have his backing, so the Earl of Northumberland chopped his head off.'

'Would Northumberland have moved against this first Robin if he'd had Warwick's backing?' Thomas asks.

'Perhaps,' Campbell says. 'Perhaps not.'

'But this Robin of Redesdale *is* related to Warwick, and so Northumberland won't move against him? Won't chop his head off?'

'Ahh,' Campbell says, 'that is the question we must all ask ourselves, isn't it? If Northumberland does go against him, then it is all over for Robin. His head'll be on a spike in York before the week is out, but what if Northumberland does nothing? What if he sits on his hands, and lets Robin of Redesdale past? Lets him run? What will happen then? Who knows?'

Hastings is right, Katherine thinks. An inn is where you discover most. But Campbell is going on, gossiping really, like a woman wringing laundry, repeating conversations he has heard many times before.

'But there is a third scenario, isn't there?' he is saying. 'What if Warwick persuades Montagu to *join* this new Robin, eh? Then we'd have the Earls of Warwick and Northumberland, combined with

75

Robin of Redesdale, rising up against King Edward, and there is only one way that will end. Save I don't suppose they'll leave Edward rotting in the Tower as he has with old King Henry, will they? They'll chop his head off and have it on a spike just as quick as you like.'

Thomas looks at Katherine again, and then back at Campbell.

'How many men has this Robin of Redesdale?' he asks.

Campbell shrugs.

'Enough, as is told, and growing more numerous by the day.'

'And where are they mustering?' Thomas goes on.

Campbell shrugs.

'It is as I say,' he says. 'Somewhere in the vale, the Vale of Mowbray, over there, through which the west road runs, you see? Which is why I say you must take the east.'

He is pleased with the circularity of his argument.

'And you have no idea of their disposition? Who they are? If they have guns and so on?'

Campbell frowns.

'Disposition? That is a very specific word, master. You begin to sound like a spy yourself now. Ah. I forget. You are Lord Hastings's man, no?'

Thomas actually blushes.

'It is not that,' Katherine lies for him. 'We are looking for some friends. Who may be involved.'

'Oh yes?' Campbell says, thinking perhaps he has her now. 'Who?'

'John,' she says. 'John Horner.'

She remembers Horner as a good man; he was not seen after Hexham, so he is probably dead, since he was not the type to desert. Campbell has never heard of him, and remains unconvinced.

'Well,' he says, reverting to his theme, 'he is not so bad a man, Edmund Riven, despite what my daughters say. But if you are determined to go, remember: the east road.'

Katherine looks at him carefully. It is hard to tell, in this gloom, whether he is telling the truth, or sending them into a trap. It strikes her that Campbell himself is not sure either. Perhaps it is a bit of both?

'Very well,' he says. 'I will leave you now. We will cook that pork at first light, to send you on your way with our blessing.'

When he is gone Thomas asks if she thinks he can be telling the truth about the mustering, about Robin of Redesdale. She cannot see why he would lie.

'But we need something more than just rumours to take to Hastings. We need . . . I don't know. Facts. Names. Numbers. Ordnance. That sort of thing. Where they are, where they are going and so on. We can't just go there and say a man called Robin, who may or may not be related to the Earl of Warwick, is gathering men somewhere.'

Katherine watches Campbell for a long moment as he busies himself with the inn's other customers, nudging the fire on, moving from board to board, placing his hand on men's shoulders in the gathering gloom, leaning over them; she sees them turning to look at him, and she sees him laughing and making his own jokes to delight them, and she sees him sending his daughters to and fro, and she thinks he is probably as good a man as most, better than some, worse than others. Yet there is something about him that she does not quite trust, some filament of doubt that remains.

And so she should not have been surprised when in the short hours of the next morning Sir Edmund Riven, with a dozen liveried men, harnessed and arrayed as if for war, came clattering into the inn's yard by the pale blue wash of the waxing moon.

7

But by then they are gone.

It was the third aproned girl – the one with the same colour hair as Rufus – who saved them. She'd come to John Stump in the cold, clear moonlight, just as he was returning from the privy by the river, trying to tie his points with his one hand, so he did not notice the girl until she was upon him. He'd gasped when she caught his arm, and then he had thought: Well, why not, after all, because . . . but she was not after that. She'd told him that her father was lying, and that Edmund Riven was not at Middleham Castle, as he'd said, but at Pickering Castle.

'Which is half a day's ride east,' she'd said.

'East!' John had said. 'So your father was sending us towards him!'

'You are missing my point,' she'd said. 'Pickering is half a day's ride. *Half* a day's ride. If Riven is coming, he will be here before morning.'

And John had understood her then, and had come running, and they'd climbed off their beds and tied up their clothes and pulled on their boots, and in the light of rush lamps they'd saddled their horses and they'd wheeled the cart out into the yard, still loaded with the coffers, and when Campbell appeared crying out about the fear of fire, Thomas had raised a fist and told him that they ought to kill him, and the innkeeper had almost crumpled in the mud, weeping, so that in the end Thomas could not even kick him.

They'd hitched the cart to the bemused pack horse and Katherine had bundled Rufus up on to the seat they'd made there, and Nettie took him, and they'd turned for the road when the third aproned girl appeared again and this time she had a thick cloak she must have stolen from her father and a bundle with her, and she'd said: 'Take me with you.'

After a moment's hesitation, when John had looked first at Thomas and then at Jack, as if for permission, he had nodded, and she had swung up on to his horse, and so here they were now, riding as fast as they dare along a pocked road westwards, the cart's wheels jumping and grinding on the grit below, their fading moon-shadows flitting across the pebbles and rocks of its surface, and already there is the palest suggestion of dawn in the sky.

The third sister shouts out that they will never get clear.

'Not with that cart. Riven's men will come too fast.'

Thomas knows she is right. They should have left the cart, but then how would they have managed with Rufus? With pregnant Nettie? This girl in her apron and her father's coat? He looks around.

'Can we fight them off?' he wonders. 'Shoot one or two of them? Shoot Riven himself?'

John frowns.

'D'you think you could pick him out?'

Both turn to look speculatively at dawn blooming in the east. The sun will shine on them at first, as they wait, but they could let Riven and his men past, and then shoot them in the back. That would work, but only if Riven rides on. And only if there are not too many of them.

'Don't be fools,' Katherine says, appearing alongside. 'You can't shoot ten men – or perhaps you can, but there would be a hundred more where they came from. They will follow us to the gates of hell.'

'But you could try,' the third sister says.

'Where does this road lead?' Katherine asks her.

'Kirby,' she says. 'Then on to Thirsk and whatnot.'

'Would we be safe in Kirby?'

The girl thinks so, but Katherine is not convinced.

'Are there any drovers' tracks?' she asks, directing a pale hand at the hills to the north. 'Anything we could take to get us off this road?'

The girl does not seem to know. She thinks not. Thomas can see the white of her eyes as her gaze flits about the road and the looming hills to the north. The sky above is paler now, a shade of dirty lavender perhaps, so that he can see the hillcrests. Surely, he thinks, there must be some way off this road.

Around the bluff they find one: an unheralded break in the gorse where already the birdsong is growing loud. Through it is a pale stripe of gritty earth, worn by the passing of many thousands of sheep over the years, that subsequently vanishes into the shadows of a narrow defile between the hills. It is easy to imagine it winding its way to the top and over.

'We'd never get the cart up there,' Jack says.

'No,' the girl agrees. 'Exactly.'

'Forget the cart,' John says.

'It's everything we own,' Jack says. 'And Nettie'll not get far without it. Not on foot.'

Thomas looks over at Nettie. She's been weeping pretty solidly since she was woken up and now she is grizzling.

'We could find her somewhere in Kirby,' the girl suggests.

'How far is it?' Thomas asks.

Again the girl is vague.

'I'll not leave her,' Jack tells them.

'No,' Thomas agrees.

'But Riven is looking for a party of seven,' Katherine supposes. 'And if we are not a party of seven—?'

'Split up?' Thomas asks.

'No,' the girl says. 'That'd be stupid. He'd still find you.'

But Jack talks over her.

'You're right,' he tells Katherine. 'Riven doesn't know me from Adam. I could go on to Kirby. Me and Nettie. You and Thomas can take the path. It's you he wants, after all.'

Thomas thinks Jack's right.

'And John? Would you come with us?' Jack asks.

John thinks a moment before he agrees.

'Will you be all right?' he asks Thomas.

'I don't like it,' the girl says.

Thomas is still not sure. Perhaps the girl is right? Should they not just try to get to this Kirby? Find a yard or something? Raise the townspeople to help them? But what has it to do with this girl? And anyway, what choice do they have? He does not want to drag Jack into this any more than he has already. Let them go free.

'All right,' he tells Jack. 'Take the cart. Go on to this Kirby. And then south, yes? Get to York if you can. Go all day. As long as the horses hold out. We'll meet you there. Three days from now. At noon, say, under that gate where they spike the heads. If we're not there, or you're not there, then try the next day. After that . . . I don't know. But wait for us.'

He thinks perhaps they should wait for as much as a week. Jack and John look at one another. After a moment they both nod. They look as if they too feel guilty, and seeing them so, Thomas feels less guilty himself. Perhaps he and Katherine are undertaking the riskier venture?

Katherine slips from her saddle and gathers the sleeping child from the bed of the cart.

'Are you sure about this?' he asks.

Of course she is not, but what choice do they have?

The girl is peering anxiously back into the rising sun. Any minute and Riven will be there. John is still looking grim.

'What if he catches you?' he asks. 'What if he does not fall for this? It is just you and Katherine, against him and his men. He'll – you know?'

Thomas thinks of Rufus and of Katherine, of their skin blistering under a glowing coal, and he is lucky not to be able to picture it.

81

'Go on,' Thomas says. 'Stop worrying. We'll be fine. It is you I worry for.'

Thomas collects his bow from the cart. After a moment's hesitation, he leaves his pollaxe. But Katherine shakes her head. She is suddenly very certain.

'You must bring it,' she says. 'It is ill luck to be parted from it again.'

So he slides it out, and is once again almost nervous in its company. It is an astonishing thing, he thinks, designed for one terrible purpose, with an aura of its own, and every eye is drawn to it, even now, in the grey-blue gloom. He slides it across the back of his saddle, almost with a shudder, alongside his bow and the bag of arrows.

'Hurry,' Jack calls.

Before he goes, Thomas scoops a palmful of coins from his purse and presses them on Jack.

'No,' Jack says. 'I have enough.'

'Take it,' Thomas insists.

It is blood money, a salve for Thomas's conscience, and he is pleased to do it. He mounts up again, and he lifts his hand to the others, and they lift theirs in return, their faces just pale discs, and for some reason they are whispering as they wish one another well, and Godspeed; and he is grateful the parting must be swift, and that it is still dark, for he feels fear stroke his spine at the thought of Warwick's hard-faced men riding grimly through the night, led by Riven, and then he feels the nauseating grip of guilt.

The girl is still casting about, looking anxious. She is studying him closely, he feels, as if she is trying to decide with whom she should come. Thomas does not want to have her on his conscience too.

'Go with them,' he tells her. 'Go with Jack.'

She makes a face he does not understand, and with one last lingering look at his horse, as if that of all things was what she most wished for, she turns and crosses to where Jack is now waiting.

'Can we really just leave them?' he asks Katherine.

'We must,' she says. 'And quickly. Riven will not want them. He will only want us.'

She turns and heels her horse off the road, and after a moment watching the cart roll down the track, Thomas follows her down into a dark dip that from above looks as if it might never end, before rising up again to find the old drovers' path, narrow where the sheep have scoured the soil from around the stones just as a stream might. It is not good for horses in the dark, and they must dismount again, but soon he is grateful for its twisting ways, and for the wind-shriven hawthorns that rise up on either side, sheltering them from view.

They carry on upwards for a while, away from Jack and John and Nettie and the aproned girl, and ahead Thomas can hear Katherine encouraging Rufus, who is nodding off, almost falling from the saddle.

'I'll take him if you like,' he says.

Thomas takes Rufus in his arms. He weighs nothing. He is like a shrimp. Rufus buries his face in Thomas's shoulder and throws his little arms around Thomas's neck, and he is almost still asleep, so Thomas holds him for a bit, as any parent might, in happier circumstances. In the dawn's light he sees Katherine's cheeks are glazed with tears. He feels a deep wrench of shame.

'They will be all right,' he says.

She nods and sniffs.

'I know,' she says. 'I know.'

'Come on, then,' he says. 'Let's keep moving.'

And nothing more is said for a while but as they continue north, hurrying up the moorside, away from Riven, and away from their friends Thomas feels ashes in his mouth. At the top of the first hill they stop again where the path levels and where the birds are loud, lifting and fluttering in alarm. They can see the road again, but there is no sign of Jack and John Stump and their women, or of Riven and his men either.

'Perhaps they have made it to this Kirby place?'

'Let us pray to God,' she says.

They stand watching a moment, and the sun rises so quickly you can see its cloud-softened rays reach out, slicing through the dawn, illuminating the pouches of mist that hang among the trees and in the hollows below. It shines flat across the hills and catches Katherine's high-boned face; and, seeing the tilt of her chin, the angle of her head, and the defiance of her expression, despite everything, despite every reversal, Thomas cannot imagine standing here in the rising sun, with disaster all around, without her. He smiles at her, and she almost smiles at him, and he feels Rufus wriggle against his chest, and he thinks back on something John Stump said what seems like months ago, about how this amount of happiness – these five years – might well be a man's allotment for one life, and he supposes that if after all that's right, then he cannot complain of his luck.

'Come on,' he says. 'Riven could be anywhere.'

So they carry on up the hill, until at last, at the top of the steepest incline, the path emerges from the stunted hawthorns and dissolves into a plateau of broad upland pasture; there are sheep everywhere, with brown faces and tight curled horns, and this is home to sky-larks that take wing, and other flying insects, bright spots where they catch the sun. Rufus wakes, and wriggles around to watch, and is enchanted. Thomas puts him back in the saddle.

'Pipes,' Rufus says.

And sure enough a little later they can hear the thin whistle of a shepherd's pipes playing a simple little tune and they look around for him, but he'll be in the shadow of some rocks perhaps, and they never see him, and so they set off again, and the grass is long, silvered with dew, and it whips against their legs as they continue north. They ride all morning among the sheep through the long grass, up and down, seeing no one, not a soul, save those sheep.

Eventually they can look back and see where they've come from. The path is empty. They are not being followed. Riven has gone after Jack and John Stump and Nettie and the aproned sister. Thomas feels his guilt redoubled, and he can hardly look at Katherine, and neither says anything, so they ride on in silence.

The sun's heat becomes heavier with each step. It is like a warm palm on the back of Thomas's neck. Rufus is hungry and Thomas has a little dried bread in his bag that he gives the boy, but it is probably not enough. He wishes he had a straw hat instead of this woollen cap. He wonders how Katherine can stand those skirts, but she is probably used to them by now. Rufus is sneezing already with the hay fever, an explosive little plush that sets his horse's ears twitching.

They find another path, down into the beginnings of a valley that runs northwest to southeast, at the bottom of which is a lively trickle of cool clean water where they let the horses drink and they wash themselves and also drink, wishing they had some more bread. Thomas can see his skin is burning in the sun's heat, becoming pink and hot, and out of the sun, the water is good, but saints! It is so hot! Even down here.

Katherine remains quiet and thoughtful, watching Rufus wander a little way off, exploring the stream's pools where there are some tiny black fish. Behind them the horses crop the grass, their lips blue-black and amazingly mobile.

'So where to now?' Katherine asks.

Thomas is finding it hard to concentrate.

'We loop west,' he says.

'Then come back south, to York? It seems a long way around.'

Thomas agrees.

'And I've been thinking,' he says.

'About what?'

He tries to remember what he has been thinking of. Then he does.

'Campbell said Robin of Redesdale was gathering men in the Vale of Mowbray, didn't he? Which is to the west.'

He points east. Katherine corrects him, pointing uphill and to the west. The thought of a climb daunts Thomas. He splashes his face with a double handful of the stream's water but seems to be only hotter for it. He imagines steam rising from his back. He is feeling sluggish and his body radiates heat.

'Are you quite well, Thomas?' Katherine asks.

He nods weakly. His head feels stuffed with wool, and it is so hot. Too hot to think. Sweat in his eyes. The land seems to swim.

'William Hastings,' he says. 'He will want us to learn something more about this – this Robin of Redesdale, won't he? What if we could learn his numbers? His whereabouts. Who is with him. That sort of thing.'

Katherine is still watching him anxiously.

'We might even discover if he has the backing of Warwick,' Thomas supposes. 'Such news would be of interest to Hastings, for certain.'

'But if he is gathering men there,' Katherine says, 'do we want to be drawn in? You know what it is like with these sorts of armies.'

'We need only ask a few questions. Have a look at them, I mean. See if there are any wearing the Earl of Warwick's livery, or the Earl of Northumberland's.'

He can tell she does not like it. Being anywhere near troops mustering – particularly if they are mustering in rebellion – is hazardous.

'We have to be able to tell him something,' he says.

She nods. They mount up in silence, and ride on, westwards now, with the sun beating on their left shoulders, with buzzards high overhead, their cries curiously bleak despite the sun's heat. The land wavers in a haze of heat and it seems they have been riding all afternoon. The horses are sweating creamy swags. So is he. At length they find the faintest path, and then after a long while during which still not a word is spoken they come to more sheep clustered in the shade of some aspens, and the path becomes clearer, and there are stone walls built up ahead, in good order, and more sheep yet, recently sheared, who look up from their shade, and there is a shearing rack to one side, and it seems they are coming to a village.

Sure enough, over a rise, below them in the valley they find a scattering of low stone buildings around a stumpy little church, all ringed and ranged about with pens made by the same dry-stone walls. The air wavers in the heat and there are people here, just as there should be: men and women going about their business slowly in the broiling temperature, and they can hear dogs barking lazily, and the sun is so hot. So hot.

Thomas feels drained, exhausted. He sits slumped in his saddle and he can hardly focus. He can hardly kick on. He wishes he were not carrying Rufus for the boy too is so heavy and hot.

They ride down. The track swells to become a well-worn thoroughfare. A swineherd sits in the shade of a wall and laughs to see Thomas so sunburned. Dogs bark, but in greeting; however, sitting straight and heeling his horse is all Thomas can manage. They ride into the cool of the shadow of the tower, where pigs lie panting and geese and chickens intermingle, and there is a blue-eyed dog in a chained collar in a pen of his own, who looks at them levelly from behind three bars, just as if he is in the stocks, and Thomas thinks absently that he looks if he is planning some terrible revenge.

'Ale,' Thomas says.

There is a brewster, with a broom outside her well-appointed house to show she has ale for sale, and Thomas can hardly swing his leg off his saddle, but the ale is cool and he does not care how much it costs. He drinks three mugs, scarcely pausing. The brewster's servant is a pretty girl, who also laughs at the redness of Thomas's skin, but the brewster is more anxious, as is Katherine, and after Thomas has drunk a fourth ale, he tells them he feels steam rising, though he feels better, but then – they stand back – he is doubled over with nausea and he vomits every squirt of ale straight back up and he manages to walk two steps from the vomit before he stumbles and collapses on the ground.

*

'It is only the heat,' Katherine tells them.

Thomas is made to lie outside in a patch of shade thrown by the high stone walls of the brewster's husband's surprisingly large and comfortable hall. Thomas is hatless, wearing only his hose, shirt rolled up and pourpoint untied, and he is dark and glossy with the sweat that seems to pour off his blistered skin. He has his bare feet in a bucket of cold water, and there is more ale at his side, a large jug of it, though Thomas will not touch it, in case he throws it up again.

The brewster – Goodwife Watkins – and her husband stand off, eyeing him anxiously. Her husband, John Watkins, is unexpected, and not the sort of man Katherine would imagine to own so much land. He is maybe nearly forty, big, running to fat, with a blotchy face and a scar on his jaw that runs dead straight, hard-edged and livid, through his whiskers. If she did not know he owned this hall and all this land, she would assume he was a churl, but there he is, in a snug-fitting velvet jacket that must have been made for him when he was younger.

'Up to me, I'd never let him in,' Watkins barks.

But it is Goodwife Watkins who makes these sorts of decisions, while Watkins drinks and looks on through eyes like a pig.

'Will he be all right?' Goodwife Watkins asks.

'Bloody well better be,' Watkins interrupts. 'I'll not have him die in my house.'

Katherine asks if they might have a mattress for him and the servants bring out a straw mattress and set it down by the unlit fire in the stone chimney. They will not assist when Katherine helps Thomas to his feet and into the hall. They are too anxious. Who knows what this sickness is? They agree with their master: they should never have let him into the yard, let alone the house. Rufus watches, mute and anxious again. She gives him a smile.

'He will be well in the morning,' she says.

She lies Thomas down. His eyes are open, and he is able to thank her.

Sorry,' he says.

'It is nothing. Not your fault. The sun. Come, close your eyes. Sleep.'

Rufus says his prayers, and then lies beside Thomas, a little way off, because, as he says, his father is too hot tonight. She kisses Rufus and strokes his forehead. In a moment, he, too, is asleep, and she blesses him and goes to a stool at the board, where she is to eat with Watkins and his wife, and she is suddenly starving, despite the heat.

Goodwife Watkins is a plain, pious soul who, like her husband, seems out of place in such a fine hall. She takes her time over prayers before supper, but Watkins himself is less careful, and when the food is brought – a duck, roasted and glazed with the spiced jam of red fruit, and a dish of greens and eggs – he is quick to serve himself, and spoons his food into his mouth as if he has been ploughing all day. He drinks like that, too, and after he has drunk enough ale he turns to her, and she sees that he is shy of her.

'So what brings you and himself there to our parts?' he demands, not looking her in the eye but reaching for some milk and almond dish.

Katherine can see no reason not to tell him the truth.

'Disappointment, really,' she says. 'We hoped for a position a little south of here, but – but it was not to be.'

Watkins grunts.

'And so you are riding around to see what opportunities the Lord thrusts your way?'

'In a manner of speaking,' she agrees.

He grunts and drinks more. She wonders what else there is to say. Then she supposes Watkins might know something useful of this Robin of Redesdale.

'Though we seem to have picked the wrong season for it?' she probes.

'Aye,' Watkins says. 'You can say that two times.'

He eats his pudding, drinks more ale, his face hidden by his mug, but she can see his piggy little eyes blinking. Perhaps you do not talk of such things at supper? And yet Sir John always did. Or maybe because she is a woman? So she carries on.

'We heard men are gathering under the banner of the old King?'

Watkins puts his mug down. He looks at his wife, who tips her head, as if to say: Talk to her.

'Oh aye,' Watkins mutters. 'Robin of bloody Redesdale. Only he's not raising his banner for old King Henry, is he? He's raising it for the Earl of Warwick. He's a cousin of his or sommat, put up there in the wind like a bowman's finger, to test which way the Earl of Northumberland'll jump if Warwick comes out in rebellion against King Edward.'

'But Warwick and Northumberland are brothers, aren't they?' she asks. 'Surely a brother would always come out in favour of a brother?'

Watkins taps his nose.

'You'd think,' he answers, 'but the Earl of Northumberland owes King Edward dear, doesn't he? It were King Edward who raised him up so high.'

'But wouldn't Warwick make him something even greater, if he were to join him?'

Watkins ponders this.

'There's nowt much greater Warwick *could* offer him,' he says after a moment. 'Or that he'd want. Being Earl of Northumberland is everything up here, you know? And I know what he's like, from when he was Lord Montagu, see? I served under him for five years, a while ago now, and I'll tell you what he's like: he's like Carlisle. Ever been to Carlisle? No? Well, bloody well don't. But that's what he's like. Like bloody Carlisle.'

Katherine has no idea what this grudging praise means. Watkins takes another long draught of ale.

'So he won't join Warwick?' she prods.

'I didn't say that,' Watkins tells her.

'So he will?'

'Didn't say that neither.'

She tries another track.

'And how many men has he?' she tries. 'This Redesdale?'

'I don't know,' Watkins snaps. 'Who are you? Some sort of spy or something?'

'Husband!' Goodwife Watkins snaps.

'I am not, I assure you,' Katherine lies. 'I am just – anxious that my husband is not to be caught up in any – any fighting.'

Watkins bangs his fist down.

'Oh, we're all anxious about that!' he says. 'While this bloody Robin of bloody Redesdale is pissing about playing silly bastards, every man around here will be rushing to his colours for the chance of some fun and bloody games down south, won't he? And so the bloody harvest won't be taken in, will it? And I'll have to pay double – *double*, d'you hear? – to get anyone with fingers enough to shear a single one of my bloody sheep! That is what *I* am anxious about!'

He lapses into silence and the servant comes again with some sweet cake and another jug of ale. Katherine can think of nothing to say. She wishes they would all go to bed, but the candles – three of them – are lit and Watkins calls for the fire to be lit as well and then he goes outside, unsteady on his feet, to relieve himself.

'He is out of temper,' Goodwife Watkins says. 'We have already lost men to Redesdale. They seem to be flocking to him. His colours, I mean. From far and wide. They say there are thousands of men in the Vale of Mowbray, all just awaiting the word.'

'Thousands?'

'Oh yes, I should say. It is a shame we are so far out of the way, or I'd be selling my ale by the tun.' She laughs, sadly. 'Anyway,' she continues. 'Never mind old Watkins. His bark is worse than his bite. But the thing is, he feels it, you see? He was with Lord Montagu's men up north. It is how he got his chin.' She traces her husband's scar on her own chin.

Katherine tells her she should not have asked so many questions.

'Oh no,' Goodwife Watkins says. 'He likes to talk.'

They both smile. Thomas starts coughing. Katherine goes over to him. He lies stunned, unconscious to everything, panting like a dog in the heat. She moistens his lips with ale. His licks it off and so she sits him up and makes him drink. He is a dead weight. His eyes roll to awareness though, and he drinks.

'Bless you,' he croaks.

She smiles and lays him back down. He shuts his eyes and is back asleep before Watkins returns to turn his chair to face the fire. He seems calmer than before, as if the act has soothed him, and his accent, wavering before supper, seems to have settled into the coarse, honest groove of his youth.

'I tell you this,' he says, 'I hope Northumberland doesn't fall for Redesdale's trick.'

There is a spin on his words, as if he wants her to ask more.

'Why not?' she asks.

'Why not? I'll tell you why not. Because I am still indentured to the old bastard, aren't I? I've got his bloody jacket somewhere, if the mice haven't had it, from the last time I was out in the field with him.'

He strokes the bristles on his chin and it is possible to see in the glaze on his eyes that he is away.

'It was where I got this. It's a scratch, I know, nowt but a nick – though by Christ, it pissed blood, pardon my tongue.'

'Oh, John, do not go on. Goodwife Everingham does not want to hear your old stories.'

'No,' Katherine says. 'I do.'

Watkins does not heed the exchange.

'It was a big lad who did it,' he says. 'Handy with his fists in a tavern, I'd vow, but we were in a coal mine, weren't we? Can you believe? A bloody coal mine. It was back in sixty-four, after the battle of Hexham. Ever hear of it?'

Katherine nods. She remembers Hexham, and how she ran with Thomas from the rout, and how she was sicker than she had ever been before or since.

'It was afterwards, though,' Watkins goes on. 'When we were out riding down Somerset's runaways – and by God there were enough o' them – and we were on the trail of a party of horsemen, up in Tynedale, in the forest there. Further north.'

He gestures, and she imagines she knows those woods. Perhaps they were those they had had to ride through themselves after they'd run from Hexham that day? Thomas would know, but he sleeps, his breathing a regular haul. Strange to think Watkins might have been trying to ride them down.

'We followed 'em through endless bloody trees,' Watkins continues, 'with endless bloody leaves, and they never thought to hide their tracks, did they? It was like we were following a team of oxen and a bloody plough. So it weren't hard, and they went slow because they were so encumbered.'

He rolls out the odd word 'encumbered' as if he only uses it for best, perhaps only when he's telling this story. Goodwife Watkins sighs as if she's heard it a thousand times, resting her head on her hand, her elbow on the board.

'So we come up on them,' Watkins continues, 'and they're stood around in the middle of a clearing, arguing about something, and there's a nob who's shouting at the others as is always the bloody case, telling them this and that – and there are about ten of them, all gathered there with their horses and they've got a line of mules with them, haven't they?'

He is reliving it as it happens, but breaks off to take a drink, his eyes wet with some feeling – shame? Remorse? She cannot tell.

'Now,' he resumes, 'because the nob is shouting so much and they're shouting back, we've got time, so we surround them, and then we come at them and catch them unawares. We lost a couple of men in the fight, God rest them, but we killed them all. Or so we thought. But when it was done, and all these bodies were lying around, we thought: That's odd. The mules aren't encumbered any more, are they? And where's that nob gone?'

'A mystery,' Goodwife Watkins murmurs.

'Aye,' Watkins agrees. 'Only then we see these tracks going into what looks like some sort o' cave, but one of the lads says it's a coal pit, and so we know we've got him, and whatever the mules were carrying.'

'What were they carrying?' Katherine asks.

He holds up a fat palm.

'All in good time,' he says, and takes another drink. 'We start shouting at him to come out, but he won't, will he? He knows what's waiting. So we have to go in. Now. No one wants to go, so we must draw straws. And who should draw the shortest?'

He indicates himself.

'So I must go first. Quick prayer to St Barbara who someone says is the saint them that mine coal pray to, and in I go, hands and knees. It is not quite dark as pitch, as there's a light – a hole in the roof of the cave, thank God, or St Barbara, take your pick – but before I can see anything, I see this shape, don't I? Coming at me with a bill-hook, shouting and screaming and all sorts. But his weapon catches on something, or the Lord in His merciful wisdom diverts it, and the blade goes like this . . .' He draws a finger along the line of his chin.

'A miracle,' his wife intones.

He glances at her before taking up the story again.

'Now: I've got a ballock dagger,' he says, 'and in a space like that – a coal mine, remember – well, there isn't much better than a ballock dagger, I can tell you, because by my Christ I made sure of him. I must have stabbed him a hundred times. A thousand. I was that scared.'

He needs another drink.

'When it was over, I looked up, and I could see there was one more of them, hiding in the cave. His face was in that pool of light from above and I knew right away that this was the nob, the man who'd been leading the party, the one who'd been shouting, and I thought: Oh Christ, he will kill me now, because you know what them sort are like. They practise their fighting all day. And so I was about to call out for help from the others, when he just – yields. Just like that. Doesn't put up any fight at all.

'So I tell him to come out and he does. And then when he is past me, and into the fresh air of the clearing again, he stands there, surrounded by men who'd chop him down as soon as look at him, and he demands – you know what they are like – he *demands* to be taken to see Lord Montagu, that instant. So we ask him who he is and he tells us he is Sir William Tailboys. Ever heard of him?'

Katherine vaguely remembers the name. He was always the aloof one in camp, wasn't he? The one with the best tents; the one whom all the others resented. Her only memories of the time are of ailing, of vomiting, and of wanting to sleep all the hours through. Any other recollections are fogged, or glossed, or made mad with the rage of it all.

And now Watkins is going on about how they decided they would not kill this Tailboys, but they'd ransom him and fill their purses with the proceeds, even though the thought of ransoming an Englishman stuck in their craws.

'But it was not to be,' he says almost sadly, 'because the Earl of Warwick was inclined to chop his head off, so we would never have got our money anyway, but by then we didn't care about any share in any piddling little ransom, did we?'

Watkins is looking at her beady-eyed now, as if he has been very clever.

'No?' Katherine asks.

'No,' he says. 'No, we did not. Because do you know what was on those mules?'

Despite herself she is caught up in the story now.

'Tell me,' she says.

And Watkins leans forward out of his chair, and he holds her gaze, and he says: 'Three thousand marks!'

Katherine is momentarily at a loss. Three thousand marks. Such a sum is impossible to grasp. Is there that much money in all the world?

'Three thousand marks?' she checks. 'Three *thousand* marks?'

Watkins cackles.

'Wherever – wherever did it come from?' she asks.

'It was old King Henry's war chest, wasn't it? Tailboys had loaded it up on to them mules after the rout at Hexham and dragged it off into the woods so it wouldn't fall into our hands, hadn't he? I don't know if he'd meant to hide it in the mine all along, and come back for it God knows when, but if so, we stopped that, didn't we?'

'And – and whatever did you do with so much money?'

Watkins looks upwards into the dark beams of the hall and gestures in a circular wave to take in the rest of the hall to signify: This.

'We shared it out among us, and old Lord Montagu, as he was then, stood by and said it was a salve for our troubles. He's a good man, like I say. Like Carlisle. So each of us got enough, some to live out our days in comfort, others to drink themselves to an early grave. But everything you see here: this board, these dishes, this salt pot, these clothes, even, they all come from that one day. It changed my life. Made me what I am today, and it is why I will never go back to soldiering. I'll never beat them days. Never.'

It is late, and the fire has died down. The candles have winked themselves to death, and Goodwife Watkins snores gently, her head resting on plump arms folded on the board, peaceful in the low amber light. Watkins finishes his wine, bangs his mug to stir her, and then the servants come to prepare the master and mistress for bed, and the two of them make their way up to their room at the top of the steps, and then the servants roll out the mattresses, and at last the cloche is put on the embers and darkness falls.

Katherine lies awake, bending her thoughts to the road that Jack and John Stump and Nettie have taken, and she prays for them, and hopes they are already in York, or perhaps at an inn along the way; but it is not long before she starts thinking about luck, and how some have it and others don't, and she is not so good a soul that she does not resent Fortune's Wheel forever turning against her while turning in favour of a man such as Watkins. She tries to imagine what it would be like to find three thousand marks in a hole in the ground in the woods, but she cannot, and she falls asleep wondering if she ought to repeat Watkins's story to Thomas or not, and then deciding probably not: he is sore about money at the moment and it would only make him more so, and above all else she wants him to be happy – in so far as that is ever possible.

8

Thomas wakes at dawn with a start. Where is he? Katherine is with him, Rufus too, both safe and sound, but he has no idea where he is or how he got here. He recalls the day before, but not how it ended. He rouses Katherine. She sits up. Explains. He lies back again and presses his hands to his face.

'Dear God,' he says.

They rise and say their prayers and dress, and then Katherine dresses Rufus while all around the Watkins household gets ready for the new day, and after breakfast of bread and ale, they are on their way, with an extra flagon of ale from Goodwife Watkins and a gruff apology from Watkins himself.

'Sorry for talking so last night,' he tells Katherine. 'The wife has already given me an earful.'

'No.' She laughs. Thomas wonders what they are talking about, and asks after they have said their thanks and farewells.

'Oh, nothing,' she tells him. 'He was talking about his days in Lord Montagu's army. He was at Hedgeley Moor and Hexham, you know? Not an archer though, so he cannot be blamed for Jack's leg.'

They ride on for a bit.

'It is odd, isn't it?' Thomas says. 'That he feeds us and gives us ale and lets us sleep by his fire, when only a short time ago we were trying to kill one another.'

'Would you rather he were consistent?' she asks.

Thomas supposes not. He feels rueful and thoughtful this morning after his sickness the day before. It is going to be another hot day and already their shadows are sharp on the road's sheep-cropped verge. Thomas is anxious, but at the outskirts of the village they find a red-headed girl sitting in the shade of a house, who is able, there and then, to twist the rushes between her clever fingers to make broad-brimmed hats to fit their heads, each one taking her no longer than it might to say a decade of the rosary. While they wait, the church bell rings out, setting doves flapping, and the girl tells them they are ringing for SS Peter and Paul, whose day it is today.

'Time passes, eh?' she says. 'Nights'll soon be drawing in.'

In this heat it is impossible to imagine what the winters might be like up here.

When the girl has finished and placed Rufus's hat upon his head, she tickles him under the chin and they ride on westwards, shaded by their new headgear, following the road as it snakes through the valley towards a gap between the distant hills.

They ride all that morning, and he is aware that Katherine is keeping an eye on him, and to tell the truth he does not feel well, and the horse is so hot, but on they go. By noon they come up and over the most westerly pass of the moors, and below, where the hills shelve away, is the broad cloth of the plain stretching for many miles toward a distant line of blue shaded hills. Above the plain, seemingly at Thomas's eye level, are white balls of cloud that move sedately southwards on a gentle breeze.

'Like sheep through a gate,' Thomas notes.

They linger a while, watching the shadows of the clouds as they move over the gentle countryside below. It is very green down there, mostly wooded save for a distant smudge of smoke over a spider-shaped fretwork of roads and tracks that come together in what must be a town. There might be a river a little way beyond, and two or three smaller villages on its course. Elsewhere the pattern of woods and furlongs, fields and pens – it looks familiar, comprehensible, heartening.

But he can see no sign of an army sheltering in its folds, no columns of smoke, no rows of tents, no lines of horses or columns of trudging men. There are no carts, no crowds of camp followers filling the roads as they would, were they there.

'Are you sure Redesdale is down there?' she asks.

'Unless he has already moved on? Or we are lost?'

'What about Riven?' she asks. 'Will he be down there?'

'There's only one way to find out,' he tells her.

He swings his leg off his horse, leaving Rufus perched in the saddle, and he loosens the ties on the pollaxe, and he takes his bow out and bends it around his body and grunts with the effort of nocking the bowstring. The illness, whatever it was, has left him weak. He hopes he does not have to use the thing in anger. He has not drawn it in weeks, but now, nocked, it is alive in hand again, thrumming with that potent energy, and he wonders whether he dare loose an arrow, and lose it, just for the pleasure of it? Then he remembers the cost of each arrow, and the threat of Riven. Imagine if he needed just one more?

Katherine is watching him with one eyebrow cocked.

So he slides the bow back on the saddle, near at hand, and with as strong a pace as possible he sets off, Katherine following, likewise dismounted, down into the cooling shadows of the valley, where God alone knows what awaits.

When the ground levels, they mount up and find a track that fords the stream, and they ride splashing through the water and Rufus gurgles with pleasure; and then they are into thick woods where they can smell charcoal burners at work, but there is no one to be seen. After a while Thomas stops and they stare down the length of the tree-pressed track, where the shade is dappled and birds chatter but otherwise all is silent.

They look at one another, and shrug, and kick on. After a while the track brings them to a road laid with old stones, running north to south through the vale, empty. Thomas is about to ride out on to it, when he sees something, down there, among the grit. He pulls on his reins. The horse steps back. He dismounts. Under his feet, in the dust and dirt of the road, are many hoof prints, all heading south, and each planted recently. Among them, too, are the long snaking lines of wheel rims, and then there are two wide grooves of shuffled footprints. Together they mean only one thing: men moving as an army.

He looks at her, she at him.

'How many?' she asks.

'Hundreds?' he supposes.

'Is it Robin of Redesdale?'

'I'd thought there might be more,' he admits.

Part of Thomas feels deflation. Hastings will not be overly interested to hear they have found an army that numbers in its hundreds. That number rode with him when he came to Marton, and that was for a ride in the countryside. No. It is clear that if this is Redesdale's army, then he is no threat to the realm.

'Well,' Thomas says. 'Perhaps Hastings will welcome good news?'

Katherine nods and gives him a tight half-smile.

'Come on, then,' he says. 'We'd best be off. Go and find Jack and John.'

He is about to step up into the stirrup again when Rufus says: 'Listen.' They look up at him and he has an eager little smile on his face, and so they listen.

'Now it is drums,' he says.

And they are dead still, bolt upright, straining to hear, and now there it is, coming on the wind: a tuneless ripple of sticks on skin. A drum. More than one. From the north. Katherine turns to Thomas, wide-eyed. They know what it means: troops. They are the only people who follow drums like that. Men under orders.

Thomas swings up into his saddle and kicks his horse around and they ride back splashing through the ford and then up along the track, keeping as low as they can, noses pressed to the horses' withers, until they reach the trees where the charcoalers are at work. He slides from his saddle and leads the horse off the road, ducking under the low fronds of a laurel tree, along a dark path twisting into the green heart of the wood.

They follow it to the charcoalers' camp: a large stump in which a hatchet is buried, a few blackened pots and a pile of stuff under a spread of sooty linen, cleaner and neater than he'd imagined from the tales people told about charcoal burners – and the two men who are standing there with their blades drawn look nothing like the figures from the horror stories you hear in inns. They are skinny, wraithlike, with jug ears, and far more frightened than frightening. One of them is wearing only a soldier's jack that hangs to his enormous, naked knees, the other a pair of hose that are rolled up at the ankles.

There is a tense moment.

'God give you good blessing,' Thomas says.

The drum is beating still. Growing louder. Coming closer.

The charcoalers hear it too, and are equally concerned, their gazes flicking to one another, their weapons – such as they are – clutched tighter. Thomas gestures, asking to go through their camp. They just stare. He assumes permission, and leads his horse towards the far side of the wood, where he hopes he'll find a view of the road and the men upon it. Katherine follows him past piles of already charcoaled branches, past the great smoking dome of their underground oven and then out under clearer skies towards the southern edge of the wood, where the trees have been coppiced. The stream loops around this edge, enclosing it nicely, and two children are fishing in the turbid waters, both naked and smudged and sooted with charcoal. Their bellies bulge and their legs are crooked, and they look up with big eyes, and say not a word.

Thomas looks over their heads, west, to the road that cuts south. The drum is still beating, and they can hear more than one, more than two, and there're pipes too, likewise more than two. A pale cloud of dust writhes through the afternoon sky.

And then he sees them. A whole column of men and horses.

'By Christ,' he breathes. 'Look at them. There must be a thousand.'

'Where have they come from?' she asks.

He doesn't know.

'Can you see who they are?'

Katherine has better eyes than him.

'Red,' she says. 'White. Bits of it. Blue, too, but – they are mostly – you know. A mix. Russet. Linen. Nothing really. No flags. They are just . . .' She shrugs.

'Who are they then? They can't be Warwick's? No. No. His men – well, they are proper soldiers. Montagu's too, surely? D'you remember them? They – they must be Redesdale's.'

They watch the men filing along the road, sunlight catching on a helmet here, a bill there. He can imagine them, imagine how mixed their feelings are and how that will affect the way they stride out. A man will swagger, caught up in it, or he will shuffle, wondering just what in the name of God he has got himself into.

'But Watkins said Redesdale would never take the field, that he was doing all this to make Northumberland jump one way or the other.'

'Well, Christ, look at them. They mean business. Look at those carts. They're loaded up with God knows what.'

He can imagine iron ingots, sharpening stones, arrowheads, hides, wheat, ale. All sorts of things. Guns, even. They watch for a long while, standing in the gloom with the children watching them, and as the men on the road trudge past, and the drums rattle, Thomas becomes no longer frightened, only taken over by a strange sadness. Katherine too.

'So it is starting all over again,' he says.

She puts a hand on his shoulder.

'You won't have to be there,' she says eventually.

He feels – what? Sadness at all this, but also relief. He has something for Hastings now.

'Hastings,' he says. 'We must tell him about this.'

'We'll have to get past them,' she says, nodding at the road. 'You know how they are, these armies? You remember when Queen Margaret came down to London? The time she beat Warwick on the field? Her army pillaged everything fifteen miles each side of the road.'

'How then?'

'Perhaps – perhaps we could join them?'

She points to the camp followers that have stumbled into view on the road, struggling to keep up along with their oxen and carts, dragging the tents, the pots, the bags of oatmeal. Along with the wives and children, there'll be bakers and butchers and brewers, bowyers, fletchers and stringfellows. There will be chancers and thieves, priests, pardoners and purse-cutters. There will be the whole soup of human life into which a man and his wife and child might easily melt, if only that man wore a suitable livery coat, or was with friends to vouch for him.

But even a column such as this will have prickers riding to and fro, each of them hefting the long lance from which they get their names, and if they do not think he is some interloping spy, they will press him into their own company, and he has spent long enough in that situation.

He is thinking how to get by when there is a disturbance on the road: a shrill trumpet, hard blown. A standard is carried aloft. Some noble it is, trying to get up the road in a hurry, with half his retinue to clear the way, the other half to trail in his wake. 'Can you see the colours?' Thomas asks.

'Blue background,' she says, 'with a few yellow curls like this.'

She draws a shape in the air. It means nothing to him either.

The column winds on past. By now the charcoalers' children have come back across the stream to climb the bank and disappear back into the trees. Thomas's horse defecates fragrantly. Katherine hears the clatter of a pot back in the charcoalers' camp. Rufus says he is hungry. She is suddenly fiercely hungry too.

'Is there another road south?' she asks. 'A path or something?'

'Perhaps these people will know?' Thomas asks, gesturing at the charcoal burners. 'Some secret path?'

He asks. The charcoalers do not appear to speak English, or only a strange form of it. There is much pointing but if they do know of another road south, they are unable to say where it might be. It is hopeless.

'God give you good day,' Thomas says, anxious to be away. There is a smell in the air that catches his throat and makes him feel sick, but Katherine's attention has been caught: the children from the stream are back under the linen shelter. You couldn't call it a tent: it is too basic for that. They are bent over something on the ground, some lump, and their posture is supplicatory and fretful, as if they are concerned for something, or someone. They are offering something, holding it out. Could it be one of the fish they've just caught? And could it be that – someone else is there? Then he thinks: The mother. Where is she?

Katherine walks over to the children to see what they are doing. The two charcoalers follow her with their eyes. There is a stream of talk. One is agitated, the other calming. Thomas cannot decide how dangerous they are. Of greater concern is Katherine. He turns and he almost groans. She has found someone who needs her help. Christ. What is it this time? He walks over, one eye on the two charcoalers, the other on Katherine.

He sees they are gathered around the head of what turns out to be a supine woman, who is so motionless she could be dead. The children hold out their fish, silvery in the dark, but they look up at Katherine. The smell under the awning makes Thomas flinch: rotting flesh and excrement on excrement. The children retreat, pushing themselves back with their heels. They are both still naked.

A bluebottle buffets his lips before he can clamp a palm over his mouth.

He watches Katherine with a sinking sensation as she crouches next to the woman. The woman moves at last, retracting her toes with a whimper. Not dead then. She is lying on her side. Her clothes are black. Her skin is black.

'What is it?' Katherine asks her.

It takes Thomas a moment to see the woman is cupping her filthy cheek with both hands. The cheek is bulbous, so swollen it fills both palms and closes her eye above, from which the tears have washed tracks in the soot. The other eye is open, blue as sky, glaring furiously. Katherine makes to move the hands, but the woman hisses something and swings her elbow. Katherine glances up at the children. They stare white- and wide-eyed. No one has ever tried to touch their mother.

Katherine tries again.

'I can help,' she says.

But again the woman's elbow comes up.

Suddenly one of the charcoalers is there under the tent. Thomas grabs his knife, but the man is no threat. He is bent, looking at Katherine quizzically. His jack flaps open and – Christ! – he too is naked. It is grotesque. Katherine ignores this, and makes slow gestures.

'I can help,' she says. 'I have medicines. Medicines?'

If the man does not understand exactly, he understands enough. He says something to the woman. She moans a protest. He is sharp with her. He leans forward, takes her elbows and pulls them away. The woman wails in pain and it seems the man might hit her at any moment. Katherine says something soothing and the man holds the woman's hands, and then kneels on them, and grabs her face, turning it to Katherine. He slides his black fingers into her mouth and forces it open. The woman bites down. They are fighting, without moving. Every muscle of each body is tensed against the other.

106

Katherine peers in. Even Thomas can see that the woman's teeth are terrible, the gums black and engorged. He cannot help murmur an expression of disgust.

'Katherine,' he says. 'Can we not just——?'

'She is in pain, Thomas,' Katherine tells him.

'I can see that,' he says. 'But you are not a tooth-puller and we——'

'I have salve,' she says. 'And dwale.'

'You do?'

'From an apothecary in Lincoln. Isabella paid for it, when she knew we were going. In a roll in the bag on my horse.'

The roll, within the saddle bag, is new made, in calfskin. Within are five small bottles with wooden stoppers held in place with leather straps, and there are also some cloth packets of various powders and two knives, sheathed in leather. The smell is sharp and cleansing.

The woman is struggling.

'I wish I had some – some tools. Pliers. Something like that. I could remove the tooth. Clean the wound.'

'We do not have time for this,' he tells her.

Thomas cannot stand to be under the linen a moment longer, with the bumbling flies, the struggling man and woman, the stench from the woman's mouth. He cannot understand how Katherine can bear it.

'Christ,' he says and he turns to find Rufus standing on tiptoes, trying to see in to the woman's mouth. 'Not you, too,' he mutters.

He wonders what Katherine knows about tooth pulling. What is there to know? Nothing. You just pull the tooth. But she cannot seem to get hold of it. Her fingers are not strong enough. He thinks for a moment if he has anything like a pair of pliers. Of course not. What else then? He remembers extracting a tree stump with Jack. They used a rope and an ox. Pulled it out that way. One of them dug around it, loosened it, while the other drove the ox. Took a morning perhaps. He saunters back towards the stream again, where the column still marches. How long now? he wonders. The sun is still high. Two hours? They are moving slowly. He remembers Katherine telling him that it took a day to ride from end to end of the column of men and wagons moving up to fight at Towton.

Katherine comes to him and clambers down to wash the blood from her hands. She is flushed and angry.

'What is the cure?' Thomas asks. He is being patient.

She sighs.

'I have given her some henbane, and some poppy seed. But she has some hole at the base of a tooth. That or a worm.'

'So what next?'

'An iron nail, engraved with the words *Agla Sabaoth Athanatos*, placed under the tooth.'

'What good will that do?' Thomas wonders.

'Nothing, until it is hammered into an oak tree, and a prayer is said.'

'Do you have an iron nail?'

'No. Nor do I have a tree frog, which might also work.'

'A tree frog? We could find one. I bet the charcoalers make soup of them.'

She waves her hand.

'I don't believe these things work. Well. Perhaps the tree frog has some unknown quantity that will balance her humours, but I cannot get at the tooth to remove it.'

He tells her about the tree stump and ox.

'We don't have a rope. Or an ox,' she tells him.

'I've a bowstring,' he says.

And she stops her rinsing and looks at him. He unwraps one from his right wrist and passes it over. She takes it, twists it, makes a loop, and then returns to the tent. Thomas follows. He watches her crouch, bend her back, fiddle in the woman's mouth, curse twice, place a knee on the woman's chest, and then haul back. He hears the noise, and then the woman screams and thrashes, but a black gobbet spins through the air and Katherine is bobbing away. The woman kicks her legs and shouts and screams a little more, but by now the henbane and the poppy-seed juice have worked a little.

Thomas returns to watching the road. He feels safe leaving her in the company of the charcoal burners now. They are like woodland animals, he thinks: squirrels, which they are supposed to eat, or badgers. Perhaps it is the white eyes in the midst of their sharp, black faces? And as they go about their business, they make curious communicative noises to one another, more like those woodland creatures than men. Jesus, they are odd. Katherine sits by the woman and the children offer her that fish, which she cannot accept, but then one of the men brings her something in a dish she thinks they are suggesting she eats. There is some for Thomas, too: a wodge of something dense and cold, smelling faintly fungal, but they eat it like bread, so Thomas does too, breaking it apart along woody grains with his fingers, and it is some sort of fungus after all.

By the time they are finished, the woman is sitting up, and the column of troops and camp followers has passed.

'Well,' Thomas says. 'That is that.'

He feels a curious despair.

'We can always catch them up,' she says.

She gathers Rufus to her, and they make to leave the charcoalers' camp, but one of them – the one with the jack – is now on his feet. He is rummaging for something among their few possessions. What is it? It is as if he wants to give them a gift, something to thank her for his wife's recovery. He finds what he is looking for, there among his things, and he holds it out reverentially, as if to him it is utterly precious. She can see why. In a world of black things, here is something red. A fold of dark red linen, kept that way, Katherine imagines, since he first acquired it. He holds it out, his black thumbs smudging it, and he lets it drop so that it hangs from his outstretched hands: it is a livery coat, a simple tabard, two pieces of cloth stitched together at the hips and shoulders, big enough for Thomas to wear. It has, though, a patch of white cloth sewn on to its breast: a tree stump. The badge of the Earl of Warwick.

She looks at Thomas, and Thomas at her. He smiles.

'That should help,' he says.

There is the inevitable bloodstain on the back, and the hole around which it clings is ragged and round: an arrow that caught the man perhaps a little to the right of his spine. She wonders how the charcoaler came upon it. Did he find the body and strip it? If so, an odd thing to keep when you think of all the other things he must have been wearing. Then she realises. This is the livery jacket that went over the soldier's jack that the man is wearing now. When she puts her finger through the hole and gestures at his jack, he grins toothlessly and turns, and there, sure enough, among the black is a deeper patch of black around a rip in the linen from which tufts of tow spew. Then he points and says something to suggest it happened a long way from here and that it was nothing to do with them, they only found the body, and perhaps they even buried it.

'Bet they ate him,' Thomas supposes.

He thanks the man and takes the livery coat. The man nods vigorously and grins. Dust rises from his fringe and his gums around his rotten teeth are very pink.

'We can pretend I am carrying messages,' Thomas tells her. 'They will yield the road for a messenger, surely?'

He shrugs himself into the tabard. It fits him loosely, since he is not wearing an archer's padded jack, and he looks nothing like he imagines a messenger of the Earl of Warwick might look. He leads the horses away from the charcoalers – the woman is on her feet now, grinning sloppily, the drool and blood having cleaned her chin – who follow them up to the fringes of the wood from where they watch Thomas heft Rufus into the saddle and then swing up after him. Thomas and Katherine pause for a moment to thank the charcoalers but it is difficult to see them in the gloom of the trees at the end of this sunlit afternoon.

They retrace their steps down the track and across the ford to the road where the tracks are dug deeper with the passing of the army and its followers. Then they turn south, following them down the old road.

'We must aim to pass them just as they have found a place for the night,' Thomas tells her. 'That way we might slide by unchallenged.'

It seems a forlorn hope, for no messenger of the Earl of Warwick would ride with his wife and child, and at the first question asked, the falsehood will be apparent, but that is almost all they can do: hope.

As the afternoon shades to evening, they come to a long, dead-straight stretch of the road; they see in the distance that it is blocked by the backs of the camp followers, but they are lucky, for the followers are engaged in some sort of activity, and Thomas thinks it can only mean they have found the right spot in which to camp. So he and Katherine dismount and wait a few moments to let the horses crop the verge in the shadow of a large chestnut. They watch as the carts and wagons are shunted to one side, canvas and cooking pots unloaded. This is the time when everyone there will be squabbling for space, squabbling to be near the watch tent, near the central fire, squabbling not to be too near the place where men will most likely relieve themselves all night and in the morning.

Any moment now there will be a lull between when the prickers come in and before the pickets are sent out – the hour between dog and wolf – and that will be the time to pass by on the road as if on urgent business.

'Well,' Thomas says, tightening himself for it. 'Here we go.'

She places a hand on his arm and speaks so that Rufus cannot hear or be spooked.

'Thomas,' she says. 'You know the risks you run?'

111

He pulls on the red cloth of the tabard.

'This?'

She nods.

'They will know you are not Warwick's man and hang you for a spy.'

'What else is there?' he asks her. 'We have been given this as – as a gift from God. It is like being given a pass. We must use it.'

'Since when were charcoal burners agents of God?'

'It will go well,' he says. 'All will be well.'

She nods again, and he places his arms around her and pulls her to him, and they are like that for a long moment before she tells him she cannot breathe.

He lets her go and they climb into their saddles.

'Shall I take you?' Katherine asks Rufus, and then to Thomas: 'It will look more – seemly?'

Thomas nods.

'You go with your mother,' he tells the boy. 'And watch me send these men scattering.'

He passes Rufus over and she settles him on her saddle. He smiles at her.

'Come on,' he says. 'Now is the time. I have an urgent message to deliver on behalf of that bastard the Earl of Warwick, whose word must never be delayed.'

She laughs to humour him.

'So steady now,' he tells her, 'but fast, yes? We are not aiming to tire the horses, only get to the next inn – or stables, better yet – before nightfall.'

He pushes Rufus's rush hat back and rubs the boy's head, then he replaces the hat. He smiles once more, and catches her eye, and then he turns and, just before they set off up the road at a reasonable, confident pace, he crosses himself and Katherine does likewise.

He rides, Katherine and Rufus trailing and a little to one side, just off from the line of sight. Despite being on the move most of the day the horses are still fresh and they enjoy the canter. As they approach he sees across the hedgerows and laid hedges that the men are clustered across a few furlongs: some are putting up their tents; smoke rises where others have already got their fires under way; while yet others are beginning to pull down a hovel for its firewood. His gaze flits over the scene. It is familiar to him, but there is nothing he recognises: no colour of livery or flash of banner or flag.

There are still some men on the road, scattered around, watching while others see to the last oxen as they are cleared off it for the night; they turn and face Thomas and his companions and there is a confused hesitation, each man looking at his neighbour for a steer, and this is it: this is when it will go either one way or the other, and all it will take is some bald-headed terrier of a man who will want to interfere out of bloody-mindedness, and who will barrel up to the challenge and stand in the middle of the road with his legs apart and his hands outstretched, daring Thomas to ride over him, and he'll shout something, and all the others will come and stand alongside, and then – it will be over.

'Stand aside!' Thomas shouts when they are twenty paces from the nearest, who still hesitates; Thomas gesticulates, waving them aside. 'Stand aside! I've a message from the Earl of Warwick!'

There is a long moment when the turned men watch, unmoving, peering to see what he is wearing, and he thinks: They'll not see I am wearing Warwick's badge because it'll be hidden by the horse's head. So he starts riding aslant the road, puffing out his chest to let them glimpse his livery coat and badge, and it seems there is no one among them who wants to stop him for the sake of it for they part before him, and as they pass the men there recognise the badge and they shout, 'A Warwick!' 'A Warwick!' – it has been some time since he heard that – and then some whistle at Katherine and Thomas thinks: For Christ's sake, she has a child here.

But they are through the knot of men. They keep going, as they must, and only Rufus turns to look back, because Katherine and Thomas know they must not.

They ride on. Thomas is laughing.

'Did you see their faces?'

'And at least we can be sure they count Warwick among their friends,' she calls.

But then the elation fades, for from nowhere – a clump of oaks and three small houses – comes a mounted picket. The road ahead is blocked and there's no way forward, and there's no way back.

9

There are six. Two remain ahead, two ride behind, and two dismount. They have done this before, Katherine thinks. The dismounted pair – one tall, the other short – walk with that slow bowl of men who know they have the whip hand. To begin with Thomas keeps his nerve, playing his part as well as any mummer. He tells them he has an urgent message from the Earl of Warwick, but the taller of the two, who has a fleshless hatchet face, just laughs.

'Personal message, is it? Come fresh from Middleham, have you?'

Thomas does not see the trap.

'Yes,' he says.

And the man laughs again. So do the others.

'It's funny that the Earl of Warwick isn't at Middleham, isn't it, eh? Funny he's in France.'

Thomas backtracks.

'A message on his behalf,' he says.

'No, no,' the other one says, turning to his shorter companion, 'you heard him, didn't you, John? Said he'd come straight from the bedside of the Earl himself. Get him off his fucking horse.'

And the other man, the shorter one with one hooked eyebrow and a nose broken and healed like a cobblestone, seizes Thomas's arm. Thomas pulls free, and instantly there's a sword blade against his face. Thomas is still for a long moment, and Katherine can see him wondering if he can do it: fight and break free; and she looks at the face of the man holding the blade and she knows his sort, and she knows there is almost nothing he would like more than to slash it across Thomas's face, and she thinks: Good God, no, Thomas, please, because you can't beat men like this. You are the rabbit, the bear, and they are the ferrets and the dogs.

Thomas makes the right choice.

'I will get off myself,' he tells them.

The first man turns to Katherine.

'You too, mistress,' he says. 'Off your horse.'

She can hardly move. She cannot let Rufus go.

'What do they want?' Rufus asks her.

The man leers at the boy.

'What do we want?' the man mimics. 'I'll tell you what we want. We want to know what it is your father and mother are doing charging around the countryside dressed in one thing when I believe they are another.'

'The black men gave my father the red jacket,' Rufus tells him.

Katherine feels her heart sink. *No, Rufus, you are supposed to lie.*

'Is that so?' The man laughs. 'The black men, eh?'

'Leave my wife alone,' Thomas tells him.

The man turns on him. He is rigid with fury.

'It ain't up to you to tell me what to do,' he spits. 'So if you fucking well try again, I will split you from your bollocks to your chops. With this.'

A length of rusted blade appears in his hand as if by magic.

'Got that?' he asks. 'Fucking got that, have you?'

Thomas does not let his expression waver, even as the blade passes across his lips.

'We should do them here,' the smaller of the two says. 'Right now. Here. Look – in the ditch. There.'

He is as bright-eyed as a ferret in the rabbit net, and is almost bouncing with the thought of it. The taller one considers it, conflicting thoughts reflected in the twitching, wiry muscles in his face. He looks around: first at the ditch; then at the small crowd that is beginning to gather. Men in russet and brown, all armed with rough bills, and two women in blue dresses with laces as loose as can be. The taller one removes his hat. His hair is shaved off at the side, left long and lank on top, like summer grass gone over.

'No,' he says at length. 'They've got a tale to tell, and someone'll want to hear it first.'

The smaller one is let down.

'And *then* we'll do them!' The taller one laughs.

'The kid and all?'

'No, you fucking fool. Not the kid. No one kills a fucking kid. Christ.'

The crowd parts to let them through into the field where they are setting up camp. The smaller of the two leads the way, the taller one behind with the horses and his knife. Men and women and children look up from their tasks – erecting tents, bringing water, lighting fires, skinning rabbits – to watch the excitement. Katherine clutches Rufus's hand. Her legs feel very weak. It reminds her of the time she was nearly hanged by the Earl of Warwick's men for deserting his army, long ago now, only this – this is worse.

'Don't say anything,' Thomas murmurs by her side. 'Not a word? D'you understand? Rufus? Yes?'

Rufus nods. It is not clear if he knows what is happening.

'There's a good boy,' Thomas says.

'Shut the fuck up,' the tall one says.

Thomas stops and turns to him.

'Don't talk to me like that,' he says.

'Fuck off,' the other man says.

Thomas looks at him a long moment.

'What? What?' the tall one demands of him. 'Adding me to your list of men you're going to kill? Is that it? Well, you can get to the back of the fucking queue, sunshine, by God's fucking truth, because I am on a hundred such lists, and do you know what they all have in common? All these lists? Let me tell you: they've all been foreclosed because any cunt who's crossed me ends up that way,

117

don't they? So if you want to shit out of one hole tonight, not two, I'd get a fucking move on.'

Another, different, knife appears in his hand. A rondel dagger: a long steel spike with a flat-ended pommel so a man might use his fist to bang it down – or up – into another man's flesh without feeling any discomfort.

Thomas has no choice. He turns and they all walk on. They have an escort following them now, of men and the two women, calling to their friends in the camp to join them. Ahead are the bigger tents.

'Listen,' Thomas says. 'I am just an ordinary man, trying to get home, trying to get my wife and child to safety. We are no threat to you.'

'Why're you wearing this old livery coat, then?' someone asks.

'It is as the boy says,' Thomas tells them. 'We had it from the charcoalers.'

'It's looted,' another man says. 'Look.'

They are pointing to the hole in the back.

'We did not ask where they found it,' Thomas says.

'Why'd you put it on?'

'Because I hoped it would get us past your picket.'

'Well, that didn't work, did it?'

This gets a laugh.

'You some sort of spy?' someone else asks. 'Running to report our numbers to King Edward, are you?'

'No,' Thomas lies. 'I am just as you see me. Simply trying to get my wife and child to the safety of their home.'

'Don't pretend you ain't an archer. Look at you. Spent half your life in the butts.'

'We've all spent half our lives in the butts,' Thomas answers.

'I haven't,' one of the women says.

This gets a laugh, too.

'All right, that's e-fucking-nough,' the taller of the two pickets tells them. They are come to the larger tents now: simple linen things, each large enough for ten men, stained by use and wear. The taller of the two guards straightens his jack, clears his throat, and then opens the tent's linen flap and steps in, letting it fall behind. There is talk within. The smaller of the two men leers at Katherine, and she feels faint and grips Rufus's hand all the tighter. She knows she's taking more support from him than he from her. Thomas puts his hand on her shoulder.

'It was a good idea,' he says, 'and we are not sunk yet.'

But she thinks: By Christ, we are. We will be swinging from the branches of the trees that fringe this stretch of common land before the curfew bell is rung. She cannot help but place her hand on the soft skin of her throat. What will happen to Rufus? Dear God.

Then the tent flap opens. The tall guard emerges first. He looks pleased. A bad sign. He holds the tent flap open and, after a moment, the commander comes ducking through.

He straightens: a tall man, broad shoulders, long face, no cap, instantly familiar.

It is, of all people, John Horner.

He stares at them, open-mouthed. His eyes widen and Katherine can feel her own hair rippling to stand on end.

'By Christ!' he whispers. 'By Christ!'

He breaks into a face-splitting grin.

'Thomas bloody Everingham!' he shouts out. 'Thomas bloody Everingham! I believed you were dead!'

He steps forward and throws his arms around Thomas. Thomas wraps his own around Horner. Their back thumps are enough to raise dust from up off their cloth. The guard curls his lip in disgust. After a moment Horner pushes Thomas away so that he can look at him more clearly. She can see Horner wears a blue livery jacket with a curious yellow smear over the chest. She has seen a couple of these in the crowd. To whom do they belong?

'By all that is holy!' he shouts.

And now Katherine cannot stop the sob in her throat, and the tears splash her cheeks.

Horner turns to her.

'Goodwife Everingham! There is no need for tears! This is a happy event!'

'I am sorry,' she says. 'I have been this way since – since Rufus was born.'

And Horner pauses before he kisses her; he looks down at Rufus and gives a shout of pleasure.

'He is the spit!' He laughs. 'The spit. But I cannot say of whom! It is a young Kit! That is it!'

Now he kisses her and she sees he has acquired deep lines at the sides of his mouth, and his hair is grey at the temples. She feels his eyes ranging over her face, taking in the changes, and she wonders for a moment if he is still wondering if she is Kit, or Kit is her, but whatever conclusion he comes to, it hardly matters because he can prove nothing, even if he wanted to.

So he crouches down and looks into Rufus's eyes on the boy's own level.

'We are old friends, me and your father,' he tells him. 'We spent many a long day cooped up in a huge castle and then we went into battle together, to fight for the right of King Henry to rule his realm. We lost that time, but we will not lose this time. You wait and see.'

Rufus looks concerned but says nothing and after a moment Horner stands and gives him a pat on the head.

'You are a good boy,' Horner says. 'You do look like your uncle, though. Have you met him? He is a fine, fine surgeon. The finest I ever heard of.'

Katherine feels a flare of anxiety, but Rufus merely shakes his head slowly, his eyes big and round, and he remains silent, as instructed, and that, for the moment, is enough.

'We believed you dead after the rout at Hexham,' Thomas tells Horner, 'so we made our way back to Bamburgh. We supposed that if you lived, you would come too?'

Horner is cagey. He sees that the audience still waits.

'Come,' he says. 'Let me find you ale. And something to eat perhaps. We will sit and talk. Come. Come.'

He opens the flap of the tent for them and holds it as they file in. There is a coffer, a stool, three sheepskins, a jug of ale. Two cups. A bit of old bread in a bowl, and a boy doing something to a piece of plate metal, and there are a couple of rush lamps, yet to be lit. There are many rolls of paper on a board and trestles, on which are written many names, just as in the ledger, Katherine thinks.

They sit where they may, Rufus on her lap, Thomas on another sheepskin, and they leave the stool to Horner. The moment the tent flap is dropped, the two pickets are cut off, though she can hear them and the others still complaining about something and Horner raising his voice and telling them to take the horses to the lines and that one of them – Taplow? – will be held responsible for anything missing in the morning.

When Horner returns he sends the boy for more ale and cups and settles himself on the stool.

'So here we are!' he says. He asks them what happened after the battle of Hexham. Thomas describes the fall of Bamburgh, and how Sir Ralph Grey, who had been Horner's lord, had been knocked senseless by the stone from a cannon.

'And that old bastard Neville of Brancepeth, he turned him over, didn't he?' Horner asks. 'My God. My God, I wish I had been there. I would have stopped that.'

Despite everything, Horner still seems fond of Grey. Thomas does not tell him that it was he, Thomas, who tied Grey to his horse and sent him out of the castle, but instead, in a very few words, tells him what they've been doing for the last five years, and then he asks again what happened to Horner at the battle of Hexham. When he has more ale in his cup, Horner confesses that he broke with the rest of Sir Ralph Grey's men, and then simply carried on running. He stripped off his plate and threw his livery coat in the river, and then he sought sanctuary in the abbey in Hexham. He climbed into the belfry, he tells them, and then out on to the roof.

'Sometime on the second day,' he says, 'they brought the Duke of Somerset out into the square, and the headsman killed him.'

After that, he tells them, he became sick. He thought it was something he'd caught from the pigeons, some vapour they gave off. He thought he'd die, and would have been happy to, but a priest found him and nursed him back to health. But by then he was sick of it all, and the thought of going back to find Grey, if he was still alive, which he doubted, was most sickening of all. So he went home.

'And when I got there, I had nothing. Less than nothing. And then suddenly Lord Montagu's men came through, each as rich as Croesus, swaggering about the place, buying land and building houses, and then by Christ I knew I'd been on the wrong bloody side.'

Horner stretches out his long, stiff legs. He is thin, she sees, as if deprived during these past years, and his clothes are worn and patched – with little skill, so perhaps he has no wife as yet – and his boots remain in need of a cordwainer's attention. Food arrives with the boy: fresh baked bread and good bean and bacon pottage, which they eat straight from the communal bowl with their spoons.

'But how came you to be here?' Thomas asks, wiping his mouth.

'When my indenture with Grey ended – because he was dead – I needed the goodlordship of another, and the man whom we are calling Robin of Redesdale was seeking to expand his influence, so . . . I was pleased when the offer came. I thought: Here is my chance. To undo what I'd done, and to get back at Lord Montagu and his swaggering bastards. I tell you, it has been a tough few years.'

That explains the lines in his face, Katherine thinks.

'And have you?' Thomas asks. 'Got back at Montagu's men?'

'Well,' he says. 'We'll see. At the moment he is sitting on his hands, isn't he? Since he's been made Earl of Northumberland he's less likely to jump to the Earl of Warwick's command, but Redesdale has him confused, I think. He's got everyone confused, really.'

Katherine is happy to learn this is definitely Robin of Redesdale's army. If Horner does not have them hanged then this is something they can be certain of, if they ever see Hastings again.

'So where is Redesdale?' Thomas asks.

'He's already moved south,' Horner tells him. 'We are the rear, or, more honestly, the stragglers. He is an impatient man is Robin: keen to be off.'

'And how many men has he?' Thomas goes on.

Horner shrugs.

'Four thousand? And we have perhaps slightly less than half that.' He gestures at the paper rolls on the coffer.

'So together . . .?'

'Not insubstantial,' Horner says with a trace of that old smile. 'And we are attracting more every day.'

She remembers him in Bamburgh: always so optimistic, always hoping a spark would come to ignite the country against King Edward, never once admitting the cause was hopeless because King Henry was useless.

Rufus is tired, and he lies on the nearest sheepskin to her, and they watch in happy silence, all of them, as he simply drops to sleep.

'And what of yourselves?' Horner asks. 'You are not really riding for the Earl of Warwick, are you, Thomas? You are not on our side?'

'No,' Thomas says. 'It is as Rufus said. We helped some charcoal burners who gave me this. I put it on, hoping it would smooth my passage.'

'Ah, you reckoned without Taplow. My God, there is a nasty piece of work. I wear gauntlets to handle him, let me tell you.'

There is a moment's uncomfortable silence.

'So where were you going?' Horner asks.

Katherine repeats the story she had told Watkins: that they had ridden north in the hope of finding a place to live.

'But it came to nothing, so we are returning to Lincolnshire where we will throw ourselves on the charity of others.'

'Join us!' Horner says. 'By Christ! All we need now is Kit and those other two – the one-armed fellow – and it will be like old times.'

Thomas's flinch turns into a more measured frown. He shakes his head.

'I would join you,' he says, 'but we were lucky to come from Hexham with our lives, and then again, when Bamburgh fell – well. It was only by the grace of God that we were spared, and even then – it was not without cost.'

Katherine feels his gaze slide across her and she closes her mind to the memory of Giles Riven's kick.

'It is not for myself that I fear,' Thomas goes on. 'I have proved this twice, thrice, four times over, but putting Katherine and Rufus at risk when I need not – I cannot square it with my conscience.'

'Later, perhaps?' Horner asks. 'When you have found them refuge among these people in Lincolnshire? We have not given permission for the men to loot, as Queen Margaret did before Towton, so as not to antagonise the south, but there will be the usual third of everything that comes to us in battle, and afterwards there will be opportunity for such advancement! And this time, this time, we will succeed.'

'You sound very certain?' Thomas says, and Katherine starts to feel uncomfortable: they are taxing Horner for information to use against him. Imagine if sometime in the future Thomas were to find himself facing Horner in the field? How would they feel then?

Horner leans forward and becomes conspiratorial.

'I have spoken to Robin of Redesdale,' he tells them. 'And he says the Earl of Warwick is to issue a manifesto from Calais, calling on the whole country to rise up against King Edward. He is going to raise the men of Kent, and a man named Tudor is landing in Wales, to gather troops there. This is it, don't you see? The spark!'

It is unbelievable. She cannot imagine it. It would mean the Earl of Warwick undoing all he has done these last ten years.

'So he has openly come out against King Edward?'

'Yes! Although, well, he has not taken the field himself, not yet at any event, because he is in Calais.'

'But if he is in open rebellion, should he not be here in England?' Katherine asks.

Horner grins.

'But this is it!' he says. 'This is it, you see! You'll never guess what he is doing in Calais!'

'He is issuing this manifesto?'

'Apart from that. No? Well, let me tell you, though it is not to be spoken of ever until – until later. He is marrying his daughter to the Duke of Clarence! Against King Edward's specific enjoinder!'

This is too confusing. Katherine opens her mouth to try to tease it apart, but Thomas speaks first.

'So that is the extent of his rebellion?' he asks. 'While you are taking the field, risking life and limb, he is attending the wedding of his daughter to King Edward's brother?'

Horner sits back with a sly smile.

'It may not sound much,' he agrees, 'but there is something else. Something . . . something I can't – oughtn't – tell you: a deeper plan afoot.'

'What is that?'

'A rumour afloat—' Horner begins, and then stops; he turns and sends the boy out. The boy looks like the sort who will only go around the back of the tent to listen from the other side of the linen, but Horner is caught up in this. He so badly wants Thomas to join him that he is made foolish. When the boy has gone, he continues.

'A rumour that King Edward is a bastard.'

Both Katherine and Thomas feign incredulous shock.

'No!'

'Yes,' Horner says. 'And there is proof.'

There is a moment's hesitation before Thomas coughs and asks, 'What proof?'

And with a gesture at those rolls of paper on the coffer, those lists of serving men, Horner tells them of a record of troop movements from the late days of English rule in Normandy that shows Richard, Duke of York, supposedly King Edward's father, was not within a month's travel of Edward's mother when the boy was conceived.

Katherine can feel the blood rushing to her face.

'And is this proof – to hand?' she asks.

Horner frowns.

'Not quite,' he admits. 'But we are looking for it – and we are close to it. When it is found, it will be presented to the Lords and the Commons and it will show that Edward is not fit for the throne. And who, then, should take his place? His brother, George, Duke of Clarence, to whom, of course, Warwick has married his daughter.'

He laughs at the cunning of it.

Katherine can think of nothing to say.

Now, it seems, Horner's loyalty to the old King has worn thin as his cloth, and he has attached himself to the cause of unseating King Edward, not caring who takes his place.

'So you see?' Horner says, turning back to Thomas. 'You had best join us! Be here at the start of things and there is no telling where you will end up! A knight! A lord! An earl!'

Katherine's mind is racing.

'But if that is so – if Warwick can dethrone Edward that way, then why are you marching south with an army of this size?'

Horner is thoughtful.

'I don't think – I don't think Warwick knew Robin of Redesdale would be so – so busy? I don't think he knew we would attract such numbers and be able to move so swiftly. When he suggested Redesdale come out against King Edward, I think he thought he might stay in Richmondshire, and his presence might force Montagu's hand, one way or the other. Besides, despite our efforts we have not found this record yet, to prove Edward's bastardy, so . . .'

He trails off with a shrug. Katherine feels a stone in her throat and she cannot swallow, but Thomas asks what steps are being taken to locate it, and when Horner tells them that Edmund Riven is tasked with finding it, he makes the connection.

'He's the son of the man Kit cut when we were in Bamburgh! Do you remember? Sir Giles Riven, do you remember? A nasty piece of work, you'd think, but the son! God deliver us, he is from a night-mare. He has some old wound – here – that weeps stinking pus, and when he speaks, there is something cut loose in his cheek that flaps, some piece of skin. Kit would've stitched it up in a moment, I am sure, but no one has done anything for him, and it has made him bitter as bark.'

It is growing dark now and the light of the fire outside glows against the cloth of the tent, and the rush lights ought to be lit. Horner leans forward, takes another drink and goes on.

'Anyway,' he says, 'Riven is now looking for the proof – this ledger – among those who were with Ralph Grey in the last days at Bamburgh,' he tells them. 'That is where it was last seen.'

They are silent for a long moment. Then he looks up with a frown.

'But – so you were there, too?' he asks. 'I mean, you went back, didn't you?'

'We did,' Thomas agrees. He is very casual.

'And did you see any – any ledger? Anyone with anything like that?'

Thomas shakes his head.

'What did Grey say it looked like?' Katherine asks.

Horner tuts.

'They say he was out of his wits. So he could remember almost nothing about it. He could only tell Warwick that he had it, but had lost it. He could not even tell him where he had got it. Well, he did, he said he'd got it from Giles Riven. But of course, that cannot be the case because then surely Edmund Riven would know of it? But that is what he said, apparently.'

Hearing these words, Katherine feels a great swelling of relief. If Grey had told Warwick that he had got the book from his surgeon, then he would have passed this on to Edmund Riven, and Edmund Riven would have known to come looking for Thomas Everingham, and this 'surgeon' whom he assisted. But what Grey had said was true: he did get it from Giles Riven, but only because Giles Riven had, in effect, stolen it from her. She spares a moment to thank the Lord for Grey's ill-sprung memory. It seems that He is protecting them after all, in His own way.

'It's a mystery,' Thomas says, as if that might end the matter, but Horner is less gloomy.

'Oh, he'll find it,' he says, 'if it has not been burned or anything. And even if it has, Edmund Riven will find it. He has been going among Robin of Redesdale's men as they mustered in Richmond, you know? So many of them are Hungerford's and Roos's, who were there with Grey at the end.'

He looks at them carefully now.

'I am surprised he has not come looking for you,' he says, 'but you will have the pleasure when we reach York.'

10

'Riven's in York!' Katherine repeats.

It is the next morning and they are washing themselves in the stream above the camp, the first time they have been alone long enough to exchange anything more significant than the swiftest of meaningful looks.

'He can't be,' Thomas says. 'He just can't be. He's in Pickering.'

But in a way he hopes he is wrong. If Riven is in York, then at least Jack and John and Nettie will have evaded capture; but then he and Katherine – and Jack and John – are riding straight into his net.

'We can ride with Horner until York, and then slip away,' he supposes. 'Horner has accepted we are not intending to join him.'

'Has he? You saw his expression? And that man – with the hatchet face – he has been ever present. He'd rather kill you than see you go.'

Taplow has been at hand, it is true, but can Horner have asked him to keep an eye on Thomas? Or is it personal? Something Thomas said that warrants revenge? But anyway, surely they'll be able to absent themselves from Horner's column in the jumble of lanes and alleys that lead off the road from York's north gate. That will be the best place, so long as Taplow is not there, on their shoulder, watching.

So they ride with Horner as the column he is commanding moves south through the Vale of Mowbray at the speed of the slowest oxen pulling the heaviest load: a great gun that takes eighteen men on ropes to lift. Food is plentiful, as is ale, and more men join them as they ride. They are gathered at the roadside as if by previous appointment, and by the time they see York, their numbers are swelled to two thousand or more who might be called upon to fight, and the same number attending behind. The journey has been enlivened by fighting among the various retinues, small though they are, and Horner has had to intervene daily.

'I'd hang a few if I thought it would help,' he says.

They are a ragbag of men, with few sharing the same livery, and though they mostly look like men who can fight in wayside inns and so on, that is not the same as soldiering, and Thomas wonders what will happen to this lot should they take the field against King Edward's household men. He hopes they will run without a fight, even Taplow, who has hardly left their side, though not perhaps his sidekick, who is staring at Katherine now as if he means to pull her limb from limb. Thomas still does not quite know how he will evade them when the time comes. But as they approach the city walls a messenger arrives for Horner from Robin of Redesdale. Still in the saddle, Horner takes it and reads it without moving his lips. When he's finished he looks bleak and he returns the paper to the messenger for re-use.

'He's already moved on,' he tells them. 'South.'

Horner is downcast, puzzled even, but Thomas cannot stop himself smiling: Riven is not in York.

They camp that night on common ground to the north of the city, under some windmills which delight Rufus, outside the Bootham Bar with the river on their right, and at Angelus, they all stop what they are doing to listen to the great bells of the city ring out across the water meadows.

The next morning, after the bread and ale has been given out, and Mass said, Thomas finds Horner dressed in full harness, readying himself to play his part for the townsfolk of York; the boy is just tying the last points of one of Warwick's red livery coats around Horner's steel-cinched waist.

'Nice,' Thomas says.

'Thank you,' Horner replies.

'We will leave you here, John, if you do not object?' he asks.

Horner looks at him very solemnly. It is the effect of wearing plate. Thomas has seen it before: Horner even speaks with added gravitas.

'If you must, you must, Thomas,' he says. 'But I hope to see you again. Robin of Redesdale is moving to Leicester. I know you wish to deposit your wife, and I envy you that luxury, but it would mean a great deal to me if you were to join us there. I always felt safe with you at my back when we were in Bamburgh, Thomas.'

The boy finishes his tying and Horner straightens the coat over his hips and then lets the boy strap on the two belts from which he will hang his various swords and daggers, and then he extends his hand and grips Thomas's. Thomas feels almost as emotional, and grips his back just as firmly. They look one another in the eye.

'Promise me, Thomas,' Horner says. 'Promise you will be there. Swear on it by God and on St George and on the life of your child.'

Thomas is caught out. On the life of his child? On the life of Rufus? But there is no room to wheedle out of this. No room to lie. Horner is too close. He will see it in his eyes if he looks away even for a moment. So what can he say?

'I do,' he says. 'I will.'

He feels a free-falling panic. I do not. I will not.

And Horner nods sharply.

'Good,' he says, and he turns and swings up into his saddle. From there he looks down at him. 'God bless you, Tom, and see you in Leicester.' And he rakes his horse with those long spurs – new-bought in Ripon – and rides out of the camp.

Thomas watches him leave before going to look for his own horse. He feels the ground is no longer so solid under his feet. To hold a man's eye and make an oath like that . . . but, dear God, what choice did he have? When he finds his horse, Taplow is standing there, one hand on its rump, proprietorially examining the pollaxe, which he has removed from its oiled linen bag.

'Fucking do a man some damage with that,' he says.

'Get your hands off my horse,' Thomas tells him.

Taplow drops the bag on the ground.

'I meant what I said, you know. You can swagger around here with Horner's protection like you own the place, but give me just one moment and I will fucking gut you like a pig at Martinmas.'

Thomas looks at him. He is as simple as a dog.

'Taplow,' he starts, 'why does it always have to be like this? Why can't you just – I don't know. Be normal.'

Taplow looks at him up and down with small, pale eyes.

'You think you deserve it all, don't you?' he asks. 'Your horse, your woman, your clothes, all this, and you think everywhere you go, you deserve to go safe, like you're in the palm of God Himself. But what about the rest of us? What about me? What about Gradle there? We're no more than bushes to you and your sort, are we? Just fucking scenery. Things to be got around. Or over. Or through.'

Thomas hardly knows what to say. He had not imagined Taplow capable of such thoughts – so proving him right, of course – but also . . . Christ! Imagine anyone thinking of him that way, with his borrowed horse and his empty purse.

'If you knew—' he begins.

'Oh, fuck off,' Taplow interrupts. 'I don't fucking care. But just remember me when we take the field.'

This is more like it, more expected: a simple threat.

'You know what happened to the last man who threatened me?' Thomas asks.

'You told your priest about him?'

Thomas thinks of Giles Riven's Scottish murderers whom he and Jack had to kill in that foul little guardroom of the outward postern gate at Bamburgh Castle. He remembers a spray of blood on the stone ceiling and the man in twitching agonies on the flagstones.

'I did,' Thomas says, 'but only after he was dead.'

Taplow is delighted.

'You fucker,' he says. 'But just remember: when it comes to it, I'll be there. Just me and this.'

A third knife appears in his hand, again as if from nowhere: a short dark blade, good for one thing only. He grins at Thomas and does something with his tongue that Thomas does not quite understand. Then he tucks the knife away, and walks away backwards, still leering, his teeth long and yellow and in surprisingly good condition.

Thomas wonders if a man like Taplow threatens everyone he meets, and if he has become so vicious because he already looked so vicious, or if he has come to look vicious because he is so vicious? Does his face tell his character, or his character his face?

Horner's army of camp followers gathers itself for the off. The carts are loaded and fastened to the oxen, and everyone is a little more intent this morning for few have seen a city like York before, let alone been within such walls. As they approach they are all but silenced by the solid and convincing bulk of the minster, but then confused by the number of church steeples beyond.

'Where is your parish?' they ask. 'Where does one hear Mass? Where does one go to pray? To see one's priest? Is it here? Or there? Is it St Martin's? St Helen's? Or is it All Saints? You just don't know, do you?'

Thomas has set Rufus on his saddle, and he walks alongside, leading the horse through the tight streets and the thick air of the city, and the townspeople have turned out to watch them pass, but they remain unswayed, for this is the second time in a week they've watched an army pass, and this one is smaller than the first, and suffers by comparison. The abiding emotion seems to be pity.

'They seem very – accepting?' Thomas suggests. 'As if they care neither one way nor the other.'

'I suppose they have seen it all before,' Katherine tells him. 'This was where everyone came after Towton.'

He, of course, does not remember that.

He starts looking for Jack and John when they are across the river, in Micklegate, which leads down to the bar where they stick the heads of the executed. It is where the Duke of Somerset stuck the heads of King Edward's brother and father. Thomas wonders if Horner will remember that when he thinks about the Duke being killed in the market square at Hexham.

'What if they are not here?' he asks Katherine.

'We shall have to get lodging,' she says, 'and wait for tomorrow.'

Thomas winces, thinking about money again. Another anxiety to gnaw at him when he has other things to worry about.

Micklegate is only a few hundred paces long, and by the time they reach the bar, and pass under the shadow of its gate and out into the barbican, he knows Jack and John and Nettie are not there.

'It is not yet noon,' she says.

And that is when they see the aproned sister. She is standing on the bed of their cart, complete with the coffers and sacks and every-thing else they own, at the side of the road, alone, waiting. She looks tired, and there is a bruise under her right eye; her apron is gone, and when she sees them she seems to take a step back, and swallows; and Thomas thinks: Oh Christ! They are dead.

But they are not.

'Riven took 'em,' the girl tells them before they can even ask. 'He were on us before we got to Kirby. He was out after that book of which he always spoke, and Jack said he didn't know what he were talking about, but Riven had a man with him who recognised John — recognised his stump. Said he'd been in some castle and had seen the arm taken off by a boy with a kitchen knife. Said he'd seen it with his own eyes. And that is when the book he seeks was lost.'

'But they said Riven was with Robin of Redesdale!' Thomas says.

'Well, he might have been, and he might be now, but he weren't that night. He were on the road to Thirsk with that bloody bastard giant of his.'

'He has a giant?' Katherine asks.

'Aye,' the girl says. 'He keeps him like a bear, only he smells worse than a bear.'

'His father kept one likewise,' Katherine says. She's turned ashen at this memory. 'He was a monster.'

'It cannot be the same one, surely?' Thomas asks.

'He is young, I'd say,' the girl tells them. 'But a monster, too.'

'Why does he keep him?' Thomas asks.

'To do his bidding,' the girl shrugs.

'But then where has he taken them?'

'To Middleham,' the girl supposes. 'That is where he keeps his prisoners.'

'What about you?' Katherine asks. 'Why did they not take you?'

'Riven knows me,' she admits. 'Knows my father.'

'So what happened to your cheek?'

The girl compresses her eyes and tilts her chin at her. She looks fierce up there on the cart, despite her torn dress and bruised face.

'He did what his kind always do,' she tells them.

There is a long silence.

Then the girl smiles down at Rufus.

'Hello, boy,' she says.

'Hello, Liz,' Rufus says.

So that is her name.

'What is Middleham like?' Thomas asks.

'I've never been there, of course, as why would I? But my father says it is like any castle, save perhaps bigger.'

'Is it – easy to come and go from? In and out, I mean.'

He is not sure what he means. He can only think of Jack and John and Nettie in a castle, there because of him, suffering on his behalf.

'Thomas,' Katherine says, 'you cannot mean to . . . You cannot mean to go and – what? Rescue them?'

'You will not succeed in that,' Liz tells him. 'No.'

'No,' Katherine agrees, almost pleading. 'You must not even think of it. Dear God. You know what these places are like. We can only – we can only hope that – that Robin of Redesdale is defeated, and that Warwick is defeated, too. Only then. Only then can we hope to see them come out.'

'But they'll be dead by then!'

'Aye, mebbe,' Liz agrees. 'But there's shit all else you can do about it now, and on your own.'

They stare at her. She stares back at them, and then turns and smiles down at Rufus again.

'Have you been having a nice time, boy? Did you see the windmills on the way in? I saw 'em meself, and I thought of you.'

Rufus twinkles with pleasure.

'But what – what if Robin of Redesdale's army beats King Edward's?' Thomas asks. 'What then?'

'Well,' Katherine says. 'We will have to pray.'

'Much good that'll do you,' Liz says.

'Well' – Thomas turns to her – 'what do you suggest?'

'You could kill one or two of 'em now,' she says. 'That one there. Only got to look at him to know he's a bastard with a blade up his sleeve.'

He turns to where the straggling tail of Horner's column roll past and he sees she is gesturing at Taplow.

'You could follow them with that great bow of yours and you could pick 'em off, one by one.'

He absently tries to imagine this. How long would it take? How many arrows?

But Katherine is right. The only thing he can do is to warn Hastings and King Edward of what is coming. If he can bring men such as John Brunt – Rufus's godfather – to the fight, then there is a chance he and King Edward can beat this crowd of village murderers.

'All right,' Thomas says. 'All right. But we must go now then. Down to London to find Hastings. And we'll have to ride fast to overtake this lot, and Redesdale too.'

'And how shall we manage that?' Liz asks.

'*We?*'

'Yes,' she says. 'We. Unless you mean to leave all this here' – she stamps a clog on the coffer – 'and do not mind if I take it to market and set myself up as a fine lady?'

He looks at the cart. It is the sum total of his – their – worldly goods.

'You'll not move fast enough with it in tow,' Liz goes on. 'So you must take it somewhere?'

'Marton,' Katherine says. 'We must take it back to Marton.'

Liz looks pleased someone is making sense.

'Right,' she says. 'Where is this Marton place? Is it far?'

They tell her.

Thomas knows what must be said and done next, but he cannot bring himself to suggest it. Liz can though.

'Will you be coming with me then, goodwife? You and Rufus? We can leave Thomas here to find his fine lord on his ownsome? Quicker that way, and safer too.'

Katherine cannot help smile at Liz.

'You have arranged it all so well,' she says.

'No point messing, is there?'

Thomas stands wondering what else he need add.

'I bought a loaf,' Liz says. 'Two, in fact. One for you, and one for us. The boy Jack left me his money. D'you want it back?'

And she holds out a palmful of coins. The same that he gave Jack. And with that, she cements his trust.

Thomas says goodbye to Katherine and Rufus while Liz turns her back and pretends to do something with the horse attached to the cart.

'You will be all right?' Thomas asks.

Katherine rolls her eyes at Liz's back.

'I expect so,' she tells him. 'I feel we have been commandeered.'

He offers to ride with them back to Marton.

'No,' Katherine tells him. 'She is right. You must find Hastings, and quickly. London is how many days' ride? Five? Six?'

He shrugs. He is not sure. Something like that.

'And anyway,' she goes on, 'there is no telling if Isabella, or her sons, will have us back.'

She leaves hanging the thought that they are less likely to do so if Thomas is there with them, and Thomas nods, accepting the truth of it.

'You know the route?'

'We follow this lot south, to Doncaster, and from there, I think I know the way by now.'

'And you will explain to Isabella? Tell her what's happened?'

'Of course.'

'She will have you back, I know it.'

'She is a good woman.'

'And once I have found Hastings——' he starts, but then stops. He does not know what Hastings will say when he finds him, though it is not hard to guess.

'I will come for you there,' he tells her. 'As soon as I can.'

She nods.

'I will wait,' she says. 'Every day. Rufus and I. We will come to the road to keep a lookout for you.'

Thomas laughs.

'Thomas,' she says. 'Don't get drawn into anything for William Hastings's sake. Don't get drawn into any fighting. It is not your fight. And God forbid anything should befall you – I will not be there, and you will not help Jack and John and Nettie that way.'

It is his turn to nod.

'So go now,' she says. 'Go, and come back safe. And may God go with you.'

PART THREE

After the Visitation, Summer, 1469

11

Thomas takes a different road to the one that Horner and his army take, one that swings him westwards, so that he may overtake the column, and – he hopes – Robin of Redesdale, before rejoining the London road further south. Thomas rides quickly, and soon the city drops away behind him, but as he goes he is overtaken by a creeping horror. He rides for a while with tears in his eyes that are nothing to do with the wind, and he thinks it is because he has left Katherine, but nor is it that. It is when he looks around him at the furlongs and fields, at the trees and the softly undulating land that he feels it most, and when he comes to the crest of a rise, he is almost struck from his horse, and can hardly find the strength to breathe, for his chest is crushed.

He finds himself climbing from his saddle and staggering along the road, westwards, towards the edge of the escarpment, where it drops into a steep little valley. The grass is lush and long underfoot and he stands there with these tears flooding his eyes and pouring down his cheeks, and he stares into the valley, at the winding beck that fiddles its way through twisted hawthorns and alders; a soft wind blows from the south, and there are fat crows and rooks in the tree-tops, but he sees nothing of these, only feels a desperate sorrow of the sort that might press him to his knees and make him pray aloud. And it gets no better the longer he stays, so he turns and makes his way back to his horse, stumbling, stricken. He trips on something in the grass and falls to his knees, and then turns to pick it up. It is a twisted strip of rusted metal – a piece of old plate – with a great pock in the middle. As it comes free, it releases an old, old smell. He looks about him: at the low sloping field and the single hawthorn, and then he tosses the metal aside, climbs into his saddle, nudges his horse into a trot and rides down the hill, away from the dismal spot towards a hamlet gathered around a tiny church.

There is a boy to tell him the name of the village is Lead.

'And what is up there?' Thomas points to the fields through which he has just ridden.

'That is Towton way,' the boy says. 'We don't go there. Not any more.'

Thomas reaches Doncaster in the late afternoon, and hears news of Robin of Redesdale from the White Friars who give him a bed for the night.

'How many men?' he asks their almoner.

'Five thousand,' the man tells him in return for one of Thomas's last coins.

'That is in all?'

'That is just fighting men. In all, perhaps ten thousand.'

Thomas doesn't know whether to believe him, but there is no reason not to.

'Where are they bent?' he asks.

'How should I know?' the man says. 'But they left by St Sepulchre's on the road running west.'

West? Thomas does not understand why Redesdale would go west, when his objective must be to the south, but he is pleased, anyway, for it means the road is clear for him to find Hastings, so he rides through Doncaster's southern gate, and out on to the London road, following a small party of pilgrims on their way to Lincoln, trying to puzzle it for himself. Horner said something about someone – Tudor? Was that it? The name is familiar – raising Wales in rebellion against King Edward and so perhaps Robin of Redesdale and this Tudor intend to combine and move on London from the west? Is that likely? Possible, even? Thomas has no idea. William Hastings will know, he thinks, or he will know someone who does.

The pilgrims turn east towards Gainsborough, on the same road that leads to Marton, but he continues south through the early afternoon until he reaches Newark, where he thinks he will have to change horses. But even before he crosses the new wooden bridge, he can see there is something afoot: there are men hoisting a flag in the castle battlements and at the bridge's far end is a clot of men in blue and murrey livery, more than might make up your usual city Watch, and far better armed. They are King Edward's men.

Thomas is half-relieved, half-disappointed. He wanted his news to come as a surprise, but it seems King Edward must already know.

'What are you doing here?' he asks. There are five or six of them, big, useful-looking men, of the type he knows well, and they are heavily armed, but there is also something leisurely about them, as if this is a Sunday in the butts, not as if they are coming north to suppress an armed rebellion against their king.

'Might ask the same of you,' one of them – the one they defer to – asks. 'You want to get down off there?'

Thomas swings his leg over the back of his horse and drops down. They are all in new-made jackets, and their helmets are polished as if new-minted. Perhaps this is how it is with King Edward's men? One of them raises his chin to point at Thomas's bow and pollaxe.

'Fighting man, are you?' he asks.

Thomas tells them that he is William Hastings's man.

'Well, he is not here,' they tell him.

'Where is he?'

They don't know, and are even puzzled to be asked. But he should be, Thomas knows, if King Edward is moving up to fight Robin of Redesdale.

'But King Edward is here?'

'He is,' the man says. 'If it is a concern of yours?'

Thomas tells them he has ridden from Doncaster that morning.

'I have seen Robin of Redesdale's army.'

Another laughs.

'Oh, that villain! We are set to spank his arse for him!'

'How many of you are there?' Thomas asks.

'Over a thousand,' the youngest boasts. 'With more coming.'

'But Robin of Redesdale has an army of five – no – seven thousand. Men-at-arms and bowmen.'

There is a moment when their mouths are as open as their eyes.

'Blood of Christ! You are – not serious?'

'They are just the other side of the river,' Thomas tells them. 'Did you not – *know?*'

Now they are more active. Thomas is taken to find an officer – a tall man, young, well dressed, indoor skin, someone's son – who greets his news with incredulity that gives way to scepticism, then becomes flailing panic. Thomas is passed up a line to some sort of steward, who walks accompanied by six bored men in blue and murrey livery, each armed with an identical bill. Again his news is met with derision, then doubt, then panicked acceptance, and so he is passed on up to another steward – younger even, very richly dressed in tight red hose, piked shoes and billowing silk sleeves, who reminds Thomas of one of Isabella's sons – who tells him King Edward is spending the afternoon with his hawks.

Ten men in pristine blue and murrey livery accompany Thomas back to his horse and then out to the water meadows upriver to find King Edward. He is nervous, of course, seeing King Edward. He has seen him before, has spoken to him before – been hugged by the man, he has been told – but he cannot recall any of this and now, as they ride out through boggy flood plains to find him, Thomas is gripped by anxiety.

They find him on horseback, on a reed-fringed, black-mud islet, surrounded by a clutch of gentlemen, with, some way apart, another clutch of less important gentlemen, and, further off still, a small army of servants carrying bags and wicker boxes and those frames for the hawks. Dog-handlers stand about, too, and their muddy charges are swimming through the turbid waters and emerging on the banks to shake themselves; while some are finding this reasonably amusing – who is going to be soaked? – others are intent on the sky, following the distant dots of the hawks as they go about their business. The afternoon is heavy and warm, and insects make clouds in the air.

Thomas is told to wait where he is, for he must not approach the King, and he waits while various negotiations are undertaken with members from one group going to the next and each time he sees their disbelief and their craned heads as he is studied and then successively finer gentlemen come splashing over to him to ask him the same questions until at last someone finally alerts King Edward, who is up there in the saddle of his beautiful mud-spattered horse, taller than them all, gauntleted hand shading his eyes, and on his head a cap the size of a woman's cushion with an extravagant feather.

He turns in his saddle when he hears what is said, and he demands repetition before he looks over; he has to shade his eyes again, and when he sees Thomas, he sort of starts, and then gestures that Thomas should come into his presence, now, and all the servants and lesser gentlemen and finer gentlemen step back so that an avenue is cleared between them; Thomas splashes forward through the mud, and King Edward meets him halfway there, leaning forward, the hawks forgotten, his expression intent and fierce.

'Dear God!' King Edward says. 'I know you.'

Thomas nods, because he knows this to be true, though he cannot remember it himself.

'Your grace,' he says, and he knows to remove his hat and clutch it to his chest while bowing his head in imitation of all the other servants and less fine gentlemen. King Edward swings his leg over the front of his saddle and drops heavily into the mud. As he does so, everyone else dismounts. He is a tall man, King Edward, taller even than Thomas, and broad-shouldered, and he is well padded with muscle but also a skim of fat that tells of time spent at the dinner

145

board. His eyes are little in his broad face, and his mouth, small and soft, pursed slightly, as if in the middle of a self-deprecating joke. And yet he is the victor of Towton, a warrior king, Sir John used to say, to rival the victors of Agincourt or any of those other battles won in the French wars.

Yet does he also look like a bastard? Thomas wonders. The son of a man other than his father?

'Thomas Everingham,' King Edward says. 'Dear God. I am glad to see you alive.'

He stretches out a gloved hand, studded with rings, and Thomas does not know if he should shake it or kiss it. He opts for the former and King Edward seems happy enough. A circle of faces has formed around them and King Edward arches an eyebrow.

'Well?' he asks. 'What have you for me?'

Thomas tells him about Robin of Redesdale's numbers.

King Edward is startled, as are the others, who look to one another seeking someone to blame.

'That is more than three times as many as we were told!' he says. 'How is this possible?'

No one says a thing.

Then: 'It is merely worse than feared,' one says.

'More than *three* times worse!' King Edward shouts. '*Three* times! Dear God!'

'We can raise more men, your grace, if we move quickly, and we can smash this Robin of Redesdale and have his head on a spike before the month is out.'

King Edward looks at this man a long moment, calming himself down, drawing encouragement from him, and then thanking him for his certainty, calling him William. He's a big man, with a full beard and weather-chapped cheeks that seem unusual in such a gathering of smooth-skinned gentles.

Another speaks: a dapper little man with a silk hat and dark eyes that he fixes on this first bearded man with dislike.

'How many men can my lord of Pembroke hope to raise in so short a time?' he asks.

The big, bearded man – Pembroke – says he has already sent orders to his estates for two thousand men, yet learning now the severity of the crisis, he undertakes to raise a further one thousand, making three in all.

'Men-at-arms?'

'In the main.'

'Then I will match that number with bowmen,' the dapper little man says with a sort of bow to King Edward.

King Edward is again grateful and thanks him, calling him my lord of Devon.

Others offer their own men, but few can match such numbers; after a moment Pembroke begs to be excused, since he wishes to set off at once, and King Edward allows it. The dapper one, Devon, does likewise.

'Hurry,' King Edward tells them. 'We will gather at Nottingham ten days from now, unless I send message otherwise.'

Thomas watches Devon and Pembroke splash away, each detaching a retinue from the group of lesser gentles and the servile commons.

King Edward turns to another man.

'Send letters this day,' he says. 'Send them now. To everyone you can think of. Cities too. Coventry. Gloucester. Norfolk. Everywhere. Tell them to send men to meet me at Nottingham. I need bowmen. A hundred each and more if they may, to be sent to me at once. Fuck the cost. You know what to say.'

The man nods and passes his hawk to another and he hurries away followed by three servants.

'What of my lord of Northumberland?' King Edward asks. 'He has not come out against this – this villain Redesdale, and nor has he sent message.'

'They say he is sitting on his hands,' Thomas tells him.

'Ungrateful bastard,' King Edward says. 'I will put him back where he belongs.'

The sun is oppressive now and the birds are returning with beating wings, lured back by their keepers, and they have been capped, and the news that the day's sport is over has spread. But it seems they know nothing of Warwick's involvement.

'Men of his livery pass freely among Robin of Redesdale's men,' Thomas says. 'It is almost as if he is with them.'

King Edward is startled.

'No!' he says. 'Can this be true? My lord of Warwick's men go among them?'

Thomas looks at him for a long moment, trying to read something in those evasive eyes. He remembers Hastings telling them, what seems like many years ago now, that King Edward did not want to hear anything ill said of the Earl of Warwick, and so perhaps no one has told him? Does he even know that Warwick has married his daughter to the Duke of Clarence, King Edward's own brother? That Warwick is going to send a proclamation telling the country to rise up against King Edward's councillors? That Warwick is going to land in Sandwich and raise the men of Kent? Has no one told King Edward anything?

'Your grace,' Thomas begins, and he tells him all that he has heard about the marriage between his brother the Duke of Clarence and Warwick's daughter, and the manifesto issued in Calais, and as he does so King Edward stands in silence while behind him his gentlemen huff and sigh and they unstick their boots and shift their weight from foot to foot, but Thomas goes on. And King Edward's expression hardens: his mouth becomes thin as a buttonhole and his eyes mere needle pricks of flint-hard anger. He seems to grow in stature, too, to puff up, to tower over Thomas. Now this, Thomas thinks, now this *is* the victor of Towton, the man ruthless enough to give the order not to spare the commons, the man who set Englishmen to kill other Englishmen until it was too dark to see. A jolt of hot fright billows within him and he takes a step back.

And King Edward has taken a step towards him. His hand is at his dagger's hilt, and Thomas sees that he is in such a temper that he could kill him now and turn the knife on any man who said a thing to stop him. Thomas swallows and anticipates the pain of the stab, for he knows he cannot – must not – defend himself against it. But then King Edward's simple anger is cooled by a harder, crueller, more calculating expression that is yet more frightening still, and Thomas feels himself naked and wholly vulnerable before this man's power. King Edward moves his hand slowly away from the knife, and he stares at Thomas, interested in his reaction now, and he says through compressed lips, and very slowly, very quietly, but very clearly:

'Do you *know* how we punish sedition?'

Now everyone is still. This is no longer a stand-off between two men in the mud. This is a man against a king. The spit dries in Thomas's mouth. King Edward is waiting, his gaze pins Thomas fast.

'Well?'

Thomas is about to shake his head, because, for the love of God above, he does not even know what sedition is. Yet he must say something, and he knows that whatever it is, his life depends upon it. He wonders what to say, and decides on the truth.

'It is the truth, sir, as I've been told.'

King Edward is a handspan away from him. He is rigid with rage, pink with it. Thomas feels as if he is looking into the eyes of one of those bear-baiting dogs, and he remembers: Just keep calm. Show no fear. So he looks back at King Edward, eye to eye. And he thinks: Just because you can have me killed in a snap of your fingers, you will not, because you know it would be a sin. And King Edward's gaze, which had been so constant, now flicks around his face, as if studying Thomas for the first time, seeing him afresh and finding himself surprised at what is there, but the confrontation is, for the moment, over. Thomas feels not merely relief, but a species of triumph.

King Edward points to the fob of white hair.

'What is that?' he asks.

'A memento of Towton,' Thomas tells him.

King Edward nods but then after a while says:

'I have seen worse.'

Thomas says nothing. He has never boasted of it.

'So you come here,' King Edward goes on, 'spouting lies about my friends and my kinsmen, and about – about manifestos, and it is as if you are able to see into the future?'

'I only tell what I have been told. It may not come to pass. I know nothing further. I know nothing of how it might be, how it is supposed to be, what any of it even means. I only tell you as I was told.'

'So you keep saying,' one of King Edward's gentlemen says. He still has his bird on his fist; its chest is gory, and there are pink scraps of flesh in its talons. He and the bird look the same, both dark-eyed and hooked nosed.

'What should we do with him, my lord of Worcester?' King Edward asks from the side of his mouth.

'To get to the truth, sir? Or to punish him?'

Thomas is astonished.

'I only tell you what I have been told,' he repeats. He suddenly feels very simple. There is something here he does not understand. Dear God! He wishes he had never come here, never tried to help. King Edward remains looking at him.

'No,' he says, after a moment. 'We will leave it a few days. I recall you are William Hastings's man. We will wait his arrival and see what he suggests.'

The hawk-faced man, who is dressed in a curious jacket of layered leather tabs that hang like his bird's feathers down his chest, looks disappointed. He has lost his prey. King Edward makes some secret signal that Thomas does not see, and suddenly Thomas is surrounded by the big men in their blue and murrey; they press in on him in silence and he cannot even move his arms and they stand there while King Edward and his gentlemen climb up into their saddles and ride back through the mud and water to the dry ground by the castle.

*

He is first taken to a corner of a whitewashed guardroom in the castle gatehouse and left to sit there while there is much running and shouting in the yard without. Doors are slammed. Horses' hooves clatter on the cobbles and men come and go. He tries to think why everything has gone so badly.

'Stuck your member in a hornets' nest, haven't you?' one of the blue and murrey guards tells him when they come with bread and ale. 'Still, lucky old Worcester didn't take you away with him. He would have made a bowstring of your guts.'

Thomas is given a blanket and sleeps on the flagstones and the next day they return his horse – though the bow and the pollaxe are on another man's saddle – and he rides with them to the city of Nottingham. King Edward is there, far ahead in the column, and messengers canter to and fro, and there is a drum being beaten and the atmosphere is more like it, Thomas thinks, though dear God how bitterly he wishes he were elsewhere.

He thinks of Katherine and Rufus and hopes they are safe in Marton, and he tries to imagine how it would be had they been here with him. Would Katherine have known not to press the King? Probably. Then he thinks of Jack and Nettie and John Stump and he almost shudders to think of Edmund Riven and all that he has heard about him, and then he tries to imagine what perhaps he should have done to save them. But surely this was the only way? It could not have been expected that the King would react so, could it? Could it? And so his thoughts ever circle back to himself and his own plight.

They reach Nottingham late in the day, and they ride up to the castle above its cliff of stone and once again Thomas is placed in a guardroom of the gatehouse, but by now, being harmless, he is largely ignored. The guards come and go, and their conversation is familiar and soothing, and Thomas listens and knows almost to the word what each will say next and the response it will get from the others. They gossip and speculate on the maids, of course, and they tease the virgin among them, and they boast of their various prowesses, sexual and martial, and then they discuss the relative merits of their towns and counties – they come from a wide spread across the country – and then what they think will happen next: where they will be sent, whom they will have to fight, and what they will do to the men they are fighting.

As that first day wears into the evening and then the night and the next morning, Thomas hears first how things stand: how King Edward has sent scouts forward across the river to see if the rumours are true and when after noon the scouts return with the news that they can find no trace of any army, let alone a big one, the guards laugh, half-relieved, half-disappointed. Then they remember that Thomas was the source of the rumours and so they turn to jeer at him, and they predict a visit from this Earl of Worcester, of whom they are all terrified, but Thomas remains adamant, and at length they seem to accept him as some sort of lunatic, touched by the moon, perhaps, and they give him bread and ale and they start to treat him as an idiot mascot, or a pet. Other men are brought in to look at him, sitting there, and he might even have had his hair ruffled were he not so big.

The guards are delighted when more adventurous scouts return from further afield later in the evening, having discovered an army, only it is nothing like so large as feared, and the thought of taking that on is very pleasing. Later still another pair bring the news that this small army is only the rearguard of a much larger army, and they are downcast.

Thomas feels vindicated, but he is still in the guardroom the next night and he becomes less popular as it begins to dawn on the men that they will definitely have to fight this large army, and the older among them express the hope that the Earls of Devon and of Pembroke will get back with their promised reinforcements before this Robin of Redesdale swings his men south.

'What do you think, Thomas? You seem to know everything?'

Thomas does not, of course, but still they ask him, and now he begins to take on a difficult talismanic role in their company.

'And what about the Earl of Warwick? Will he bring his men?'

Again Thomas does not know, and even if he could say for sure that Warwick would or would not bring his much-feared troops, he cannot say for sure on which side they would fight. None in the various guardrooms can believe the Earl of Warwick could be guilty of such treachery, as is rumoured, certainly not the older among them, who knew of him when he was fighting alongside King Edward at Northampton and Towton.

But one of the younger men has stood guard with some of that big, bearded Earl of Pembroke's men, and says they are all talking of how the Earl of Warwick hates King Edward's queen and all her family, most especially her father and her brother, and of how the Earl of Pembroke thwarted Warwick's plans in Wales while the Earl of Devon has done something terrible to his interests elsewhere.

'So it is all turn and turn about.'

And Thomas is left wondering what, in the name of God, all this is for.

The next day a newly come messenger arrives in the guardroom in search of ale and something to eat. He is sun-pinked and sweaty from his ride, and he shrugs off his coat and sits heavily on a stool, ignoring Thomas while he drinks from his own leather mazer, and it is a moment before Thomas sees he has the familiar black bull's head badge stitched into the folds of his jacket.

'You are Hastings's man?'

The man looks over and grunts agreement.

'Come from London with a message for the King,' he says. 'Bugger me, it is hot.'

'Is William Hastings here?' Thomas asks.

The man shakes his head.

'Coming tomorrow,' he says. 'Too much for him to do in London, my word.'

Before he can explain, one of the other guards returns.

'Come on, you,' he tells Thomas. 'You're called for.'

Two more men in blue and murrey wait to escort him through the bailey to the hall where he is passed to another steward and then on to another, who guides him to a door on which he taps and opens a small way, poking his head through the gap, and then, after a whispered conversation, opens wide. Inside are some of the men from the hunt the other day, though their number is shrunk, and King Edward stands apart, staring out of a window, a piece of paper hanging from one hand. All turn and stare at Thomas when he comes in.

'Ah,' King Edward says. 'Thomas Everingham.'

He walks to him quickly. He is wearing blue today, with low black shoes, not too pointed, and at his belt a sword in a long red scabbard, which seems odd inside, Thomas thinks, but is maybe intended as a sign of his resolve.

'I wanted you to be here,' he says, 'when I relay the news sent this day from London by our right well-beloved William, Lord Hastings.'

He flaps the square of paper. There are few lines on it. No seal. Thomas knows this means it was written in haste.

'So my lords,' he says, turning to his audience and tapping the paper with the back of his fingers. 'Our lord of Hastings writes this day with great good news, of which we may have had intimation, thanks to our right loyal friend Thomas Everingham here, that has come to him in London from our town of Calais, where it seems our brother George, my lord of Clarence, is this week blessed in holy wedlock!'

The gentlemen avoid looking at one another and King Edward must wait a long moment before the first thud of hands indicates a formal show of their pleasure at the news.

'And who is the lucky bride?' King Edward asks himself. 'Why, none other than the Lady Isabel Neville, daughter of our most loyal cousin, my lord of Warwick. I suppose we must now get used to calling her the Duchess of Clarence.'

There is a furrow of brows.

'But, your grace,' the Earl of Worcester – still in his jacket that looks like the feathers of a hawk's chest – begins, 'you expressly forbade the match.'

'Yes, yes, my lord, I thought I had, but evidently I did not make myself absolutely clear to all parties involved.'

King Edward's smile is made of glass.

'And has the Pope granted his dispensation?' Worcester continues. 'Without that it is—'

'In March,' King Edward interrupts, holding up that piece of paper. 'It was granted in March.'

'In *March*!' Worcester breathes. 'Four months ago and . . . Christ! And who married them?'

King Edward is pleased with the question.

'Ah,' he says. 'That would be the bride's uncle, my lord the Archbishop of York.'

'And was Earl Warwick there?' This question is from the youngest of the party.

'The father of the bride would hardly miss the occasion, don't you think?'

There is a long moment of mutterings in the crowd.

King Edward turns to Thomas.

'So, my friend, it transpires that you were right,' he says. 'And I was wrong for which I am heartily sorry. I falsely accused you of something the other day and, though King, I am humble enough to admit my crime before this audience. I hope God will forgive me my pride and anger, and that you will forgive me any inconvenience to which you have been put. I would not blame you if now you chose to turn and go on your way, having done me a great service already, but I should welcome the chance to make amends and reward your service in some way?'

Thomas can feel his face becoming full.

'I did nothing with any thought of reward,' he lies.

King Edward sees through him without any effort.

'Well,' he says. 'We shall discuss this further at a kinder time. But please, sir, you mentioned – a manifesto?'

Thomas has little more to add on the subject of the manifesto, but the Earl of Worcester steps forward to ask him when he heard about the manifesto, and how he heard about it, and though Thomas is tired, and hungry, he is elated at the recognition he has received and so he talks without thinking how each sentence will end, without thinking how each ending will build up a story, and how that story will end, and he stands there before this dark-eyed, hawk-nosed, fierce little man, and he talks and talks. He does not notice the sharpening of the little man's expression as he tells them the story of his few days in the north, nor does he pay mind to the scribe standing by Worcester's side, who is noting down the names Horner and Riven, even Campbell. Then Worcester wants to know where Katherine is, and Jack and Nettie, and John Stump, and Thomas tells him and it is almost too late for any back-tracking when Worcester smiles finally and asks:

'Why did you flee the inn so precipitously?'

And Thomas must tell him they were scared of Edmund Riven.

'But *why* were *you* so scared of Edmund Riven?'

'He – he burns people,' Thomas says. 'He takes two – a mother and her son, say – and he burns the one to get the other to talk.'

Worcester pauses to picture the scene, and then smiles appreciatively.

'Oh, yes,' he says. 'That is good. But does this Edmund Riven do that to every man he meets? Surely not! Why, if he did, he would be the hardest-working man in Christendom.'

'No,' Thomas says. 'Not everyone.'

'So what', Worcester probes, 'makes you so special that Riven might burn you?'

And at last Thomas sees the trap he has constructed for himself, but it is too late. Now Worcester's gaze seems to flay him, to strip him of all protection, and the Earl's voice seems to slide between his joints and scrape his nerves.

'Well?'

'I don't know,' Thomas admits. 'I just feared him. I had a wife and a child.'

'A wife and a child. A wife and a child. And did you in your time in those Northern Parts learn who – or what – it was that this Edmund Riven was looking for?'

And now Thomas wishes to God he were at home with Katherine, or she were here with him, for she would know what to say, and that this – this *predator* was not circling over him, with his gore-crusted chest and the scraps of pink flesh like worms in his talons, and that look in his eye.

'I didn't,' Thomas breathes. 'I was more concerned to learn that there was an army of rebellion against King Edward.'

Worcester opens his mouth to say some terrible sarcastic thing but King Edward has had enough.

'Leave him, Worcester, please,' he says. 'You are beginning to scare even me.'

'But, sir—'

King Edward holds up his hand. Enough. And, of course, Thomas sees, Worcester cannot go on to explain his meaning, because King Edward does not know of the ledger, and the secret they are all struggling to contain, but he, Worcester, does.

That night, Thomas is permitted to leave the guardroom a free man and a steward comes to bring him to board in the great hall where there is much sweetly spiced meat and fish, and bright red wine that is as sharp as a nettle at first, but he gets used to it quite quickly. He sits between two gentlemen who were perhaps in the second group of falconers that day, those not permitted access to the King, and they are, initially, offended to be seated with a man wearing travelling clothes in which he has obviously slept while they have made some effort, but they soon relent, and they pump Thomas for information about Robin of Redesdale's army. Both become anxious at the thought of taking the field against three times their number.

'But what of those Earls who have each promised three thousand men?' Thomas wonders.

'If my lords of Pembroke and Devon raise that number, they'll only set them against each other,' one says. The other agrees.

It is no wonder the mood in the room is muted. Thomas looks over at King Edward, who sits at the end of the hall, raised on the usual dais, half-hidden by silverware, surrounded by his gentlemen, hovered over by servants, in glum, food-picking silence. He sits with the youngest of his gentlemen at his right hand, and the hawk-nosed Earl of Worcester a little way along. Halfway through the meal, King Edward sends Thomas a dish – beef bones in cinnamon – and raises his cup in a toast. Thomas is honoured, but he catches Worcester's eye with a lurch and turns quickly away, and he knows without looking again that Worcester is smiling to himself, and that he's given himself away. Thomas sits and regards the beef dish. He feels naked, exposed, and frightened of what Worcester now intends.

Also, is that the extent of the reward that King Edward had promised? A dish of beef bones?

The man beside him seems to understand.

'Fine words butter no parsnips,' he says, leaning forward to stab a chunk of meat the size of a fist and transfer it to his own bowl.

The next morning dawns fine again, and Thomas tries to leave Nottingham, to ride back to Marton, to get away from Worcester, but he is delayed searching for his horse and then when at last he has found it, not in the stables but in among the lines in the castle's bailey, he must negotiate with a short-tempered ostler reluctant to give up any mount, and then he must find his bow and the bag of arrows, and his pollaxe without which he will not leave, since only a fool would go out on to the roads unarmed when there are armies milling around, and anyway, he cannot imagine where he will find the money to get a new one.

By the time he has done this, the castle is in chaos, with men coming and going, and its gates are jammed with traffic, as are the streets below, all the way back to the bridge across the river to the south, where the roads have become impassable with carts bringing the stuff an army needs to fight a war. There are flocks of sheep and herds of cattle to block the ways, too, as well as bored and anxious soldiers with sharpened weapons and ale in their bellies.

Into this, riding from the south, comes William, Lord Hastings, with five hundred men on good horses. Because of the crush of soldiery within and around the castle, Hastings has to leave most of his men to set up camp on the common land the other side of the bridge, and he forces his way up through the crowds with only a handful of men, and he emerges through the gatehouse looking harrowed and angry, just as Thomas is trying to get out.

The two men stare at one another.

'My lord,' Thomas says. He has to raise his voice above the din of men and horses.

'Thomas,' Hastings calls, 'what in the name of God above are you doing here?' He pushes his horse through the crowd.

'I came to find you,' Thomas tells him, 'but I found the King instead.'

Hastings dismounts and passes his reins to a steward.

'You have news?'

'None that you have not already heard,' Thomas tells him, 'save that the Earl of Warwick is supposed to be about to issue some manifesto in Calais, calling all the true men of England to rise up against King Edward.'

Hastings nods.

159

'I have it here,' he says, indicating the bag around one of his escort's shoulders. He looks grim. 'How did King Edward take the Duke of Clarence's news?' he asks.

'He accused me of sedition.'

Hastings's eyes become round.

'Sedition!' he says. 'Is my lord of Worcester here, by any chance?'

'He is.'

'But you are free to go?'

'The news I brought was confirmed, and the King toasted me with wine last night.'

Hastings laughs.

'You are ever the lucky one, Thomas. Now, where is the King?'

Thomas indicates the hall, where he supposes him to be.

'Come with me, then,' Hastings orders. 'I would benefit from your luck.'

Thomas tries to explain.

'There is no point you leaving now,' Hastings tells him. 'You will never get through the town. A cart is jammed on the bridge and has broken its hub. The carter will not let anyone tip it over into the river unless they pay him for it and its load of goose feathers.'

Thomas hesitates. He does not want to face Worcester again.

'Won't they float?' he asks.

Hastings laughs.

'Come, please. Wear my livery. Just for this day. It will make me invincible!'

He makes the man carrying the messages give the bag and his coat to Thomas, and he waits while Thomas puts it on, and then they walk up the steps together to find King Edward. There is a press of bodies through which they must make their way.

'This is like old times, Thomas,' Hastings says. 'I recall standing with you in Westminster, with old Sir John Fakenham – may God keep his soul – waiting for an audience with King Edward's late father. Do you remember? It was the night the Earl of Rutland told Warwick to keep quiet. Ha! A long time ago now. Here we are.'

But he hesitates.

'Oh,' he says, as if something has just occurred to him. 'Before we go in. Thomas, have you had any word of that other matter we mentioned?'

The ledger. By Christ, Thomas thinks. Why does it always come back to the ledger?

'No,' he says, shaking his head sorrowfully, and seeing the lines between Hastings's eyebrows sharpen.

'No?' he asks. 'You are sure?'

Thomas nods.

'Yes, sir. We were not in Senning long enough.'

Hastings nods in his turn, but there is a twinge of sorrow in his expression, and Thomas sees he does not quite believe him, and so everything gets just a notch worse. One of Hastings's other men opens the door and they resume their bustle into the centre of the room, and Thomas finds himself standing slightly behind Hastings's right shoulder, bending his head before King Edward for the second time in two days. Sunlight filters through the tall windows, falling in reds and blues on King Edward and his gentlemen as they sit in tight groups, coiled and tense.

'William!' King Edward calls, and he advances down the steps and embraces his old friend. You can see some of the lightness return to him with this reunion. Hastings greets the other gentlemen, including a youngster, who is the Duke of Gloucester, and of course the Earl of Worcester, who smiles at him and holds his hand a little too long, so that Hastings has to wrench it free.

'Have you brought the manifesto?' King Edward asks.

'I have.'

Thomas takes it from the bag he has been given, and passes it to Hastings. It is a broad square of good-quality paper that has been softened from recent handling. Hastings takes it and passes it on to

King Edward, who unrolls it and begins to read in silence, his lips moving quickly. His frown deepens.

'That goddamned little weasel,' King Edward says. 'I will settle with him. Oh yes. I will settle with him. If it is the last thing I ever do. I will settle with him.'

'It is Warwick's hand, isn't it?' Hastings asks.

'Of course it is his hand! Have you read it? Look at it! It is just as we sent out back in 1460, when we came back from Calais and wanted the commons of England to rise up against bloody old King Henry. Yes, yes. "We come not to evict the King but his deceitful and covetous council, whom he has been favouring with largesse over these past years" – as if I have not given him everything I could and more! – "and because of this the country is plunged into turmoil, and law and order has broken down", as if *he* were not responsible for breaking it down, the little shit! Yes. Yes. It is all there. And look! Look at these conditions! You cannot tell me that some hairy-arsed Yorkshireman with a made-up name like Robin of Redesdale is worried about anyone diverting tunnage and fucking poundage from the keeping of the seas! He is behind it! Of course he is, the mercantile, devious, slithering little shit snake!'

King Edward balls the paper and throws it on the floor and then he scuffs it towards the fire.

'There is more, I am sore to say,' Hastings tells him, 'an addendum.'

He opens the bag Thomas holds and removes a smaller piece of paper that he passes over with a wince of regret.

'It is nothing we did not suspect,' he says.

King Edward takes it, opens it, reads the few words once, frowns, looks again. Then he is incredulous for a moment, holding the paper in slack fingers, looking blank-faced into the distance.

'Great God above,' he murmurs. 'Great God above. George! What have you done? You – You bloody fool.'

No one says a word. They wait.

After a moment King Edward gathers himself, and turns first to Hastings.

'You have read this too?'

Hastings nods.

Then he looks to the youngster, the Duke of Gloucester, to whom he says:

'It is George again.'

And the boy – not as young as he looks, in fact, but small – shakes his head sadly.

'What this time?' he asks.

'I think this may be the worst yet,' King Edward says. 'Our brother George has joined forces with my lord of Warwick and together they mean to come with their armies and force me to accept these – these terms.' He takes another kick at the first paper among the rushes.

'What shall we do?' Gloucester asks.

And King Edward is silent for a moment, because however angry he is, he cannot bring himself to tell one brother that, together, they must kill another brother.

12

Katherine and Rufus and their newfound companion Liz cross the river at Gainsborough in bright sunshine and a light breeze. Katherine bargains with the ferryman, and gets a good price, seeing as they are two women on their own, but Liz is not having it, and after a further exchange the price is dropped lower still. The ferryman offers to steer the cart on to his craft, but Liz tells him she would rather dally with a pig than yield the reins to him. He will not look at them after that as they bring their horse and cart aboard, but others are more admiring, and happy to say so, until Liz turns on them, and then they turn their backs and watch the river surge by, and comment no more.

Katherine stares into the swirling turbid waters, too, until Liz tells her not to fret about Thomas.

'He seems capable,' she says. 'Able to handle himself.'

Katherine is not so sure.

'The last time I saw him go off like this, I lost him for two years.'

'But he came back in the end,' Liz says. 'Plenty didn't.'

And Katherine supposes this is true.

Liz has already told her about how Riven took them. Twenty well-armed men on big, fast horses had overtaken them easily, just as they feared. Jack and John Stump had not even tried to fight. They were just swallowed up.

'Jack tried to stop them taking me into the bushes, but Edmund Riven held a blade to the pregnant girl's throat and gave him the choice. It was either me, or her. I volunteered in the end just to stop her crying, and him having to make the choice. It wasn't the first time, so I knew what to expect. And in the end it was only one of them – a right dirty bastard, but at least it weren't that bloody giant of his.'

'Does he keep the giant in memory of his father or something?' Katherine wonders.

'Maybe it's a family tradition?' Liz thinks. 'You know what them families are like.'

'Does he – does he put out men's eyes?'

Liz frowns.

'The giant? Not that I know of, but Riven's been known to slit noses.' She draws her finger down the length of her nose.

'You were lucky,' Katherine tells her.

'Yes,' Liz is quick to agree. 'But he knew I were just a local, since he knows my father, like, so he were not so excited at finding me, but he was all het up about the others, and when he found he'd let you slip through his fingers, well. He – I've never seen anything like it.'

Katherine swallows hard. Dear God.

'But there is no profit in you worrying,' Liz tells her. 'You did what you could. Anything else is on them. They understood that.'

Katherine nods, and wishes she could believe her.

'So what is this place we are coming to then, Kate?' Liz asks.

No one has ever called her Kate before. It feels odd, but also, from Liz, soothing.

'It is home,' Rufus tells Liz. He is clutching the little bow that John Brunt gave him, and in his blue jacket, with the russet hose, he looks like a small, unlined version of Thomas. Katherine puts a hand on his capped head.

'It has been strange, this journey, hasn't it, Rufus?'

He nods, but says nothing. Once they are unloaded from the ferry, they turn south, past a grand and new-built hall, and men stare at two women and a child riding a cart, and they open their mouths to say something, but Liz is usually in there first. A friar on a mule is resting in the shade of an oak tree, and tells them he marvels to see such a sight, though he wonders if it is pleasing to God. Liz tells him to be away now and wash his balls.

They follow the river's meanders until they reach Marton. Everything is plump with life, saturated with it, burgeoning and verdant, and the wayside is filled with briar rose and alder, and there are butterflies below and swallows above, and the warm air is scented by lime trees and meadowsweet. Rufus shouts out that he has seen a kingfisher.

But Katherine feels unease billowing within like a species of nausea. Will Isabella allow them back? She will have retired from life, properly, completely and finally, as she said she would, and she will have left her sons to make decisions. What will they say when the wife and child of the man who killed their hounds comes rolling back, begging for charity? And what about Borthwick? Isabella's sons sent him away after their dogs had been killed, since there was nothing for him to do, but perhaps they have new dogs and have called him back?

They come to the village from the north, past the windmill Sir John had had built on a small rise above the river, and Rufus asks if they may stop to speak to the miller as he has in the past. Katherine is usually charmed by the pleasure he takes in windmills, even though she does not share it, for close to the towering linen sails seem alive, and remind her of the dragon's wings in a mural she once saw in a church named after St George. Thomas, of course, was there to tell her that it was the other way around: that wings should remind her of the sails, because the painter painted the wings to look like the sails.

In any event, today the sails are stilled and when they approach, the miller is absent.

'Where is he?' Rufus asks.

'I don't know,' Katherine says. Though, surely, on a day such as this, he ought to be at work, grinding his grain?

They stand on the small hillock while Liz waits with the cart below and they look out across what were once Sir John's lands, and odd things catch Katherine's eye. The pea crop: it is unharvested, and the plants are mobbed with birds when there should be a boy with a stick to keep them at bay. And the hay in the pastures beyond – which should have been cut by now, surely? – lies where it is, beaten and desiccated in parts, rotting in others. And where are the oxen? Katherine tries to think how long it is since they left. It seems ages, for they have been through much, but it cannot be more than a month, surely? And yet – look at the place: it is neglected just at the time of year when most needs be done. She shields her eyes and peers at the trees that mask the hall from this direction, and she is relieved to see a pale wash of wood smoke.

'Come on,' Katherine tells him. 'Let us go and find Isabella.'

When they reach the hall, she is perplexed.

'Where is everybody?'

The stable doors are shut, as are those to the hall, and there is a sense of dry, dusty abandonment about the place, as if no one has been here for months; yet a thin line of smoke slips from the chimney that Thomas and Jack and John were so pleased to build, and so someone must be within. Katherine knocks. There is a long moment's charged quiet.

Katherine shouts.

'It is me, Katherine Everingham. Who is within?'

And then comes the sound of a shuffle, a creak, and the doorbar being drawn, but there is some fumbling, and it is done hesitantly, or weakly, at the cost of some effort, and then the door is opened on sighing hinges and a face appears in the gap. It is Isabella, opening her own door. Her face is pale and her blank white eyes are rimmed red from crying. She gasps when she makes out Katherine, as if she cannot really believe who it is; then she opens the door wide and pulls Katherine into a desperate hug.

'Isabella! What is wrong? What has happened?'

Isabella has her in a drowning grip, and she sobs unashamedly.

'Katherine, Katherine,' she says. 'Oh great God above, thank you for coming back.'

When she has soothed her a little, Katherine goes within, where everything is as she left it – almost precisely so. Nothing has changed, been moved, been cleared away. The air is claggy. There are a few sticks of wood left to burn from the great pile that usually filled the bay, and there are a few crusts of old bread, small, burned, stale, like the shells of walnuts, mouldering on the table that had in the past been the scene of such feasts and discussions. Isabella herself is a shrunken filament, bent and dried with some affliction, perhaps. She turns away from Katherine and covers herself so as not to be seen, not to be looked at.

'Oh, Isabella,' Katherine says, taking her in her arms, 'what is wrong? What has happened? Why are you here alone? Where is everybody?'

Rufus comes to the door but stops in the frame, aghast at the sight of the place and at its smell. Liz looms up behind him.

'Come on, lad,' she says. 'Let us leave these two. You show me around.'

But Rufus slips away and runs to Isabella and throws his arms around her, and she nearly falls, but Katherine has her, and Rufus has made her weep all the louder; they guide her back to the settle where Sir John used to sit and they lower her into it, and her bones are like those of a bird, and as they let her down Katherine can feel them creak and grind beneath her palms.

Liz watches a moment and then turns and Katherine knows she is getting ale and bread from the cart. Isabella mutters something. It takes some gentle persuasion to get her to repeat it so Katherine can hear.

'I am so ashamed,' she whispers.

Katherine has to blink away her tears.

'Why?' she asks. 'Whatever has happened?'

Katherine crouches next to the old lady, who is tormenting a string of dark rosary beads in her lap with fingers gnarled as roots while tears splash on the dusty dark stuff of her dress, and Katherine knows whom to blame.

168

'Where are they?' she asks. 'Where are William and Robert? Where have they gone?'

This sets off a fresh bout of sobs. The story emerges slowly over the next few hours. Once Thomas had gone, his knowledge of the land went with him, or his ease with it, and his ease with the tenants, too, and he had been replaced by the houndsman Borthwick, of all men, whom they recalled but was not equipped to act as reeve in any form. Then it transpired that her sons had already pre-sold parcels of Sir John's acreage and some – many – all of his interests, too, including the windmill, the stock ponds, the oxen, and so when St John's Day came, there were barely any rents to be gathered in, for the boys had sold much of the land, and whatever money was gathered turned out to be owed elsewhere, for falcons, and finery, and to men in London for things about which Isabella could only guess.

Her sons had made all sorts of further demands on her purse, which she had met, but when she asked about the pea crop, and about the haymaking, they shouted at her that it was none of her business.

'They are like locusts,' Isabella says. 'A plague. They have taken everything they can and sold it for fine clothing, and armour. Armour! What do they think they will need it for? I don't know. I never thought they were those sorts of boys. They, well . . . And all Sir John's work, and all your work! All of it just—Nothing left save his house and his gardens now.'

Isabella is not so sad about the loss of those scattered furlongs and properties that Sir John had collected throughout his lifetime, since they were merely revenue, but she is ashamed of the way the tenants have been treated and of how she – Katherine – and Thomas were ejected, for which she blames herself, and she is humiliated by her sons' careless treatment of her own self. Her sons' behaviour has shattered every view she held dear, she tells them, and she weeps constantly, and the rosary beads that she ceaselessly turns serve as more of a comfort than a prayer cycle.

Her eyesight has deteriorated, too, and it seems the cataracts are now like dots of milk within the eyes, placed there by an unnecessarily cruel God.

'I can still see a bit,' Isabella says, 'and I do not mind it so if it will spare me further suffering in purgatory. It is only that I miss seeing the host lifted at Mass, and I miss looking on the painting of St Christopher that we had done in the church.'

And yet, what else has she missed? The hall is filthy, which is one thing, but the other is that under the aged skin of Isabella's hands, and specifically her wrists, blue and green bruises flourish. She keeps knocking into things, she says, but Liz shakes her head when she sees them. She tells Katherine they are thumbprints, where Isabella has been grabbed, and she shows her one on her own wrist, from when she was taken by Riven, fading now.

Katherine wonders if there is anything to be done, other than pay close attention to the old lady's movements. She remembers Mayhew telling her about how one might couch a cataract, but she did not pay much attention since at the time they were engaged in removing arrows from the wounded, and he said that the cutting cured blindness only twice in ten.

Still, though.

Isabella asks about Thomas and why they have returned. She claps both hands to her cheeks to think of Jack and John Stump taken in the night, but most especially of Nettie, of course, who will soon be on her childbed. She has heard of Edmund Riven, but never spoken of him since Sir John would not allow it.

'What can we do?' she asks.

Katherine tells her about Thomas and his mission.

Isabella is not convinced, but she is so diminished she can only mew sorrowfully and regret that she should live long enough to see such things. After a moment, though, she has a better idea.

'I will send message to my cousin,' she says at last. 'Well, he is my cousin's husband, Baron Willoughby. He is an adherant of the Earl of

Warwick, and I will press him for information about them. I am sure he will help, if he can.'

So together they draft a letter to this Baron Willoughby of Tattershall Castle in the County of Lincoln, but with no one to send it personally when it is finished, Katherine must go to the road south, and see if anyone is going that way and whether or not they will take a message. It is fraught with uncertainty, but short of taking it themselves, there is no alternative. Katherine waits, letting a group of soldiers pass, before battening on a sumpter man with a long line of mules and donkeys carrying God knows what. She's seen the man before, on these roads, and assumes she might again. He reluctantly agrees to take the message, and supposes it will be three days before he can get it to Tattershall 'on account of the roads, which are wet down there'.

Over the following days Katherine and Liz set to work on the hall, restoring it to order, partly because it needs be done, partly to keep themselves occupied, though during the works Katherine cannot help but break off and ride down the track to the road to wait for Thomas, and to ambush travellers for news from the south or from this baron of Isabella's; but on these daily trips she sees neither Thomas nor the sumpter man, and nor does she hear anything of what is happening elsewhere in the country. At prayer times, Thomas's name is never far from their lips, and whenever there is a noise without, she feels a spike of hope that it is he come back to find them all, or at least the sumpter man with news.

After a few days, they have the hall as Katherine remembers it. She and Liz have got the walking wheel working again, and they sit in the sun trying to spin some yarn, though it is hopeless for the wool is mostly kemp. Isabella sits in her accustomed seat in the shade. They have been talking – again – about her two sons, William and Robert, and how Isabella thinks their father, who'd been killed fighting for King Henry at that first battle of St Albans, was at fault for their want of kindness.

171

'He was a fierce man,' she says. 'Wrathful if he could not under-stand something, and proud of being good at only one thing, which was fighting.'

'And he weren't much good at that, was he?' Liz says. 'If he got himself killed.'

There is a moment's silence while they check the wool.

Then Liz tells them about her family: how her mother died in her childbed, and how her father never remarried because he said he had enough women in his life with four daughters, though one of them died too, when they had a bad year and the rye got wet in the barn and her leg fell off. She is fond of her father, still; it is obvious.

'Do you have a family, Katherine?' Isabella asks.

Katherine is caught out. She had not foreseen this.

'I have Thomas, and Rufus,' she tells her.

'No,' Isabella presses. 'I mean your people. Your parents? Where did you come up?'

Katherine tells her she does not know. As she does so, she feels a sort of rushing in her ears, a build-up of pressure within, which in the long silence that follows increases to almost a roar, and she feels she may scream or fall over, just to stop the flow of this conversation. She knows what is coming. She has felt this before – with Thomas, hinting, probing, wondering, suggesting she find her family – and she would rather be anywhere right now but here, only she cannot leave. It is not that she is holding the yarn (though she is), it is that Isabella is so fragile, so like to break at any harsh word, particularly from her, Katherine, who has become almost all Isabella has in the world right now.

And now here is Isabella, looking at her with those terrible sad eyes, and Katherine knows that Isabella is going to say something wise. She is going to relay something she's learned from hard-won experience, and Katherine knows she will probably be right but she cannot stand to hear it if it is about her own family, of whom she still dreams when she is at her most exhausted: that same, damned, recurring dream that gets her nowhere, of the stone fireplace and the glazed window, and then of the handing over of a bag of letters and a purse of money to an old woman in black who she knows must have been the Prioress before *her* prioress, who'd seemed fretful but kindly, and who had taken her in and then . . . nothing, only terrible, absent blankness.

So she feels a sort of horror when Isabella keeps looking at her and Liz chips in to tell them that she believes a woman must know her own mother if she is not to repeat the same stupid mistakes the woman made, and marry a man with a concave chest like her father, and Katherine hopes this is enough to break the tension she feels. But it is not. Isabella continues looking at her with those eyes and Katherine can stand it no longer.

'I was brought up an oblate,' she says. 'I never knew my mother or father.'

There. She has told them. Told someone. And for a few beats of the heart she is free. This thing she has hidden so long is out of its cover, and it means nothing. This great secret shame that has pressed down on her, that she has hidden from herself as well as others, all its power is gone. She is like anyone else. Anyone else.

But Isabella leans forward and whispers:

'You poor child.'

And Katherine cannot bear it. She flings the wool from her and stalks off through the yard, leaving the spool on the ground and the two women in silence. She walks to the house she and Thomas built, empty now, though sound and dry within, and she shunts open the door and is alone with her thoughts and the dust and spiders and dried leaves that have blown in, and she is there for the rest of the day until she hears the Angelus bell, tinny and distant, when Liz comes to find her.

She does not mention what has passed, and together they find Rufus watching some red butterflies on the lower branches of a shiny-leafed flowering bush, and he tells Katherine that they have been to the village to buy ale, but that the usual woman is dead, so they must learn to make it themselves and until then they must drink water.

'It is not so bad,' he says.

But there is wine with the pottage that night, some that Sir John had left tucked away where Isabella's sons did not find it, almost as if he knew a night like this would come, and they light candles and sit and eat and drink and Katherine is at ease for a while, but then she starts to feel the slow accretion of those little pauses, those little awkwardnesses as the wine makes Isabella and Liz no longer care to cover up their thinking about what happened today and finally the silence that falls is too deep to be overlooked.

'Well,' Liz says.

Katherine knows she should apologise and explain, but she is not going to. It is something she will not talk about. Only Liz does not see it like that.

'What made you run off like that?' she goes on. 'Have you got some secret past or something? You the daughter of a priest? Is that it? A priest and a nun? Though looking at you, I'd say a bishop and an abbess. But they are at it all the time, too, since they've no proper work with which to occupy their hands and minds.'

Isabella feigns shock, but cannot help a slight smile.

Katherine says nothing. She feels penned in, pressed back against a wall.

'Please,' she begins, but Isabella does not see her expression, of course, and she continues.

'It is rare,' she says, 'in this day, for a child to be avowed to a monastery.'

'Why'd anyone do it?' Liz asks. 'Imagine sending Rufus away now, to be looked after by such as them.'

'It is done only in exceptional circumstances,' Isabella tells them.

'Like what?' Liz asks.

And now Isabella is reluctant to speculate, for such speculation is almost an accusation.

'I don't know,' she says. 'It might be that a child is born and is not wanted?'

'But plenty are bastard born,' Liz says. 'That hardly matters.'

'No,' Isabella says. 'It hardly matters in some places, in some parts. But in others it does. But it might not be that. It might be that a child is simple, or the thought of another girl is too much, or perhaps the mother died in childbed. It might be anything.'

Katherine is not interested. The block she has placed on her thoughts about who she is, and why she is as she is, and why she is where she is, is far too stubborn to be moved by a conversation over wine between a couple of women.

'Are you not interested, even for the sake of Rufus?' Isabella asks.

Katherine has not thought of that. She puts it aside for now, but will return to it later, she thinks, perhaps when Thomas is back. If he comes back.

'Do you know if Kate's even your real name, Kate?' Liz asks.

'Please,' Katherine says. 'I don't want to think about this. Not now.'

'So you don't?' Liz goes on.

'They used to give the child the mother's name,' Isabella tells Liz just as if Katherine were not there.

'And is Katherine a common name among such as them?'

'Them?'

'Them what can afford to send a child off to a nunnery like that. You have to pay for it, am I right?'

'That is true. I hadn't thought of that,' Isabella says. 'Only the very wealthiest might afford it, and since the practice is so disapproved of by the Church, they must have had influence with whoever took you in, whoever they were.'

'Quite exciting, really,' Liz says. 'Where was you put, Kate?'

The two women are looking at Katherine, waiting, Liz with her sharp gaze, Isabella peering through the clouds in her eyes, listening more than looking.

175

Katherine says nothing. She feels only a curious emptiness.

'You going to tell us,' Liz asks, 'or what?'

Katherine takes a deep breath.

'It was the Priory of St Mary, at Haverhurst.'

Liz shakes her head, pursing her lips.

'Never heard of it,' she says, as if this is Katherine's fault.

But Isabella has.

'Great God above,' she breathes. 'If they had wanted to put you in a more dismal spot they could not have found one. Even the Cistercians fled from there.'

'How did you get away?' Liz asks.

'I ran,' Katherine tells them. She does not tell them how, or why. She has never spoken of it, never shared it, and now it is as if access to the memories of those times has calcified, or grown over, or rusted shut, and all she can do is shake her head when they try to press her further. Then Liz and Isabella become aware she is crying, and no more is said of it.

That night Katherine dreams of the priory again. It is not the first time she has done so since she left for the second time, but this night the dreams are more vivid, and set earlier, back when she was a child, and it is as if she is now granted a clearer view of those times, and she sees herself being delivered and she sees what she is wearing, and she sees the letters passed and many incidental details, and in the morning when she wakes, she remembers not one thing.

When she sees Isabella she wonders why they have not heard back from her cousin, the supposedly close ally of the Earl of Warwick.

'Why don't we go to see this fine gentleman,' Liz suggests, 'so we can tell him ourselves?'

'Oh, but he lives south of Lincoln,' Isabella says, as if that does for the scheme.

'But we have a horse and cart,' Liz tells her. 'We could take you.'

Katherine looks at Liz. She is an astonishing girl, in some ways.

'But what about the roads? There is supposed to be trouble.'

'We've got John's crossbow,' Liz says. 'Takes a bit of strength, but once it's spanned it can send a bolt through a tree. Wave that about and no one'll come within fifty paces.'

'But my eyes,' Isabella says.

'You'll not need to steer the cart or shoot the bolt.'

'We must do something for Jack and John and Nettie,' Katherine tells her. 'Imagine if all we've heard of Riven is true?'

'And it is, Kate, so come on,' Liz says. 'What'll we lose but time?'

At length Isabella agrees to the idea of the trip, and they leave the next morning: a grey day, with spitty rain from the east that they hope will clear by noon. Isabella sits in the cart on Sir John's old trunk and together all three women eye John's crossbow as they might a coiled snake; it is spanned and ready, with the goat's foot mechanism and a bag of bolts nearby.

'We will be in Lincoln by noon,' Katherine tells them, and they roll back down the road, and she half hopes to meet Thomas coming their way, but they don't. They see the spires of the cathedral and the castle's tower just as the sext bell rings and they pass under the Newport arch where Isabella must pay the murrage to a tiny old man with one tooth in his gums, witnessed by a group of men with rust-hazed sallets and bills who constitute the Watch. Then as they pass along the bustling bailgate they meet five men in green livery, one carrying a flag, who are clearing the way for a canopied coach to pass.

'Make way,' they shout, and they expect to be obeyed, not merely because they have horses and sharp steel, but because everybody usually does. For a moment Katherine thinks Liz will not, that she will assert some equal or prior right to passage, but no, after a moment Liz steers the cart to one side, shouting at a barrow boy to move himself if he does not want to be tramped flat, and they watch the soldiers and the coach's iron rims grind past. The coach is freshly painted in green and yellow, and the canopy is of pale gauzy material that billows and riffles like silk. Within are three women, perhaps just like she, Liz and Isabella, travelling the other way, and behind another five men on horseback and another cart, pulled by four horses.

Liz laughs.

'Could be your sisters.'

Katherine says nothing. They pull back on to the road, and continue between the crowding buildings to the precinct between castle and cathedral, where Liz is properly astonished, even frightened, as her gaze moves from the cathedral's broad base right up the full height of the looming spires, so tall their vanes are lost in cloud. Around them the streets are busy with friars and priests, but Isabella is determined to say her prayers in the cathedral, and to light a candle each for Thomas, for Jack and Nettie and for John Stump.

So they leave the cart with a mildly trustworthy-looking boy, and they go through the precinct and up the steps through the west door into the vast scented gloom of the nave where hundreds of men in black and grey and white come and go. Liz and Rufus stand in their scudding midst as if lost, stunned by the light falling through the rose windows, Liz's mouth open like some simple pilgrim from afar.

After a moment a man approaches Isabella and takes off his hat and tries to engage her in conversation, and Liz is shaken from her torpor by the man's smell, which is bad, for he does not look to have washed in a month; Liz turns on him and whispers something fierce in his face, and he stumbles back like a whipped dog, vanishing into the shadows.

'Who was that?' Katherine asks.

'Someone who should by rights be hanged,' Liz tells her.

'You know him?'

'His kind. He's claiming sanctuary from his debts, most like, by the look of him.'

They find a side chapel where Isabella buys four overpriced tallow candles that they light from a bank of the same, already lit, and they place them before the little altar and the statue of Our Lady, and then kneel, watched over by a monk, and each prays for their missing husband, father, friends.

They see no more of the sanctuary-seeker, and when they are done, they come out in the precinct again and Katherine remembers when she first came here, how she was still terrified of the clerics, imagining they could see through her shabby disguise. She remembers the stationers' stalls set up against the wall, and sees that they are still there, busier than ever perhaps, with new trades – ink-sellers, pen merchants – strolling with their trays, calling out their wares. They are in the same spot where Thomas once bought a book from an old stationer who dealt in books from Bruges, she recalls, and who sniffed when they showed him the ledger and pronounced it trash, but he had tried to buy Thomas's drawing of the rose window in St Paul's Cathedral in London, and she welcomes this revisit as a slim link in the long chain to her absent husband.

She leaves Rufus with Liz and guides Isabella over to the stall to see if the man is there, but he is not, only a much younger fellow, dressed in a poorly dyed black coat that shows green in parts. His stock is just as varied though: he has one or two fine-tooled covers, a few books of simpler design, and many stitch-bound pamphlets. She has ever been drawn to the unfinished nature of these sorts of thing, which to her mind seem part of an ongoing conversation, whereas if a man binds a book, claps it in hard covers, it is as if he is saying: Here, this is my final word on the matter, and I am right. Whereas, Katherine finds, the things you read in such bound books are so often wrong.

'Ah!' the stationer says, seeing them dither over his table. 'Yes. I see you have good taste.'

The stationer tells them what he has, and what they might like, starting naturally with the second most expensive book – a copy of a book of hours done in the Flemish style – and descending to the rougher texts, merely paper-bound in what looks like bowstring, all the while leaving the finest and most expensive book unmentioned, lying there resting on a nest of dark velvet, and with each passing moment it assumes a greater significance, and Isabella is trying to make it out, peering very closely, then askance, at it, trying to see around the wretched discs of horn in her own eyes. The stationer talks and talks. New methods of production. Trips to Bruges. The improved quality of paper – as they can see from his stock – and the scarcity of good vellum these days. None of this Isabella hears. At last she asks what that book is, and the stationer cannot suppress a smile.

'Didn't I say it when I first saw you?' he asks. 'You have excellent taste.'

He takes it down with exaggerated care. It is a breviary. Smaller than the first, the size of a woman's hand, it is elm bound, with ornate hinges and clips of polished silver. Within, the paper is very fine, and the colours vivid, the scenes beautifully painted, the lettering regular, precise, fluid.

'A thing of beauty, is it not?' the stationer asks.

But Katherine can see Isabella is stricken.

'What is it?' Katherine asks.

'It is mine,' Isabella sobs. 'Sir John – he gave it to me when we were married. I thought I had hidden it safe.'

The book seems to vanish into the air and the stationer's expression has closed like a fold.

'What are you talking about, you blind old hag? Are you calling me a thief?'

Isabella is half-collapsed. Katherine must hold her up.

'It was one of the boys,' Isabella moans. 'They will have stolen it and sold it for their – their dicing debts or their falcons.'

The stationer, seeing he is no longer the accused, opens up again.

'It was a young man with a half-beard,' he says, indicating his chin. 'Dressed like a princeling or a doge.'

And Isabella sobs again.

'How could he? It was a wedding present.'

'I paid a fair price for it,' the stationer tells them.

And they cannot afford to buy it back, even though he offers it to them at the price he bought it.

'Keep it for us,' Katherine says.

He says he will, for two weeks – until the Feast of the Seven Sleepers of Ephesus, at the end of the month.

'I must make a fair living.'

They are leaving when he calls Katherine back.

'I have something that might interest you in the meantime,' he says, and he gives her a handful of rough-tied sheets of sawn-edged paper covered with tiny letters from the very top of the first page, to the very bottom of the last, save for, on the fifth or sixth spread, a drawing of the eye of a man, or perhaps it is even a goat – it is not very clear – and the man/goat has what looks like a devil's tongue, but what is of interest is that all around the eye are various labelled circles.

'A treatise on complaints of the eye,' he tells her.

Isabella stands mute, still too shocked to engage with anything said, let alone to speak. Katherine looks from the paper to Isabella's eyes, those opaque discs, and then back again.

'How much?' she asks.

He names a price. Katherine feels a gathering of purpose, of intent, of excitement even. She pays the man half what he asks and he accepts, and then the hour bell rings in the towers and a thousand pigeons erupt into the sky and she guides Isabella back to the cart where Liz is waiting, already mounted. She helps the old lady up, and they are about to kick the horse on when Katherine is struck by a thought. She returns to the bookseller.

'I'll not take it back,' he says.

She does not want him to. She wants to know about the old stationer, who used to be here.

'My father,' the man says. 'I am glad you remember him. He has a very fine eye for a book.'

'Is he still with us?'

The stationer smiles.

'Indeed he is. He is across the Narrow Sea, in a town named Strasbourg, at the book fair.'

'When will he return, do you think? I should like to speak to him about a matter.'

'A matter to buy or sell?'

'Neither. An old matter.'

The stationer is disappointed.

'My mother prays he will be back before Michaelmas, and that he will not have to travel in winter.'

'I will come back then,' Katherine tells him.

'Who should I say was asking after him?'

'He will not remember me,' she says.

'I will keep your breviary,' he tells her. 'Until you can afford it.'

She thanks him, and leaves him with the hope that his father's trip is blessed by God, and so is the rest of his day.

When she gets back to the cart, Liz is worrying about Isabella.

'And what've you done to her, Kate?'

Isabella is mute with misery, her mouth curved down like a cordwainer's needle, her hands fluttering and flattening the linen of her dress because she has left her rosary beads behind. Katherine tells Liz about the two sons and Liz opens her mouth to insult them, but every insult that comes to mind – bastard, perhaps, or whoreson – rebounds on Isabella, so she is left to grind her teeth and growl.

'You'd not treat your old ma like that, would you, Rufus my boy?' Liz is asking, and Rufus is shaking his head, though Katherine is not sure how much he understands.

'Where are we bound?' she asks Isabella, who manages to point south down the hill as she continues weeping. Katherine wonders if the tears might wash away the cataracts, and she finds she is still clutching the pamphlet the stationer sold her and so she pushes it into her bag, and checks Rufus is safe on the cart and then she and Liz

182

lead the horse across the precinct and on, down the steep cobbled street that will take them to the river and the city gates.

She has walked this street before, of course, with Thomas, many times, but the first was nearly ten years ago, when she stood just here, and he stood just there, and a messenger came barrelling up the hill from the south, careless of the cobbles, coming to tell the Bishop or someone that Richard of York had landed in England, come to try to kick the old King off the throne and take it for himself. They'd looked at one another, and she'd known the wars would come again, though he did not believe her. And now here they are, ten years later, and the wars are come again, again.

Down here is the pardoner's house where she went that day with Thomas to return the ledger. Dear God. If only the old man's widow had taken it! How much trouble would they now be spared? They would not have Edmund Riven burning their friends on one side, nor this bloodhound of Hastings closing in on them from the other. How easy their lives might be then!

The old house is unchanged: the whitewash more streaked green perhaps, and the lower-storey windows more firmly grimed with dust and cobwebs, and perhaps the woodwork has peeled back a little more. Could his widow still be there? Katherine steps off the road and looks at the house's upper storey, jutting out a little above, and her heart suddenly fills her throat. There at the window is the widow, looking down, just as if she'd been expecting Katherine for the last ten years, her face as pale as ever. And then, suddenly, she is gone. But it is not as if she has taken a step back. She is just – gone. Melted as if she were never there.

Katherine cannot suppress a shiver. She feels it ripple across her back, up her neck, into her scalp. She crosses herself twice and begs the Lord to save her. By Christ! Was it her imagination? She ought to bang on the door, demand an explanation, but – but she is too scared. There is something about that house. She turns and hurries after the cart where Isabella is still weeping silently and Rufus is stroking her arm and telling her not to cry and that they will soon be home.

Once through the gate across the high bridge they all climb back up on to the cart and they travel south through land that is very wet this year, and even though it is July, the mud on the road is thick, and there are long stretches where it is only a suggestion through swathes of rushes under a choppy soup of muddy water. Carts coming the other way are splashed and sodden, and anyone walking north is wet up to the knees, and looking forward to reaching the city's heights. King Edward is blamed for much of the flooding, but no one reports any trouble further south, and for that they must thank God.

'Where to now?' Liz asks.

And Isabella at last wakes to the world.

'To the manor of Tattershall,' she says. 'It is east of here. There is a turning up ahead somewhere. A few miles yet, I believe, and then there will be a marker stone. You will have to look out for it with all this water.'

'Have you been there before?' Katherine asks.

'Many years ago,' she says. 'My family – We are connected to the Willoughbys and I was with Joan Willoughby for a while, before I went to my first husband's household. She is dead now, but her husband Baron Willoughby lives on, and has the ear of the Earl of Warwick.'

'The ear of the Earl of Warwick,' Liz repeats. 'I'd not mind that. I'd screw it in a little ball and chuck it to the pigs.'

They travel on into the pale sun-inflected sky, through a mile of rushes that will soon be harvested, and Katherine thinks of the eel-trapper she once took in when she was in Cornford, who took with him Eelby's baby. She wonders what has happened to him. She descends into a kind of reverie, remembering those days at Cornford, and she looks up just as Liz turns the cart off the road and on to the track leading east.

And she suddenly knows where they are going.

'No!' she says. She stands in the cart, nearly falling.

'Sit down, you daft woman,' Liz says. 'You'll frighten the horse. By Our Lady.'

'This track,' she says. 'It leads past – it leads past the priory. I'll not take it.'

Liz brings the horse to a stop. There is only a low marsh of brackish water to be seen around here, and in among it a few islets of feather-topped, vivid green rushes. It is impossible to stay here.

'We are not going into the priory, Katherine,' Isabella tells her. 'But this is the only road to Tattershall, and so must pass it.'

'D'you imagine the Prioress is still out and about looking for you, Kate? Is that it? That she'll be in the rushes there with an army of angry nuns waiting to spring out with their washing beetles and drag you back in for the shame you've brought on them?'

Liz is laughing. Isabella is trying to look sympathetic. Katherine wants to tell Liz that she has no idea what it was like, but Liz has been through worse, surely, and the words sound so foolish in her teeth that she swallows them. She turns from the women and from Rufus, who is more confused than ever, pulls her cloak around her and stares south as Liz kicks the horse on. They follow the track east and she can feel the priory coming nearer, as if she herself is being stalked, and she feels it as a kind of clamour, a tumult within her, until at last she can stand it no longer. She is about to throw off her cloak and run, run up the track through the lapping waters and back to Lincoln, when Liz says:

'Blood of Christ, look at that.'

13

Thomas is in the butts when the summons comes. He is sitting on a log, well polished by a thousand buttocks over the years, down by the river, outside the city of Nottingham, watching men in blue and murrey livery send shaft after shaft booming from their bows to thump into the dampened earth mounds two hundred paces beyond. The air is filled with the noise of clean strings and fierce swearing. He is with William Hastings's men, Rufus's godfather John Brunt among them, and they have already had their turn, and now are stripped to their hose and pourpoints, still flushed from their exertions, taking bread and ale and watching King Edward's men do their best.

'Not too bad,' Brunt thinks.

The messenger who comes is a young lad, not fifteen, with plump ruby cheeks and an almost impenetrable accent. He tells Thomas that Lord Hastings has sent for him and he is to make his way to the castle keep with all despatch. Thomas gathers his jacket and bow.

'Good luck, Thomas,' Brunt tells him, 'and may God go with you.'

Brunt and the others know Thomas has been petitioning William Hastings to let him return to Katherine, but Hastings has been closeted with King Edward and others in the castle these last days, and has had little time except to tell him that King Edward is not disposed to let any of his men leave at this hour. No one is surprised by this, because it is now well known that the Earl of Warwick and King Edward's brother George, Duke of Clarence, have returned from Calais and, as feared, have raised the commons of Kent in rebellion against King Edward.

So now, Thomas can see, there are no fewer than five armies abroad in the land, convening who knows where. One is led by the Earl of Pembroke, him with the beard and the extravagant promise of many troops, and this army reputedly numbers three thousand trained fighting men-at-arms, loyal to King Edward. Another, of a similar number of bowmen, marches under the banner of Humphrey Stafford, the dapper little Earl of Devon, likewise loyal to King Edward. A third – an unknown number of men under Robin of Redesdale – comes from the north with the express intention of unseating King Edward; while the fourth, under King Edward's old ally, the Earl of Warwick, converges from the southeast, and is like to be large enough to vanquish the few troops King Edward has with him in Nottingham, which make up an army of perhaps fifteen hundred.

Knowing all this, there has been a heightened atmosphere in the city as the days have passed. Everyone from king to knave is waiting to hear news from elsewhere that will inform their lives, one way or the other, and all are distracting themselves as best they can. Butchers, wine merchants and plump young women who look as if they've never done a day's work in their lives have been busy satisfying King Edward's orders in the castle, while men such as Thomas have been in the butts, or out on the furlongs fighting with padded weapons. The din of the smiths is constant, and the air is filled with acrid smoke and the smell of metal on stone, of burning charcoal, of sweat, human waste, blood and guts of animals and new-brewed ale. Boys run everywhere. Carts and wagons are at standstill for lack of space in the city, and messengers must force their ways to and fro. Companies of men in livery arrive, but never in large numbers, and though tents are erected around the city walls like mushrooms in autumn, news of Devon's men and Pembroke's men is not to be had, and in its place, rumour is rife.

'They are a day's march away.'

'They have fallen on one another and all are dead.'

'They have fallen in with this Robin of Redesdale.'

'Warwick has already destroyed them.'

'They are coming to kill us all.'

As is usual in moments of crisis, the castle's yard is given over to the horses and servants of King Edward's household and the atmosphere is strained as each man marks out his territory and keeps it from encroachment. Armour is being cleaned and weapons sharpened and as Thomas comes through the gate a delivery of firewood is being made and there is a scuffle as he shoulders his way through the mob.

He finds Hastings in one of the solars, half-heartedly playing dice with three other men in fine, though unwashed, clothes and hair newly cut in the military-style: shaved at the sides, left long on top. Hastings is reading messages that another man – a secretary – standing behind his shoulder keeps sliding on to the board among the cups and bowls before him, and occasionally he swears softly. Meanwhile the air smells slept-in and a lurcher puppy is chasing his own tail on the rushes before the fireplace, half-ignored, and the sunlight through the windows falls heavy, like a physical force.

'Ah, Thomas,' Hastings greets him. 'Good of you to bring your bow.'

It does feel a bit foolish, inside, but he would not leave it outside with all the staffs against the wall for someone to steal. Hastings looks debauched, whey-faced with dark circles under his eyes, and he has a job for him, Thomas supposes, as he has done before, but he asks anyway.

'My lord,' he says, 'I beg leave to request—'

'Never mind all that,' Hastings says. 'You know how the situation is. I need something done, and you're the perfect man for it. Afterwards, who knows? Perhaps King Edward will let you go then.'

Thomas knows better than to argue. Hastings asks him how morale is in the camp and Thomas tells him it seems pretty good, though it would be better if the men knew when the troops of the

Earls of Devon and Pembroke will arrive, and for that moment to be before the Earl of Warwick's Kentish men make themselves present.

Hastings nods.

'We all want to know that,' he says.

'Are Pembroke and Devon not sending reports of their progress?'

'They are. Messages to say they are here, there and everywhere, but I think they are lying, saying such things as King Edward wishes to hear, hoping to steal a march on one another for the usual things. King Edward is . . . Well, he trusts them to arrive before this Redesdale character does, but I'd like to know for certain. Pembroke has crossed the Severn at Gloucester, that I know, but where is he now? Devon – pfffft. He could be anywhere.'

Thomas can see where this is going. 'I do not know the land well,' he points out.

'No. No. Well. I have a guide to go with you. Someone who knows the roads. Or at least has land near Oxford.'

'Why not just send him?'

Hastings looks slightly ashamed.

'He is – not as reliable as you.'

That does not sound good, Thomas thinks.

'And in truth I need him out of the way,' Hastings goes on.

What does that mean? Thomas wonders. Out of the way as in out of the castle? Or out of the way in case there is any fighting? Thomas hopes the latter, but suspects the former. Hastings nods to the secretary, who slips quickly away. When he comes back he has in tow a tall, astonishingly well-made and well-dressed youth whom he introduces as Sir John Flood.

Flood beams at Hastings with genuine fondness, but Hastings seems awkward in his company, shamefaced, and he cannot meet his eye. Sir John Flood is slightly taller than Thomas, in the full flush of youth, with a square jaw, blond hair cut in that same military style, and clear blue eyes. Thomas is taken aback. Flood is the chivalric ideal, he sees: the perfect gentle knight.

Flood tells Thomas he is pleased to meet him and that he has heard a little of his exploits from his cousin. He indicates Hastings. Hastings shifts uncomfortably on his stool.

'So, John,' Hastings says. 'You are to go with Thomas and four others of his choice, and you are to find Pembroke, and enquire of him why he dawdles. Well, not exactly that, but attempt to hasten him along. And when you've delivered such messages as I will give you, come back here with any he has for us. Is that understood?'

Flood nods. The secretary gives him various pieces of paper that he will need – passes for checkpoints, a chit to get horses from the ostler and so on – and a fat purse of coins and then they are dismissed.

'Keep an eye on him, Thomas, will you?' Hastings asks. 'His mother would never forgive me if anything happened to him.'

So that is it, Thomas thinks. He feels put upon. He does not want to have to look after Flood when he should be looking after Katherine and Rufus.

Flood is waiting for him in the passageway.

'I would like to bring my servant,' he says. 'So you need only round up three if you like? Men you trust, eh?'

They agree to meet in the bailey when they have the men and materiel they need, and Thomas hurries back to the butts to collect Brunt and two others of his choice: Brunt's closest friend Caldwell, taller by a head than the next tallest man and startlingly gangly, but able to shoot an arrow further than any man Thomas has yet met; and O'Driscoll, who is compact and springy with muscles from having worked all his life in his father's smithy. He walks on the balls of his feet with his chin and chest out, and is Irish, the first Irishman Thomas has knowingly met.

'It doesn't sound as if it'll be much fun,' Caldwell says. His Adam's apple is as large as a clenched fist, and bobs six inches up and down his long neck.

'I am not promising you that,' Thomas agrees.

190

'And your man Flood!' O'Driscoll says. 'He's more suited to the tilt yard than the tavern.'

'But have you seen the man's wife?' Brunt asks. He raises his eyebrows three or four times and O'Driscoll laughs a lecherous chug. And there she is when they meet Flood and his servant in the yard. Every man present is stilled for the moment, giving her room so he may stand back and gaze on her; even Thomas feels the spit dry in his mouth. All around her the men react in different ways, some adopting vague, distant smiles, others putting on shows with barking laughs and displays of physical strength, others standing and staring open-mouthed. There is something collectively predatory about this, and Thomas does not envy the poor girl, who is head down, with her cheeks blazing, her great doe eyes fixed on Flood alone, and you can see why: now he is dressed for riding, he is like something from a tapestry, the embodiment of a young Alexander or Caesar perhaps, come to life with such symmetry and grace that he has an effect on the men around him, too. He is wearing plate on his legs and feet, with long spurs, and a tight-fitting metal-studded brigandine the colour of wine around his body, with two belts on his hips from which hang his daggers and swords in beautifully worked sheaths. His hair is a golden helmet, and the sun seems to shine from him, so that if his wife were an iota less beautiful she might become a mere adornment.

'Blood and nails,' Brunt mutters.

Seeing the two say their goodbyes is actually painful.

'How long have they been married?' Thomas asks the servant, a hunched little man with a cap like a loaf.

'A week,' he tells them, rolling his eyes.

Thomas wonders if Hastings will be there to see them off, and looks around; he sees in an upper window not Hastings but King Edward, staring down at Flood and his wife, and Thomas notes his expression and knows now that he was wrong about why Hastings wanted the boy out of the way. Is there a single thing he can do about it? Take her with them, he supposes, but he can't do that.

191

'Come on,' Thomas says. 'Sooner we get this done, the sooner we'll get you back.'

They have been afforded access to the stables and the stores and they have chosen good strong horses, and are laden with a loaf of fresh bread and a great costrel of ale each; all have two bows across the backs of their horses and two sheaves of arrows apiece. They have sallets, and brigandines, though none so fine as Flood's, and each has been given a tabard of Hastings's livery in good broadcloth. They walk their horses – Flood's is white, the others' are brown – down through the city gates and out on to the bridge and across the river in spate. Flood wishes to say a prayer at the chapel and Thomas lets him, and stays on the bridge and stares down into the waters as they swirl around the many piers below, and thinks it odd that the sea comes this far upriver, and even odder that if he were to commit himself to its flow, he would be taken back, north and east, to Marton.

When Flood returns from his prayers Brunt asks where they will find this Earl of Pembroke.

'Lord Hastings says the Earl has crossed the River Severn at Gloucester and is moving along the west road towards us, and that the Earl of Devon is coming with his bowmen from further south. The roads meet at Oxford, two days' ride from here.'

O'Driscoll makes a joke about riding for two days that touches tangentially on Flood's wife, but Flood doesn't bother trying to understand. Thomas wonders if he should tell Flood about what sort of man King Edward is, but he does not. It is not his place. Flood swings up into his saddle nimble as you like, and they are off again. Flood rides beautifully, horse and man moving seamlessly as if both enjoy it. He could ride forever without tiring, Thomas thinks. The others, including Thomas, follow him bouncing like sacks in their saddles. Flood knows the name of every plant they pass and every bird they see. He can whistle some of their tunes, and he takes delight in any small churches they pass, always finding something to praise, and Thomas has to stop him going into each and lighting a candle for this or that relation who has either passed on, or is unwell, or is, in one case, unhappy. He speaks tenderly of his wife, Maude, and every time he does so, Flood insists they stop at the next chapel to light a candle for her, and once Thomas does likewise, hoping against hope that she will somehow find the strength to resist King Edward's advances.

They follow the road south through the rest of the day at a good pace until they reach the gates of Leicester, where, before they can find an inn, Flood again gets them to stop so that he can pray in the cathedral.

'Pious sort, isn't he?' Brunt asks the servant.

The servant rolls his eyes again.

At the inn, the attention that Flood receives is unnerving. Every man, woman, child and dog flocks to him, circles him, does what he, she or it can for him; he need only smile and all is his. He smiles often, and is granted whatever he wishes, and Thomas thinks of Taplow, with his knives, and wonders what he would have to say to Flood, but Flood does not seem to notice that the favours he is offered are offered nowhere else, and you can see he thinks that this is what life is like for everyone. Matters reach a head at the end of the night, when he pays for the food and the ale from his own purse, and then he takes none of three young women up on their offer of a bed for the night.

'Chriiiiist,' Brunt groans.

The next morning they are up and away before dawn. The sun comes up lilac and gold, and soon it shines hot in their faces. Thomas makes them stop to buy some of those broad-brimmed rush hats and even though they are worn only by men and women in the fields, when Flood puts his on it does not make him look like a peasant, but suits him, and he buys one to take back for Maude and all the other men look away.

They ride all morning – passing through Rugby and Daventry – until early afternoon when they come to the first signs of something amiss: a cart, pulled by two oxen, driven by a boy, with, sitting in the back, a fat priest and his boxes and coffers. They must ride off the road to let the cart past, and as he goes the priest in brown clutches something to his breast and looks at them fearfully.

'What are you running from?' O'Driscoll jeers.

The priest says nothing, only wraps his arms around whatever it is all the tighter, and the cart rolls north. But seeing this, Thomas gets them to take off their rush hats and strap on their helmets. They tie on their livery tabards and make sure the black bull badges can be seen, and Thomas loosens the pollaxe on the back of his saddle.

'Why?' Caldwell asks.

'He's running from an army, isn't he?' Thomas tells him. 'But there's no telling which army it is, is there?'

Caldwell takes his point, and dismounts to nock his bow.

'What do Pembroke's men wear?'

'Azure and gules,' Flood tells them.

'And Devon?'

'Azure and vert.'

They come to the first prickers late in the afternoon, when the heat has gone out of the day, at the far end of a track that runs through a village. They are in blue and red: Pembroke's men, well harnessed and heavily armed, as if expecting trouble.

'Who the fuck are you?' the first one asks.

Thomas explains and shows him the passes and letters from Hastings. The man can't read but is swayed by Flood's presence.

'Come on then,' he says. 'Though if you've a message for the Earl of fucking Devon, you've missed him.'

'Missed him?'

'He's taken his men and gone off somewhere. He wasn't happy with something. He's been arguing with Pembroke ever since we left Oxford.'

'So – what? He is just – gone?'

'It is as I say. I do not know. They argued over something and now he is gone, taking his bowmen with him.'

'But he is still coming?' Flood asks. 'I mean, King Edward – he needs them. He is relying on them! Robin of Redesdale is abroad with ten thousand northerners, and now the Earl of Warwick! He too has come out against his grace!'

The pricker had not heard this news.

'Warwick is now against King Edward? Mary, Mother of Jesus, I never thought I'd see that. How many men has he?'

'No one knows,' Flood tells him. 'But he's moving up from London to join Redesdale, and without Devon's bowmen we are—'

'Fucked.'

Thomas intervenes.

'Where is Pembroke?' he asks.

'He is camped off the road, on the hill up there.' The pricker nods to a distant rise to the south. Elsewhere the land is flat, a few trees, meadowland and good pasture for cows. There is a meandering river marked by a few field maples, ash and willows and perhaps another village to the southeast.

'How many have you?' Thomas asks.

'Just shy of four thousand?' the pricker supposes.

They ford the river and then take a track towards the camp.

'Will Devon come back, do you suppose?' Flood asks.

The pricker knows nothing.

'He may have gone home, for all I know. You might be our only archers.'

No one laughs. The camp is chaotic. There are only a few tents, and most men are preparing to sleep out wrapped in their cloaks. That is why they have chosen high ground, so as not to wake hidden in mist and soaked in dew, but Pembroke's tent is the only tent on the flat, while the others are on the slope; uphill pegs give in the soft earth so they've had to use such arrows as they have instead.

'Lush around here, isn't it?' one of Pembroke's squires opines.

They stand waiting for the Earl, and from their vantage can see many leagues of gentle land cut through by the road heading north to Leicester and beyond, and below them, the meandering river. It is very good land, they agree. Pembroke emerges, looking thunderous, and he is immune to Flood's charms. He recognises Thomas though.

'Got any more good news for us?' he asks.

Thomas tells him about Warwick's arrival from France, and Pembroke actually growls.

'Where is he?' he demands.

'He left London three days ago.'

Pembroke calculates and then rubs his forehead.

'Christ,' he says. 'He could be in . . . He could be anywhere. And if he and bloody Redesdale combine—' He almost shudders.

Flood asks him about the Earl of Devon.

'Don't even mention that bastard,' Pembroke tells them. 'God damn his eyes. Do you know what he has done?'

'We heard he has taken his men elsewhere.'

'Do you know *why* he has taken his men elsewhere?'

They shake their heads. Pembroke jabs a thick finger at his tent.

'Because my tent is on the flat, while his would have been on the slant. Because of that. Because of that he marched his men off as if – as if . . . I don't know. As if I'd taken his doll!'

'He has left you with no archers, because you . . . because you have the best tent?'

'Exactly.'

There is a moment's silence while they try to understand this.

'But he is still bringing his men to King Edward?' Flood asks.

'You'll have to ask him that.'

'Where is he?'

'I am fucked if I know. He went that way.' Pembroke points the same thick finger south.

'But that is not towards King Edward!' Flood says. 'That is away from him.'

Pembroke says no more, but takes Hastings's letters and retreats into his tent, leaving them around the beginnings of the cooking fire.

'What shall we do?' Flood asks.

'We ought to get back to King Edward,' Thomas tells them.

'Tonight?'

'There is daylight enough for a few miles.'

It is agreed. They are walking their horses back down the hill when they see some riders coming fast from the east. A party of prickers. One – no, two – are carrying themselves as if wounded, and there is an empty saddle. Thomas and the others clear the track and let them pass. One has a gash on his shoulder and his arm is cupped on his lap, the other has blood all over his face, and the usual smell of horses and sweat is tainted with that of blood.

'Redesdale! Redesdale!' one of them shouts. 'Down there. Across the river.'

Can Robin of Redesdale have come this far south so quickly?

'We'd best be going,' Thomas says.

They agree, but Flood will not let them.

'If this lot are caught in battle,' he says, gesturing at Pembroke's men, 'they will need our help. We must join them.'

'You've never been in a fight before, have you?' Brunt asks.

Flood has not.

'Now is not the perfect time for it,' Thomas tells him.

But still Flood will not budge, and before they can persuade him another party of prickers returns from the north and their escape is barred.

'Come on,' the commander says. 'You are all the bowmen we have!'

They return muttering to Pembroke's camp. The wounded prickers are telling those who will listen that they found trace of an army and followed it until they met a party of ten horsemen in blue, with a yellow badge across their chests – 'like a smear' – and they attacked them, even though they were outnumbered.

'They are just over the river!'

Messengers are sent for Devon, to recall him, but by now it is dusk. Some men go down to the river, where there is a bridge, and

Pembroke sends another party down to brace them. Two hundred in all. He sets his men to build big fires, and to tend them, to make Robin of Redesdale believe that Devon is with him, but he tells his commanders that they must be ready at first light.

'We will catch them before they are ready,' Pembroke says. 'Before they learn we have no bowmen.'

Thomas and the others are to sit with the first party of prickers they met, all of them Welshmen, and they must keep the fire going all night. They sing incomprehensible songs and one of them recites endless poetry in their own queer language, and they toast their bread on the fires and then slice cheese over it, and in fact this is not so bad, Thomas thinks, if only they'd shut up.

Thomas keeps the last watch, over the cooling ashes of the fire, and the country is loud with birdsong. He sees the dawn come first as a pale smear, very ordinary, and below there is a mist rising up where the river meanders through its meadows, and he is on his knees in the wet grass, offering up prayers to God for his own safety that he may return to Katherine and Rufus, when the quietude of the morning is broken by distant shouting and the batter of weapons from down by the bridge.

That is how it starts.

The camp erupts around him. Men surge to their feet. They throw off their cloaks, and others call for servants, squires, ale, bread, their own boots. Pembroke is there among them, roaring his head off, bellowing for messengers to be sent to my lord of Devon, demanding that his lesser knights and gentlemen bring order to the camp and get their men together, and the camp resounds with Welshmen bellowing at one another, and over it all: the smell of cheese toasting. Very few women have come, because the men were mustered late and fast, and so it is just a lot of men with dark shaggy hair strapping on their armour and gathering their bills and spears and hammers and swords and struggling to find their friends among so many doing likewise and appearing so similar.

It is surprising how quickly they organise themselves, though, and before the sun is properly up they are lined across the field. There are perhaps three thousand of them formed up in three battles. Pembroke stalks the ground before them. He is in full harness, with a pollaxe. His squire carries his helmet and his bevor. Another tries to tie a strap at his calf but Pembroke will not stop his prowling.

The noise of the fighting below is a constant irregular rattle. Men are already limping away to collapse in the grass or trying to drag themselves up the hill. The trees hide what is happening on the bridge itself, but as the mist clears Thomas can see a horde of men surging through the furlongs the other side of the river, making for the bridge, and there is a great surge of sound as they come. Thomas wonders why Pembroke does not stop them on the bridge. Then he thinks that the Earl is not trying to stop them. He wants them to cross the bridge, and to form up, and then he will send his men down on them to kill them.

But what about bowmen? It is not much good having the advantage of height if you have no bowmen.

Pembroke stops and turns his back on the fighting and faces his men. He is a big man, made more so by his harness, and his face is broad, too, and now, weather-chapped and mottled, with his hair on end, he appeals to his men.

'Men of Wales!' he bellows. 'Men of Wales, I thank God that you are with me today. Here in this shitty little part of shitty little England. I could have no finer company. None braver, none better beside me. And I thank God for that. D'you hear? I thank God that you sons of David are with me. Each and every one of you. You.' He points. 'You.' He points elsewhere. 'And you.' At someone else.

'Today you are my brothers. Today we are all brothers. All of us here. All of us in this line. We are brothers. We are a family. A nation. A race. A race of men. A race of men the world has come to fear. A race of men the world has reason to fear. And on this day we

199

will write another legend in the annals of our proud nation's history. Another chapter.'

Thomas wonders where men such as Pembroke learn all this sort of stuff. Is rhetoric thrown into their upbringing along with drills in the use of the long sword and the battle axe?

Pembroke continues. He acknowledges that Devon is not yet there, but tells his troops that now is the hour they must acquit themselves as men, and that when the battle is done, Devon and his men will come to regret their petulance, and that they, being perfidious Englishmen, will come to lie about this day, and say they were here on this field, and that they saw what the sons of Wales can do.

There is much shouting and waving of weapons.

Thomas and the few others who make up Pembroke's bowmen are standing a little off, on the right hand of the right-hand battle. They nock their bows, fluff out the fletches, and begin rolling their shoulders to warm them.

'We are to hold the flank,' Thomas mutters. He might laugh if it were not so desperate.

Flood is in full harness now, and of course, someone has spent money with an armourer to make his plate just the finest you could possibly imagine. In it, he looks awe-inspiring. He moves with such facility that even though Thomas knows there must be the usual weak spots – the groin and armpit – it is impossible to imagine him being still for long enough for anyone to threaten them. He has a pollaxe as fine as Thomas's and a horseman's hammer in his belt. His servant has taken the sheaths from sword and dagger and they hang from rings.

'You are not to go down there,' Thomas tells him.

Flood looks at him with those widespread blue eyes and for a moment Thomas feels he is falling into them. Flood tries to appeal to him.

'Thomas,' he says. 'Thomas, sir?'

'No,' Thomas tells him. 'Lord Hastings charged me with bringing you back whole and alive. I don't care how good at this you are, and how much you want to get your harness bloody. You are not risking your neck here and now. There will be plenty of chance for that later.'

Flood blinks.

Thomas sees he has a piece of gauzy cloth tied to his pollaxe. Can it be from Maude? It is. Oh dear God. Does he know what that weapon will do to a man? Does he want to get something so pure all splattered with gore? With brains? With the stuff that spills from torn entrails? Really?

'Give me your axe,' Thomas says.

'No.'

Pembroke is still shouting, but in Welsh, and the Welshmen are shouting something in return. The men at the bridge are still putting up a fight, but soon Robin of Redesdale's men will force a crossing. It is only a question of time.

Thomas holds out his hand for Flood's axe.

'This is not your fight,' Thomas tells him. These are words that would persuade him, but Flood is young. He has not yet fought anywhere other than the tilt yard.

'Come on,' Thomas says, and he puts his hand on the axe, closing his fingers around the shaft. Flood does not let go. It is a strange position. If Flood wanted to kill him now, he could. Thomas watches him consider it. But Brunt and Caldwell move slightly behind Flood's shoulder and Flood sees the movement and turns to them, one on one side, the other on the other, and they smile innocently at him, but all four know what's just happened, and Flood looks back at Thomas and smiles.

'Very well,' he says, letting him take the pollaxe. 'But keep it close.'

Pembroke has finished rousing his rabble and the men at the bridge have finally been overwhelmed and are now scattering across the lower reaches of the hill pursued by Robin of Redesdale's men, who have taken the bridge by weight of numbers and are spreading into the field below.

'Come on,' Caldwell mutters. He has a long arrow nocked in his enormous bow, and if only Pembroke would give the signal, he could send it into those who are even now killing the wounded men.

Pembroke gives the signal. He steps back and levels his hammer at Thomas and his little band, and then lowers it, and so now Thomas drops Flood's axe in the grass next to his own and snatches up his bow and nocks an arrow. Already Caldwell has sent that first shaft down the hill, carefully aimed, into the chest of a man with a hammer about to despatch another crawling through the long grass. Brunt laughs. O'Driscoll cheers. That is the way to do it, Thomas supposes. They are only four bowmen and they each have fewer than fifty arrows apiece, so laying down salvoes will do no good. They must pick their targets and shoot accurately.

He is become judge and executioner.

He sees a man, decides he does not like him, draws his bow and sends an arrow skimming down the hill to kill him. On what basis? He has never liked those helmets with cheek pieces. Barbutes, they call them. He picks a man wearing one, draws and looses. The man is snatched away from what he is doing – trying to organise his men – and sent staggering. He sees another urging men forward, but not moving himself. Him he catches on the helmet. He may not be dead, but he will not be getting up any time soon. He imagines he sees Taplow, or someone very like him – but there are so many who are like him down there! – and he looses a shaft at him, aiming for his chest and sending him scuttling backwards. Then there is another Taplow, and so he looses at him too. And then he remembers Horner, down there, just trying to make a living, and he wavers, remembering his promise not to fight the man, but he thinks: Well, there is nothing for it. He must do what he must, and take the repercussions as they come.

And he draws and looses. He does not know these men. It is better not to speculate. It is better to loose as if he were a fulling stock: rising and falling, pulling and loosing. He just ceases to think and concentrates only on sending arrows as well as he is able and as fast as he is able: shaft after shaft down into the faces of those trying to come up the hill to kill him.

But they have nowhere near enough arrows. And soon arrows are being loosed back at them in return. A dark cloud. A dirty blur in the morning sky. A man is dropped on Pembroke's front rank, an armstretch from Pembroke himself, and all along the battles there is a slight retreat, a flinching, a wincing, as the front rank withdraw from the arrow shafts that come slicing down and bury themselves where they will. A man screams. There is a bellow, a bleat, and another runs for a moment before he falls thrashing. Pembroke remains, standing with his arm raised and showing no fear, and God gives him luck, but they all know if they stand for long, without Devon's bowmen, they will all be hit and the Earl knows without Devon's bowmen he cannot hold this height, so he shouts above the noise:

'For God! For King Edward! And St David!'

And his Welshmen surge forward with a bellowed roar. They storm down the hill towards where Robin of Redesdale is drawing up his men, and Thomas looses his last arrow and sees with admiration how well Pembroke has timed his charge, for Robin of Redesdale's bowmen have not had time to do their worst, and nor are his men-at-arms ready to receive this onslaught. Pembroke's men arrive in a hard, broad front with momentum behind them, and they break the loose formation below. The noise is terrible, a rolling batter of steel on steel. The screams will come later. Robin of Redesdale's men are pushed back into the trees, into the river, the lucky ones back across the bridge.

Thomas and Brunt and the others are bent with their hands on their knees, faces flushed as apple skins, breathing hard, steaming in the early morning like oxen, watching the events below.

It is only then that Thomas sees Flood is not there.

14

The priory is no more.

It is gone, burned through, a collection of blackened stumps, a cancerous growth on a low islet in the encroaching fen. The church tower is shorn at an angle, the roofs elsewhere are collapsed and the outer wall is crumbled to stone and mortar. The damp air smells of soot and ash and disturbed gulls wheel above, shrieking.

'Was it always like that?' Liz asks, letting the horse come to a stop on the road below. Katherine does not reply. She just shivers. Now that she has finally seen it again, she cannot take her eyes from it. This is the place in which she grew up, the place that has sent a black shadow like a pike shaft through her life since, the place that has filled her nightmares and sometimes her waking hells. It is gone. Just like that. She cannot grasp it.

'What is that place?' Rufus asks.

Isabella and Liz look at Katherine for an answer and when it comes it surprises them all, even her.

'It was once my world,' she says.

'Not a very nice one,' Rufus says.

Liz smiles.

'Was there a fire?' he asks.

'Big one, by the look of it,' Liz says.

Everywhere is black. The whole place, from gate to grate, from footing to spire, all of it, tumbled down and thick with layered soot.

'What a shame,' Isabella murmurs. She cannot abide waste.

Katherine says nothing.

'Shall we go up and see?' Liz asks.

'See what?' Katherine asks. 'What is there to see?'

But they do. They leave her with the horse down on the track and she watches them go.

Rufus tells her not to be sad and she tells him she isn't.

'Then why are you crying?'

And she realises she is. She stands watching for a long while. It is cold today. No sign of the sun, and the wind stirs the water around about and the rushes sigh as they move. She shivers as if her dress is wet.

After a while the two women come out through the gates again. Their blue and green dresses and white linen headdresses are dabs of colour against the drab black world. They come down the track. Liz has soot on her elbow and shoulder, and their boots are black with it.

'By the Mass, what a place,' Liz says.

'It was worse before the fire,' Katherine tells them.

Liz laughs, but Katherine can tell they hoped to find something. What? A coffer full of papers relating to her family?

'Are you sure you don't want to go up?' Isabella asks. 'It might be better for you. It is – There is nothing still standing. Even the floor of the church is broken up.'

Katherine shakes her head. They climb back into the cart; Liz settles and flicks the horse into a slow plod.

'No one's been in since it burned down,' she says. 'Odd, you know? Because there's wood to be had, and stones there for building.'

'Who's building around here?'

They look about. The mill is there, but it is abandoned too, and its wheel has folded over and the roof tiles slithered off.

'Like it were made of cheese,' Liz says.

Other than that, there is nothing.

'Cornford Castle is that way,' Katherine tells them. She is thinking aloud, really; reminding herself of her past life. Isabella lets out a long sigh.

'Let's leave that for another day, shall we?'

Katherine cranes her head around to watch the priory slip out of view. She can see the sisters' half of the priory now. The field where she first met the Rivens, and Thomas of course. Ten years ago, or thereabouts. Dear God. And as they roll on, she begins to feel that something is now missing from the middle of her life, and she starts to feel as if she is floating – or falling; she cannot decide which. She cannot believe the priory is gone.

'Wonder what happened to all them monks?' Liz asks.

'They must have escaped the blaze,' Isabella imagines.

'It had a bad atmosphere,' Liz counters.

'It always had a bad atmosphere,' Katherine tells her.

'Perhaps Baron Willoughby will know?' Isabella says.

But when they finally make it to Tattershall, Baron Willoughby is absent, and with him every able-bodied man, and most of the women, too, so all that remains of his household are the elderly, the infirm, a few women, and an old priest with pink-rimmed eyes like a dog. When Isabella asks about the priory, he crosses himself and turns around three times and spits on the ground.

'The devil himself came unto that place,' he tells her through loose lips, but that is all he will tell them – because they are women, Katherine supposes – and he does not want to shock them. Liz, who goes first to the kitchens, tells them afterwards, though only once she has clapped her hands around Rufus's ears.

'The Prioress was sent out of her wits for the love of another sister!' she tells them later. 'And that sister was so scandalised, she were driven to drown herself in the river where they washed their linens. The Prior of All came and investigated but nothing could be proved, but still he sent the Prioress back to where she'd come from.'

'That was all?'

Liz shrugs.

'They say this Prior of All were terrified of her. And he were right to be so, because they said that before she left she cursed the place – that she damned the canons and sisters all to hell and what have you.'

Rufus wriggles free.

'Within a month they were visited by a one-eyed beggar who came for alms,' Liz goes on, 'only he brought with him the pestilence.'

'Dear God.' Isabella crosses herself at its mention.

'And by the end of the month, every monk was dead save one. Can you imagine what that must have been like? Trapped in there? Alone and just waiting for them black spots to come up on your skin? Burying a body every day? Anyway. He went mad, of course, too, this monk, after a month or so.'

And she grabs Rufus again, more than just playfully, and she presses him to her and covers his ears again.

'And he set fire to the whole place. He said it were cursed, just as everyone knew it were, and everyone within were damned. Well, they were after that, that's for sure, because the fire took hold and the sisters on their side couldn't get out because the Prioress had put in locks, hadn't she, because someone had once absconded, and she'd taken the keys with her, hadn't she? And before it happened the Prior of All had said there were no need for them to leave the priory any-how, and that they should try to be like the first sisters of that order, and live in total isolation. And since there were no contact between the sisters and the canons, it was thought they'd not get the pesti-lence, and so when the fire took hold, they were all burned alive. Every last one of them.'

There is a long silence.

'Dear God,' is all Isabella can repeat.

'Save the Prioress,' Katherine says.

Liz looks up at her.

'Yes,' she says. 'Save her.'

They stay that night at the castle in Tattershall. It is a meagre din-ner, in low light, during which the priest becomes drunk and after which prayers are said for Baron Willoughby and the men he has taken with him in arms across the country. It is generally assumed within the castle that everyone knows the men have gone west to help the Earl of Warwick remove King Edward's corrupt councillors from his side, and to restore the Earl to that position, and though Katherine has scarcely registered a word spoken all night, she looks up then, surprised to hear the enterprise spoken of so freely, since she had imagined it would be thought of as treason.

'Will he succeed?' she asks the priest.

'Oh yes,' he says.

But all she can think about is fire ravaging the priory. She can imagine it taking the sisters, and she remembers the time they gathered in the nave when they thought they were being attacked by the men who turned out to be the Rivens. How they had cowered, snivelling, waiting to be – what? She shudders to think of it, yet cannot clear the images from her mind. She imagines them clawing at the walls, leaving marks in the plaster. She sees them trying to escape those narrow windows. And all that time the flames coming closer. The heat. Dear God. And worse. Afterwards. She can imagine it afterwards. Boiled blood, congealed fat, blackened bones. Their scattered, sooted skulls with bared teeth, and their spines curled in agony.

But not the Prioress.

Afterwards Katherine, Rufus and Liz bed down in the great hall with the other servants, while Isabella, on account of who she tells them she is, is given a room with a strung bed in the southern range of the castle where the stones retain the sun's warmth, even into the night. Katherine lies awake, too scared to close her eyes for the dreams she knows will come, and when dawn breaks on her at last, and the servants begin their creeping day, she is up with them as they light the fires with faggots of hawthorn, and she gives thanks to God for guiding her through her lonely vigil, for she has in those short hours discovered something about herself that has been a long time in the coming.

On their return from Tattershall the next day, they must once again pass the priory. The iron hoops of the cart's wheels hiss through the wet Lincolnshire slop and they all sit in silence and stare at it as they go by, even Rufus, who has heard something of the previous night's conversation, turning their heads to watch it slip behind them, and as they go, Katherine's fearful memories seem to fly from her, like rags in the wind, and she starts to believe that when it is gone, when she can see it no more, she will be free of it. For in the night what she had come to see was that the priory was not a heaven-sent punishment for a sin she could never remember committing, as she had always believed, but that it was merely a world of the Prioress's creation, a reflection of her, and of nothing more than that.

This past of hers, so long a source of shame, has become nothing she need hide from the eyes of such as Thomas, or Rufus, or Isabella or, even, Liz. It was a time in which she was under the power of another who mistreated her, and the fault of it was not her own.

And so now she stands with the others on the bed of that cart, and she turns and watches the priory as it dwindles, shrinks and finally subsides behind the horizon, and she feels exultant. She feels like bellowing at the top of her voice that it will be well, all will be well.

'But now you'll never find out who you are,' Liz says.

'I don't care!' she tells her. 'I don't care.'

But Liz looks sceptical, as if she ought to care, and so they all lapse into silence, lost in their separate thoughts, and by the time they reach Lincoln the sun is out, shining on their backs, and by the time they are in sight of the hall at Marton, their shadows lie long on the right-hand verge of the track and Isabella has nodded off, her head drooping like a fritillary.

That is when they see the men and horses, up by the hall, five or six of them.

'Are you expecting anyone, my lady?' Liz asks.

Isabella wakes up, and looks panicked. She is not.

Katherine feels a welling of delight.

'It is Thomas!' she says.

'Ah, good,' Liz says, satisfied, and she flicks the horse on.

But it is not Thomas. It is Isabella's sons, William and Robert, and they even have Borthwick with them, though no new hounds, and the falconer is there with his charges. Isabella has not been expecting them, but is happy they are back despite what they have done. They greet their mother with tense restraint. They want to know why she was abroad, and where she went. Isabella tells them. There is a slight quaver when Lord Willoughby is mentioned.

'He was not there?'

She tells them he has gone to Warwick's banner.

'He said he would summon us,' one of them whines. 'Were he to go to Warwick's colours, he said he would. We – are his indentured retainers!'

'He promised he would send for us!' the other one says.

'Well, I am grateful he did not,' Isabella says. 'I have seen too many men I love go off and be – become lost in these stupid, stupid wars.'

The boys are angry and ashamed of themselves, and turn on Isabella.

'He did not call us because he knew we could only provide a handful of men, that is why.'

'A handful of poorly armed men at that.'

'We need more money.'

Isabella tells them she has none to spare.

And that, for the moment, is that.

From then on, though, the cords of the three women's triumvirate are broken, as Katherine and Liz become servants again, banished from the fire's side while the sons sit idle and Isabella sighs and twists her rosary into knots in her lap, too frightened to bring up the subject of her breviary, trying to think what else she can do to make them happy.

'They're a couple of shits,' Liz says, having watched them at it for a few days. 'And she's so blind she can't see them for what they are!'

She is carrying a broad wooden bucket filled with bowls and mugs back towards the yard. Katherine tells her to beware Borthwick.

'The fatty who smells of dogs? I've already dealt with that one.'

Katherine envies Liz her facility. If she had had it, rather than recourse to that blunt eating knife, then – then how different would things be?

'What do you think they want?' Liz asks. 'Not much more they can take, is there?'

Katherine agrees. But there is a tension in the air. The boys are definitely angling for something.

Quite what it is they are after comes slowly: in the week after the Feast of the Seven Sleepers of Ephesus at the very end of July, the day until which the stationer had agreed to hold Isabella's breviary. Candles have been called for and rush lamps bought. The bearded boy suggests that Isabella is living like a peasant and should not be. Isabella agrees. There is a fine edge to her voice that carries a weight of meaning, but not with the boys. Katherine listens from behind the screen as they ask her why she has taken Katherine back in. Isabella tells them Katherine is more help to her than anyone has ever been. Again the implicit meaning is missed.

'We think it is time you sold this place,' one of the boys says.

'Sold it?'

'While it is still worth something.'

'Where am I to live?'

'You could move into a convent. A priory.'

'I don't want to do that.'

'You can't afford to live here!'

'I can. It is you I cannot afford.'

'But we live on nothing! You give us nothing.'

'I have given you all I can.'

'Tcha!'

Liz is about to storm into the room and unleash her tongue on the men, and perhaps they deserve it, but Katherine grabs her wrist and forbids it and for once Liz takes her advice. The next morning Robert and William take their birds hunting and Isabella is left exhausted by her efforts at defence, and preoccupied.

'Perhaps they are right,' she tells Katherine.

'Do you want to go to a nunnery?'

'Of course not, but this place is too big for me alone now. I cannot manage it. Not with my eyes. And if Robert and William need the money . . .'

'Do they not have any offices themselves? Positions and the like?' Liz asks.

Isabella purses her lips.

'There was talk of something,' she says. 'But that went to another man, who was favoured by the Queen.'

It is always someone else's fault, Katherine thinks.

'So you would do it?'

There is a long moment. Isabella screws up her face, and her chin wobbles.

'Perhaps it is for the best,' she says.

So that is that, Katherine thinks. She has lost her home before, of course, and should never have allowed herself to hope. She thinks of those boys with their scarlet cloth and their falcons, and she thinks of herself and Thomas and little Rufus, and she could weep. She thinks of Senning, so perfect, and of Watkins, the man who found Sir William Tailboys and all his money hiding in a cave. Why do some men catch Fortune's Wheel as it is on the rise, while others only when it has already gone over the top and is on its descent?

After that it is hard to pass the days with Isabella, even though Katherine can see she is caught in the gap between a mother's love for her sons and her judgement of them as men. Isabella weeps constantly and becomes so helpless she cannot do the simplest of things, so Katherine resorts to spending more time alone in the little house she and Thomas built. It is empty: all such furniture as Thomas ever managed to make, and every bowl, jug, blanket and board has been taken for use elsewhere, perhaps by Borthwick; so she sits on the floor and she thinks – about the priory and the Prioress, about Jack and Nettie and John Stump under lock and key in some dismal tower, and she tries to think of anything else they might have done differently, and she sees there are many things they could have done, had they but known.

Her gaze flits over the little cottage, the repository of so many small memories of the good years between their return from Bamburgh and Sir John's death, but it returns, as always, to the hearth, made of stone set sideways so it forms a series of ridges in the clay and sour milk from which Thomas made the floor.

Under it, wrapped in linen and oiled cloth, is the ledger.

She sits in silence and she thinks about it, and as she does so, it seems to loom larger in her mind's eye, so that she can see it there, wrapped up, and it seems to be in communication with her, as it is said some saints' bones communicate with initiates by rattling, or by letting slip blood when they are nearby. The ledger is crying out to her, she thinks, and then she understands that the way to save Jack and John and Nettie is not through having Thomas try to bring about the Earl of Warwick's destruction, and through him Edmund Riven, but through giving them what they want: the ledger. She must take it to Edmund Riven, wherever he may be, and let him discover it for himself.

She vaults to her feet. That is it! That is it! She will do it. She hugs herself, wrapping her arms right around herself, and she does a sort of shoe shuffle of leather sole on earthen floor. By God, she misses Thomas in moments like this.

But then she thinks: What then?

After she has done that, and after Thomas has returned to her, what then? Where will they all go? If Isabella sells this place that has been their home, and Hastings no longer needs Thomas's services – because, after all, what will happen to him if King Edward is declared illegitimate? – then . . . then what happens to her, and to Thomas, and to Rufus?

It is back to the same damned thing: money.

Still, they can worry about that when the time comes. They must first think about Jack and Nettie and poor old John Stump, for whom no one really cares. They must be got free from their imprisonment first. The loss of the ledger is merely the price worth paying, a price she will gladly pay.

She finds a mattock and starts to work on the floor. The clay makes a fine floor for everyday use, but it is easy enough to break it up and soon she has the hole by the side of the hearth deep enough to find the edges of the black wodge of oiled linen, plastered in clumps of dried clay, that's been buried there perhaps three years. She tugs it out and finds that their precautions have worked. It feels light within its packaging, as if it is still dry. She holds it a long moment, just staring at it.

Christ, the trouble it has brought them.

She is about to cut these wrappings open, to slice through her carefully placed stitches, to inspect it, when Liz's shadow fills the doorway.

'What're you doing all covered in—What are you doing, Kate?'

Katherine is caught. Her options flit through her mind, but she is holding the parcel like a thief caught in the act.

'What's that you've got there?' Liz goes on.

Katherine decides to tell her.

'It is – it is what all this trouble is about. It is what Edmund Riven has been looking for. Don't ask what it is, because I'll not tell you, and it is best you do not know.'

'That? Is it gold and stuff?'

Katherine hesitates.

'Yes,' she lies. 'Gold.'

'It don't look very heavy.'

'It is very well-worked gold. A book. A manuscript. Illuminated. In Bruges. By the best, most skilful monk that ever did live.'

Liz knows she is lying.

'So what are you going to do with it, now you've found it?'

'I am going to take it to Edmund Riven. I am going to give it to him, so that he no longer has a reason to keep Jack and Nettie and John.'

Liz looks at her thoughtfully.

'So you had it all along? While he were scouring the north for the thing, it were just lying here, buried under your hearth? How did you come by it?'

Katherine tells her it is a long story.

'We've plenty of time,' Liz says.

'No,' Katherine tells her. 'That is the thing. We do not. Think about Nettie. She will be childing any day now.'

Liz is surprised.

'So you – you mean to take to the road again, to ride up to Middleham in time of war to give that Edmund Riven this book, and then what? Deliver Nettie's baby?'

'I don't know,' Katherine says. 'But Nettie cannot have the child in some – some stinking dungeon. We – I – could at least get her out of there. Take her to a nunnery, or a hospital if there is one. An inn, perhaps. Your father's?'

Liz nods.

'Though what of Isabella?' Katherine asks. 'We cannot leave her like this, can we? Alone with those sons of hers. They will find her some priory.' She looks at Liz. 'Would you stay? To look after her? If I were to go?'

Liz is uncomfortable.

'It'd be odd,' she says. 'Me here, you there.'

'So you would come with me?'

'Aye,' Liz supposes.

'But what about Thomas?' Katherine wonders. 'We must wait for him.'

Now Liz looks thoughtful.

'But maybe . . .' she begins hesitantly. 'Maybe if we did it quickly? We should, with Nettie about to child, and then you could be back here for when Thomas comes?'

It is a good idea.

'But there is still Isabella,' Katherine says.

'Well,' Liz says. 'Think on it. But in the meantime, you'd best hide that bloody thing.' She points to the ledger. 'If it's as valuable as you say it is,' she goes on, 'them two boys'll have it off you and be hawking it around town before you can bless the blood and bones of Our Sacred Lord Jesus Christ.'

Katherine feels chastened. She's about to slide the package of the ledger back into its clay groove under the hearth with her own few odds and ends, including, she sees, the papers the stationer sold her, when she has an idea.

She takes the papers out again, sets them aside while she repairs the damage to the floor as best she can, and then she takes them up and follows Liz outside into the late-afternoon sunshine. She sits on a log Thomas sawed for this purpose and picks her way through the tight lettering of the bundle. Soon she comes to the section wherein the writer – unnamed – deals with couching cataracts. He – it is certainly a he – suggests a surgeon cut the lens of the eye with a thorn, from bottom to top, and push the disc blocking the eye down towards the cheek, and out of the way. He does not say what the disc is made of, or why it has formed, only that it can be moved. But a thorn though? And how would you wash the eye? Rose oil, she supposes, rather than urine.

'By Our Lady,' Liz says when she sees the papers. 'Is that a goat or a man?'

Katherine is not sure. She wonders if it matters. Do goats have the same sorts of eyes as men? They are differently conformed; but they do the same job, don't they? Liz is scandalised and reminds her that mankind is made in God's image, not some bloody goat's.

And how would you make it so that the cutting did not hurt? No one would be able to stand having anything – let alone a thorn – thrust into their eyeball without a fight. If she were to do this, she'd need to render Isabella insensible. How? Goodwife Popham had a dwale that once knocked Sir John almost dead for three days. How did she do that? Something to do with poppy seeds and henbane. Such things are not unobtainable locally, but you would need money, which, of course, she does not have. She is pondering this when she hears Isabella bleating for her from the yard; she sighs, and goes to find her.

When she does, she leads her back into the hall, where Isabella takes her seat in the gloom by a cold fire, and then fetches out a purse that she has hidden under the chair. It looks full. She tells Katherine that the breviary her sons sold has been much on her mind recently, and that reading it again will take her back to happier times. She asks Katherine if she will take the money and go back to Lincoln for her, and perhaps buy back the breviary. Katherine does not remind Isabella that she cannot read, for her eyesight is so bad, because Katherine can understand it is not the actual reading of the breviary that will bring her comfort so much as merely having it in her hands. But she does remind her that the stationer promised only to keep the breviary until the Feast of the Seven Sleepers, now a week past.

'Nevertheless,' Isabella mews. 'I feel God will have kept it for me.'

She holds out the purse and, after a moment, Katherine takes it.

'You will not tell my sons?' she asks. 'I should not like them to know that I know they have deceived me.'

It is heartbreaking, but when she says this Isabella starts to weep, and Katherine cannot stand another moment of it. She leaves Rufus with Liz and rides alone, wrapped in an old travelling cloak, sitting astride the saddle, and she goes fast. She is so indignant on Isabella's behalf that she does not pause to ask for news from any of those she passes, but still, when she gets to Lincoln the stationer is not there.

'Where is he?' she asks the man at the next stall, fat-faced, selling bee-related products for which none have need.

'He is gone to London,' the man tells her. 'To appeal his father's arrest.'

'Arrest?'

The man shrugs.

'No one knows,' he says.

She walks her horse back along towards the arch of the north gate. Whatever can it mean? Can it possibly be something to do with this bloodhound of Hastings's? She still cannot see that a connection can be made between the stationer who once saw the ledger – and did not, as far as she can remember, even touch it – and her and Thomas. She is assailed by fears though. The coincidence, it is too great.

She is also hungry, she realises, and along the street there are one or two food stalls; she stops for buttered peascod and ale and she sits and eats and drinks from the suspiciously weighted mug and then ambles along past a shop above which hangs a sign cut into the shape of a double-handed ewer. An apothecary. Its hatch is down, and it's dark within but light enough to see the rows of earthenware jars and stoppered bottles. The apothecary – elderly, with a very round face topped by a curiously small hat and tailed by a thin pointed beard – is crumbling something into a powder with long strong fingers.

'Dried fox lung,' he tells her. 'Good for breathing problems. What can I do for you?'

He has oil of roses, yes. He has gall of a boar, yes. He has the universal salve for all wounds, made up from the exact number of different ingredients as there were apostles, and he lets her smell the jar and it takes her floating straight back to the pardoner, who once dressed a wound in Thomas's head with something just like this, and may even have bought it from this man all those years ago. He has poppy seed and henbane, and he has a dwale that he swears will render a man senseless for a week with no long-term harm.

But it all costs money.

She weighs it up, and then takes out the purse hidden under her dress and passes over the coins. She feels curiously hot and breathless, doing something she knows is wrong.

'May God forgive me,' she murmurs.

The apothecary wraps the goods in tiny slips of paper and hands her a small earthenware jar sealed with wax. He asks what her master is attempting and without bothering to correct him she tells him about Isabella's eyes. He tries to sell her a cream that has come from Russia that is made up of rotting wolves' carcasses.

'Does it work?' she asks.

'It is yet to be proven,' he admits.

She does not take it. She does take a small knife though, honed so that it cuts through linen even when it is lying in a heap.

'Better than a thorn,' he tells her. 'And you will need a needle. This one. It is silver.'

And almost ruinously expensive, but she buys it anyway, and the small flask of a tincture of henbane which he also presses on her, and by the end of it, she has very little change left from the money that Isabella gave her, and so she rides home with her heart thumping against her ribcage. When she gets there, she is, for once, pleased to see Isabella's sons are there by the old woman's side, because it means Isabella cannot ask her for the money or the breviary. The atmosphere is tense though. No words are said.

'They've had another row,' Liz tells her. She is washing Rufus in a bath of warmed water, using the last of the black soap they took north and brought back. 'They want her to marry some new husband.'

'But she is an avowess!'

'They say she can break the vow in a moment.'

'But why, though?'

'Something to do with getting on in the world. You know what they're like.'

'But what would a husband get out of marrying her?'

'To sell the place and take the money, I expect.'

'And he would be happy with – with an old blind woman?' Katherine wonders.

'They said many a man prefers it that way.'

Christ, Katherine thinks, they are giving their mother away like an old ewe. But how valuable is an old ewe? Not very.

She tells Liz about the dwale and the oil of roses.

'Blood of Christ, you are not serious! You?'

Katherine lowers her voice and tells her that she has cut many a patient, saved hundreds of lives.

'But an eyeball? You ever cut one of them?'

She admits she has not.

'But that is no reason not to.'

So she does, the next day, when William and Robert and Borthwick and the falconer have left to go hunting for the day.

'You are not even going to *tell* her?' Liz asks.

'It will be easier that way,' Katherine assures her. 'And it will be over before she knows it. No longer than saying the paternoster.'

And she is right, she thinks, since Isabella will put up all sorts of reasons why she should not be cured of this. She will say her blindness is sent by God, that the discs that block her sight are a discharge from an impure soul, and that prayer and fasting are the ways to remedy them, and if they are not gone yet, it is only because she has not prayed or fasted enough. Katherine can put the dwale in her ale. It is as simple as that. Liz is still doubtful, but only, it turns out, because putting it in the ale is so easy, since Isabella is blind.

'Hardly seems fair,' she says.

They sit with Isabella until her head nods. Liz catches her as she slides from the settle.

'Like a bag of sticks,' Liz says.

For a moment Katherine feels almost faint with it all. She is in a sort of heightened state: colours are brighter, sounds sharper. But then she is gripped by a sense of purpose. Suddenly she knows what to do, and is doubtless.

Together they lift Isabella's frail old body on to the board and carry her out into the yard. It is the perfect day for it: the sun is bright, and there is no wind. They put the board on the logs where Sir John used to play chess. It is a little low for a table, but Isabella looks comfortable.

'Is she dead?' Rufus asks.

Katherine looks at her son. May God forgive me, she thinks, for she had forgotten about him.

'No,' she tells him. Though she does remember to put the bowl of water on her chest, so that she can at least see if she still breathes.

He asks what they are doing.

'We are saving Isabella's eyes,' she says. 'So she can see properly again.'

Rufus accepts this as if she'd said they were mending a basket.

'She will like that,' he says. 'Will there be any blood?'

'No.'

He comes over to watch.

'Don't touch anything,' Katherine tells him, gesturing to him to stand back from the pot of rose oil and the wine, and the knife and the needle she has laid out on a strip of clean linen. Isabella lies on her back, her mouth open, the loose skin of her face sloughing back towards her ears. Her teeth are long and yellow and she looks impossibly old and vulnerable.

'How shall we do this?' Liz asks.

In fact, it is quite easy.

Katherine stands at the end of the board above Isabella's head and leans over her, with her shadow falling across her face. Her hands are slippery with the oil and she wipes them on clean linen. Then she takes up the knife.

'Are you sure, Kate?' Liz asks.

And there is a moment now, when it is not too late.

But Katherine nods.

'I am,' she says.

'Maybe she wouldn't want you to do it?' Liz says. 'Don't you think it is more – up to her to decide? It is wrong to cure someone like this if they believe their infliction is heaven-sent. You are cutting His work out.'

Katherine pauses. The knife is perhaps three inches from Isabella's closed right eye. The fingers of Katherine's left hand are curled in a soft pinch and she knows exactly what they will do and how they will do it and how it will feel as they cut the soft skin of the eye. But Liz's words have made her look up.

What *is* she doing?

'It is like you are being God,' Liz tells her.

Katherine looks down at Isabella lying peacefully in the sun and she is assailed by doubt. What if Liz is right? She straightens. Her knife is held in a steady hand and she looks at Liz and thinks: No. I can do this. I can make her see again. It will be a miracle, but also not a miracle.

She takes the tincture the apothecary sold her, and she unseals the jar and then, bending over Liz, she peels back first her right eyelid. She watches the murky circle in the middle of the blue circle shrink to a tiny pinprick. So she does as the apothecary advised, and she taps a drop of the tincture of henbane from the puckered mouth of the jar on to the sightless ball of Isabella's eye. When the drop lands, there is a slight resistance on the lid, as if Isabella were trying to blink. Katherine does the same with the other eye. It feels no less strange to be rummaging among such privacies. She stands back.

'Is that it?' Liz asks.

'No,' Katherine tells her. 'We must wait for as long as it takes to say an Ave.'

A moment later she checks on the eye, peeling back the lid, and is astonished at what she sees. The dark circle at its centre has become enormous and the blue of the eye is now rendered a tiny thin rim around it. And there, in its dark centre, is the cataract in full view. It looks like a chalky pebble, or very fine ladies' button.

Katherine reaches for the needle.

'Oh God,' Liz says, unable to look at this.

For some reason Katherine is pleased to find Liz so squeamish.

She washes the needle in the warm wine and lubricates it in the rose oil. Then she turns and leans over Isabella from the side, so close she can see her breath stirring the fine down on the old woman's cheek, and her hand is surprisingly steady, given how fast her heart is beating,

'Hold her eyelid,' she asks Liz. 'Open, like this.'

Liz is wary but does so. Then Katherine steels herself, takes the needle and eases it through the front of the eye, just inside the slender rim of blue. It is like pushing the needle through the skin of a grape, or a ripe medlar, and within, under this resistant cover, the pulp is a thick liquid. She was fearful there might be blood but there is none. Isabella surprises her by snoring suddenly but then settles back.

Katherine advances the needle until she can feel its tip against the solid, opaque lens. She gives a tentative push and the lens recedes but then returns as she eases the pressure. She advances the needle again, now pushing firmly at the edge of the lens where it is attached. She withdraws the needle, re-angles it, and pushes in a similar manner at the other side of the lens. Then, once again, she pushes at the middle of that milky ball; she pushes firmly, and suddenly, to her delight, the lens pops into the back of the eye and disappears down behind the lower rim of the hole which now appears black.

Katherine very slowly withdraws the needle. She takes a drop of the rose oil and moistens the eyeball, then she lets the lid close.

She looks up. And breathes.

'That's it?' Liz asks.

'For that one,' she says.

'And it's worked?'

'I think so.'

'Bloody hell,' Liz says, and then straightens because they can hear hoof beats approaching on the track beyond, and a moment later William and Robert return, Borthwick and the falconer trailing behind. The four men stop, and stand shoulder to shoulder, staring at them in silence.

15

Where is he? Where is he?

'Flood! Flood, you bloody fool!'

But if there is a sign of him, it is impossible to see. Flood has snatched up his pollaxe and gone running down the hill with the rest of Pembroke's men and now here is Thomas, standing at the top of this hill, sweating from his exertions, poorly armed and in too little plate, making himself a conspicuous target for any enterprising bowman from the fields beyond the river or at the bottom of the hill.

'We have to go down,' he tells Brunt.

'Not on your life,' Brunt tells him.

They are none of them harnessed for this kind of mêlée. Archers' jacks and wool hose are almost useless where there are hammers and daggers and bills.

'Leave him,' O'Driscoll advises. 'Is he not having the time of his life?'

'I promised Hastings,' Thomas tells them.

'He'd understand.' Caldwell is sure. 'And if he wanted us to go down there and fight it out, he'd've given us more than these.' He raps his knuckles on his sallet.

Thomas is not sure. He doesn't want to go down there: that is for sure. He turns and together they watch the fight at the bottom of the hill. The sun is coming up and the mist is sliding back into the river and their view is becoming even clearer. By the looks of it, it is very close between the two sides, but these things are hard to judge. Pembroke did the right thing, coming off the hill when he did,

Thomas thinks. He's neutered Robin of Redesdale's bowmen, who would have massacred them had they stayed up here, and he's taken advantage of impetus as his men have come charging down the hill to crash into Redesdale's line.

Still, Thomas finds himself collecting all his gear together, and he sees the others have done likewise. If the battle turns against Pembroke, they must be away and fast.

But what of Flood?

'Can you see him?' he asks.

It is just not possible. There is a mob of men, backs turned, the dark lines of their weapons rising and falling, hacking and chopping at the other mob of men, faces towards them but hidden by visors, the dark lines of their weapons cross-hatching with those of Pembroke's men. You cannot see any individual fight, or any particular combat: it is all one grinding crash, and awful when you think about what the men in those ranks are facing, and what they are doing. The line wavers, bends and buckles. Wounded men drop out of the back and wheel away clutching parts of their bodies: faces mostly. Others need to be dragged out of the fray, while others are simply left where they lie, perhaps already dead.

Thomas sees a group of Redesdale's men running along behind the backs of their own men. There are perhaps thirty of them – someone's household – and they are coming to try to flank Pembroke's line below where he and Brunt are standing. The fight is so close that something like this will tip it irreversibly in Redesdale's favour. And there! There he is! Flood! Thomas is sure of it. He is on the right flank. Precisely where these thirty men are now aiming their weapons.

'Oh Christ,' Thomas says. 'Come on!'

He starts down the hill, but then stops and puts his pollaxe aside. He snatches up an arrow that one of Robin of Redesdale's bowmen sent over, nocks it and takes careful aim with the first lift of his bow, then looses it with the second, sending the arrow shaft slicing down the hill, a foot above Flood's head. It cracks into the man facing him, and knocks him reeling.

'Ha!' Brunt says. 'You are his guardian angel.'

He too picks up an arrow and sends it down.

'Jesus, he's an idiot, that boy,' O'Driscoll says, 'and he'll get us all killed, but you've got to love him, have you not?'

Until he gets us all killed, Thomas thinks.

But he is grateful the others have come. He scavenges three more arrow shafts and slides them in his belt behind his back. Down he goes, through the long grass. The smell of men fighting drifts to him: the metallic tang of blood and the onion smell of sweat and then the vinegar they use to clean their plate, and the wet wool and the chipped steel and the low faecal waft. Thank God they do not have—

The first gun erupts with a stilling boom. A sharp stab of smoke in the ranks and a sudden bellying of the line away. In that pulse of nothing as men pause in their thrashing of one another Thomas hears the first roars of pain. Then the noise resumes, like a heavy surf breaking on pebbles. He finds another arrow, nocks and looses it. Flood is only fifty paces away, waving that pollaxe, trying to find someone to hit. Thomas stops and readies himself for the men coming around the side when an arrow buzzes past his nose, coming from the bowmen in the trees to their right.

'Christ's blood!' He'd forgotten about them.

Then a gun's ball fired from the trees catches O'Driscoll and flips him tumbling across the grass. He lies face down, as if he's been rubbed in the dirt, and he thrashes and twitches, and they stop to stare at him a moment, but there's nothing to be done.

Brunt and Caldwell turn and run, back up the hill.

Thomas shouts after them, but they keep going. Another arrow thrums past his face. He sees he is a duck caught on water. It is amazing they have missed him. He sprints down the hill and launches himself forward into the line. He shouts at the men there, to urge them to turn to the right, to face the archers and the men attempting to flank them,

227

but they're caught up in their own fights, gripped with that lust to at least land a blow on an enemy, whom they still think are in front. He has to pull them by their breastplates, by their shoulder straps, he has to shout in their faces, but their eyes slide past him to the front where the noise of battering weapons is coming from.And then he sees Flood go down. He doesn't see what hits him, only that he's knocked back. He sees him throw up a hand as if to call a halt to the day, as if he is yielding in the tilt yard, but that's not how these things work. Someone will kill him, any moment. A fat-bladed bill in the unguarded face. A dagger in the groin. Or he'll simply be clumsily battered to death.

Thomas must move fast now or his mad rush down to save Flood will have been in vain and even suicidal. He comes barging into the line where men are fighting over Flood's supine body, and Flood's still lying there with his hand raised, not expecting to be murdered as any other man might, but expecting to be saved. Expecting to be dragged out. One man steps on him the better to jab at his enemy and Thomas thinks if Flood grabs the man's ankle, the man will kill him.

Thomas forces his way through. He is a fool! A fool! He doesn't even have gloves. He cuts in at an angle and reaches Flood just as he grabs the ankle of the man standing on him, and the man looks down and is about to dig into him with a billhook when he is stabbed by another assailant. Thomas shoves him forward, blocking the bills and swords that swing and probe, and he hauls Flood out from under their feet as if he were reclaiming a doll.

He shoves his way through, battering men out of his way, pulling Flood behind him. Men push back and kick at Flood, but at last Thomas has him out of the line, where there is space. He drags the dead weight of Flood sliding through the long wet grass. Five, ten, fifteen paces.

Then he stops. He rolls Flood on to his back and lifts his visor. Eyes are shut, but the boy is breathing. He checks his plate for anything. There's a dent in the helmet. How bad is it? He can't tell. He starts stripping the plate. Unbuckling the gorget, tossing it aside, cutting the sallet strap under the chin, slicing through the leather and points of the breastplate and all the other bits. He flips away the various plates of steel with a distant sorrow at the waste. Someone is going to do well out of today, but it will not be him. When he has Flood down to his arming jacket he hauls him up and over his shoulder. Thomas leaves his bow with infinite regret, but will not leave the pollaxe. He gets to his feet. Christ. Flood is heavy.

With one last glance at the fighting, he starts up the hill. There'll be someone up there – a surgeon – to look at him. But there's no blood so what's a surgeon going to say? By God, whatever he is, he is heavy. Imagine him in harness! Thomas is granted a sort of mercy from the bowmen and the gunners behind the trees, who have turned their attention elsewhere, perhaps, or are Christian Englishmen. Then he sees Brunt and Caldwell have stopped above him, and are sending arrows whistling down into the trees to keep the bowmen from aiming his way. Sweat stings his eyes. He wishes he were not wearing this bloody helmet. Come on, he tells himself. Come on. Only a few more paces. An arrow hums past.

'Brunt!' he shouts.

Brunt looses a shaft over his head, and Caldwell gives a little cheer and looses his. They are collecting strays among the grass, and are in some danger themselves. And at least they have the decency to look shamefaced at their cowardice, or caution, and as Thomas nears them they abandon their search for second-hand arrows and come scuttling down to help.

'What a fucking idiot he is!'

'Is he alive?'

Thomas lets Flood on to the ground and stands gasping for breath. Caldwell slaps Flood's pale cheeks.

'Come on, you daft bastard, wake up.'

'Leave him a bit,' Brunt says. 'He'll come around.'

They stand over him and look across his body to the fight that rolls on below. It has been going for half an hour perhaps. The sun is up, the mist evaporated, the day very fine now.

'Beautiful country hereabouts,' Brunt opines.

Caldwell seems to agree.

At the foot of the hill Pembroke's men seem to have gained the upper hand. It is marginal still, but Thomas knows once these things turn, they turn very quickly, and Robin of Redesdale's men – who have been on the road for weeks, and are made up of disparate households and fellowships – will be tired and less bonded. The only thing that will keep them together when the moment comes will be desperation and a lust for life.

And now, as they stand watching, he sees Redesdale's men have stepped back. Suddenly there is a broad scattering of them with their backs turned. Some have been wounded and are making their way to the rear of their lines, but little knots of the unwounded are fragmenting from the lines, and those who ought to be joining are hesitant, as if they are taking a view of the situation, and it might be that soon they will try to run for it.

'Where are all those bloody bowmen Devon promised?' Caldwell says. 'When they get here it's going to be a slaughter! Like Towton!' He is still loosing arrows into the trees. He's trying to avenge O'Driscoll.

Flood groans.

'Ah!' Brunt says. 'He lives!'

'Better keep an eye on him,' Caldwell says, 'or he'll be off down there to try his luck again.'

There is something of a feast day atmosphere up on the hill. It is like no battle Thomas has ever experienced. He can remember only two – in both of which he was on the losing side and compelled to run for it. This one looks as if he will be on the winning side and he cannot help be pleased. He wonders if he will benefit somehow. The spoils of war are traditionally divided into thirds. But under whose command is he?

It is something that Brunt and Caldwell are worrying about too, when there is a disturbance at the very top of the hill, where men are shouting and pointing to the east, to a point behind Redesdale's fracturing line.

'Here he comes!' Caldwell shouts. 'Devon at last!'

'Now we'll have some fun,' Brunt says.

'But why's he coming from that way?' Thomas wonders. 'They said he was south of here.'

'He must have come around,' Brunt says.

'He's coming right up behind them!' Caldwell laughs. 'God's Truth! This will be a slaughter!'

But the men on the top are not celebrating. They're throwing their possessions aside, and running for their horses. The tents are abandoned.

'What the fuck?' Caldwell asks, pausing mid-nock.

Then they hear it is not Devon.

It is Warwick.

And so the day turns.

'Those Kent bastards!' Brunt shouts. 'By Christ! Come on, Thomas, we've done as much as we can here.'

Word travels quickly down the hill to the men who are still fighting, pressing Robin of Redesdale's men back over the bridge, men who thought they were winning a battle. The news spreads and with it, space, because those at the back no longer press those at the front of the little army: they've turned and are now running up the hill, spilling what they do not instantly need. Helmets, and polearms first. Men keep only the barest minimum to survive. There is the usual pushing and shoving, slipping and falling. Men are terrified. Again the stronger push aside the weaker, just as they had done to get to the fight below.

And the cheers! Robin of Redesdale's army has also heard the news, and now those at the back, who had been hoping to melt away and were considering their own options, are now revitalised for the fight, and they come pressing behind those on the bridge and the noise reaches Thomas in great waves as they bellow, 'A Warwick! A Warwick!'

Men are streaming past now. The stoppage at the bridge has been cleared, and Robin of Redesdale's men are through into the field again, hacking at anyone they can reach. A knot of men is putting up a fight – Pembroke's, Thomas must suppose – but the flanks have crumbled, the rearguard gone, and the devil is left to take the hindmost.

'Come on,' he says. 'Help me.'

They haul Flood to his feet but it is no good. He is boneless.

'Leave him,' Brunt says.

'Or kill him now,' Caldwell says.

Thomas cuts the last pieces of plate from him, and rips his arming jacket off, and his hose that will fall down without it anyway, so that he is in braies and shirt.

'I'll do first shift,' Thomas says.

Brunt and Caldwell exchange a look before they agree. Brunt takes Thomas's pollaxe. Thomas lifts Flood on to his shoulders and he staggers up the hill, making for its crest and beyond. He has no destination in mind, just anywhere away from Robin of Redesdale's men. He imagines they will come up the hill after them and hamstring anyone still running, or send arrow shafts into them to send them bowling. He is, for a moment, glad to have Flood's weight on his shoulders, offering some protection at least.

They crest the hill – the most dangerous moment, when they are silhouettes for bowmen to hit – and then they are down on to the sunny southern slope. For a moment it is easier downhill. But then Flood's weight only seems to increase.

'Leave him, Thomas,' Brunt shouts from further down the hill. 'They won't kill him.'

But they might, and so Thomas staggers on, digging his heels into the soggy turf, the smooth soles of his boots slipping and sliding on the warming summer grass. At the bottom of the hill they pause. Men follow them down from the hilltop, all running south, leaving a trail of discarded plate, weaponry and blood-clotted clothing, as if after a flood. Some are wounded, clutching arms and faces, stumbling and tripping. One falls and lies there shuddering. Thomas steps over him.

There is a small stream to the left that will take them off the path beaten down by Pembroke's scattering remnants.

'This way,' Thomas says.

They follow it, keeping to the shelter of its trees. It leads them further east, away from the rest of the army. Will they be followed? They can only pray not. Flood is very heavy now.

'What is even wrong with him?' Caldwell asks. He refuses to carry him. Brunt is reluctant. Thomas wonders if they have come far enough so that they can rest. He has to anyway. They can hear no more shouts or those startling crashes of weapons. Only birds in the hawthorns and the gentle trill of the stream below. He sets Flood down against a stout oak's trunk, in the shade, and then pushes his way through the scrubby thorn trees to the stream where the water flows sweet and pure. He drinks some, and then fills his hat and brings it back for Flood. He's still insensible. Thomas feels through his sweated hair, but can find nothing amiss other than the bulge of the bruise. Christ, he wishes Katherine were here instead of Brunt and Caldwell. He pours some water on to Flood's lips; he moves them for some more and Thomas takes this as a good sign.

'Where are we going, Thomas?' Brunt asks.

'I don't know. But if we follow this stream, we'll come to somewhere. We can maybe find a horse?'

'For him?'

'Why not?

'Why not us? We're just as like to be killed.'

'Caldwell, I'll kill you myself, now, if you go on. For the love of God, do you want to come back to Hastings with a dead boy?'

'I'd rather not come back at all,' Caldwell says. 'If Pembroke's beaten, how long will it be before they turn on King Edward and Hastings and the like?'

'And he's slowing us down!' Brunt says. 'Come on! We'll all be caught with him like this. They'll come and chop us down. Let's just fucking leave him.'

Thomas knows they are right. But how will he live with himself if he does this?

'You go then,' he tells them. 'I am sick of your whining.'

He is not sure what he expects them to do, but they look at one another, and nod, and perhaps Brunt is going to say something, some admission of shame, but Thomas shakes his head. He does not want to hear it. So they leave the shelter of the trees and hurry south across the field.

Thomas watches them go. They look like the sort of men who might rob a grave. As he watches, four horsemen in red livery come thundering across the field. Each has a long lance – a pricker – and when Brunt and Caldwell see them they start to run, but they are in the middle of a field and there is nowhere to hide; the first horseman catches Caldwell and sticks him so deeply that the spear is torn from the horseman's hands and Caldwell is flung to the ground. One of the other riders misses Brunt, who trips, but when he is back on his feet and running for the hedge, another rider catches him and knocks him down with a hammer in the back of the head. It has taken as long as it takes an arrow to fly three hundred paces and now both are dead.

Thomas remains still.

One horseman comes back and dismounts to retrieve his spear. The other, the one with the hammer, does not even bother to dismount. He turns his horse back and looks down at Brunt's body from up there in his saddle; then he looks at the hammer's pick, to see if there is any damage, perhaps; and then he shows it to one of the other riders and their laughter reaches Thomas in his hiding place. The second of these two riders imitates the first's swing. And again the laughter. The third joins them, and he shakes the first by the hand in congratulation, and they ride around for a bit, looking down at Brunt as he dies, and then, when he is dead, there is nothing else to do, so they ride off.

Thomas watches them go, and he feels absolutely nothing.

16

The next morning Thomas is woken by a big red pig. He was exhausted the night before, having walked all day with Flood on his shoulders, and for want of any better shelter, he staggered off the track and lay down and covered himself and Flood with leaves, and now this pig has come rootling for beechnuts.

Thomas shoos the animal away and turns to Flood.

His eyes are open.

'Thank the Lord,' Thomas says.

Flood asks him where they are. Thomas doesn't know.

'Can you move?' he asks.

Flood lifts one hand.

'Come on then,' Thomas tells him. 'We'd best be off.'

'Where are we going?'

'To Nottingham, I suppose. Wherever King Edward is.'

Flood nods, and then groans. He asks what happened and where Brunt and Caldwell are.

Thomas tells him about the Earl of Warwick's army arriving to defeat Pembroke's, and about Brunt and Caldwell being killed.

Flood looks glum.

'I will pay for Masses to be heard for their souls,' he says.

'They'll need your prayers,' Thomas tells him.

Flood is very slow getting up.

'Christ, it hurts,' he says.

He can hardly walk for the pain. They manage a few paces, Flood's arm around Thomas's shoulder, but after a moment they hear horses on the track through the trees and they stop still. The pig is still snootling about. Then the horses move off. They look at one another.

'Quietly, then,' Thomas says. With each step Flood gasps with pain, and they have hardly gone thirty paces when they hear the horses again. A raised voice. Someone is complaining. There is nothing for it: Thomas picks Flood up and he sets off through the trees at a slow run.

Flood groans constantly.

'I wish you were insensible still,' Thomas tells him.

'So do I,' Flood agrees.

But what is his plan? He has no idea. To get away. The riders do not follow him. He keeps the stream on his left. It meanders and he crosses fields to cut the path short, and at length, some time before noon, they come to a river. It is not especially broad or fast-flowing, but it is enough of a barrier.

'Can we cross it?' Flood asks.

Thomas is bent with exhaustion. He does not know if he will be able to cross it, let alone carry Flood over. But he must do some-thing. He turns downriver, northeastwards. Flood starts asking him questions. About where he was brought up. Who his people are. If he has ever been to London. Calais. How far he can send an arrow shaft.

'Please, Flood,' Thomas says. 'Just – no more.'

Flood apologises. He tells him about his childhood in somewhere Thomas has never heard of and he tells him about how he and Maude were betrothed when they were six but they hated one another then. He tells Thomas that he would like Maude, and that she would like him. He asks Thomas if he is married and what Katherine is like and Thomas wonders what she would make of Flood, and he finds him-self laughing, and then after a while the laughter fades and he wishes he were not trudging along this bloody riverbank carrying a man on his shoulders, and he wishes that he were back home in Marton, with

Katherine and Rufus, and that Sir John were still alive, and Lurcher were there too.

'Take heart, Thomas,' Flood says. 'Look: a boat.'

Thomas almost drops him. There among the rushes, tied to a withered stump, is a flat-bottomed punt such as rush farmers use.

'Come on, then,' Thomas says, and he picks Flood up again and helps him down into it. It is brittle with age, its planks silvered with lichens or something, and there is a deal of ale-coloured water in the bottom, but it does not sink.

'There's no pole,' Flood complains.

'I've this,' Thomas says, and he untethers the rope, steps into the boat and pushes off using the pollaxe. Flood lies at one end of the boat, Thomas the other.

'How do you come to serve Lord Hastings?' Flood asks.

Thomas tells him it just happened.

Flood tells him that he thinks Lord Hastings might be his father.

Thomas had guessed.

'He's a good man,' he tells Flood.

The current is not fast. They dawdle through the river's wide bends and slow-flowing waters, and then they speed up as they slide through constricted banks. They come to another village, and they slip straight over the ford watched by three boys. There is no sign of any horsemen, and all seems everyday and ordinary.

'Whose boat do you suppose this to be?' Flood asks. 'We should have left them something.'

'Such as what?'

He is silent for a while.

'Where do you think we will end up?' he then asks.

Thomas looks about them. It is well past noon, and he guesses the river is flowing in a long loop but it still seems to be taking them northeastwards, but only very slowly. He shrugs.

'I don't know,' he says. 'Just so long as it is not towards Warwick, or Redesdale.'

He thinks about Brunt and Caldwell, who struggled through their lives only to be murdered in a muddy field. Was that God's plan for them, or were they part of His plan for the men that killed them? Will something come from what those prickers did that day? Will one of them suffer remorse, say, and hold off killing someone else who will go on to found a chantry? Build a bridge? Is that it?

And what about Jack and Nettie and John Stump? Now Warwick has won this battle, what will become of them? He thinks about each individually: about Jack, whom he has failed through no fault of his own, and about Nettie, who is probably childing even as he sits here, and John Stump, who wished to cross the Narrow Sea to fight along-side the Duke of Burgundy, but who will never get that chance now. He sees he has already given up hope of his plan succeeding. He sees that he has given them up, and that they are already, in his mind, dead.

But then he stops himself and sits up. He is looking at this in the wrong way. He is looking at it, he sees, as if they have gone passively to their deaths, when that is not the case. If they are dead it is because they have been murdered. Murdered by Edmund Riven.

Christ! The things for which that man must be made to pay!

For a moment he allows himself to be gripped by a murderous rage, and he imagines himself repeating what he did to the father – with this pollaxe here – to the son. After a while the hopelessness of his situation acts to soothe him. There is nothing, not one thing, he can do while stuck in this punt, on these waters with Flood.

He tries to remain vigilant. Warwick's prickers could be anywhere, but he is tired. His eyes are closing. He wakes Flood, who does not recognise him for a moment, and tries to climb out of the punt.

When he is calm again, Thomas tells him he must keep watch.

'Any horsemen, you wake me,' he tells him.

Flood nods. After a while Thomas finds a comfortable position, feet out of the water at the bottom of the punt, and falls asleep. When he wakes, Flood is asleep too, and they are caught on some shallows under a willow tree where the smell of river mud and fox mix to almost overpowering effect, and the light is shaded green. He parts the fronds and sees they have entered a broad lake. There are the traces of eel farms sticking above the waters, and across it, where dense clouds of insects circle in the thick summer air, are five or six rush farmers, cutting and filling their punts with bundles of fresh green bulrushes until it looks as if they will sink. Thomas watches them for a while. Flood wakes.

'Sorry,' he says. 'I must have fallen asleep.'

He is better this time of waking, though still he groans when he moves to join Thomas watching the rush-cutters.

'Where does it hurt?' Thomas asks.

Flood thinks for a while.

'The only bit that does not hurt is here,' he says, pointing to his left forearm.

'Can you walk?'

'I'm sure,' he says, but he can't.

They watch the cutters at work for a moment in silence.

'Busy around here, isn't it?' Flood says.

Thomas grunts. He is thinking exactly that. He is thinking they ought to stay where they are, hidden by this tree, and carry on only when it is dark. Food and drink will become a problem, but – well, they are on a river, they can drink that, and it is not as if they have not gone hungry before. He closes his eyes again, and is woken just as dusk falls by Flood singing a song about ale. He wants no pies, no stewed mutton, only good ale brought to him and his friends, and he wants it now. He has a nice singing voice.

When it is properly dark, with a newish moon smiling above the willow tops, Thomas pushes them off and out to try and find the sluggish stream that winds through the lake. It is so shallow he can use the pollaxe to push them through the waters, but the current is elusive, and it is hard to see where they must steer. Often their way becomes blocked by the fringes of a massed bank of reeds and they must retrace their non-existent steps. After a long while Thomas gives up; he removes his boots, pourpoint and hose, and drops into the cold waters, up to his waist, and he guides the punt that way, his toes in the mud and the roots.

Flood is touchingly, pointlessly, concerned for him.

At length Thomas finds the river's exit. By now his teeth are chattering and he is chilled to the marrow. He clambers back into the boat and begins rubbing himself dry as the punt is drawn through the banks of rushes and into a narrow channel between two more willows. He dresses himself. It is not easy in the dark and on a punt. When he is dry and a bit warmer, he realises that he is properly starving.

'Like Lent in one day,' Flood agrees.

They drift along all night, until the birdsong starts up and the dawn emerges as a pale luminescence and then as a beautiful flare of magenta and silver, ahead and slightly to the right, so they know they are still going northeast, and Thomas supposes they must soon look for somewhere to pass the daylight hours, but then again, he thinks, surely they have come far enough now? The river remains deserted at this time of day. Its green surface is oily and smooth, but as the sun rises, it begins sparkling. Two swans float past. Their cygnets, still fluffy and grey, follow in line. Thomas thinks of Katherine and Rufus. His hunger is gnawing at him now. Flood looks pale too, and is licking his lips constantly.

They say their prayers.

Then there is a bridge, the first they've come to. Where there is a bridge there will be someone to charge pontage, both to cross and go under it, and where there is someone to charge pontage, there is a village.

'We have to find some food,' Thomas tells Flood.

'Christ, yes,' Flood agrees. 'I'd kill for a simple bowl of pottage, you know? With some good white bread? And ale. Or wine. And perhaps a rabbit, roasted? Or even woodcock? Two of each maybe?'

Thomas plants his axe in the water and uses it as a rudder to steer the punt to the north bank, where there is even a little jetty. He runs the punt up against the jetty and clambers out. He ties it up and helps Flood. The boy is better, but two nights in the rough cannot have helped whatever ails him, and he is still very tentative. Thomas puts an arm under him and they totter up the jetty on to the path between strips of farmed furlong. It is misty, and across more common land where a single long-horned cow is feeding, is a gathering of low stone buildings gathered under the bodkin point of a church spire.

A boy calls out to them not to go too near the cow. She is like to go for them.

'Where are we?' Thomas asks.

'Olney,' the boy says.

'How far are we from Nottingham?'

'Nottingham? Where's that?'

The church bells ring from the east.

'Can we have some food?' Flood asks. 'We've come a distance.'

The cowherd laughs.

'Not much of that around here now.'

'Why not?'

'Why not? The King's army's taken it all, haven't they? Everything that isn't hidden's gone into their gullets. Them fuckers took the rest of my cows. Only saved her because she was being so hard to handle.'

Thomas looks at the cow. He'd've just killed it with an arrow. Still could, he's that hungry. Though he no longer has a bow.

'When did the King come through?' he asks the boy.

The boy scoffs.

'He's still here,' he says. 'Taken over the inn.'

He jerks his head towards the village. Thomas can only think the boy is lying or mad. Flood is speechless, for once.

They leave the boy and make their way towards the church. Neither speaks. Can King Edward really be here?

They are stopped by two men in blue and murrey, with sallets and bills. King Edward's men all right.

'Forgot to get yourself dressed, did you?' one of them asks.

'We've just come from – from over there,' Thomas tells them. 'From the Earl of Pembroke.'

The guards are amused. They think Thomas is simple.

'Oh yes,' the elder of the two says, 'and how is he?'

Thomas is gripped by that same sense of incredulity he felt when he brought news that Robin of Redesdale's army was thrice the size predicted, and much closer than supposed.

'Well,' he says, 'he's probably dead by now.'

The guards remain smiling.

'Dead? What do you mean?'

'Have you not heard?' Flood asks.

And again the incredulous shock is the same, and again the same process is repeated as they are passed up the chain of command, but each time they tell the story, Thomas sees they are leaving something in their wake: the men who've just heard the news exchange informal glances, covert nods. As he and Flood are conducted from one room to the next, from one building to the next, they leave a trail of men springing into a frenzy of packing up. Coffer lids are slammed. Horses are shouted for.

Finally they are taken before Lord Hastings, who's taken an upper room in a stone-built inn in the shadow of the church's spire.

'What in God's name is it now?' he demands to know before he's seen who they are. He looks tired but not unusually fretful until he recognises them. Then it is: 'Dear God!'

He sends for ale and bread while Thomas explains about the battle. He tells him about Devon dividing the army by taking his men away, so that Pembroke faced archers with none of his own, and yet how near it had been until the arrival of the Earl of Warwick's army. Hastings pales and ages before their eyes.

'Is this – true, Thomas?' he asks. 'Not some result of – of I don't know what?'

242

Thomas can only nod. Hastings gets up and stalks across to the window. He looks down into the yard. Now they can hear the shouts and hooves of men clearing out.

'And you told them?' he asks, indicating the men below.

'They wouldn't have let us see you if we hadn't,' Flood says.

Thomas joins Hastings at the window. Beneath them men are hurrying about the place as ants might. Hastings sniffs.

'Christ,' he says. 'Where have you been sleeping?'

A servant arrives with a pie and some ale. Flood breaks the pie apart and passes some to Thomas. It is delicious beyond belief. The ale too.

'What in God's name will we tell the King?' Hastings murmurs. He is still at the window, craning his neck to watch the scene below. Thomas senses he is fixing in his memory the names of those he sees discarding their livery coats and badges, packing up their gear and readying themselves to abandon their king.

'Will they all leave?' he asks.

'Most of them. Not that I blame them. Without Pembroke or Devon we haven't one-fifth of Warwick's numbers.'

'So that's it?'

Hastings nods.

'We've been fools,' he says. 'Misjudged the whole thing. We should have realised as soon – Dear God. Even the aldermen in London knew! They stopped any weapons leaving the city last month. And still we did nothing. No, that's not quite true. We ordered a few jackets and went on a pilgrimage. Meanwhile Warwick was mustering men and marrying his daughter to the Duke of bloody Clarence. He was ten – twenty – steps ahead of us. God damn him.'

'What about you? Will you go?'

'No,' Hastings sighs. 'I am with and of Edward. All that I have, I owe to him. And besides, it's the Queen's family that Warwick's after. Them and poor old Pembroke. He isn't a bad sort, really, Pembroke. I wonder if he surrendered or went down in the mêlée?'

'I did not see him run.'

'No. Well. For his sake, I hope he went down fighting.'

'Warwick cannot mean to do anything to him? He was fighting for the King.'

'Perhaps you don't know my lord of Warwick? He is not one to forgive, or forget, or overlook a slight. And he feels he has been slighted. So . . .'

'And what about King Edward? What will he do?'

'Well,' Hastings says, 'Warwick will probably place him in the Tower along with old King Henry. Ha! Two kings under his lock! How he will love that.'

'Will he make himself king then?'

Hastings bobs his head in thought.

'No,' he decides. 'Not even he would try that, surely? No. He must be thinking of George, his new son-in-law. If he could prove—'

He stops, struck by a realisation, and turns to Thomas.

'And you are sure you had no luck with that – with that other task?'

It takes Thomas a moment to recall the ledger. He is glad. It makes his denial seem all the more convincing. Meanwhile Flood has sat on the hearthstone and closed his eyes. He is still in his muddy braies. He manages to look even more handsome than usual.

'Thank you for bringing him back, Thomas.'

Thomas cannot think of anything to say in reply. It was not nothing.

'Can I go now?' he asks. 'My wife—?' He gestures, as if surely Hastings can understand his need to be with Katherine. But Hastings frowns.

'You'll not leave too, surely?' he asks.

'Everyone else is.'

Hastings nods.

'I suppose so, but – someone has to stay.'

Thomas feels panicked.

'Not me though, surely? King Edward – he has all his gentlemen with him?'

Hastings nods to the window, through which can be seen King Edward's gentlemen deserting him.

There is a noise at the door.

'William? By the Mass, where is everybody? I have been shouting for an hour yet no one comes?'

It is King Edward. He is in a nightshirt, standing at the doorway to the other room. He looks puffy, debauched, tousled and red-faced. His focus sharpens when it fixes on Thomas.

'Everingham?' he says. 'What brings you here? Not more bad news.'

At that moment, words desert Thomas.

'I am sad to say so, your grace,' Hastings says, and he tells him about Pembroke. King Edward sits down next to Flood. Flood does not open his eyes even when King Edward takes his mug of ale and drinks from it himself.

'Pembroke?' King Edward whispers. 'He is – destroyed?'

Thomas cannot believe he is the first to be bringing this news. And then thinks: My God, Pembroke's army must have been utterly routed if there was no one to get away to deliver this message.

'What about Devon? Where is he?'

'We never saw him again,' Thomas tells him.

Edward is aghast. He looks to Hastings.

'Not Devon too?'

Hastings is cautious.

'We've heard nothing,' he says. 'He may have arrived too late to help. Is that possible, Thomas?'

Thomas nods.

'In which case, he will not have engaged, will he?' Hastings goes on. It is what he wants to believe.

'You mean he would have scuttled back to that horrible stew in which he lives?' King Edward demands.

Hastings shrugs.

'Minehead,' he says. 'Yes. It is possible.'

There is a long silence. The noise outside is quietening down. King Edward looks up.

'Has everybody gone?' he asks.

Hastings peers out of the window again.

'It seems so,' he says.

Christ, Thomas thinks, he is witnessing the collapse of the King's world. This is a man who until now has had a roster of men to watch over him while he sleeps, to lay out his linens, to pass him a sponge after a shit. And now he has no one. He has been betrayed by his brother, his erstwhile closest ally, and now his entire army. He is left with – who? Just Hastings, and a few of his men, and Thomas and Flood. Just then the man Thomas recognises as King Edward's youngest brother, the Duke of Gloucester, comes in. He is looking shaken.

'Where is everyone?'

'Fucked off,' King Edward says.

Gloucester straightens awkwardly.

'Oh,' he says.

There is another long silence.

'Richard,' the King begins. 'Now I do not want you to lose your rag, but there has been a something of a reversal.' He tells Gloucester what has happened.

'By all the saints,' Gloucester says. 'Are we to fight?'

He is pink in the face, furious. King Edward tries to soothe him.

'I know you like a challenge, but I think there may be one too many ranged against us for that,' he says.

'Then what?'

'Then we shall have to wait and see,' he says.

They do not have to wait long. Before noon, a party of horsemen in red livery comes swirling into the inn's yard. Thomas joins Hastings at the window. One of the horsemen is in perfect armour, with a hammer, visor down. Even Hastings has to whistle in admiration as the man dismounts. He has spurs a foot long, a flanged mace, and is encased in steel, yet still he manages elegance as he stops in the yard and looks up at them, and then tips his visor open. It is a form of a salute. King Edward is at Thomas's shoulder, likewise looking down, and he grunts when he sees who it is.

'Who's that?' Thomas asks.

'His Grace the Archbishop of York,' King Edward says. 'He has come to take us into his care.'

And he turns to the door, and readies himself for captivity.

PART FOUR

Before and After the Assumption, Summer, 1469

17

Thomas stands with Lord Hastings perhaps ten yards from King
Edward, slightly behind his right shoulder. It is raining and they
are in a place known as Gosford Green, where they've been since
dawn, standing before a straw-scattered scaffold on which sits a
log of green yew. When they first saw it, they all believed it was
for King Edward, and Thomas watched the King's face drain pale,
but Warwick's steward, a plump, elderly little priest with jug ears
and no way to say the letter R, assured them it was not. He sim-
pered and capered and laughed at the thought, and his servant
offered the King some sweetmeat or other, and a cup of something
that the King took and knocked back. Strict order has been main-
tained since the moment the Archbishop of York – who turns out
to be the Earl of Warwick's brother – took King Edward into his
custody in the yard of that inn at Olney. Knees have been bent,
praises lavished. Hastings says King Edward has eaten better food
and drunk finer wine since going into captivity than before it, and
King Edward, now relieved of duty, has joked that imprisonment
has much to recommend it.

But this is grim.

There is an edge to the air and, even though it is late summer,
a blustery rain-filled wind blows from the west. There are perhaps
five hundred of Warwick's men set about, all in his colours, all well
harnessed, standing in ranks to leave three sides of a square around
King Edward and the scaffold. Behind is a great crowd of the commons, craning necks to watch. There are five drummers over there

251

who have been beating a slow thud for the past while now and King Edward is made to stand alone and wait.

Hastings mutters something about getting on with it, and at last there is some movement: the execution party, led by two priests, one swinging a censer, and six men-at-arms, coming from the chapel behind. The drummers pick up their rhythm. Behind the six men-at-arms come two hatless men wearing only well-cut pourpoints, fine hose and what look like other men's shoes.

'Dear God,' Hastings breathes.

King Edward turns. He opens his mouth and closes his eyes, as if he cannot believe what he is seeing. Then he opens his eyes and closes his mouth into a hard, tight little line. His fists turn to hammers. The soldiers nearest him – the most finely dressed in polished plate under their livery coats – move slightly, the merest shifts of balance. They are carrying pollaxes, of course. King Edward is in linen, and unarmed.

The two men are brought past Thomas and then Hastings and then King Edward. One is elderly, big-bellied, a man who has lived well. The other is about Thomas's age, only with his hair in that warlike crop. There is a family resemblance. They might be father and son. Each of them looks at King Edward as he passes. You can see their Adam's apples bob as they swallow, and they nod to him, and after a moment's hesitation he nods back. His entire face is clenched. His jaw muscles flex under the blanched skin.

Behind the two condemned men comes the headsman: a big fellow with long arms that reach his knees and on the end the hands of a wrestler. He too wears only his pourpoint but he has a pair of fine leather riding boots that he must have swapped with one of the two men he is following. Behind him come more men-at-arms, all in Warwick's colours.

'Who are they?' Thomas asks.

'Earl Rivers is the old one,' Hastings tells him. 'John Woodville the younger. The Queen's father and brother, respectively.'

Thomas watches as the two men are led to the foot of the scaffold where a log is laid as a step. The men-at-arms step aside to form a narrow passage through which the two men must walk. There is a moment when both stop. The father turns to the son. They hold one another, chest to chest, then by the arms, and there are tears in both sets of eyes as they step apart. The father goes first: no man could stand to see his son die like that. There is a moment, after he stops looking at his son, and after he has stepped up on to the scaffold, when he is not of this world, though he is still on it.

He keeps his gaze fixed on the block and approaches it aslant, and then he looks up at the headsman and almost seems to ask him permission to approach, raising his eyebrow and nodding at the block. The headsman nods too. Earl Rivers stands above it, looking down at it as might a man about to jump from a height, and takes a deep breath; he looks up, and around at everyone gathered. His expression is free of meaning. He allows the priest to approach and he kneels before him, suddenly very brusque, and he accepts benediction from the cleric, whose muffled chant is barely audible above the shift of men's feet and the gusting wind. Unseen by him the headsman has stepped back and picked up the axe from under the straw where it lay hidden.

When the priest makes the sign of the cross over him, Earl Rivers crosses himself likewise, and then he settles himself on the log, turning his head slightly for comfort, so that he is looking away from King Edward. The priest steps back and away, and then the headsman moves fast; with three quick steps, he dances across the straw and swings the axe. There is a crump and a wash of blood on the straw, and a collective drawing in of breath by the crowd, but the old man's head is still attached to his neck by a taut, pinkish fatty braid of something. The headsman chops through it with a second short blow and the head thumps on the platform below. The body slides back with a brief judder and blood continues to gutter on the straw.

There is a moment of unrehearsed confusion before the six men-at-arms climb up on to the platform, leaving the son alone, and they pick up the body by its clothes and take it to one side. Under the scaffold is a simple wooden coffin. One of them drags it out and they roll Earl Rivers's body off the platform edge and in. They fold his arms within, and one of them collects the head by the red-sodden white hair and puts it in with the body and they close the lid. There are red fingerprints all over the pale wood of the coffin, and blood beads at a seam between two planks.

Seeing what he has seen, the son is now less cooperative and he has to be manhandled up the steps. More straw is laid down but the smell of the boy's father's gore is strong, and John Woodville is rearing back and turning his head away from it. They've tied his hands. Perhaps they always knew whoever was going to go second would react like this? He is digging his heels in, but the platform is slick with blood-wet straw, and his shoes slide before him as two men-at-arms shove him forward. They stand him over the block and they have to force him down and on to it. He resists until the moment he is pressed into his father's blood, and that it seems is what is bothering him most, for when it is done, and his shirt front and pourpoint are smeared with it, he stops struggling and instead becomes almost too cooperative; he lays his head at an angle just as his father did and he sobs, great fat tears sliding from his eyes, and he ignores the priest, who stands and prays over him before stepping back to let the headsman take a very deliberate aim. The executioner's hands are wide on the axe shaft, but close together as he swings the weapon high and hard down through the neck and into the log, letting a great flood of blood splash him all over his new boots, and the head rolls clear with a bounce, and the body jerks three or four times. Blood pumps from the stump against the buried axe head, and it sprays back and sideways and all the men-at-arms and even the priests are marked with it.

'Christ,' Hastings mutters.

When the bodies are cleared away, King Edward's party, which includes the Duke of Gloucester, is escorted in silence back to their horses. This is where Thomas supposes he will be able to say good-bye to Hastings, and begin the journey for Marton, for of those left alive, it is only King Edward whom the Earl of Warwick insists on keeping hostage.

But Hastings remains reluctant to let him go.

'The King wants you by his side,' Hastings tells him.

'But I have a wife, and a son,' Thomas says.

'So do I,' Hastings says. 'So does he – well, a wife, anyway, but look, Thomas, Edward is the King. Everybody gives him what he wants, save obviously the Earl of Warwick, who has other ideas, and that is just how it is arranged. He wants you with him. So – you are with him. He says you bring him good luck.'

Thomas half laughs. He has brought King Edward nothing but bad luck so far.

'It is Fortune's Wheel, isn't it?' Hastings goes on. 'You were there when he was on the up, weren't you? At Newnham, he says, and then at Northampton and then at Mortimer's Cross when you saved the day again. He says if he keeps you with him now, while he is at the bottom of the turn, then the rise will be all the faster.'

'But that doesn't make sense,' Thomas says.

'Do you want to tell him that yourself? He has taken those deaths hard. He was fond of Earl Rivers, and now he'll have to tell the Queen – and her mother, dear God – that the Earl of Warwick has had her father and brother murdered. They won't like that.'

'But I left my wife in – in uncertainties,' Thomas tells Hastings.

'Uncertainties! Come, Thomas, Goodwife Everingham is not the one to be daunted by a little uncertainty, is she?'

'Nevertheless.'

'But think of the hunting! My lord of Gloucester says Middleham has the best in country!'

'I don't hunt like you—What was that you said? Where are we being taken?'

'My lord of Warwick does not trust us to remain under his roof down here,' Hastings tells him, 'so he is taking the King to his northern fastness at Middleham, from which there is no escape, and from which none of King Edward's friends will be able to conspire to break him free.'

Everything Hastings says has a little twinkle of sarcasm, Thomas thinks. It is as if none of this is serious. Yet they have just seen two men have their heads struck off.

'So King Edward will actually *be* in Middleham Castle?' Thomas asks.

'Yes,' Hastings says. 'Do you know it? You have been my lord of Warwick's guest there? Taken supper in the great chamber of which he boasts? Heard Mass in the new chapel? Or sat on one of his many, *many* latrines?'

Hastings is smirking. Then he stops.

'Thomas,' he says, 'are you quite well? You are flushed. An imbalance of humours?'

Middleham. Where Jack and Nettie and John Stump are either still imprisoned, or where they have been murdered. Dear God. What should he do? If he goes . . . But he can't. He must find Katherine and Rufus. But then if he does not go and the others are still alive and then they are later killed – how will he live with himself then? How would he be able to forgive himself? And Katherine, what would she think if he had come home to her rather than gone to find those friends who sacrificed themselves for him?

And Riven will be there, too. Edmund Riven.

Thomas feels himself burning with something. He is feverish with it. His fingers are tingling. He transmits his nerves to the horse, which skitters on the road beside him, hauling on the bridle.

'I will come with you,' Thomas tells him.

'That's the spirit,' Hastings says, but then he looks ashamed, 'only I won't be there.'

Thomas is incredulous. How quickly he has come to rely on Hastings!

'Warwick is not holding you?'

'No,' Hastings says. 'Nor Gloucester. We are as surprised as you. I think my lord of Warwick has been caught out by events. By Robin of Redesdale moving so fast and then destroying Pembroke in the field. He had not prepared for such success, you see? And the truth is: he rather likes me. I can tell. He wants me on his side. Same with Gloucester. Likes him too. Wants to stay his friend. He is not a fool, old Warwick, even if he has acted like one with this.'

And now Hastings leans in and once more becomes confidential, and Thomas is instantly made anxious again.

'And also, look,' Hastings murmurs, 'I have heard news from that agent in France. Who was looking out for the record, do you recall? He says the trail is shortening. He has narrowed down the names of this dealer to five or six, and I need to be there when the moment comes, you see? This has to be wrapped up as if we are a townsman drowning kittens. Not a peep must escape.'

Thomas can say nothing.

'Don't look like that, Thomas, please. It will not be long, and I am sending Flood with you.'

'Flood?'

Thomas is fond of Flood, of course, but he is a responsibility rather than a boon.

'Yes,' Hastings says. 'We need to get him away from home. He will be distressed, but he too has formed an attachment to you. Says you saved his life? So there you are. You'll never do that again, will you?'

Thomas probably won't, he thinks.

'So now,' Hastings goes on, 'King Edward. He is headstrong, of course, but he is no fool. If – if he develops any scheme to evade Warwick's clutches, be in accord with him, yes? He will push the bounds wherever he can, I know, but he is the King, and so have faith in him, and serve him well.'

Thomas watches Hastings kiss King Edward farewell, with some whispered words of encouragement, and then he rides off with his own men with the look of a man whom the devil has released back to life.

They ride all that day. Fifty or so of Warwick's men on the road ahead, and fifty behind, and, caught between them, King Edward's party, led by King Edward himself on a bay gelding, accompanied by a lord and various sirs who are there to deliver him safe to Middleham, and a chinless priest he has been sent by the Archbishop of York. Thomas and Flood ride side by side, and behind them the few servants Warwick has permitted him.

'At least we will not have to dress him, or pass him the wiping cloth,' Thomas tells Flood, who looks at him as if this is something to be regretted.

It takes four long days of steady riding before they reach the Earl of Warwick's castle in the north, and in all that time King Edward hardly speaks. He does not call for company or raise his gaze from his horse's withers. He has asked by what right the Earl of Warwick ordered the deaths of Earl Rivers and John Woodville, but no one has an answer much beyond there is nothing to be done about it now, anyway, and so his humiliation has been complete and he rides with his chin sunk on his chest, just as old King Henry might have done after his first and second captures, though King Edward has not sought solace in prayer and fasting, but rather has been drinking very heavily since Olney, and now his eyes are slow, and under-swagged with puffed mauve bruises.

The country along the way is familiar to Thomas from having been there with Katherine, and she is in his mind almost all the time when he is not trying to imagine what he will find when he gets to Middleham Castle. Hastings has paid for him to send messages to Marton Hall, to tell her he is alive and well, and to tell her where he is, and where he is bound; he has sent her money, too, that Hastings has given him. He is a generous man, Hastings, but seems always surprised that Thomas has no money of his own, or has no access to it.

They stay not at inns, or monasteries, or at the sides of roads as Thomas has done when travelling in the past, but at great stone castles along the way. It is astonishing to travel this way, without the hardships and uncertainties of earlier journeys, but each castle holds some odd memory or meaning for King Edward, some good, some bad – especially at Sandal, where his father was killed – and then at York, and at each place Thomas is expected to sleep with Flood and the chinless priest in the rooms immediately outside that taken by King Edward, who rightly evicts his host to take the best bed in the best room of each castle. Young women are sometimes ushered in and out by a chamberlain, and there is much to be eaten and drunk, but it seems King Edward only drinks, usually alone, and often late into the night.

'At least they are treating him like a king,' Flood says. 'And this weather is treating us kindly as well.'

They ride up back through the Vale of Mowbray, following the same roads Thomas rode with Katherine and Horner. He wonders what's happened to Horner. He wishes him well, whatever it is. If he thinks on the promise he made not to fight against Horner, it is with a rueful shrug, because, after all, here Thomas is, separated from his wife and child, riding north, as a prisoner of the man whom Horner served.

They come to Middleham at dusk on that fourth day. All are tired from being in the saddle for four days, but Thomas is riding stiff-backed, his heart is booming and he is dry-mouthed, and he constantly pats the saddle behind, as if he will find the pollaxe, his pollaxe, and every time he does so he misses it, and feels the swoop of anxious loss when he remembers it is not there. One of the Archbishop of York's retinue prised it from his fingers with the threat of force, and there is no chance he will see it again, not a second time. But now – when he is just about to find and face Edmund Riven – is when he needs it most, and what has he in its place? Nothing but a blunt eating knife.

But as they swing up the slope towards the town and above it the castle, its tower tops showing pinpricks of lantern light in the late-evening gloom, Thomas sees King Edward, too, sitting agitated and ready, with shoulders stiff, jaw set, reins gripped in clenched fists. He, too, is ready for his confrontation with his one-time ally and now over-mighty enemy.

The streets of Warwick's northern town are thronged with people waiting to see the humiliated King come, and a gusting noise rises from them as King Edward's party rides up the hill. Thomas wonders if they will shout and jeer, throw insults, dung, bricks, but the atmosphere is not so much rowdy as uncertain, and while some seem to enjoy the sight of their vanquished enemy, others cry out to King Edward, blessing him in the name of God, and there are faces puzzled to see him apparently so reduced when last they saw him standing under his banner, in his blood-glazed harness perhaps, after the great battle at Towton. Is it a right and proper thing to have God's anointed King of England under one's lock? Is it right and proper to now have *two* of them?

They go on through the town and up to the castle, where the bridge is down over the ditch, and the divers gates in the corner tower are open, and a reception party of perhaps another fifty men in various shades of red livery coats waits for them with lanterns lit. Some of them, at the back, carry billhooks also, like the guards in the Tower in London.

Thomas leans forward in his saddle and fillets the crowd, looking for the man with a weeping eye.

At first he does not see him and he feels himself sink, half in relief, half in disappointment.

But then comes a sudden spike of fear, mixed with dry-mouthed excitement, for there – there he is.

Edmund Riven.

It can only be him. Tall like his father, he stands three paces back from the crowd, always apart, unpopular, exiled, but always watching, observing, with a pad of white cloth pressed against his right cheek, his left thumb hooked over his belt at its buckle, and his body angled, perhaps to express resentment at being obliged to turn out and join this reception party. In the gloom it is not possible to see more.

Thomas feels both burning hot and ice cold. He has seen Edmund Riven before, but only once that he can remember, and that glimpse had been fleeting, after the fall of Bamburgh, at a time he thought Katherine was dying, and so saving his wife was more important than killing a man, any man. By the time he knew Katherine would live, Edmund Riven had long gone, and though it was he who had first attacked Katherine, all those years ago in the snow in the fields below the priory at Haverhurst, and though Riven had killed a great number of Thomas's friends since then, Thomas had never been afforded the chance to avenge them. And it is just the same now. He cannot kill the man here, now, surrounded by his own men, in the Earl of Warwick's castle, and expect to live. So Riven, for the moment, will live too, and Thomas looks at him as a man to fear, as a man to be got around if Jack and Nettie and John Stump are to be brought out of their suffering and back into the world.

When that is done, he tells himself, then he will deal with Edmund Riven.

King Edward dismounts. Greetings are delivered, hats removed, knees bent, formalities observed, and when they are done King Edward asks after his lord of Warwick. The constable, Sir John Bellman, regrets that his lordship did not expect them to make such swift progress and remains in London, but he says he is expected soon. In the four days they have been riding King Edward has recovered some of his truculence, and he has steeled himself for a conversation with the Earl, so now, finding it denied him, he cannot help but

261

curl his lip, and it is obvious from the humming and hawing that follows that Bellman and his men have some sympathy with this view.

When they are done, Bellman leads them through the parted wings of the waiting company, past Edmund Riven, who steps back and seems to sneer, though it is hard to tell in the gloom with the cloth against his cheek, and they pass on over the drawbridge, through the gatehouse into the narrow confines of the courtyard beyond. Here the keep looms large above, its tall windows bright with candle- and firelight, and the outbuildings, solid against the surrounding curtain walls, are so numerous they leave only a narrow gravelled area in which to gather, unlike a normal bailey. There are dogs here, and a couple of boys wrestling with tied bales of hay, but the absence of the usual castle stench is instantly striking, and Thomas recalls Hastings's mention of Warwick's many, many latrines.

To the right are covered steps up through a porter's lodge leading to the great chambers of the keep, and ahead is a building that looks like a chapel. Thomas looks for evidence of a dungeon or an oubliette, or some terrible bloodstained chamber where Riven goes about his work, but there are so many possibilities in this lavishly accoutred castle that, if they are within, Jack and Nettie and John could be almost anywhere. They might even now be in some tower, looking out through a slip of a vent, able perhaps to see him, Thomas, standing there with King Edward. He listens for any cry, but there is so much scraping of feet and hooves and nervous laughter from the men that he is unlike to hear a thing.

Servants are waiting to take their horses and their baggage, such as it is, and then the constable ushers King Edward into the keep. Thomas and Flood follow and as they walk up the steps, there is a racket behind as the bridge is drawn up and the outer gates boom shut, and the iron gate is dropped, and it is clear that they are now closed in, and not just for the night.

Supper is capon, quail, half an ox. There is wine, warm wine, and ale. The bread is white. Afterwards, strange sugary shapes – of

St George cutting off the dragon's head, and of the castle itself – are laid before King Edward, who cannot resist them, and hippocras and then more wine and music. They eat in the great hall in the keep. It is the largest room beyond a cathedral nave that Thomas has stepped into, with a fire in the middle, black and white flagstones, bright tapestries on two walls, tall windows set in both others. Servants scurry to and from the kitchens and the diners sit on boards arranged around the walls. King Edward is on his dais with Sir John Something and a few of the other gentlemen, and two young women who don't quite fit in. Flood is cross to be relegated with Thomas to the shadows.

And Riven is there, too, at another table just down from the dais, the second highest table, with more well-dressed young men and women, who bend away from him while he sits silent, alone, vigilant. He is beyond the circle of human companionship, excluded from it, perhaps happily so, and he is utterly still, save for his gaze that flicks around the great hall, his focus sharpening on what catches his attention before relaxing its grip and moving on. He does not once look at Thomas, and after a while Thomas can stand it no more. For reasons he cannot explain, even to himself, he wants to catch the scent of that wound, to smell if all they say about it is true – that it curdles milk, brings on miscarriages, causes cats to bark.

He asks the man next to him if he knows Riven, and the man betrays anxiety.

'I know of him,' he says, and he reaches for some meat and turns his shoulder.

By the time supper is done, Riven is gone.

Thomas and Flood are to share a chamber not in the keep with King Edward, but in one of the ranges of domestic buildings on the west wall, where the henxmen are usually put, but have been cleared away elsewhere while King Edward's men are here. The room is on the third storey, is large, has a window that can be blocked with a piece of pine wood, a door that cannot be locked, and along the passageway there is one of the latrines Hastings talked of. The flagstones underfoot are gritty, though, and the stone of the walls, even in high summer, is cool enough to numb pain.

Thomas goes to the window and stares out at the keep across the bailey. What he imagines he will see he does not know. Flood meanwhile stretches out on the bed and groans. His feet smell very strongly, but baths of scented water are promised for the morning and, besides, Thomas knows he smells too.

They are woken in the morning by church bells in the town. A moment later a bandy-legged servant passes their door with a yoke from which hang a pair of steaming buckets, and calls them to follow him if they are desirous of a bath. Thomas follows him along the passage to a room in which a fire burns in a wall-set hearth and before it is a long tub that might have been made by an apprentice of the finest cooper in all England.

Thomas asks if there is a dungeon in the castle.

'A dungeon? Are you not happy with your quarters?'

'It is not that,' Thomas says.

'Well, good,' the man says, 'because we have no such things here.'

Thomas is surprised.

'I thought . . . What of Sir Edmund Riven?'

A quick intake of breath.

'Oh yes,' the servant admits. 'We have him with us all right, but if what you're after's being locked up for the night and having your bones stretched or your skin flayed in the morning, then you'd best be joining the queue, for he is like a one-eyed cat, that one, dragging in half the wounded birds in the county and filling that tower of his with cripples and what have you. Makes the auditor mad, having to feed 'em all, too. Says some of 'em come to enjoy it: they start off grateful for a belly full of soup, as you might, then they come to expect it, then they demand it.'

The servant pours the water into the wooden bath. Steam rises. It is scented with meadowsweet and wood smoke and there is some of that soap that is so precious that Isabella gave them some as a wedding gift, and Thomas takes off his long-worn clothes and puts a toe in. The shock of hot water on his foot is extraordinarily wonderful. He has not had a hot bath since he cannot remember, having always washed in barrels, in rivers, in ponds, always cool, sometimes cold. This – this is incredible.

He slumps in, lies down, and the water is up to his chest. The servant goes below for more water. Flood comes and wants to get in with him but there is no room in the tub, so he stands waiting, his body very white, long smooth slabs of muscle, unmarked by any scars, much bigger on the right-hand side. When Thomas is washed and steam drips from the ceiling and the walls, and there is a grey scum on the cooling water, he reluctantly gets out. The bandy-legged servant arrives with more water. He tips the first bathful out and it runs down a drain and vanishes gurgling through a hole. He fills up the bath with new water and Flood climbs in while Thomas dries himself on a linen towel.

'Mother of God,' Flood groans.

He too has not had a warm bath for some time.

'Which tower is Riven's?' Thomas asks the servant.

'Southeast,' he says. 'So his victims may have a fine view of their last dawn.'

'And do you know who is in the tower now?' Thomas asks. 'Some friends of mine were taken up. More than a month ago perhaps. A man with very dark hair, and his wife, who is with child, and a man with an arm like so.' He demonstrates and the man sucks his teeth again.

'I never see 'em come or go,' he says, 'since that is done through the east gate, but there was some talk of a one-armed man – Riven wanting to see if losing one arm'd make him fear losing the other more, like, or less.'

Thomas does not understand exactly what is being said for a moment. Then he does. He stops drying himself.

265

'He would cut it off?'

'No, no. Just burn it a bit. That is what he does. They say the screaming is something shocking. Not that I've heard it meself, if I'm honest. I've put some clean braies and hose for you on the bed. Should fit.'

Thomas is left to walk back to the chamber where there are two piles of folded linens and hose. Nothing is old or worn, everything is clean and – can it be scented with something? The pourpoint has the badge of the ragged staff embroidered on the breast. He puts on his braies, shirt, pourpoint, then ties his hose up, laces the codpiece. Flood comes in.

'This is all right,' he says.

They hear Mass in the chapel set against the east wall. King Edward is not there – he hears it in a private chapel somewhere in the keep – but Riven is. He is dressed simply, as if for work, and again he stands a little apart from everyone with that cloth pressed to his face. Thomas weaves his way through the crowd to stand near enough so that he can finally smell it, and when he does – there – his innards rebel: it is rotten flesh, putrid eggs, dog faeces, all mixed together. It is like finding a month-old corpse bobbing to the surface of a tanner's vat. His cheeks bulge, his gorge rises, and he stumbles away.

Riven turns and Thomas cannot help but look back, straight into that single dark eye. For a moment it is as if it can see through him, straight into his soul, and Thomas wavers, but then its expression seems to change, and it is possible to read hurt in there, mixed with resignation and sorrow, as Riven turns away, back to the priest who is warbling his solemn way through the Eucharist.

And then suddenly there is an enormous man in front of Thomas, stepping between him and Edmund Riven, and something inside Thomas almost gives way, something deep within. He does not know why, but it is caused by the sight of this man's bare feet, even in church, and the fact that his hose are ripped and frayed, and he wears only a shirt and pourpoint, and he has a shaggy black beard and wild hair that springs from all around the stained arming cap tied under his chin. He provokes some reaction in Thomas that Thomas does not understand, some mixture of terror and hatred. The man gurns at him and mumbles something unintelligible and then presses him back with a huge hand that covers Thomas's chest, and Thomas is propelled through the crowd, clutching at them as he staggers and only coming to a stop against Flood, who catches him, straightens him and gives him a searching look.

But Thomas cannot stay in the church a moment longer. He has to get out into the air. He thrusts his way through the throng, out of the church doors, down the stairhead, through the keep and back out into the courtyard in which they gathered the night before.

His head is spinning and his breath comes hard. What is wrong with him? Why did that man, that giant send him off so? He wanders around the keep, past the gatehouse, still shut yet guarded by perhaps ten men, and then he goes left, along the north wall past the auditor's chambers, then left again, under his own chamber and there's a bridge above him, linking the keep to the wall, and then on past the bakery where the smell is disorientating, and then he turns the next corner, and there it is: the southeast tower.

Riven's tower.

18

'It is good you know the way so well,' Liz says.

'You have no need to stay with us,' Katherine tells her. 'We will do well enough on our own.'

'I'm not so sure about that,' Liz scoffs. 'And anyway, I want to see what you'll do next.'

They are on foot, their backs turned on Marton Hall, walking north. Katherine has a staff, a russet travelling cloak, a bag of her few possessions, including the ledger, still wrapped like a corpse, and a little money left over from that which Isabella gave her to buy back the breviary. Rufus also has his cloak, and he carries the practice bow that John Brunt gave him (though he has lost the string) and he taps it on the ground as he goes, wearing away the horn nock – but that is the least of their problems. Liz has her cloak too, and her large clogs crump on the stones. They might almost be an ordinary party on their way to market, say, were it not for John Stump's crossbow, which Liz carries crooked over her shoulder.

Katherine hardly knows what it is that she will do next, but she is pleased Liz will stay with them. This last exile was as unplanned as it was sudden, and so here they are, walking back towards Gainsborough again, aiming to cross the river they came over only a few weeks or so before, and from there, back up north.

'Will Father be there?' Rufus asks.

Katherine is loath to say no, but she must.

'He will come and meet us. Catch us up maybe,' she says. 'In a day or two.'

And Rufus seems reasonably content, and so they press on through the sunshine, though the two women exchange a look with one another, for they have already heard so many conflicting or impossible reports from passing traders, merchants and pilgrims that it is impossible to know how it stands in the south. One man told them there had been a battle after which the King had cut off the Earl of Warwick's head, another that it had been the other way around. Some said Robin of Redesdale had been killed in this battle, others that it was his father, or brother, or son. Some said the Queen herself was dead, or in sanctuary, like the man who had bothered Isabella in the cathedral, while others that the Queen's family had all been executed, while still others that King Edward had been abandoned by his men and had fallen into Earl Warwick's hands and was in a dungeon in the Tower next to the old King.

With each piece of news, and with each insight into what it might mean for ordinary folk, Liz becomes steadily more impatient.

'Let 'em get on with it,' she says, 'without 'em bothering us.'

And the effect of the gentles' struggle is plain to see as they follow the road north. They pass men with stiffening wounds. There are stove-in faces, with hammers, Katherine supposes. Some have mangled hands carried as if their owners believe that with the right prayer the fingers will grow back. There are woman and children, too, returning home without their men, grey faces smudged with snot and tears, facing God alone knows what sort of future. She and Liz and Rufus take up with these sorts of groups, moving slowly, it is true, but securely, unbothered by the men who have been put beyond the King's grace, and who are said to haunt the forests along the road's lonelier stretches.

'Funny how them that were right there know the least, isn't it?' Liz asks.

It is true. No one really knows anything. They know of the fight that took place down south, and they know that an Earl of Pembroke was there, and that his Welshmen were right fierce, and that in the

269

fight many northerners were killed, and they can name many of the dead, none of whom are known to Katherine or Liz. One man with an arrow wound in his thigh tells them this Earl of Pembroke surrendered, only to have his head chopped off the next day, though no one can be sure why, since he was fighting for the cause of King Edward, who is anointed king, and so it cannot have been treason. And no one knows what has since happened to King Edward, but they are certain he was not there. No one tells of having seen anything of Lord Hastings, either, or any of his men with the head of a bull as a badge, save one – a boy who described a knight in armour that shone, whom he saw levelled. But that does not sound like Thomas, Katherine thinks.

'Well,' Liz supposes, 'that is something.'

They trudge on, weary and heartsore, through the endless forest towards York, and she thinks it seems to get longer each time she walks this road, and she wonders if they are lost. She thinks of Thomas, and where he might be. Liz is doing the same.

'How will he know to find us?' she asks.

Katherine does not know. If he returns to Marton – as he said he would – then will Isabella's sons even let him on to the land? Or will they just cut him down? Christ, she thinks, what they will do to him depends on whether Isabella wakes up. And if she wakes up able to see from the eye that Katherine has cut. It all depends on something Katherine has already done! She cannot change it now. She must wait to see. But worse is that she will not see, because she is now many miles from Isabella, and so will not know if she has been successful until she hears it from Thomas, or someone else.

Oh dear God, why did she ever do it? Why did she just take it into her mind to cut Isabella, without telling her, and without mentioning her notion to anyone, so that it looked like a whim, something she decided to do on the spot? She looks at her hands now, one around her cloak, the other on the staff, as if they have somehow betrayed her, as if it is their fault she took it into her head to do such a stupid, stupid thing. She cannot even say she was not warned. Liz told her no good would come of it, and now she has left Isabella lying insensible, with one blind eye, and one cut eye, to be cared for by those two boys who are so keen to see her prised out of her home they will drop her into some sort of oubliette while they destroy what remains of Sir John's estate.

Rufus has become almost mute again, asking only after Thomas, as if she has betrayed him and he no longer trusts her. He has barely said a word since Isabella's sons returned to find his mother stooped over their bloody-faced, unconscious mother with a knife and needle in her hands.

She has tried to explain what she was doing, just as she tried to explain to William and Robert, but like them the boy does not seem to have understood. Isabella's sons wanted Katherine dead, and when she thinks about it now, she still trembles with the fear of it. Had not Liz been there, and had she not seemed to know almost precisely what was going to happen before it did, and have to hand that crossbow, spanned and fitted with a bolt, then the moment might have passed very differently.

When Isabella's sons stood there, staring, she had been taken back to when she had cut open Eelby's wife, and Eelby had come in and seen the blood everywhere, and she had felt not guilt, as you might expect, or not then at least, but caught out. Found out. Disturbed. She had felt angry that she had not managed to finish what she had started. She had felt that if they had just stayed away until nightfall, then – well, there might have been a chance that no one but she, Liz and Rufus would have ever known what had happened.

Isabella might have been in some discomfort for a few days – Katherine had been prepared for that – but she would surely have overlooked it and put her restored sight down to a miracle sent by God. Katherine had even been prepared to find some amusement in this – she might have been able to smile at Isabella's pious delight – and for this to become a secret joke between her and Liz. She had even half imagined a moment when they would see her at prayer, thanking the Lord for the miracle of her restored sight, and that they would exchange just one knowing look and then never mention it again.

But that was then, and now, after seemingly endless nights spent wrapped in their cloaks by the roadside, she has come to see these thoughts as being shameful, and as evidence of an extreme form of pride, and she knows now that this uncertain tramping of the roads of England is punishment for that. The fact that Rufus is suffering too – that he has been made homeless and is now stumping alongside her – well, that is sent only to make her punishment greater.

And still she does not know how she will ever find Thomas again.

'He will be with William Hastings,' she tells Liz. 'Once we have released Jack and Nettie, then we may go and find Hastings, who will be easier to find than Thomas, that is certain, and if we find him, we'll find Thomas.'

'What if this Hastings fellow is one of those that had their heads removed?' Liz asks.

'I don't know,' Katherine admits.

When they are in sight of York Liz asks about Isabella and her eyesight.

'It was as the book said,' Katherine tells her. 'I cut the covering, and there was the disc, and I pushed that down just as suggested.'

'But you can't be sure it worked?'

'Not until she wakes.'

'She'll be awake now,' Liz says.

'Yes,' Katherine supposes, and she cannot help look behind again in case Isabella's sons have sent Borthwick or the falconer after her to call her back to cut the other eye, if the first has been successful, or to ride her down if it has not. But there is nothing odd to be seen, nothing more than the slow grind of men and carts returning north. This unknowing is just as unsettling as not knowing where Thomas might be, or what she will do when she reaches this Middleham Castle where Liz says Jack and Nettie are held.

They pass the spot they met that day only weeks before, just south of the Micklegate Bar in York, and Katherine sees there are some new heads on the spikes above, though she does not want to ask the Watch to whom they belonged for fear of attracting attention, and that night they stay in an unwelcoming inn without the city walls, where they are given beds in the eaves, and yet still the whole building shakes when the city's church bells ring at daybreak.

After they have eaten a meagre breakfast, they step out and walk through the city and as they approach the minster, Katherine half expects Liz to leave her, for she knows the road to Liz's home is northwards, through Monkgate, whereas hers, to Middleham, takes her through the other one, Bootham Bar, northwestwards and across the Vale of Mowbray.

But Liz is still intent.

'It is as I told you,' she says. 'I'm waiting to see what you do next.'

Katherine thanks her, and together they follow the road along the south bank of the river, heading west, which they are told will take them to Harrogate, only if they have gone that far, then they are lost, for they need to take the north road that will lead them up to Richmond and Darlington.

'I'm not going there, that much I will tell you,' Liz says.

It takes two days to walk to the Earl of Warwick's castle at Middleham, to the west of the north road, nestled into a fold in those hills. The houses along the way are of solid grey stone, square built and grimly defensive.

'It's the Scots, isn't it?' Liz tells her. 'They come down here and try to steal what they can. They take our pigs for their wives.'

They walk all day, and they take it in turns to carry Rufus when he can go no further himself. The pain of his weight burns their shoulders and backs but they do not stop. A flax merchant offers the boy a lift on his cart, and they walk alongside him for a few miles, heading towards a town where the man means to stop and sell his goods.

He knows Liz's father's inn, for his trade route takes him up to Scarborough to the fair there, and Liz asks after her father.

'He has two boys working for him now,' the man says.

Liz tells him that her sisters – the other two aproned girls – have been sent away, 'for their own safety'.

'Your father was not pleased,' the merchant says. 'But at least the manor house is to be occupied once more.'

Katherine feels a sore twinge in her spirits. She has loved the thought of that manor house.

'Who has occupied it?' she asks.

'Some connection of the Earl of Warwick,' the merchant tells her. 'Well. That is what Master Campbell told me, though how he is expected to know, I can't say.'

'You hear all sorts, in an inn,' Liz says.

When the merchant leaves them he promises to pass on Liz's greetings, and reassure her father that she does well.

'A pity,' Katherine says. 'About the manor.'

Liz grunts non-committally.

'There were always folk after living there,' she says.

Katherine supposes Hastings might have sent someone else, or perhaps the Earl of Warwick has taken it from him? She will only know when they find Thomas.

As they walk, they talk, and at length Liz changes the subject to one that seems to have been on her mind since first she heard of it.

'So this Prioress . . .' she begins.

A month ago such a phrase might have made Katherine feel sick with nerves, but the death of the priory has changed her, just a little, and now she feels only a constriction in her throat and a desire to change the subject.

'I can't think about her,' she tells Liz. 'All I can think of is Thomas, and whether he came through the battle of which these men speak, or about Nettie giving birth to a child in the dark on stinking straw, with only Jack to stand by.'

Liz acknowledges these are serious concerns, but she is relentless.

'Do you know anything of her?' she goes on. 'I mean, she must have gone somewhere. What sort of accent did she have? Was she local to Lincoln, or of the Northern Parts, say? Did she ever talk about home?'

'She spoke only of a place named Watton,' Katherine admits grudgingly.

'Watton? I know of Watton. That is east of here. Between here and the sea. Not much of a place.'

Katherine cannot say if that is where the Prioress came from, but she remembers why the name stuck in her mind: the story of a sister of the priory – an oblate, like herself – who fell pregnant and who was tortured half to death by the other sisters before she was made to castrate the lay brother who had put her in that state. That she had lost her child was regarded as a miracle.

'I've no special desire to see it,' she tells Liz.

'Not even if you were to find out who your people are?'

'Why would she know?'

Liz shrugs.

'She may not, but she's the only person like to know now, isn't she? You have to start somewhere.'

'But I may not want to start at all.'

'Not even for the boy's sake?' Liz asks, nodding at Rufus, who sits in silence on the cart, his anxious gaze never leaving Katherine. 'Not even if there's money in it?'

'No,' Katherine says, 'and anyway, there is no saying she came from Watton.'

'Well, why did she talk about it then?

She tells Liz the story of the nun of Watton.

'Bloody hell fires,' Liz says. 'But have you ever heard that story elsewhere?'

Katherine hasn't.

'So,' Liz says. 'She must be from them parts.'

*

275

On the second day out of York, it rains softly as they trace the western hills, and they walk all day in it, until it stops towards late afternoon and the sun comes out to steam the rainfall away. They follow a winding road with the setting sun in their faces, passing rich parkland and an abbey, and then at last they see the castle from some miles away, sitting above its tenant lands that in winter must teem with sheep, but are now just golden straw stubble. There are one or two women finishing their day's work, making their way back towards the town that hugs the skirts of the castle, but the paucity of men is expected: they must all be south, Katherine supposes, with the Earl of Warwick, or Robin of Redesdale, up to no good. They walk on, and as they approach the castle none take their gaze from it, even Rufus; it is as if it is somehow drawing them on.

It is a great square of the grey stone, planted there, and the rise and fall of its turrets and its curtain walls is oddly pleasing; but as they come closer, Katherine cannot stop herself thinking that Edmund Riven must be within, perhaps in that tower there, or that one, and she is coming to him, bringing him what he most wants, and she is unarmed, unprotected and without Thomas, and she cannot suppress a shiver. It is as if she is entering Riven's world, a world of night, and that is when she has the sudden and terrifying idea that he knows she is coming. He knows she is bringing him the ledger. The thought leaves her breathless.

Looking at the castle as they close on it, seeing its towers, its walls, its guard-kept crenellations, she starts to hope Jack and Nettie and John Stump are being kept elsewhere. She has been in this position before of course, when they were trying to bring the ledger to the attention of the old King Henry, lodged in a castle like this, though that time they wanted credit and acknowledgement for bringing it to him, whereas this time she wants to leave it – anonymously – for Riven to find.

Rufus is exhausted now, half-hanging from her hand, done in, and he's still hardly said a word since they left Marton except to ask for

Thomas. He stands with his face blank, somehow closed off, but his eyes are darting around the countryside, seeking what? Threats, she supposes.

And the first of these emerges very soon after they enter the town, from an inn, just beyond the first house they come to. Two men in red, with that white tree stump and bear stitched on to their livery cloths, emerge unsteady with drink, and while one stops to urinate at the side of the road, the other grins at them and asks what have we here.

Thank God Liz is there to call him a sweating barrel of fat and the son of a prostitute. He is momentarily silenced, and she and Katherine know not to stay in that inn, so they walk on past the two men as swiftly as Rufus will let them to another – the White Swan – further on, beyond the butter cross, with Warwick's badge made in stone above the door. Even here, though, the atmosphere in the candlelit hall is raucous, celebratory, with every man, woman and even child glazed with drink, and the innkeeper, a red-faced lump with a gingerish beard in sweaty pourpoint, is slack-lipped with it too.

'You are all drunkards,' Liz tells him when he has found them a place to sit and brought them each a bowl of pottage and a mug of ale. The innkeeper takes no offence, but beams at her.

'As we have good reason, surely?'

'And what is that?'

'Our earl!' he says. 'He has bearded another king!'

'He – has *bearded* another king?'

'Yes! He has him under lock and key, just like the old one!'

There is a roar among the throng gathered around the fire – someone has done something funny such as spilled a drink on a dog or something – and Katherine is finding it hard to concentrate.

'Say that again,' she tells the man.

He looks at her oddly, slightly put off by her accent perhaps, which is not local. He clams up a little, but Katherine presses him and he confirms the tidings of the battle in the south during which Robin of Redesdale's men saw off the Earl of Pembroke's men, and the Earl of Pembroke, who was among King Edward's most covetous and greedy advisers, and a traitor to the people of England and most especially an ill-willer to the Earl of Warwick, had his head chopped off in Coventry, and the other one – the Earl of Devon – was later caught and hanged somewhere in the West Country, and so now the Earl of Warwick, long may he live, and may God bless him, is restored to his place at King Edward's side, and as a consequence of this, the commonweal is likewise restored to health, wealth and happiness.

'And isn't that good?'

Liz nods, though she is oddly restrained, and suffers the man to put his arm around her shoulders and press himself to her.

'Though Warwick's not really restored to King Edward's side, is he?' Katherine says. 'If he has him in a dungeon?'

'Oh, he is not in any dungeon,' the man tells her. 'No! No! He is right here, in the finest chamber in the castle.'

He indicates across the yard to the castle they have come to find. Katherine assumes he is mad, or joking, or a liar.

'But it's true!' he says. 'King Edward's here! We have seen him come through the town on his way to the castle, stripped of them what live their lives at the expense of others, and now that he is in our care, and not that of the Queen and her family, we may be certain he will mend his manners, and return to the pattern of the old days.'

There is another roar from the crowd by the fire, and the innkeeper excuses himself and hurries away to repress their raucousness – or to join them – and Katherine and Liz are left face to face, with Rufus half-asleep, his head on Katherine's lap.

This is a shock. If the Earl of Warwick has King Edward at his command, then will he still be seeking the ledger? Katherine stretches her hand down and feels it in its bag.

'Still there,' Liz notes dryly.

Katherine cannot make any sense of this. Has it, at this stroke, lost its value to the Earl? Will he feel he no longer needs it, and have given up looking for it? And if he has given up looking for it, is there any further point in him keeping Jack and Nettie and John Stump? Surely he will release them? She is pleased at the thought.

'What?' Liz asks.

'It may be that we will not have to give Riven this,' she says, and again she reaches down to touch the ledger.

Liz cocks an eyebrow.

'Come all this way', she says after a moment, 'for nowt?'

'Not for nothing,' Katherine says. 'For Jack and Nettie and John.'

Liz is puzzled. Katherine tells her what Edward's captivity means.

'They could be released any moment,' Katherine says.

Liz looks to be thinking fast; her dark eyes dart in the firelight.

'They might already have been,' she supposes.

Katherine has not thought of that.

'How will we ever learn?' she wonders aloud.

'We could ask,' Liz says.

'Who, without implicating ourselves as interested?'

'Might have to go back to that other inn, the one with the fatty and his mate, pissing in the road. Ask them about it.'

Katherine sees what she is suggesting, and sits back.

'They would want something in return,' she says.

'Pshaw,' Liz says. 'We can duck away before then. They are men. Simple as muck, them sort.'

But by Christ Katherine does not want to do this, and Liz understands.

'I'll do it,' she says. 'You stay here. Look after Rufus.'

There is something about Liz now, in this light, in this place, that is unusually brilliant. There is a steel to her, a flint-like hardness. Katherine tells her she need not, and that she must not go alone, but Liz sees through that.

'Who else is going to come with me?' She drains her drink and stands up, the quicker to get it over and done with. Then she bends over and strokes Rufus's hair. 'He's a good boy,' she says. There are almost tears in her eyes.

'Oh, Liz,' Katherine says. 'You do not have to do it.'

But Liz does.

'Yes,' she says. 'Yes I do.' She loosens at the laces on her shirt, gives Katherine one last grimace, and she is gone.

Katherine sits in the gloom with Rufus still sleeping on her lap. She does her best to be inconspicuous and not to think about what Liz is enduring for her sake. She strokes Rufus's hair. He is a good boy, she thinks, yes, Liz is right. To have put up with so much. To have walked so far on such short legs. Thomas will be proud of him.

She watches the men and women in the inn, celebrating their lord's victory, and she tries to imagine what it must be like to find that your town is suddenly at the centre of the world. To know that the whole country is being governed from a mere hundred paces away. They must be proud of their earl, she supposes. Proud to know he has raised himself above all else, and that every time a messenger clatters through the streets, his missives for their lord come from the highest in all the land, the highest in Christendom, even.

Then she tries to imagine what it would be like were Jack and Nettie and John to come through the door right now, freed from Riven's clutches. If they did that, she thinks she might throw the ledger on the fire, this instant, and be done with it. Instead her hand slides to it once more, and she thinks to herself that this is just as it was when she and Thomas first took the damned thing to Bamburgh! First they must give it to King Henry, and then they must not.

And so she starts to wonder what she and Liz will do if Jack and Nettie and John are *not* freed? What will they do if Riven is still after the ledger? Because, after all, why would the Earl of Warwick give up looking for it, just because he has King Edward under lock and key? Would it not be better – from Warwick's point of view – to have both King Edward *and* the ledger? That way Warwick would have the King's body and the King's mind in his hands.

In which case, the Earl of Warwick will be keener than ever to find the ledger, so that no one else can gain control of his prisoner, or – worse! – prove his prisoner is not fit to be king, and therefore, in fact, worth nothing. So not only will Riven be keeping Jack and Nettie and John Stump wherever he has them, he will have been bending every sinew in his body to get hold of the ledger, and he will go on doing so until he has his hands on it. My God, she thinks, he will be astonished to learn that she and Liz have brought it to him.

He could not, in all truth, have planned it better if he had tried.

Just then someone comes into the hall – a young woman – and there is a cheer of welcome and Katherine thinks of Liz, and murmurs a prayer for her safety as she reminds herself what an astonishing girl she is to have done all she has for her and Thomas and little Rufus: how she brought them the cart, took her south, and stuck with her as she has come back north. And now this: going off on her own to mingle with exactly the same sort of men who raped her at the side of the road outside Senning, and to risk all that again! What must she be made of?

But as she thinks this, she feels a sort of dizziness. New thoughts slot into unfamiliar places, old ideas reorder themselves, fresh doubts emerge and she finds herself saying it again: Riven could not have planned it better if he had tried.

And then she thinks: What if he did plan it this way? And what actually *did* happen to Liz on the side of that road beyond Senning?

19

Thomas stands there in the cool of the morning, watching the comings and goings, and trying to think his way around the impossibility of breaking three people out of a tower, in a castle in which you are held, in a country you do not know and wherein you might find no succour. He has no luck. There is no way, of course, which is why they are in the tower, and he is in the castle, and the castle is where it is.

At length three men in red arrive and they hammer on the door and some time passes before it is unbolted from within. The men troop in. A moment later, some others troop out. It is a changing of the guard, Thomas supposes, for this second lot look done in. They stumble off to their beds, and Thomas is left wondering if it would not be better to discover as soon as possible whether or not Jack and Nettie and John are in the tower, and to try to do so before his face becomes well known around the castle? Now that Riven has seen him, he will remember him. And so it must be now, he thinks, suddenly gripped by the idea, while he – and that giant – are at Mass.

He steels himself, straightens his pourpoint and strides to the door to the southeast tower, climbs the steps and hammers on its planks. He waits, trying to look bored, and then after a moment he hears scuffling on the steps beyond and the bar is lifted. A face appears and looks blank. Thomas says nothing. He angles his body to come in and after a moment the man opens the door wider. Thomas steps in. Silence is the thing, he thinks. Silence and presumption.

'What is it?' the man asks. He too is only in a pourpoint and hose. His sleeves are rolled up and there is a smear of something – blood? Shit? – on his pale inner arm.

'Edmund Riven said to meet him here,' Thomas tells the man, moving past him and starting up the circular steps. This is much easier than he'd thought.

This is the old bit of the castle and, going up, it is low overhead and uneven underfoot. But as he walks he is overcome with something else: the smell. It is alarming at first, a hint of what is to come, and he almost trips.

'By God!'

Thomas grips his nose, tries not to breathe. The smell is like a species of slime coating his mouth, his tongue, his throat, his lungs.

'Bad, isn't it?' the man behind says. 'We keep the poor fucker out on the walkway.'

But this is not the smell of Edmund Riven and his milk-curdling eye. This is an older smell, and fouler still. It is the sweet, sickly stench of the black rot and just the faintest trace of it takes Thomas back to another castle, a guerite, in Alnwick Castle, where they once found John Stump on his death bed, his right arm consumed by this same stinking black rot after he'd been wounded in a fight with some of Lord Montagu's men.

'Won't be long now,' the man says. 'Be a blessing for him, poor old sod.'

The steps circle past one closed door and on up into a third storey, and the smell gets thicker until it is almost impossible to breathe. He can hear men calling to one another in muffled voices.

'What happened?' Thomas asks the man following.

'Sir Edmund burned him. His other arm. A glowing coal. Just to see. Fucker never said a word, but he shat hisself. So either he doesn't know the whereabouts of whatever it is that Sir Edmund seeks, or – he's got the bollocks of a donkey.'

Thomas feels each word like a blow. John Stump, burned. And for why? Because of them. He turns to the man and holds his gaze. He does not know what he expected a torturer to look like, but this one does not look out of the ordinary, and yet here he is talking of this as if it were nothing more than a discussion about pig-gelding.

When they reach the third storey there is no door to close, only the whitewashed and vaulted chamber itself, where there are chains set in the wall and a large table – like a butchers' block – in the middle of the straw-strewn floor.

Thomas says nothing when he sees them. He can't speak.

Jack is still alive, though, Christ, he looks terrible. He is slumped against the wall, his wrists chained together above his shoulder. He does not look up when Thomas comes in. He is half-starved though, and his filthy clothes hang off him. Nettie is next to him, likewise chained, though she is allowed a stool, and Thomas does not know whether he is relieved or not to see that she is still with child. There are two men, sitting on stools, not doing very much. One is using a knife to clean something that looks like the goat's foot mechanism for a crossbow. They look up at Thomas.

'Who're you?'

Thomas doesn't know what to say and can hardly speak anyway.

The door to the south wall hangs open. Through it he can see John Stump lying on the walkway, thrown out as if for a dung-collector and left to die.

'I'm the surgeon,' Thomas says. It is all he can think of.

'You don't look like one,' the first guard says.

'No,' Thomas agrees. He pushes the door open and goes out on the south wall walkway. He looks down at John. He has seen him like this before, of course, five years ago. Despite the wind that comes down off the hills behind, the smell is enough to make anyone gag. John is huddled in a corner, his remaining arm like a branch, held away from him as if he too feels disgust. It is wrapped with stained linen, an old pair of braies perhaps. He is sweating heavily, but his

284

teeth are chattering although it is another warmish day. Thomas folds his arm over his mouth and he squats next to John.

'John,' he says. 'John.'

John's eyes are flickering under their lids. It is impossible to know if he can hear, or if he knows what is being said. Thomas touches his good shoulder and says his name again. This time the eyelids flutter and the dust and detritus that has built up there from his crying and sweating over the last days crumbles and John blinks ten, twenty, thirty times. His teeth rattle.

'Thomas?' he says, his breath foul and his tongue thick.

'It is me,' Thomas tells him.

'Katherine? Where is she? Where is Kit?'

Thomas does not know what to say.

'Coming,' he says.

'Will she – she be able to—?'

'She will,' Thomas lies.

John gestures with his stump. Thomas knows that if John had a hand he would clutch Thomas.

'Praise *Jesu*,' John says.

'Amen,' Thomas says.

John slips back into his delirium. Thomas stands and watches him a moment. He thinks back to the time in the guerite in Alnwick. Katherine had said they needed to cut him straight away if they were to save his life. She had not even waited for food before she had done it. He looks down at his own hands – at his lumpen fingers, his calloused palms. There is no way he will be able to cut John, even if he could recall how she had done it. He remembered a knife, a saw, a candle. What else? Rose oil, linen thread, urine. Plenty of that, he supposes, what with Warwick's new-built latrines.

But no. He cannot do it. He needs Katherine. Christ. Where is she? Could he send a message? Could she get here in time? He peers at the rotting limb. The rosy glow is creeping up towards the elbow. How long has John to live? he wonders. Katherine told him that

285

Payne had told her the black rot gets into the blood and it goes to the liver, and when a man dies of this, if you cut him open after he has gone, then his liver seethes and bubbles.

The sun is shining now, throwing deep shadows on the walkway. There is a guard down the other end, stripped down to his pourpoint, leaning against the stonework, his helmet and bill on the ground next to him. Thomas wonders how long it is until the first leaves will fall. A month perhaps? Will John live long enough to see them drop? No. There is no chance, unless Thomas can do something.

He turns and goes back into the tower.

Jack is awake. His fierce blue eyes are slow-moving in his battered and bruised face, as they might be were he ill with those winter agues, but when he looks up and sees Thomas, they crease with incredulity and he opens his mouth to say something, but the guard is in there first.

'Tell us again who you are?' he asks.

Thomas has almost forgotten what he said. Nettie is weeping to see him.

'You'd let a woman child in chains?' he asks. 'With no care of a midwife?'

The two men look at one another and there is a momentary pause to suggest that they, too, have reservations. Then one of them – the man who let him in – shrugs.

'It is Sir Edmund's doing,' he says. 'He is determined. He thinks he is close to what he seeks and this man' – he aims a kick at Jack – 'and this woman, he thinks they know its whereabouts.'

'What has he done to them so far?'

Again, that pause of shame.

'Nothing, as yet,' the second man says. 'He is waiting.'

'For what?'

'For – for the child to come.'

'And then what?'

Neither will answer.

'You cannot mean to burn – to burn an *infant*?'

The men – they might even be fathers themselves – look helpless. It is not a goat's foot bracer the man is cleaning, but something else that Thomas does not recognise, though it has a blade.

'You don't know him,' one says. 'You don't know that giant he has. He laughs at this sort of thing. He wanted us to – to rape her. He said if we did not, then the giant would.'

Thomas looks at Nettie. She is looking away, her eyes screwed shut. Tears welling from them. Jack is likewise warped with shame and pain.

'Did you?' Thomas asks.

He thinks he might kill them if they say yes. The elder of the two guards shakes his head.

'The constable's wife, she heard her screams from the chapel, and so the constable came running on her command and forbade we touch her. Sir Edmund has sent message to the Earl of Warwick to make sure it is known he is able to overrule Bellman on this and such matters. We are awaiting the reply.'

Both men look sick. If they could have run from their duties, they would. Thomas goes over to Nettie and squats by her, just as he did with John. She looks at him fearfully.

'How long do you think you have, Nettie?' he whispers.

She shrugs.

Katherine would know at a glance, he thinks.

He stands. He hardly has a plan, but he thinks he has already been here too long.

'I will be back,' he tells the guards. 'Feed them, and water them, and find them fresh linens. And stop cleaning that thing, whatever it is, and look to your duties. Christ! They are still Englishmen, and still King Edward's subjects, whatever it is that Edmund Riven wishes to extract from them.'

Both Nettie and Jack twist in their chains as if they could somehow come with him. He nods at the shamefaced guards and hurries down the steps. When he comes through the door and into the clean air again, he breathes deeply until he looks to the right, and through the passage that runs under the chapel he sees the giant come looming. He sets off in the other direction, and comes around the keep; he is at the foot of the steps up to his own chamber when Flood appears. He is holding two thin bows and two bags of arrows, and looks pleased about something.

'King Edward wants to go hunting,' he says. He shows Thomas the arrowheads that are like crescent moons. 'We are to meet him in the stables to find horses.'

Hunting! Christ, that is not what he needs to be doing now. But he turns and looks over his shoulder and there, looming around the corner, is that giant.

'Come on then,' he says, and he is quick to take Flood by the shoulder and guide him away. 'I have something I must ask of the King.'

The stables are through the east gate, across a bridge and into a secondary bailey, wherein are conducted the malodorous activities that are so vital for the smooth running of the castle: the smithy, the tannery, the butcher's, where even now an ox is strung up by its hooves, its belly cut from top to tail so that its entrails flop glistening pink and grey into a vat below. Beyond the greyhounds are snapping and the horses stamping, and the marshal is shouting at the slaughterman and everyone else is laughing, and the air is filled with the smell of blood and fat slow-moving flies.

But King Edward is already outside the gates, holding a fine-looking courser, and there are stable boys with two more horses for Flood and Thomas, and the chinless priest is there also, and another couple of men too, but they are already mounted and watching closely, and neither carries a bow. Thomas wonders what promises King Edward had to make to the constable to be allowed out like this? What is to stop him riding out, all the way to York perhaps?

King Edward seems entirely changed when they are close enough to see his expression. He seems carefree, relieved of a burden. He greets them happily, without constraint or formality, as if they were Hastings himself, rather than his representatives.

'Sir John,' he greets Flood, and then: 'Master Everingham.'

Thomas copies Flood as he removes his hat and clutches it to his chest, just so.

King Edward laughs.

'Look what the huntsman has shown us!'

In his hand he has a cone of leaves wherein lie a pile of small black turds. Flood looks excited. Thomas is left unmoved.

'Come on! Mount! Let's ride. The huntsman says we should be in position.'

What follows is both confusing and simple. One of Warwick's men – though he is not in the red livery but russets and browns and green – leads them southwards from the castle, through parks and walled gardens, an orchard, then a rabbit warren, until they pass an old motte and he turns westwards, up towards a flat-topped hill. King Edward is delighted with the man's lack of respect, and he keeps turning to Thomas and to Flood and rolling his eyes; he behaves for all the world as if is he is some novice, teasing a short-tempered prior. After some riding they are brought to a shallow depression, and the huntsman tells them to dismount but stay with their horses. He sizes them up and guides them to certain spots overlooking the bracken-filled expanse. Thomas is on the extreme right, King Edward in the middle, the chinless priest next, then Flood on the extreme left. The bow Thomas has been given is a slender thing, the sort a youth might use, made, he thinks, of holly, and he knows he could bend it in a circle with no trouble whatsoever. He watches the others nock their bows and he does likewise. They stay very close to their horses, using them, Thomas supposes, to shield their smell or their shape.

It is turning into a beautiful day.

Thomas waits, but Jack and Nettie and John are much in his mind, and he cannot stop himself approaching King Edward, though Flood has told him he must not speak to him until after the unmaking, which is apparently one of the many unspoken rules of the hunt he should already know. Thomas takes a step towards the King and opens his mouth to say something, but Flood shoots him a look, and in this instance Thomas can only trust him. Nevertheless, there follows a good interval in which nothing happens, except that he hears dogs barking and the sound of a huntsman's horn in the distance.

'Here they come!' King Edward half whispers, half shouts.

And Thomas sees eight or nine brown stags, their antlers many-pointed, come bobbing quickly down the hill through the bracken, as if on springs. King Edward laughs with glee. In a moment the animals are on them, bouncing with astonishing speed. Thomas nocks one of the curious-shaped arrows. He imagines King Edward must loose first and waits. Sure enough, so do the others. King Edward draws, looses, misses. It must be dangerous for those following on behind, Thomas cannot help but think as he draws his own bow and looses an arrow that thumps into the throat of a great hart while it is thirty paces away. It havers, but then comes charging past. It is startlingly large, like a barrel planted with a tree. The arrow has vanished into its chest. The others loose too. One of the deer goes down instantly. Then the others come bounding past, so close Thomas might almost reach out and touch one. King Edward is trying to nock another arrow, but it is too late. In the time it takes him, they are gone. Thomas watches his own stag veer to the right, and then, a hundred paces further on, it slows, its legs tangle, and then collapses in the heather.

'A fine, fine shot,' King Edward calls.

They stand there a long moment. Thomas feels nothing for what he has just done. He feels none of the exultant pleasure the others seem to enjoy. All he can think of is the scene in the tower, with his friends all chained and dying in their own filth. You'd not even treat a bear like that.

'What will happen to it?' he asks when they are gathered around it. Its tongue is extended and blotted with dark blood, and there is moss or something growing on its antlers. It looks almost peaceful. The biggest thing Thomas has ever killed.

'There will be the unmaking of the animals, and then the curée,' Flood says, 'when the best parts will go to the constable's larder, naturally, and the rest will be given out to the men and the dogs.'

King Edward joins them. He has a costrel of wine and he offers it around.

'A fine shot,' he repeats.

Thomas thought it was like a butt coming at him. He could not miss. Though King Edward did, so he does not say as much.

While the hart is tied to a pole and the hounds are rounded up, King Edward asks Thomas and Flood to ride with him. The chinless priest and the two guards follow behind.

'We shall make of this what we can,' King Edward supposes. 'The hunting is fine, and look: plenty for our falcons. Otherwise the castle is – what would you say? Comfortable enough?'

Flood mumbles something appreciative.

'Yes,' King Edward goes on, 'he has certainly done himself well, my lord of Warwick.'

As they ride towards it, Thomas cannot take his gaze from the southeast tower.

'There is something about it though,' King Edward goes on, talking to himself more than to Thomas or Flood, perhaps. 'Some odd atmosphere.'

And Flood catches Thomas's eye. Now is the moment.

'It is Edmund Riven, sir,' Thomas says. 'The man with the missing eye.'

King Edward looks at him from under a raised eyebrow. He is a handsome man, but his mouth is very tight, and curls up at the ends, as if he is constantly suppressing a smile. There is something irritating about this: it suggests he is amused by all he sees, and that the better, more serious part of his life is lived elsewhere.

'Ah yes,' King Edward says. 'Bellman was complaining of him last night.'

Flood asks why Bellman might complain of Riven.

'Apparently my lord of Warwick has ordered him to offer this Riven every assistance, but he does not know why, or what he is up to, and as you might imagine he does not like this overmuch.'

'He is torturing people,' Thomas blurts. 'He has a dying man up in that tower, and a woman, about to child, and a one-armed man he's burned half to death, all of them chained to a wall.'

King Edward breathes out in disgust.

'Which eye is gone?' he asks.

'The left,' Thomas tells him.

He is unsurprised. 'The philosophers tell us that the right eye offers understanding,' he says, 'whereas the left offers affection.' King Edward enjoys philosophy.

'A woman about to child?' Flood asks.

Thomas nods.

'What has she done?' King Edward asks. 'Apart from the apparent?'

'Nothing,' Thomas says.

'Then – why is she shackled so?'

'I cannot tell.'

King Edward is thoughtful. There is a growing glimmer in his eye though, as if he has seen some opportunity.

'I will tell Bellman,' he says. 'He is not so bad a fellow, considering everything, and he might welcome some kind of intervention, I think. Also, a first test as to the whereabouts of his loyalties, hmmm?'

Thomas does not pretend to understand this last remark. They leave their horses at the stables in the outer bailey and cross back into the castle through the east gate. Thomas is hungry, he realises, and there is dinner in the great hall: cinnamon and milk soup, roasted rabbit, a dish of sweet spiced vegetables, a soft cheese, a hard cheese, a piece of one of the harts they have just killed and more bread and ale. Again King Edward takes the board on the dais, sitting next to Bellman, and Thomas is aware of glances his way, and then heads bent together.

Afterwards Bellman leaves the hall and King Edward raises his eyebrows, but nothing then happens and Thomas is left pacing until Flood asks for help writing a letter to his wife. She cannot read, Flood tells him, and, in all honesty, Flood can hardly write, so Thomas draws him a picture of a tiny, extravagantly handsome knight in harness on a horse.

'Oh, she will like that!' Flood says. 'You are as good as any monk I ever knew.'

'How will you get it to her?' Thomas asks. He has assumed communication with the outside world would be limited. Flood tells him he has found a company-starved white monk who comes and goes from nearby Jervaulx monastery, and who will happily bring and take anything, in return for alms and conversation. So Thomas writes a letter to Katherine at Marton, telling her where he is and what has happened. He leaves the letter with Flood and he borrows some blunts from the sergeant and spends the rest of the afternoon in the butts, stripped down to his hose and pourpoint. He just does not know what else to do, and every so often his gaze slides across the castle walls to where the guard watches him from the battlements by that southeast tower. Katherine would know what to do next. Yes. She would know.

And how long has John got before the rot kills him?

And Nettie? Surely she cannot have long to go?

He sends his arrows singing down the range thumping into the dampened earth mounds a hundred paces away. When he has shot twenty-four arrows, he walks down and collects them. He does it time and time again. It is a way of controlling his ferocity, he knows, and he wonders if he should not be aiming this temper elsewhere?

293

After a while others come out to join him, and they lend him a proper bow. Spending time in their company, he finds they are men not unlike many he has known before; but each wishes he were with the rest of Warwick's men in the south, where they believe there is a chance of loot. There is talk of how Lord Montagu's men once stumbled upon a fortune, and what a good man he was for letting them share it out among themselves, without taking any for himself. They imagine his brother the Earl of Warwick might do the same, should such an opportunity arise, for he is fond of gestures.

Thomas asks them about Riven.

One of them crosses himself.

'Nasty, nasty piece of work,' he says.

'Don't get on the wrong side of him,' another laughs. 'He is like to have that giant of his sodomise you to death.'

They discuss the giant and agree that he is simple, and from Ireland, though there is no evidence for this.

'He is like one of those boarhounds that never leave their master's side,' one says.

'Never says a word,' another adds. 'Just grunts.'

The afternoon grows cool. A wind picks up. Thomas shrugs back into his jacket and after a while they pack up and troop back down through the east gate again. As they come through, they catch a trace of the rot blowing from the south wall, or the southeast tower, and the men all groan and cover their mouths and noses, and Thomas looks down through the passageway under the chapel that seems to frame the door of the southeast tower, and it is open, and he thinks of John again, and he offers up a silent prayer for the man.

As it grows dark, he wanders with Flood to the great hall in the keep from which the smell of food and the sound of voices emanate, but instead of joining them, he climbs to the steps to the covered bridge that would take him across the bailey into the chambers on the southern range, where Bellman the constable and his family lived. The door is shut, of course, and Thomas stops on the bridge and looks down at the doorway to the southeast tower. That too is shut, yet the stench of the rot is all-pervasive. It seems to stain your clothes like a dye. He rests his elbows on the hoarding and looks down into the courtyard, lit by faint light coming from the windows of the tower, as there is a commotion at the door of the passageway. Three men emerge, guards they look like, leading what might be a woman in a travelling cloak. They are hurrying. One thumps the door of the southeast tower, just as Thomas had earlier in the day. They step back to wait. One of them turns to the woman and asks something. She replies sharply, dismissively, and while the man she's speaking to does not laugh, the other two do. There is something about the woman . . .

Then the door is opened. A lamp is held up, splashing light on to the upturned faces. Thomas thinks: By Christ, is that . . .? No. Surely. He does not hear what is said. The woman goes halfway up the steps, and then covers her nose. She says something and the man within grunts something back and shuts the door. The light goes. The three guards and the woman – it is definitely a woman – wait. The woman moves anxiously. A moment later the door is opened again and this time it is Sir Edmund Riven. He is pulling on his jacket. He asks a sharp question of the woman: 'Where?' and the woman replies, 'In the inn.'

There is a moment's stand off, when no one says a thing, then, after a moment Edmund Riven pushes past her. Then the giant blocks the light from the doorway as he emerges, and, together with the first three guards, all exit the courtyard by way of the passage under the chapel. The man holding the lamp stands at the doorway a moment longer, and then closes it.

It has all taken about the time it might to say the paternoster.

Thomas waits a moment, and then he returns to the great hall, where King Edward is already ruby-faced with drink, but there is no sign of Bellman. Thomas is about to slide in next to Flood, who is discussing the day's hunt with the chinless priest, when one of the servants nudges his back, and he tells him he is wanted without. There is something covert about the man's manner, as if a favour is being asked, rather than it being an official summons, and so Thomas comes quickly, following the servant down the turning steps and into the heat-blasted kitchens, which smell of frying onions or human sweat, and out through the low doors in the bailey; it is quite dark there, and he is awaited nervously by one of the men from the southeast tower, one of those who had looked so shamed by their treatment of Jack and Nettie and John Stump. He is holding a rush lantern, which casts a low glow, and he touches his cap in salute.

'You are a surgeon, you said?' he asks.

Thomas does not deny it.

'We think – we think the woman is about to birth,' the man goes on. 'And we think the other one – with the . . . you know? – we think he is not much longer for this world.'

'Is there no midwife? No . . . other surgeon?'

'Both have gone south,' the man tells him. 'They are with the Earl in London or wherever. You are the only one versed in any kind of medical matter.'

'But what about Edmund Riven?'

'He is called out on one of his – his raids, or missions, or whatever he calls them. He will soon drag in some poor flightless bird or other, but – before then? Could you come? You might at least offer them some comfort.'

Thomas knows he cannot do a thing, and that the man should find the priest, but it is the very least he can do. He has helped many a ewe give birth, and if he can help Nettie, then that at least is something.

'I do not have any instruments,' he says. 'Knives and so forth.'

'Oh dear God, we have knives,' the man says. 'But hurry! There is no telling when he will return.'

At that moment Flood of all people steps out from the kitchens. He has followed Thomas.

'Are you well, Thomas?'

Thomas tells him what he is about. Flood is astonished.

'You are a man of many parts,' Flood says.

Thomas agrees.

'Come on,' the guard urges.

'Can you bring water? As hot as you can, and linen, clean, if possible, and – and wine. Plenty of that? Ask in the kitchens.'

'Of course,' Flood says.

Thomas follows the guard around the keep and up into the top room of the tower, the lantern's glow guiding the way. He pinches his nose and closes his mouth. That smell. He can feel his heart in his chest, beating against its bone walls. He feels it may force its way out through his mouth. Christ. What is he going to do? There is a sudden scream in the darkness above. Harsh, and wounded. He thinks of tearing flesh. He stumbles, catches himself.

He hears Jack calling for Nettie.

'All will be well, Nettie! All be well!'

When they reach the top floor the door is open and the sweet foul smell billows within, and there is a lamp on the table, but the guard is crouched in the shadows next to Nettie, and Jack is on his knees at the full extent of his chain, his face wet with tears, and he is calling her name over and over again.

'Unchain them!' Thomas shouts.

'We cannot!' the guard calls back. 'We have not the key!'

'Where is it?'

'In Edmund Riven's purse! On his belt.'

'Break them! Break them!'

Nettie shrieks like an animal. Her cry echoes around the chamber. Both guards are almost mad with their shame and sorrow.

'How? How?'

'Run for the smith! Find him! Bring his hammers and – and whatever. A tool to break the rings!'

'Thomas!' Jack cries. 'Help her! Help her!'

Thomas is frozen for a moment. He looks at Nettie. There is blood everywhere. Her hands are like claws. She is pulling on her sodden skirts. The smell of John's wound is still unbearable. He hurries to her. He tries to be calm. He holds her. He talks to her in the same way he used to soothe sheep. He speaks in a low burr and calls her 'girl'.

'It will be well,' he murmurs. 'All will be well. Come now. Come now. That is it. Caterwaul if that helps.'

Nettie grips his hand with both hers, a bond sealed with her own blood, and she squeezes it and cries out, full-lunged. She's kicked away her stool and sits against the wall with her legs straight out before her and her hands are chained above her head. Thomas cries out that he is so sorry and she swears on the body and blood and bones of Christ and Jack calls over to say that she does not mean it and the other guard is weeping and Thomas knows that John Stump is dying just through the door there and he knows he has passed beyond forgiveness for what he has visited upon these three.

Just then he hears footfall on the steps, and the guards look at one another in naked fear.

Riven is back.

20

Katherine stands in the shadows of the entrance to a dyer's yard, where the stench is enough to make a nightwatchman redundant, and she prays she's wrong. She prays Liz will come traipsing back from the other inn, straightening her laces, with the news that Jack and Nettie and John Stump have been set free, and that Edmund Riven is no longer looking for the ledger. She's holding Rufus in her arms, and he's a hot deadweight with his face pressed snuffling against the bare skin of her neck, and the words of her prayer spill from her lips in a mewl of miserable desperation.

'Please, Lord, make it so,' she entreats.

But she knows her prayers are in vain. She knows she has been betrayed, tricked, traduced and even condemned to certain death when, after a long moment, she hears shouts from behind the houses up by the castle, and then, striding purposefully into the marketplace in the dusk of the late-summer's evening, comes Edmund Riven. He is unmistakable, with a patch of linen pressed to his face, on horseback, leading a party of ten or fifteen men, each carrying a lantern and billhook. They are making for the White Swan, and the giant is with them, head and shoulders above all the others, loping next to Riven with unnerving and inhuman fluency, like some stag-hunting dog.

She must move, she knows. She must be away, but where is there to go? She'll never get far along the roads she's come in on, or across the country. Riven and his men will hunt her down in moments. Where can she hide? Nowhere for very long.

There is nothing else for it. She needs sanctuary.

She slips back into the deepening darkness of the yard, where after the heat of the day the rotting stench is like uncooked egg white at the back of her throat. Rufus murmurs and shifts as she makes her way past the curdling vats and the drying racks where the skins hang and out through the back of the yard following a well-worn path to the stream where the dyer must tip his waste. There's a slippery plank across it and beyond are the shacks of his boys, where there's a chained dog yapping.

She crosses the plank and cuts away up the slope, away from the shacks, following the stream back towards the bulk of the church tower that blots out the moon-backed clouds. It is desperate, but it is all she can think of. She scrabbles over a low hazel fence, one leg at a time, and a larger dog sets to barking, and then she comes to the churchyard wall, above which black branches of yew sway and dance in the freshening wind. The dusk is filled with bats. She follows the wall around to the left, thanking God the day has been long, but now at last the darkness is closing behind her.

Rufus is awake again, so she can put him down a moment, and swing the ledger back over her shoulder with her other bag. She leads him on, and finds the church gate and fumbles with its locking bar before she can get it open.

'Come on,' she says.

'Where's Liz?'

'She – she has gone to find help.'

Rufus's accepting, anxious face reflects the faint moonlight. He is bone-weary, slumped, as if he were made of dough rather than flesh, and there is precious little of that on his bones anyway. She puts a hand on his narrow shoulder.

'We'll sleep here tonight,' she tells him. 'Then in the morning—'

She hears a noise. Something man-made above the soughing of the branches.

'Come,' she says, whispering, and she hurries through the gate and guides him through into the darkness of the churchyard where gravestones lie in the long grass pale as ghosts. The path is stone-flagged to the church's south door. She hopes it will be unlocked. If not she is prepared to break a window. She will send Rufus through the narrow aperture like a common thief, and he can open the door for her. This way at least they will be dry, and in the morning when the priest comes, she will do as the man who accosted Isabella that time in Lincoln had done, and claim sanctuary.

But then she sees a light within, through those parti-coloured windows. Someone is there. Pray God, it is the priest. She leads Rufus quickly to the door and tries it. It is locked. She knocks as loudly as she dares, a series of muffled thumps with the underside of her fist. A moment later there is a bead of light between the door and the stone floor. Someone is coming.

'Who are you and what do you want?' a voice calls from within.

She hesitates. If she shouts she'll be heard. They'll know she's here. So she says nothing and she just bangs again. After a moment she hears the bolts drawn. The door opens a crack and a slice of yellow lantern light falls out. A man presses his eye to the gap and studies her. She pushes Rufus forward, to show she means no harm. The man's eye – dark – flickers down to him and the door opens a fraction wider.

'What do you want?' he asks.

'Refuge,' she says. 'For the night. There are some men – We – we are being pursued.'

Even so he does not seem willing to open the door further.

'Go to the castle,' he says. 'The constable is a good man.'

'Please,' she says. 'For the love of Our Lord Jesus Christ. In his name. Charity. If not for me, then my son.'

The man hesitates still, so she forces the door and is across the threshold before he can shut it in her face. He is a priest, in a dark robe long enough to reach the ground.

'Thank you, Father,' she says as the priest dithers at the door. 'Lock it,' she says. 'Please. You must lock it. There are men out there. Thieves.'

301

'Thieves!' he cries, his voice high-pitched with fret. 'You've brought thieves to my door?'

'Not if you shut it,' she tells him. 'They will not violate the sanctity of the church.'

The priest has no choice. He shuts it behind her and shoots the bolts, top and bottom, and then drops the drawbar. When he has straightened he holds his lantern up to inspect her more closely and reveals himself as being in his middle years and hatless, with his dark hair disarrayed. It seems he is angry with her.

'Why are you abroad at this hour?' he demands.

'It is not by my choice,' she says. 'We've travelled from – from York. Some men on the roads took our bags, and so we are left without money for an inn.' She pulls Rufus to her. She does not want him telling the truth.

'But you can't stay here,' he says. 'Not now. Not tonight.'

His eyes flick to the darkness of the nave and back.

'You would not send us out into the dark?' she asks.

He is awkward. She can see him trying to think of a reason to eject her. She turns from him, and sets Rufus down on the floor with his back against a pillar and strokes his cheek.

'It will be all right,' she soothes. 'This nice priest will let us stay.'

When she stands up, the priest is still shifting and undecided. It is as if she has caught him out in something.

'You say you've no money?' he checks.

She shakes her head.

'All was taken. On a horse.'

'What's in there?' he asks and leans close to her to touch the ledger's bag.

'A book,' she says, pulling back. She smells wine on his breath.

'Who are these men?' he asks at length.

She tells him she doesn't know, and leaves it to his imagination. She can feel his gaze ranging over her, taking her in. She imagines he does not think she looks worth raping.

'Are they outside now?' he asks.

She nods. Now she just wants to be left alone, but the priest won't. He keeps asking questions. What did they look like? How were they dressed? When did you first see them? When did you last see them? How did you get away?

As he goes on, she can feel herself losing the strength to confect or fabricate. She feels stripped naked, so sickened with her self-sorrow that surely her shame must be obvious to anyone with eyes to see.

'I will go myself and fetch the Watch from the castle,' he volunteers.

'No!'

He stops, turns back to her.

'No? Is it the Watch you are seeking to avoid?' he asks.

'No. It is that I don't want to make nuisance.'

'Well,' he says. 'You've already done that.'

'More nuisance,' she clarifies.

There is another long silence.

'Please,' she says. 'Just for tonight. Let me sit with my son and in the morning, we'll be gone.' She is too tired to talk about sanctuary tonight. She will claim it in the morning. After a moment he says:

'Very well.'

And he turns his back on her and walks away, taking the light with him. She slumps next to Rufus, back against the pillar, boots out before her. She has not wondered what the priest is doing in the church alone at night, but now she looks up when she hears him whispering. There is someone else there, a woman, in the glow of the lamp. Can it be that she and Rufus have disturbed some tryst? She shuts her eyes and rests her head against the stone behind, and she wonders that such things still go on, while God seems bent on testing her and her alone.

She wishes they would blow out the flame in the lamp, and she thinks about Edmund Riven and that giant being out there now, in the dark, and she wonders what he would have said and done when he arrived at the White Swan to find her gone. She imagines the search he will be carrying out. Every room in the place to begin with, and then every nearby house, and then what? Would he think she's taken the road or made for the hills? She is at least lucky darkness is complete, she supposes. At least now he is faced with an array of possibilities he'll have to take his time to investigate.

It is as she is thinking this that the first bang on the door resounds around the nave. There is a shout from without. The priest stands up. There is scurrying as the woman removes herself.

'You've brought them here,' the priest accuses.

'No,' she says. 'You mustn't let them in.'

'But who are they to disturb the House of God?' he asks himself. He is sidling towards the door with the lamp in his hand, incredulous, when the door is simply knocked in with a splintering crash. The priest screams and jumps back. Next to Katherine, Rufus flexes like a fish on a riverbank and is on his feet before the second blow on the door sends it smashing from its hinges to screech across the stone-flagged floor. Light from lanterns beams across the darkened nave.

It is the giant, of course, who comes first, ducking through the door, blocking the light behind for the moment, but still caught in the priest's lantern; he is grinning at what he's done, and more men crowd in after him, lanterns held high, likewise admiring his strength. They are laughing at it.

The priest quails.

'What do you want?'

The giant says nothing. His face is huge, his brow so low and heavy it almost meets his jutting jaw.

'Where is she?' one of the other men asks.

The priest's mouth is open as he backs away from the advancing giant. He stammers something and then holds the lantern high, and in its pool of light he points across to Katherine. One of the men has a bull's-eye lamp, and he swings the beam flashing across the pillars to catch her.

Someone laughs.

'Well well!'

She can't move. It is as if the light has transfixed her. The giant moves swiftly and she feels her bowels melt. She grips Rufus and pulls him to her. The giant laughs too now and bends; with one hand he picks her up by the gathering of her cloak at the throat, and with the other picks up Rufus likewise, and he straightens and pulls them apart just as if he were yanking the head off a chicken. He holds them up, arms extended, so that Rufus is dangling a foot off the ground. The giant's laugh is like rolling thunder. He smells of kennels, and bear gardens, and strong wine.

Katherine swears at him. She tells him he is damned by God. Each time he laughs. She aims a kick at his groin and he stops laughing; he growls instead, and his lip curls, and she imagines he will drop her and pummel her to death, but he simply hoiks Rufus higher, and the boy slips in his collar and he starts to choke.

The other men come clustering down the nave to meet them, with their billhooks and lanterns, and they are still laughing too.

'That weren't so difficult,' they say.

'Please,' Katherine implores. 'He's hurting the boy.'

But they seem to have incomplete control over him, or are afraid to exercise it, and their grins become fixed and anxious.

'Let him go,' she shouts. 'Let him go!'

The giant just begins laughing again and twists his fist, tightening the ligature around Rufus's slim little neck as if he means to hang him.

'Let him go!' she shrieks again.

And this time her words are echoed by a voice from the door of the church and the giant stops laughing and looks around. He lowers Rufus, who gasps for air when his toes touch the ground. Katherine strains for him and the giant, uncertain, relents and she gathers Rufus to her. He is tearing at his clothes to loosen them from his neck and his breathing is reedy. His little tongue sticks out and his eyes bulge.

Holding him to her, she cannot stem the flow of tears. That she has led him here, to this end. May God forgive her.

The men around them – in Warwick's red – step back to allow the man from the door to approach.

'So here we are at last,' Edmund Riven says. His voice is just as she'd imagined: clipped yet sneering. He strolls towards them, but even with that wad of linen pressed to his face, and even with the giant there, she flinches when she smells him, turning her face from him, but not before she sees how angry her reaction makes him.

'Where is it?' he asks. 'Is that it?'

He gestures at the bag and indicates a man should take it from her. One steps forward and pulls it from her, tugging it over her head. He passes it over. Riven looks inside at the battered old book, but he doesn't take it out. He is not a child that he needs to see its contents right here, right now. He nods and slings the bag over his own shoulder, turning for the door.

'Take that other bag from her too,' he tells them. 'And search her person. She'll have some knife about her somewhere.'

'But we are in a church,' she says. 'We claim sanctuary.'

Riven pauses; then he starts to laugh.

'Sanctuary? Sanctuary? You want *sanctuary*!'

His laugh takes root, surprisingly high-pitched. Katherine is left there clutching Rufus while the other men laugh uneasily along with him. Riven even co-opts the priest to join in, and he does so. Then Riven stops his laughter and checks his stained linen pad, as if moving so might cause the wound to weep more copiously. The other men fall silent as soon as he does. In the shadows, the priest's woman suppresses a sob.

The giant looms over her and closes his fist on her cloak again, and he lifts her off her toes, while another man takes her knife and lets his hands wander over her at his leisure – her breasts and between her legs – and when she lashes out, the giant twists her neck and she must endure or choke.

'Sure you've not got another one, hidden up there?'

He lifts her skirt. She kicks him and he laughs again. She almost spits at him. She wishes she did have another knife.

'Come on,' Riven says. 'There will be time enough for that, you heathen brute.'

It is a fond compliment and the man laughs.

'Hear that?' he jeers.

'Bring them,' Riven calls, and the giant picks them both up again.

'No,' she says. 'I will come. Let me carry my boy.'

Riven is impatient.

'If it will speed us along,' he allows, and after a moment of slow thought the giant releases them from the great shovels of his hands and pushes them staggering forward, out through the splintered door frame and away from any idea of sanctuary she ever had, into Riven's care, and she thinks what a fool she has been.

'You've got what you want!' she calls to Riven as he swings himself up into his saddle. 'Let us go. We cannot harm you.'

Riven glances at her.

'Could you ever?' he asks.

He has turned his horse and is trotting on ahead now. Seeing him up there, triumphant, she loses her temper. She cannot stop herself.

'I did once, do you remember?'

He gestures to imply she is deranged.

'Well?' she goes on. 'D'you remember?'

She is almost jeering at him. It is because she is so powerless. She gives in to her rage, and she wants him to know what she has done to him, and what she is to him. She wants to remind him of the harm she has done him. None of this is logical. She is not thinking. She is not thinking of limiting the damage, of communicating anything, of her future at all. She wants only to show she is not this woman they are dragging back to their castle fastness, this woman whom they have beaten.

'Your face,' she calls. 'I did that. With a bucket! Remember?'

Riven's shoulders hike. The horse walks on.

'Outside the priory at Haverhurst! You and your accursed father. I was the nun you thought to attack that day.'

And now Riven does twist in his saddle and he stares at her with his one furious eye. She can see him trying to reimagine that morning so long ago, when she hit him with the bucket, but after a moment he turns away again, and it is as if, for the moment perhaps, the effort of remembering is too great. He kicks his horse on, but his back is stiff and his shoulders raised, and the guards riding by her side know this is a bad omen.

'Christ, woman,' one whispers, 'why did you tell him such a thing? He will only have us go at you all the more now.'

And she sees what she's done, and she feels her guts give with fear and self-loathing. She has fallen down into a hell of her own device and, worse, she has dragged Rufus with her. Now all she sees are burning coals pressed on soft skin, and the boy is weeping in her arms, and the air is filled with that strange gammy stench of Riven's face. There is no longer any point in asking him to let them go. He'll never do that now. Oh Christ, she thinks, as the tears spill from her lids. Oh Christ.

But now they come through the castle gatehouse, and every man of the Watch stands back to let them pass, faces falling, conversations withering, and it is as if she is being marched to the headsman's block – only this is worse, for there is no promise of the axe blade's swift release into the afterlife, only that of much pain.

Once they are through, they can hear music from the bright-lit windows of the keep, and the thought that something so everyday should continue while she and Rufus are dragged away only makes it worse. Riven dismounts and a boy appears to take his horse away to the stables and Riven walks ahead, stiff-backed still, and the giant pushes them to follow him, towards a passageway under what must be a chapel, where the coloured windows are also illuminated – for an evening service, perhaps? – and then Riven stops. He turns and manages a grimace; then he indicates with a flick of his hand and there in the shadows is Liz, standing to one side, head hanging low.

Katherine's vision narrows when she sees her, and all she wants to do is throttle Liz, to drive the life out of her, to squeeze her neck so hard the fingertips of her right hand will press against the fingertips of her left hand. She strains against the giant's grip on her collar.

'How could you?' she snarls. 'How could you?'

Liz looks up. She's been crying, perhaps, but she is no longer.

'He had my sisters,' she says, indicating Riven, who stands watching. 'Both of 'em. Told me if he didn't get what he wanted, then he'd let that' – she points to the giant – 'get what he wants. With them.'

'You could have just taken it!'

'I tried! I thought you had it in the bloody cart! In your bloody coffer!'

'So you gave him Jack and Nettie? And John? You sold them all!'

'What else could I have done? What would you have done?'

'I don't know! I don't know! But not this! Not to – not to *Rufus*! Not when I could have done *anything* else!'

'But he wanted you,' Liz says. 'Riven. He wanted to know how you'd come by it. Everything. And I could not – I could not separate you.' She chokes on her own misery for a moment, and can't speak, but then she wails: 'Don't blame me! Don't *blame* me!'

At this Katherine feels a rushing of undimmed rage. She lunges at her again but the giant's grip does not slacken, and she almost loses her footing. Liz draws back.

'Katherine,' she says. 'Please forgive me!'

'I'll never forgive you! D'you hear! Never. I'll curse you to hell! I'll – I'll – Damn you!'

But Liz is determined and she comes towards Katherine with her arms outstretched, imploring, and there are tears pouring down her face. The giant is laughing at the women's pain, and Riven too is watching with bright eyes as Liz puts her arms around Katherine. Katherine tries to fend her off but she cannot hold Rufus and push

Liz away, and Liz grips her and she is sobbing and begging Katherine to please, please forgive her, and Katherine is still fighting her when she feels her slide something into the laces of her dress. The object stays there, and then Liz breaks away and looks at her, hard, and Katherine is momentarily silenced, trying to think what in God's name she's doing when Liz steps further back. Riven grows bored of it.

'Well,' he says. 'If you are not going to fight one another . . .' He jerks his head and the giant pushes Katherine past Liz, sending her staggering down the passageway, forgetting that Rufus is there for the moment, watching all this.

He pulls her out into the next courtyard, and that is when she gets the first scent of the black rot, even above the stench that Riven trails like a vixen in heat, and she thinks back to the first time she smelled John Stump's wound in the guerite at Alnwick and she knows it is him. Somehow she is sure of it. It is the sort of thing Edmund Riven would do.

But now Riven is disconcerted by something, and the giant, too, is puzzled and brings her up short. She tries to twist free of his grip while they watch Riven walk quickly to a tower and up the few steps to where the door hangs open, and from where, Katherine supposes, the stink must be billowing.

'Bring her,' Riven says.

He disappears within. The giant pushes her on, stumbling up the steps. Rufus begins to gag at the smell that seeps down and she has to pick him up and carry him. He wriggles and kicks and she has to catch him and catch him again as he struggles to escape, and she half hopes she'll be able to do the same, but the giant is there, pushing her forward even though she is already moving upward, and she turns on him and shouts at his vast, stupid, clueless bloody face. She tells him that he is no better than an animal, and that he is the devil made flesh, and that she hopes he will spend eternity roasting in hell's fires, and everything else that she can think of, but he remains unprovoked and just continues to prod her with fingers that are as big around as her wrist.

'Shut her up,' Riven says over his shoulder.

Katherine tries to kick and elbow him but it is hard when she is carrying Rufus and the giant seems impervious to pain. Then she hears a howl of agony from above that sets her hair on end, and then Riven mutters something and the giant shoves her hard so that she nearly falls, and Rufus is still thrashing to try to get away, and so she does not see exactly what happens when Riven enters the room before the giant knocks her aside. She rights herself and checks Rufus is all right. He is gagging with the reek of the black rot. It is all he can think about. He scrabbles away from her towards a doorway that must lead out on to the walkway, from where there is a supply of fresh air: he is like a drowning man given a chance of life, and she cannot stop him.

'Rufus!'

But he's gone, and then she hears Riven shouting in the chamber.

'What in the name of God is happening here? Who are you?'

And she looks into the room, past the great bulk of the giant, and there is a man standing up and turning to face Riven, and she sees it is of all men, of all things, Thomas.

21

No one has time to say a word.

Riven turns on the guard, who looks as if he might void himself. 'Shut her up!' he shouts.

He's pointing at Nettie, who's growling deeply, her face a livid sheen, her clothes and all the straw around her wet and stained pink with blood and her waters. Any moment and she will start screaming again, for that is how it comes, the pain of childing, in waves.

When the guard does not move, the giant strides around the table and slaps the guard with the back of his hand, sending him crashing against the wall and to the floor under the window. He seems about to do the same to Nettie, when Thomas stands in his way. By Christ, he looks so small. The giant is confused for a moment, that someone should stand up to him, and then he raises his hand to hit Thomas, but Thomas is fast, and he is very strong from pulling that bow, and he punches the giant first. He hits him not in the face, which is perhaps what he was aiming for, but misses, and buries his fist in the softer regions of the man's neck, around his throat. Katherine does not know if it is a lucky punch or not, but the giant staggers back and crashes into the table and then to the floor in a sprawl of dead-weighted limbs, his trunk like a dropped sack.

There is a moment of startled silence.

Then Nettie growls again and Jack lunges to help her, only for his chains to pull him back with a taut clang. Roaring with pain and frustration he turns and begins aiming kicks at Riven, but Riven is likewise out of his reach, and he ignores Jack. He seems momentarily stunned by what has happened to his giant, who may be dead; he's staring at the broad spread of the man's body with his pad of pus held in mid-air and Katherine cannot stop her eye being drawn to the pink wet wreckage of his face, but after a moment he claps the pad over his wounds again, and now she sees his gaze rise to Thomas, and his focus sharpen. His face hardens, and he has a drawn blade in his hand, a short, broad thing, perfect for a confined space like this, and his knuckles whiten as he begins to circle the table and she knows he will kill Thomas unless Thomas runs.

But then, suddenly, there are more men coming up the steps. They are running and shouting. And then there are more on the walkway beyond, coming through the open door, and they too are sprinting. The first one into the room is an astonishingly handsome youth. He carries a bucket of steaming water. The second one is – can it be? – King Edward. He carries a great pile of linen sheets. The men on the walkway are in Warwick's livery, led by an oldish man and, astonishingly, a woman in a fine blue dress.

They all arrive at the same time and force their ways into the chamber; Riven hesitates, but then resumes his intent. He steps over the body of the giant and swipes the blade at Thomas. Thomas leaps back, wild-eyed with fear. He knows this is it. He knows he will be killed. He retreats. Riven has him in a corner.

Men are shouting. Telling Riven to stop, for the love of God, but he ignores them. He has only one thing on his mind now, and there is nothing anyone can do to stop him as he takes another step towards Thomas and stabs the sword towards his guts. Thomas presses himself against the wall. The next thrust will be the last.

Men watch with open mouths, frozen by the intensity of the violence in such close quarters.

Katherine feels her head pounding. Sounds come and go like waves on shingle. Colours warp. Shapes twist. The air seems to become heavy. She starts to move in slow motion. She reaches under her coat for the knife that Liz slid into her laces, and her fingers close on its stubby handle, and she realises this is exactly why Liz gave it to her; she draws it out, and feels from its balance that it's a clumsy little thing, and none too sharp, but it will do its task.

She knows now that this is the moment that has been coming for so many months – years even – and noise roars in her ears, and she knows this is wrong, and that there are good reasons this has not been done before, but she knows too that it is the only thing she can do. She throws herself forward across the room, and she claps her left hand on Riven's shoulder, and she drives the short fat blade into the soft of his back, just above his hip, to the right of his spine, and she punches it so hard she thinks it must come out the other side.

Riven takes three tripping steps forward, but he is already keeling backwards under pressure of her left hand, and the sword that was about to cut Thomas wavers and is then thrown aside as he tries to pluck at the knife in his back. But she just keeps pushing. And now Thomas raises his hands to Riven's chest and shoves him back. Riven is bent at the knees and is gasping as if he's choking on his own blood. She lets go of the knife and hauls his shoulders back and down and steps back to let him fall to the flagstones on to the knife, and when he does fall on it, it is driven in deeper yet, and the point does come out of his belly, but instead of cutting his pourpoint it sticks up under it, forming a tiny bloodstained pyramid.

He does not lie dead, but thrashes and twists between the table and chair leg and the giant's naked feet, and his blood is everywhere in the straw mixing with Nettie's waters, and everyone else stands immobile with their features pulled and their eyes fixed on him as he shouts imploring half-words and beseeching half-phrases, but no one here will help him and the pain is so great he cannot call on God to accept his soul or forgive any of his sins. After a long, long moment he stops his twitchings and lies still, his arms sinking slowly to his sides, and stinking pus weeps from the pink gash in his face, like foul yellow seed pearls, and at last she has killed him and at last she is exultant.

314

There is silence in the room.

She looks up at Thomas at the same time as he looks up at her and there are tears in his eyes as there are in hers. They throw themselves at one another and he folds her in his arms and she feels as if in a vice and she grips him tighter yet, and they stand like that and no one else exists: not the two dead bodies, not the gasping Nettie, not the silenced crowd who watch in silence – not even Rufus, who she prays has seen nothing. If she presses her face into the cloth of Thomas's pourpoint she can almost mask the stench of Riven and the reek blowing through the door, and she finds that he smells unaccountably clean, of good soap, and it is this that strikes her as most odd, but of course she has no time to discover why this should be, because, after he has folded her in his arms for this lasting moment, they part because, she can tell, she is needed as never before.

The guard who'd been knocked to the floor is rousing himself while the other is quick to try to redeem himself: he stoops to cut the key from Riven's purse and unlocks first Nettie and then Jack. Jack shucks off his chains and ignores the pain to crawl to Nettie's side.

Katherine calls for Rufus.

'Where is he? Where is he?'

Thomas comes with her out on to the walkway where John Stump lies, alive at least, but perhaps only just, and she has to look past him, to the walkway's far end, where, in a huddle in the shadows beside the steps up to another open doorway, she and Thomas see the slight figure of their son, curled with his arms clamped across his legs. They approach and crouch next to him.

'Rufus?'

He says nothing. They look at one another. She feels almost crushed by shame and guilt. All the febrile elation she had felt in killing Riven, and in it being so easy that surely God must have ordained it, has gone.

Thomas puts his hand on the boy's arm.

'Rufus?' he says. 'Rufus, all is well now. We are here, together. It is all over. There is nothing to mind now. Come.'

Still Rufus is silent. After a moment the woman in the blue dress appears in the circle of their lamplight. She is the constable's wife, her face as round and wrinkled and kindly as a bun.

'I will mind him, if you like?' she offers. 'I have boys of my own and we will get along very nicely and when all this is clear, and you are cleaned of – of – of stains, we will start afresh, like a new day, and put this by, eh?'

She has a wonderfully calming voice, and she sits on the step next to Rufus and she smiles at Katherine and Katherine is about to tell her thank you but no, when there is a great shout from within the tower at the other end of the walkway, and it seems Nettie must be approaching her moment of crisis, and so, with sundered feelings, Katherine accepts the woman's offer.

Katherine returns to the light of the tower, where the giant has been dragged across and shackled in the chains that so recently housed Jack, and the constable is stroking his whiskered jaw over the corpse of Edmund Riven.

'He was the Earl of Warwick's man,' he tells them. 'I was waiting word on which between us had lordship over the other, and now this. The Earl will think I had him murdered.'

King Edward, who seems cheered by all he's seen and heard, tells the constable to assume that it was he who did it.

'Warwick will understand,' he says. 'Tell him it was an accident. Tell him I slipped. Which is more than he will ever be able to say about the loss of the heads of my father-in-law and his son.'

'Thank you, sir,' the constable says. 'If you are quite sure?'

King Edward waves him away, and the constable nods to the two guards waiting to carry Riven's corpse away.

'What about him?' the King asks, nodding at the giant. 'Shall we just – kill him too? While we are about it?'

The constable is tempted, but wonders if this is not going too far.

'He's chained, isn't he?'

King Edward seems disappointed.

'If he moves, I shall kill him,' Jack says.

The King laughs.

'Another accident waiting to happen,' he says.

Then he turns to Katherine.

'Speak,' he says. 'We are at your command.'

She takes a moment, then calls for a fire to be lit, more lights brought, more wine, too, and more hot water. She calls for a broom to clear the bloodstained rushes and for someone to find her bag that the giant took from her. When it is found at the foot of the steps and brought to her, she takes out her dwale and mixes it up with such wine as is on the table and she gets Thomas to go on to the walkway and force John Stump to drink it.

There is not much she can do for Nettie now, other than make her comfortable. She cannot even ask the men to leave the room, but must deliver the baby as it comes, for she doubts Jack will ever leave Nettie's side again; even now, while she is scarlet-faced and strong-smelling, he crouches by her head and holds her hand as her growling becomes screaming. The handsome youth is there, too, keeping an eye on the still-inert giant, though he clearly wishes he were elsewhere. Katherine sets about cleaning Nettie up as the candles arrive, and the broom, brought by women from the kitchen, who set to work on the sodden rushes, and after a moment the room becomes less a charnel house and more like a birthing chamber.

Then she goes out on to the walkway to check on John Stump and she calls for more candles to be held up around his wounded limb by men with masks of cloth over their noses. The smell is choking. The constable's wife comes over to say she is taking Rufus to her chamber where she will put him in her bed, and send her women with herbs to burn.

'He is as silent as a stone,' she says, 'but sleep will knit him up.'

Katherine and Thomas thank her, but she will not hear of it.

'It is the least we can do, when we see what has been happening in our house, in our name.'

When she is gone Katherine stoops to look at John's remaining arm in the uncertain light, and she can see the dark tidemark has reached the elbow. She thinks this is very close to being fatal, but there is just a chance. She must cut him a hand's span above the elbow: that is the logical place.

John is very feverish, neither asleep nor awake.

'He drank the dwale?' she asks Thomas.

'All of it.'

She looks at John again.

'What do you think?' Thomas asks.

'We can only try.'

Thomas smiles.

'John Stumps is a better name.'

'You can tell him that when it is done.'

'It need be tonight?' he asks.

'Now,' she says.

Inside Nettie is yowling.

'And how much longer for Nettie?'

'I don't know. I have never been at a childing.'

'But I have,' he says. He means Rufus's.

'Well then?'

'Soon. I think.'

That is not as useful as it could be.

'Tell me when the dwale has worked,' she says, nodding at John. 'He needs to be almost – almost but not quite dead.'

He holds her eye a moment longer.

'Thanks be to God you are here,' he says. 'It is . . . unbelievable.'

'You likewise,' she says, 'though – why are you here?'

'It is a long story,' he says.

Nettie bellows. They clench hands and then she turns back into the chamber where the screaming is becoming screeching now, and

318

Nettie is sodden with sweat and more fluids wash on the floor. King Edward and the constable have gone – to get more water, the handsome youth says – but he is still here with Jack, who looks terrified, and both are at Nettie's head, holding her hands, for neither wants to see what is below her skirts. This is Katherine's task.

Until now, she has been so pleased by Thomas's certainty that she can save both Nettie, the baby and John Stump that she has not stopped to think what it is she is doing, but when she crouches at Nettie's ankles and pushes back the hot wet weight of her skirts, she is taken back to the moment she helped the midwife with Eelby's wife, and where that got them. But needs must, she thinks, needs must. She has rose oil. She anoints her hands with it, and then she shuffles forward, recalling the midwife's attempts to deliver Eelby's wife's baby before they abandoned her to her fate and Katherine took the knife and cut the baby out.

She senses that Nettie is approaching her time, and though there is nothing she can do, she cannot leave her to suffer with only men to attend her, and she wishes some of the women had stayed. Perhaps they will return? They *must* return.

So she stays and tells Nettie that the baby will come and that very soon this pain will be over and it will have been worth every moment of it, for then she will have a son. And Nettie nods and blows air hard and furiously, but there is nothing of the swelling and the colour changes that attended Eelby's wife when she was in labour, and so Katherine can tell Nettie that all goes well, and that she is not to mind the pain, and so on and so on. The intensity and frequency of Nettie's cries increase.

Thomas comes to tell her that John is insensible. She tells him what to fetch from the kitchens: more water, more wine; two knives, one large, one small; a whetstone; a fresh candle of the best quality; a metal dish; a butchers' saw, if there is one to be had; a length of clean linen thread; clean linen cloth; a bowstring; and some charcoal. While he is gone, she leaves Jack to reassure Nettie and she checks on John. He is, as Thomas says, insensible, but for how long? What if she starts the cut and then the baby comes? And yet she can see in the light of the braziers and the candles with which the men have now surrounded him that the black rot is seeping up the limb. If she leaves it until morning, then it will be too late to save John's life.

She must do it now.

Thomas returns bringing with him all the things she's requested, including a new saw, because of course the Earl of Warwick has a butcher of his own, and King Edward is there, too, with a sack of charcoal under one arm, a long length of linen rolled under the other, and the constable in tow with something he says will sweeten the air. They turn their eyes from Nettie and they proceed out on to the walkway, where it is now quite dark, and the constable scatters bunches of dried leaves on the braziers that crackle and flare and make the air smell better.

'So you will cut his arm off?' King Edward wants to know.

Katherine nods. She adjusts the candles and then wraps the lower, blackened part of John's remaining arm in a blanket, so that the smell is to some degree contained, and she gets one of the guards to sharpen the knives while she soaks the bowstring in the wine. She is thinking that it is too dark for this, and that she will not be able to stitch those little tubes of blood. She asks someone to fetch a poker or some such and King Edward volunteers.

'But you will not start without me?'

He is enjoying this, Katherine realises. It is so peculiar. King Edward of England, on an errand for her. But she has no real time to think about this. The guard has sharpened both knives, and the wine is warmed in its ewer. The constable's wife has sent a silver needle and she even has lengths of silk thread that have never been used. These Katherine puts in the warm wine.

The noise that Nettie is making is regular now, becoming an almost uninterrupted scream. So Katherine puts the knives back in the ewer of wine and returns to check on her. She slicks her hands with the

320

oil of roses, and she recalls her time with the midwife Beaufoy, and she slides her hands up under Nettie's sodden skirts along her parted thighs to her nethers and then she feels something she thinks perhaps should not be there. It is hard. She is tempted to knock on it, with her knuckles. Her fingers cannot get around it. Nettie is thrashing. The noise is extraordinary in the room, bouncing off the walls. It is a kind of hell. Jack is in tears now. He is holding Nettie's shoulders and caught between trying to calm her and begging Katherine to do something – but what can she do? This must take its course. But what is it that she can feel? It is smooth. It is not the elbow, or the leg. Nothing like that. Christ! She smiles at Jack. It is the baby's head. Thanks be to Jesus for that.

And then the giant wakes with a great roaring cough. He lies there in the bloody straw for a moment, staring up at his hands, which are chained to the wall, as if trying to piece the past together.

She and Jack exchange a look.

'Thomas!' she shouts.

Then the giant pulls on the chains. The links clang taut. He pulls them again. Harder. Still they clang taut. He does the same thing again. And again. On it goes.

'Stop it, you bloody simpleton!' Jack calls.

Thomas comes in and sees the giant is awake. He looks unsure what to do, and hesitates before reaching for one of the staffs propped against the wall by the chamber doorway: it seems Thomas cannot hit a chained man. But Jack has no qualm. He has a score to settle and he lowers Nettie still screaming to the ground and then takes the heavy staff from Thomas's grip and begins hitting the giant as if he were chopping wood. The blows are crisp, well timed, and they crack against the giant's arms, and the giant is driven back into the corner and withdraws into as small a ball he can manage, which only seems to anger Jack even more – and anyway he is getting his revenge for some terrible things done to him, because now he just hammers blows down on the giant's body, hitting him anywhere, a flurry of

clumsy smacks that resound through the room until he catches the
wall above the giant's head and the staff springs from his hands and
clatters to the floor. Then Jack starts kicking him. The giant is curled
up with his back to the wall, his arms across his face and head. He is
unmoving. At length Jack stops. He's red-faced, and his breathing
is ragged.

Nettie is managing to laugh despite her own pain.

'He is a devil,' Jack says.

Then Nettie shrieks again and all attention returns to her. Jack
slides down beside her and cushions her again. Katherine covers her
legs and then returns to John. The wind is got up and King Edward
is back with what she sent him for.

'Light the candles,' she says. 'Get the fire really going.'

She washes her hands in the warm wine, and then she starts by
tying John's arm off. She wraps the bowstring just above the muscle
three times, inserts a piece of wood in the loop and twists to tighten
it. The string bites into the flesh. She twists four times, and then stops
to watch. John Stump moves in his drugged sleep.

'Be ready with it,' she tells Thomas, but he already knows what
to do.

She watches the arm below the string and sure enough it starts to
fatten and turn rosy. She does not want that. It means the blood is
still pumping into the limb, but not flowing out. She quickly untwists
the length of wood and slackens the ligature. The arm subsides. She
twists again. Six turns this time, quickly. Then waits. She can hear
the men breathing as they watch. Now she has it right. The arm stays
slim, and white. The blood is stopped both ways. Good. She checks
her knives, saws, needle and thread once more, and asks Thomas to
soften the beeswax candle.

She is ready.

'Hold it,' she tells the handsome youth. 'Like this.' She bends the
arm. The smell escapes in a gust. Someone retches beyond the circle
of light and there is some laughter.

322

The handsome youth – she learns his name is Flood – crouches next to her and holds the arm up, wrapped in its grey woollen blanket sleeve, and she begins the cut above the elbow, below the ligature. The knives – the Earl of Warwick's knives – are sharp and slice through the skin and muscle of John's arm easily enough, now that the muscle is slack. When the thick tough band is sawn through, the arm flops. Flood lets it lie. There is a splurge of blood: half a jugful perhaps. She wonders if she should tie the blood vessels before she cuts the bone, but decides to get rid of the arm because the stink is turning her stomach.

Nettie is shouting now.

Katherine takes up the butchers' saw. It needs cleaning, she thinks.

'Who has the urine?' she asks.

No one. She had forgotten the need.

'Can anyone – piss on this? To clean it? I need the blade at least rinsed in urine.'

The gathered men must defer to King Edward. He shrugs.

'I am sure I can help,' he says, and he takes the saw and steps away and they sit and stand there, in their circle of wavering candlelight, listening to King Edward pissing on a saw.

'There,' he says, bringing it back and proffering the dry handle. She takes it and sets its teeth into the pink bone.

'Are you ready with the wax?' she asks.

Thomas nods, and she starts to saw. It does not take long. Perhaps fifteen cuts forward and backward. Blood gurgles in the plughole of the bone. Then she is through. She pushes the lump of lower arm away from the cut with the flat of the saw blade.

'Take it,' she tells Flood, who gathers it in its blanket and steals away towards the battlements.

'Wax,' she says, and Thomas passes the dish in which the wax is hardening again around the strip of its wick. She washes her hands in rose oil and then scoops up a few fingerfuls and moulds a ball around the wick that will prove a plug for the hole. She stoppers the bone with the long wick hanging out, and then she fishes in the ewer for the thread and the silver needle.

The noise from Nettie in the tower is now a constant bellow of effort. It is like listening to a man hauling an ox from a ditch.

'Is the poker hot?'

One of the men takes it from the brazier. It is dull red. Not as hot as a smith might wish, but it will do for this. She tells him to leave it, and another man to bring the candle closer, and in its uncertain light she concentrates on stitching off the fatter tubes that lie around the chunk of John's muscle.

'Poker,' she says, and there is a moment's confusion as the man holding it cannot pass it to her because she would burn herself, and nor can he pass her the cooler end because then he would burn himself. It is solved by moving the brazier nearer, which sends sparks up into the night air to be plucked away by the gusting breeze, and the constable tells a man to watch them. In the brazier's orange light, John is still slack-faced. The dwale is very, very potent, she thinks.

She takes the poker with a linen cloth and then bends over the stump and dabs at it, cauterising the smaller tubes, sealing them up with a hiss of meaty steam. It is a curiously intimate feeling, inhaling a man's burning flesh, and the men around her lean back to let the vapour escape without touching them. She has to reheat the poker twice before she is satisfied there is crust enough.

Then she pulls down the wrinkled sock of skin so that it hangs below the stump. She gives it a few careful turns around the candle wick, taking care not to unseat it from the bone plug; then she fishes out the needle and thread again and puts a few running stitches into the twist of skin before folding it over and adding more stitches, so that when it is done it looks very neat, with only the wick hanging free of the stitched flaps of the stump.

'By God,' someone breathes. 'And that is it?'

'Practice makes perfect,' she says, pleased with herself and the outcome. It ends almost logically, halfway between shoulder and elbow.

'Though, my God, what will it be like for him now?'

'He will fall off his horse, that is for sure.'

'He'll have to wipe his arse with his teeth.'

'Is that even possible?'

Katherine stands. Her knees are sore, her skirts bloody.

Jack calls urgently. He stands at the door of the tower chamber.

The men watch her stand, straighten her back, and then go to attend to Nettie.

No one says another word.

It is as if they are witnessing a miracle.

The baby is born in a welter of fluids and odd, fatty pastes that coat its slick little body. It is tinged blue for a bit, but it – she – has such a set of lungs on her that they are never worried that this means anything other than that the baby is merely tinged a bit blue. Katherine remembers the midwife tying off the cord, and she does so herself, and cuts it between the two ligatures as if the cord were a hank of linen, and then she wipes the baby with the rose oil from top to toe, cleaning her of all that basting. Then she wraps her in a length of clean linen and places her in Nettie's arms.

Nettie is tearful, fearful, sweaty and filthy, and exhausted by the labour, but she looks down and sees her tiny daughter's pickled face, and she smiles the sort of smile that brings tears to your eyes, and Jack is still holding her, and he too is smiling as if the girl ('We will call her Katherine') is also a miracle.

Nettie makes to get up, but it becomes clear that she is not finished yet, and Katherine must return to her skirts to deliver the rest of the matter that comes with childbirth. When that is finally done, and she has gathered everything up in a great blood-sodden pile of linen and straw and whatever else it is, she washes Nettie with rose oil – she is running very low – and waits to see if there will be any unwarranted bleeding.

There is none.

'Thanks be to God,' she says.

'Amen.'

She goes to see John Stumps. He is still insensible but someone – King Edward? – has made him comfortable: he lies under a blue cloak with white fur under his chin that moves with his breath, so that she can see instantly that he lives. Thomas is there, in a ring of men by King Edward's side, just as if they were equals of long standing, and King Edward is making light and easy talk with them and she sees they have all become friends through this long night. They turn to her and King Edward says:

'Here she is!'

And then he shouts down into the yard for warm wine and fresh rolls to be brought this instant, by God.

PART FIVE

Before the Nativity of the Blessed Virgin Mary, Late Summer, 1469

22

'To think of it here,' Thomas says. 'Right under King Edward's nose.' He swings the bag in which the ledger is kept from his shoulder and pats it.

'And you are certain he does not know?'

Thomas is not sure.

'I think he knows something is going on, but also knows enough not to enquire too deeply.'

'He might have heard rumours?' Katherine supposes.

She is lying in the bed that Thomas had, until she arrived, shared with Flood. Flood has been evicted and sent to another room in another part of the west range. She has had a bath, with hot water and soap. Thomas insisted on it, not because she was particularly filthy (though she was) but because – well, once she was in, it was obvious. She had never had a hot bath, ever.

'To think King Edward has one of these every day,' she had whispered.

After that she had slept for more or less two days. A priest had come – King Edward's chinless confessor – to satisfy himself that she was not some devil incarnate, and she had thought he had come to reclaim her for the priory. She had shouted at him that it was no longer there, that it had burned down and everyone was dead, and the Prioress had fled in pursuit of the devil. Thomas had had to usher the priest out while she 'collected herself', which meant she fell back into dreamless sleep for another day.

'Where is Rufus?' she'd asked when she woke that second time. And Rufus had come padding silently into the room and they had wrapped their arms around one another and stayed like that for what seemed an age. She'd asked him if he too had had a bath and he'd nodded solemnly and Thomas had made a face behind his back to indicate that he had not spoken for all that time.

'And Nettie does well?' she had asked, and Thomas had told her she was already up and walking.

'She did not want to stay in that chamber a moment longer than need be. And the baby – she is well, too. Very loud.'

Katherine had nodded.

'And John?'

'I am giving him the dwale,' Thomas had told her, 'and inching out the wick, as before, and he is bearing the pain better than last time. You remember how he cried out for that spirit of Ralph Grey's?'

And mention of Sir Ralph Grey, the long-dead constable of Bamburgh Castle, is what has brought them on to the subject of the ledger that now sits between them again: a resurfaced problem that won't go away.

'What shall we do with it now?' he wonders. 'Can we just – burn it? Get rid of the bloody thing?'

She has been thinking about this.

'Riven will have told the Earl of Warwick about it, won't he? That he has scent of it?'

Thomas sighs wearily.

'Probably,' he says. 'Probably.'

'So the Earl of Warwick will come for it, won't he?' Katherine goes on. 'He will have heard of Riven's death and might suppose someone – King Edward – murdered him to keep him quiet. Which will only confirm the ledger's power, confirm its strength in his mind. It will make him mad for it.'

'But he can hardly ask King Edward for it? Can he?' Thomas asks. 'If he thinks King Edward has it?'

That is a good point.

'But so many people know of it now,' she says. She is thinking aloud. 'And they are all his, aren't they? They may have hated Edmund Riven, but they do still love the Earl of Warwick, and they know King Edward doesn't have the ledger, don't they? So the Earl might come to believe that both he and the King are looking for it. And that it is here somewhere. And so he will come for it himself.'

'True.' Thomas sighs. He is looking very well, she thinks: clean, well fed, fresh-faced, but now unhappy at what this must mean: leaving this place. He sits on the edge of her bed and pinches his nose between his eyes.

'So?' she asks.

'So we must be gone before the Earl comes,' he confirms.

'When is he due?'

'I will find out,' he says. 'Bellman will tell us. He is a good man.'

'Then we will have some notice at least.'

'Yes,' he supposes.

The thought of taking to the roads again so soon, and after such glimpses of comfort and ease as they have had, is too much. She shuts her eyes to keep back the tears.

Later he comes back without Rufus.

'I still cannot believe he is dead,' she says before he can say anything. 'And that I killed him.'

Thomas looks at her very seriously, as if she might be feeling guilty.

'He deserved it a thousand times over.'

He does not need to remind her that Riven was also about to gut him.

'I know,' she says. 'I know, but still. It is unbelievable that he is gone, that he menaces us no more.'

It is like a great weight lifted from her. She can breathe.

'What happened to Liz?' Thomas asks.

She gives him a few details, but she has not thought about Liz since the girl gave her the knife with which to kill Riven. Now that she does, she still cannot decide what she feels about her. She betrayed them, and Rufus, but she had her reasons, and when she agreed to do it, she had no knowledge of them; and her tears that night when she had given her the knife were, surely, genuine enough.

'So she is gone back to her father and sisters at Senning?'

'I suppose.'

Then he asks about the priory's destruction, and he is incredulous.

'So it is true? What you said? They are dead? Every one of them?'

'Not the Prioress. She fled.'

He smiles.

'In pursuit of the devil, you said?'

'Did I? I have been having some strange dreams.'

'But if they are all dead, and the place is burned to the ground, then you will never – never find out who you are.'

Not this again, she thinks.

'I know who I am.'

'Well, yes, but you know what I mean.'

'There is still the Prioress. She lived through it, they said, and was sent home, or to some other priory. Wherever she came from. If anyone still knows, it is her. But perhaps I was never meant to know, not even for Rufus's sake.'

Thomas shakes his head. He has never truly been able to accept she does not care, but she really does not. It is unfathomable to her why anyone would care about something that would never make a difference. It is all in the past. To cleave to it would be to give some-thing else – someone else, perhaps – power over your person they do not deserve.

'Must we go?' she asks.

He nods sadly.

'But where?' she asks. 'Where can we go?'

'What about Marton?' Thomas asks. 'Could we go back there? Would Isabella have us?'

She has not had a moment to tell him about cutting Isabella's cataract without asking her first, and then being caught at it by those two sons. Thomas will not want to hear of that now, so she shakes her head.

'It would not do us any good, anyway,' she says. 'Even though Riven's dead, if Warwick wants the ledger he will find Liz, and Liz knows where to find Marton, and so if we went there, he will find us in a trice.'

He nods.

'So,' he says. 'Somewhere else.'

'But where?'

In the event they do not have to think very fast, because King Edward will not permit them to leave him, and so they must sweat out that August in Middleham, waking each day and coming to Mass to hear Bellman admit that the Earl of Warwick has sent message to say he is delayed, and is not yet ready to join his king.

'So we may go to him?' King Edward asks.

'Ah, no, your grace, he bids you rest at peace here until he comes.'

And both men laugh at the situation and at Bellman's discomfort, for the King has found the pace of life at Middleham to his taste: he insists on hunting every day save Sunday, when he joins Thomas and the men of the castle and the village in the butts south of the Earl's formal gardens. He is not the worst bowman there, Thomas tells Katherine, but he is far from being the best. He is slow, for one, and clumsy at nocking, and though he is reasonably accurate in the butts when he can see how far he must shoot, when it comes to shooting on the rove, when they all walk around the parkland shooting three arrows apiece at specific marks, he spends more time looking for his arrows than anyone else, for they are often spread far and wide, and usually short.

Still, he is relentlessly cheerful and easy among his subjects, and he mocks himself and his own inadequacy before any man can say a word; and anyway, everyone there knows that shooting arrows is not everything. They have seen him ride with the hounds, and throw a spear, and some men there saw him at Towton, and no man doubts him.

There remains no sign of the Earl of Warwick, which King Edward puts down to cowardice, but Flood tells them that the Earl is occupied trying to coerce parliament to meet – or not meet – to do his business and there is a trouble everywhere, in every part of the country, with everyone taking advantage of King Edward's absence to pursue their own claims to their neighbours' property.

'My lord of Warwick is not the King. That's the thing, you see?' Flood explains.

Flood also says that King Edward thinks the people do not understand why, having risen in support of Warwick's ousting of King Edward's infamous and unpopular favourites, and this having been achieved, with them – the favourites – being dead or exiled, King Edward remains a captive. It makes King Edward laugh.

'Bloody Warwick. See how he likes ruling a kingdom filled with bastards,' he says.

Meanwhile Nettie has regained her strength and Katherine is slowly reducing the amount of the dwale that John Stumps is allowed. He sits up now, pale but with no sign of the fever that nearly killed him the first time she cut an arm off, and he can touch his stumps together.

'You are like a seal,' Jack tells him, and he barks like those they used to see below Bamburgh. John says nothing, because King Edward laughs.

Being there with King Edward has, Thomas tells Katherine, been odd. For a while he had no name for the sensation he was feeling as they rode up into the hills behind the castle and hunted various animals with various other animals, until one day, when they were riding back after a long hunt, trailing behind them a line of horses over which were heaped the corpses of a number of deer, wild boar and badger, Flood turned to him and said the day had been fun.

'Fun?' Thomas had repeated.

'Ha!' Flood had laughed. 'You say it as if you have never heard the word!'

But there was more to it than just fun. Every day he has seen Katherine and Rufus resting and recovering from the rigours and uncertainties of their recent travels. They have eaten well and slept well and there were no chores to do, so that the two of them spent their time with Nettie and her baby, walking in the Earl's garden, playing gently, their idleness enforced by a guilty Bellman not certain of their social status. After a week, Thomas overhears Rufus speaking very quietly to Katherine, though he had still not said a word to anyone else.

But these days, when it is believed that kingfishers might roost on calm seas, cannot last, of course. Messengers come and go, clattering across the bridge with missives for King Edward and for the constable. There are too many tensions pulling at King Edward, pulling at one another, unseen forces working from as far away as Rome, London, Calais, and even back in the north where a name from the past, Sir Humphrey Neville of Brancepeth – the man whom everyone hated in Bamburgh Castle when it was besieged – has risen again in support of old King Henry.

This is a rebellion the Earl of Warwick cannot suppress without the King's moral authority and so he sends word for the constable, and Bellman comes to tell King Edward that it has been decided he is free to go about his business, though could he first please issue these commissions of array, so that troops may be raised in the Midlands to come north to quell Humphrey Neville and his rebels?

'And in all this time, he's never come to meet my eye!' King Edward scoffs of the Earl of Warwick. 'In all this time!'

'Soon be home, I reckon,' Flood says. 'By Christ, I cannot wait to see my wife.'

Thomas nods. He hopes it will be a happy reunion. He himself hardly knows where he should go next.

'Could we go back to Marton?' Jack asks.

And Katherine shakes her head, and they all want to know why not, and so now she must tell them. They listen in silence, even when she describes cutting the eye, and when it is over, Jack starts laughing sibilantly.

'Mother of God, Katherine,' he says. 'This gift of yours! It is a double-edged blade!'

Katherine can hardly look at them for shame.

'Mother did right,' they hear a voice say. 'She only wanted Isabella to be able to see.'

It takes a moment to realise it is Rufus who speaks. He looks up at each of them in the eye, almost one by one. He is not shy, and nor is he challenging. He is just very clear about this. There are indigo circles under his dark eyes, and he looks elfin and otherworldly, and Thomas is half-proud of his son, half-frightened of him and for him.

The mood changes.

Jack says that he will take Nettie and his daughter back to Nettie's father and mother, who farm strips of land in a village near Marton, and he supposes he will stay there and help work the furlongs until something comes up.

'Perhaps I will go across the Narrow Sea and fight with that Duke of yours, John,' he says.

John says he thinks there will be plenty of fighting in this country, if that is what he wants.

'No,' Nettie says. 'That is not what he wants.'

She is holding their little pip of a daughter and Jack cannot but smile and agree.

'And what about you, Thomas?' John Stumps asks. 'What'll you do now?'

'We will go with Jack and Nettie as far as Lincoln,' Thomas tells him, 'but from there – well. I don't know. We must throw ourselves on the goodlordship of William Hastings, I suppose. What about you?'

And he thinks again what it will be like for John Stumps, with no arms.

'I could become a monk,' John says. 'The sort that only pray. You do not absolutely need hands to pray.'

'Can you read?'

'Letters? Words? No.'

There is a long silence, and Thomas sees John does not trust himself to speak.

'Come with us,' he says. 'I do not know where we are going, or what we're to do, but stay with us. We will see to you. Take care of you.'

23

It is only on the day before they are to leave for Lincoln that Thomas receives an answer to the letter he sent to Katherine at Marton Hall just before she came to the castle, which he had entrusted to Flood, and had then forgotten about. When Katherine sees him being handed it by the boy, she flushes red. He breaks the dab of wax holding the edge and unfolds it.

It is from Isabella.

'Is it in her hand?' she asks.

'Yes,' he tells her, for he recognises her shapely letter Ts, and Katherine sits back, lets her shoulders droop and squeezes her eyes tight shut.

'Thanks be to God,' she murmurs. 'What does it say?'

Thomas reads. Isabella first commends herself to him with all her heart and trusts that God keeps him well. She tells him his letter arrived at Marton in the second week after the Assumption, and that she was pleased to receive it brought by a cloth merchant, from whom she bought a length of finest scarlet in addition to a half-pound of best pins. She has been pleased to hear that God has spared Thomas the divers hazards that may be encountered on any field of war, with which she has some intimacy, having buried two husbands who were not so blessed. She was pleased to hear that Thomas is with his grace King Edward, who has likewise avoided such torments, and that his grace King Edward now does well under the care of his lordship the Earl of Warwick. She is sending this letter with the self-same merchant in the hope that it might reach him at Middleham at speed.

'Is that it?' Katherine asks. She takes it from him. She looks at it closely, then at Thomas. She is disappointed.

'She is alive at least,' Thomas says. 'That is something. You are not a murderer. Or not of Isabella, at least. Not yet.'

Katherine does not smile.

'And look,' he goes on. 'She can see well enough to write, so your cutting must have worked.'

'But why has she said nothing about us? About me? About her eyes? About Marton?'

'Perhaps there is another message to come?'

And there is. It arrives the next day, at dawn, brought by the white monk on a pony from Jervaulx, along with many others for King Edward sealed with chunky coins of wax. This one is much longer, and time has been taken, so Thomas imagines she sent this the next day.

Again Isabella recommends herself to Thomas with all her heart, and trusts that God continues to keep him safe. She then tells him that his wife — may God also keep her safe — has left Marton Hall, with a job only half done, and should it be within his powers to find said wife, she would be forever in his debt if he might persuade her to return to Marton to do whatever she did to the one eye, to the other. And, she writes, though she has no right to ask such a thing, and though she has prayed to God to forgive her for not having done as well by Thomas and Katherine as she might have hoped, she says this last favour is a matter that might be best resolved before Martinmas, since, she writes, that is when she will be quitting Marton Hall.

'She is leaving Marton!' Thomas tells the others as they gather in the bailey before the northeast gate.

There are gasps, and claims of incredulity.

'No!'

'Why?'

Thomas reads on. Isabella is doing so because, despite her sins of neglect in regard Thomas and his family, she has been truly blessed by God: she intends to renounce her state of avowal and to marry again – for the last time, she sincerely hopes. This time her husband is a knight with property in the south. She trusts Thomas will bless her in this union, and, though she knows it will bear no fruit, she avers that her new husband is an upright and Christian soul, beloved of God, and she welcomes the prospect of his consoling presence, since, she writes, she found the divers privations of widowhood burdensome beyond all anticipation.

'She is getting married!' Thomas tells them all. 'To a Sir John Ffytche, of the County of Dorset.'

Again there is astonishment, but Katherine had expected such. Thomas tells them what Isabella says of him.

'It sounds as if it has worked nicely for her,' Katherine says. 'And at least she will be away from those sons of hers.'

'And she will make no mistake when she murmurs his name,' Jack laughs.

'But I wonder how it came about? And what is in the bargain for this Sir John Ffytche? Taking on an elderly widow?'

No one knows, but Thomas feels the loss of Marton as a physical blow, a scooping out of something from within him. He is not alone. Every mouth is downturned. It has been their home for many years. In Katherine's case, her only home. That it was already lost to them seems not to matter. They wanted Isabella to be there, at the very least. They wanted to know that whatever happened to them, some things carried on the same. But no. It is not to be. Someone else will be sleeping in their houses, tilling their fields, gathering around that chimney.

'So that is that,' he says.

'We should buy it,' Jack says. 'Gather all our money together and just buy it.'

He shows them that he has a silver groat.

'We'd need a bit more than that,' John says.

'We will need at least five hundred marks,' Jack says. 'That is what one of those boys of hers reckoned they might get for it.'

Thomas feels sick.

'Well,' he says, 'how long would it take you to earn that on your shilling a day from the Duke of Burgundy, John?'

John looks bleak, but Katherine laughs.

'Some come back from war as rich men,' she says.

'Not us,' Thomas says. 'And not in England.'

'No,' she agrees, 'but remember John Watkins's story?'

Thomas doesn't even remember John Watkins.

'The man who let us stay in his hall after you were out of your wits with the sun that day in the hills.'

'What was the story?' Thomas asks.

And then she tells them all of how John Watkins and a few of Lord Montagu's men had found Sir William Tailboys hiding with old King Henry's coin in a coal mine after the battle of Hexham, and as she speaks, Thomas hears a pounding in his ears. He feels burning heat throughout his body, and Jack is likewise staring at her, open-mouthed and flushed, as if he has some sickness.

'Say that again,' he says, and so she does.

When she has finished, he is staring at her, his eyes round, his cheeks red.

'Why didn't you – tell me before?' he asks.

'I did not want to upset you,' she says.

In fact she feels guilty that she has shared it with him now, since no good can come of envy.

'But we saw them,' Thomas says. 'We saw Tailboys and his men after Hexham. In the woods. They rode past while we were in that hovel. At dawn. Do you not remember?'

She shakes her head. She does not recall. Of course not, otherwise she would have said something. But why is he so excited?

'Because one of the mules slipped and fell down a mine hole! Right where we were! And Tailboys nearly killed the man responsible. One of the mules carrying the money! It will be down there still!'

*

They ride out of Middleham behind King Edward, watched by the townspeople just as they had when Thomas and the King arrived a month earlier. Their attempts to exert any independence of their own have been quashed by King Edward, who insists they stay with him.

'You will be paid, I'm sure,' he tells them, 'and we all want to see our wives and dogs and so on, but the commonweal must be tidied up, eh? And I am keen to show bloody old Warwick that I can do what he cannot, for all his ability to shuffle dockets.'

King Edward has already sent for his brother Gloucester, his brother-in-law Suffolk, and his various earls and barons, including Arundel, Northumberland, Essex and Mountjoy, and, of course, William Hastings. He is keen to show that he is not going against this rebellion underpowered as he did the last.

'They are bringing their men to York,' he tells them as they ride. 'I will show that smiling shit-snake my lord of Warwick that King Edward of England is not too grand to learn his lessons in the hope that he bloody well learns his.'

All the uncertainty has flown from him. His shoulders are back; his smile is wide. Perhaps this captivity has actually been good for him, Thomas thinks. Not everyone is comfortable being in his company though. John seems to freeze when he speaks, because he was not there with King Edward as the others were when his arm was being cut off, and so not did not bond with him as a brother in that peculiar adversity; while Jack tries to make King Edward laugh with jokes that fall flat for being too familiar. Katherine stiffens and exudes doubt and suspicion whenever he comes close, but, far from being offended, he seems to understand, sympathise even, and after a few moments in his company she too relaxes, so after a while it comes to be normal that they are talking to King Edward of England.

He turns and addresses them now, twisted in the saddle of his prancing white stallion.

'Sirs,' he says. 'There is nothing so poor in all the world as a king who is on his own, and so I wish you fellows to be my fellows. You will forever have a place at my side, Thomas Everingham, for you bring me great luck, through every grind of Fortune's Wheel. And I require especially you, Goodwife Everingham, for your skill as a surgeon is enough to shame the great Galen himself. And you, Jack Whatever-your-name-is, I have seen pull a bowstring back further than your ear, so you are most welcome on my flank. And John Stumps, do not despair. I need a new jester. You would have your work cut out, it is true, since you are a stranger to merriment as such, but that is perhaps understandable, given your situation, and there cannot be a man in all England – in all Christendom – to match your impersonation of a seal.'

So they must ride with King Edward, back to York again, east and then south on that road, and then east again, with the river on their left. There is no choice.

'Besides,' Thomas tells them, 'Brancepeth lies between here and Hexham, so we would have to get past the rebels anyway. At least this way we march with an army, and thus in safety, and we will be paid for our time. Sixpence a day, since we are on horses.'

But they are no longer interested in sixpences.

'By Christ, Thomas, what do you think the chances are?'

Every time he is reminded of it, he feels a constriction or a flutter in his chest. Already his fingertips are fizzing, and he can hardly sit in his saddle.

'We can only hope,' he says.

'And are you sure the mule had money in its sacks?'

He cannot say for sure, but he remembers Tailboys's fury as the mule went down the hole.

'Look,' he tells Jack. 'I don't know. I don't know, do I? It is more than five years ago. Someone might have started work in the mine at any time.'

'How likely is that?' Jack asks.

'I don't know! I have never mined coal. I do not know anyone who has.'

'Do you think you will be able to find it again? Do you remember that forest? It was vast.'

'We can only try,' Thomas says. 'We can only try.'

'But what are the chances?'

'Oh, for the love of God.'

They see the minster and the spires of York's other churches as it grows dark, but King Edward is expected, and the men of the Watch have braziers and torches lit, and the gates stand open, and there are crowds along the road's side to cheer him as he rides through the city and across the bridge to the outer bailey of the castle. And at the foot of the great mound of Clifford's Tower, there are all King Edward's nobles, including his youngest brother, and even William Hastings, and King Edward spurs his horse forward and jumps from the saddle to embrace them; and Thomas and Katherine and Jack and Nettie and John are left with Flood, hungry and saddle-weary, sitting in the darkness as the pool of light that ever surrounds King Edward withdraws and follows him up the steps, in through the great doors in the castle gatehouse, and is then gone.

'Well,' Thomas says. 'Here we are again.'

They find stables for their horses and board within the castle, and the next days are passed watching messengers come and go, and waiting to be allowed to go north. Hastings summons Thomas on the second day, and Thomas is fearful this will be about the ledger.

'He will have spoken to King Edward,' Thomas says. 'King Edward will have told him about that night, and he will want to know why Riven was questioning Jack and John.'

'What will you say?' Katherine asks.

'I had hoped you'd tell me,' he says. He is serious.

'Well,' she says. 'You could tell him that Riven took them because they were asking the same sort of questions he was. You could suggest that he thought they might be after the ledger too, and that he wanted to know on whose behalf they searched.'

He nods.

'You'd best let me take it then,' she says.

She holds her hands out for the ledger and he takes it off his shoulder and passes it over. He feels reluctant. Now that he has been reconciled with it, it is comforting on his back again. But he does so, and he takes Jack with him, just in case – though in case of what, he does not know.

In the event, Hastings is pleased to see him, and greets him like an old friend. First he apologises that they are unable to return to Senning.

'As soon as he could, my lord of Warwick confirmed the attainder had been reversed. There was nothing I could do or say.'

Thomas is so relieved Hastings does not want to talk about the ledger, or the events of the night in the southeastern tower, that he waves aside Hastings's apology, and when Hastings goes on to ask him to take command of more than a hundred of his men, should they need to take the field, he is pleased to comply.

'We should not see too much of the rebels,' Hastings says. 'King Edward has issued a general pardon for all commotions, save the leaders, so they will melt away, by and by. You may reassure Goodwife Everingham on that score.'

He always mentions Katherine, whenever they speak, and it unsettles Thomas. It is as if Hastings knows something about her that he does not. And her attitude to him is odd, too. Still. Hastings gives him a heavy purse of silver coins with which to buy such accoutrements of war as might be needed, and once again there are livery vests to be worn, and once again Katherine becomes beady-eyed at the sight of the black boar's head on Thomas's chest.

'It was the only way,' he tells her.

They ride out three days later, in companies, in a long column of men belonging to King Edward's brother Gloucester and the other nobles who've gathered in York, on roads that have by now become wearyingly familiar. Katherine rides with Rufus on the saddle before her, and Thomas rides with John's horse on a lead rein. John is humiliated, and has to work hard to stay upright, but there is nothing else for it unless he wants to walk.

'How many times have we been up here?' Thomas asks Katherine.

She hardly knows, of course. She is too worried about Rufus, who seems to have retreated within again. He moves flightily, as if under threat, and when he walks he is on tiptoes, and she is freighted with guilt for having let him see all that he has seen, but Thomas tells her there are plenty his age who are already drummer boys, and who carry arrows to bowmen in battles.

'Imagine the things they have seen,' he says. He does not add that they are usually half-wild things, undernourished and sickly, and most times short-lived.

They move up into the Vale of Mowbray, past the fields in which they met Horner again, wearing the livery jacket they were given by the charcoalers, and then past the exact wood where the charcoalers must still be at work, silent, secret save for the pale smoke of their underground fires, and Thomas asks Katherine if she would like to visit them, see if they have any more teeth they need pulling?

'It seems an age ago, doesn't it?'

At nights they hobble their horses and sleep by the sides of the tents that those who can afford them have brought, and King Edward's brother Gloucester organises the pickets. There is plenty of bread and ale at this time of year, and the days are still warm, if the nights are less so, and in the morning they wake wet with dew. The second day, they smell bitter smoke of burning rushes and wattle and daub, and suppose this to be the southern limit of the rebellion. There are fresh-dug graves and a definite change of atmosphere as wary women and children watch them ride by. Their men are elsewhere.

'Feels like we're invading their lands, doesn't it?' Jack asks.

They see five bodies hanging from a roadside oak. One of them is Taplow, wearing only his braies, recognisable because of his oddly cut hair. Flies hum in the air. Thomas stops to consider him. He is covered in nicks and scars, the story of a lifetime of trouble there to be read in his skin. His face is blown up, purpled, and his tongue is out. The man with the cobble nose is there, too, next to him, pigeon-toed, his skin drooping like lard in sunshine.

Katherine clutches Rufus to her so that he cannot see the corpses, and they ride by.

'It was a matter of when, not if, I suppose,' Thomas supposes.

Men start to join them, in dribs and drabs, standing at the roadside, waiting permission. None wear livery. They are obviously Sir Humphrey's men, deserting in numbers now, and no one is surprised, or even holds their sins against them.

'I suppose we have all been there before,' Jack says.

Sir Humphrey Neville and his brother Charles soon see the way this is going, and they desert their remaining men and try to escape to Scotland, but they are as unpopular in their own lands as they were in Bamburgh and they are betrayed before they get ten miles from their abandoned camp. Brought before King Edward in Darlington – the town that Liz would never visit – he has them executed after hearing Mass together at St Cuthbert's, and men think that only fair.

Thomas and Katherine take Rufus elsewhere, walking against the crowds who flock to see it done, and afterwards William Hastings calls for him, worried they have already gone back south now that the rebellion has been crushed so easily, and Thomas finds him alone in a chamber in the White Hart on the road south. He looks sombre, despite everything, and it is obvious he has now heard King Edward's story of the night they delivered the baby and cut John's remaining arm off.

'It is a pity your Sir Edmund Riven is dead, Thomas,' Hastings begins.

Thomas shrugs.

'No,' Hastings agrees. 'Well. Not a pity. But I should have liked the chance to ask him a question or two. Did you know what he was doing in Middleham?'

'He was looking for the same thing as you asked us to find. A book. That is why he took Jack and John and questioned them, because he heard we were asking the same questions, looking for the same thing.'

Hastings looks at Thomas. Can he tell he is lying? Thomas cannot be sure.

'What did they tell him?' Hastings asks.

'Nothing,' Thomas says. 'They had nothing to tell him. Which is why one of them has lost his remaining arm, and the other's wife was delivered of a baby while she was in chains.'

Not that the last is quite true, but Hastings is abashed. He is a good man, after all.

'I am sorry for their troubles,' he says. 'I will make it up to them, insofar as I am able.'

Thomas does not ask about Hastings's bloodhound, the one coming after the ledger from the other end, and nor does Hastings mention him either, and Thomas prays that with Riven gone, the matter of the ledger is dead. Hastings thanks Thomas for his service, and releases him from it for the time being, and reassures him of his own goodlordship, and Thomas is so mightily relieved he is grinning as he pumps Hastings's hand, and he promises he will be there for him whenever he should need.

'Let us pray it will not be for some time,' Hastings says, extracting his hand from Thomas's palm.

Thomas is exultant. Now that there is peace between King Edward and the Earl of Warwick, Hastings has let the search for the ledger drop. Thomas breathes deeply, and feels wonderfully unencumbered. Does it mean they are finally free of it? That they might even return to Marton, to return the ledger to its place and leave it there undisturbed, to be forgotten?

*

When he returns to his inn to find Katherine, Jack has everyone mounted up and ready to ride. They are itching with excitement to be gone in search of the dead mule in the forests of Tynedale.

'Come on,' Jack calls. 'Come on!'

They heave John into his saddle and leave Darlington, which really wasn't so bad, and they follow a path that hugs the feet of the hills to the west. They ride for the rest of the day. The countryside is bitter barren up here, with berms of spoil from coal mines like the burial mounds of the ancients, and the heather in the hills is fading from purple to ochre. In the late afternoon there is something in the light that makes them know they are into autumn. Still though, they have much to look forward to, literally, and Jack rides at the front with his wife and daughter with him on his horse, peering ahead, itching for the forest to blot the skyline.

That happens on the second day's ride, after another night in the open, when they are told by some friars that the town on the ridge ahead is indeed Hexham.

'Odd, being here again,' Jack says.

They ride past the old battlefield, from where Thomas ran, and then cross the bridge, which they'd last seen jammed with troops fleeing the rout, and the water below is quite low at this time of year, and then they are in among the trees on the road that leads up the hill towards the town. Ahead the gates are open and there is a wary Watch who want to know their identities, loyalties and purpose. It is assumed they are rebels, but their accents, from the south, betray them, and there is some suspicion and confusion, though they hardly look threatening: two men capable of bearing arms, perhaps, a man with no arms, two women, a child and a baby. Eventually the story of their travelling to Alnwick in search of a man who owes them money is believed.

'But we must go careful,' Katherine says. 'If anyone takes it into their head to accuse us of anything, we are done for.'

They spend the night in an inn below the abbey and while Thomas thinks of Horner watching the Duke of Somerset having his head

349

chopped off in the market square beyond, Jack and John bicker good-naturedly about the money they think they will find the next day, and they start in with the questions he – Thomas – cannot possibly answer, such as how much he thinks will be there, and whether it will be in gold nobles or silver groats.

The next morning they are up before dawn, ready to ride out at first light, and are across the bridge and into the forest beyond almost before Rufus knows he is awake. Thomas scans the side of the road, trying to remember where the path diverged.

In the pell mell of the scattering of Somerset's men after the rout of Hexham, they'd come hurtling across the bridge, terrified they'd be skewered by Montagu's prickers, who'd been let loose to do their worst on their fleeing enemy. He and Jack and John Stumps had led a woozily pregnant Katherine along this road northwards until they'd decided to get off the road, and they'd seen a path through the woods that looked unpromising, the sort no one would think of using, and they'd taken it.

So now they are looking for it again. Is it that one? John shakes his head. Then that one, a little further on? Or that one? There is almost any number of paths and tracks leading off this road.

They stop. They argue about it. John's memory is so skewed he thinks the track led off the road to the east. Jack thinks this one ahead might be it. Thomas feels sure it was in a gulley. It is difficult in early autumn to see what was there in late spring, when the leaves were so vivid green. They decide this one might be the track, and venture down it, only to lose heart as the trees close in and it dwindles to nothing, and they must retrace their steps.

'At least no one's been down here,' John says, nodding at the unbroken cloth of leaves, disturbed only by deer and perhaps boar, but not man or horse. They regain the road north and ride up it over a hill and then down into a shallow valley through which a small stream runs.

'This is it,' Thomas and John say at once.

Now Jack is doubtful.

'Thought you said it was on the other side?'

'I'm sure now,' John says. Thomas is, too.

'But we left it, do you remember? To find somewhere to shelter for the night. So we have to keep a lookout for that too, even supposing this is the right one.'

Katherine sighs.

'I wish I had gone south now,' she says, 'or stayed in Hexham.'

They misadventure twice, coming to two dead ends. Along the third path they do at least find a coal mine, but it is not the right one. It is getting on towards the end of the afternoon when they find what they think they are looking for. There is a small trickling stream, and the path is quite steep, through dense foliage. Thomas feels his blood warm. This is it, he is certain. He swings his leg off his horse and the others do likewise, except Nettie, who clings to her baby as it suckles, and Jack leads them up the track behind.

'This is it! This is it!' John is suddenly sure, too.

They follow him, shouting and babbling with excitement, and they come to a clearing, wherein is a dark circle of a deep pit. The leaves form a dense layer, undisturbed for many a month at least, and beyond is the hovel in which they sheltered. This is it, all right.

They hobble their horses and both Jack and John rush to the mine's edge. They peer down.

'Well?'

'I can't see anything.'

Jack lies on his belly, with his head and shoulders over the edge of the hole.

'Be careful!' Nettie calls.

Thomas looks down into the hole, too. He can remember it all so clearly. The mules being driven by, with Tailboys screaming at his men, before hearing Montagu's soldiers on the track below. He wonders about Tailboys's men now. How did they ever think they would

351

evade capture? Their tracks were like way markers. It was almost as if they wanted to be caught.

He can hardly make out anything down there in the hole, where the soil and rocks are very black. How far is it down? He plucks a stone from its damp berth and drops it. Thirty feet? How are they to get down there? Of course they have not brought a rope.

In the end they use a tree: a beech that they finally bring down just before dark, hacking away at it with various blades and pushing it from its roots. Thomas and Jack drag it back down the slope and drop it down. It is just long enough, its bushy top above the lip of the hole.

Jack suggests they send Rufus down first, but Katherine will not have it, and once they have said not Rufus, they cannot say Jack, so it is up to Thomas. He climbs down backwards. The tree slips first, a jolt that nearly throws him. The sides of the shaft are crumbling black stones and soil. The tree bends under his weight. Without taking a step he is below the lip already. How will he ever get back up? We should have got a rope, he tells himself again. He lets his feet slide down the trunk to the next branch, and then the one after that. Some branches break and the tree lurches.

Jack tells him to hang on.

The darkness closes in on him, the walls seeming to circle around. He looks up. Three heads break the circle of light above, peering down at him. Various odd smells rise up. Something has died down here, he can tell, but how long ago? When he reaches the trunk of the tree he has to grip it with his legs and shuffle lower. If he looks down he can see the circle of light reflected in black pools of water. They can't be too deep since they are small, like fragments of glass in the bottom of a well. He slides off the tree and lands with both feet on a rough pile of something he hopes is dry. It is not. Thick green mud grips his boots.

'Can you see it?'

'Is it there?'

He takes up a slick black stick that stands clear of the water and stirs the murk. The base of the hole is perhaps five paces across, roughly round, thirty-five feet deep. Roots of trees protrude from the sides and its bottom is filled with all sorts of God knows what. Thomas pokes around in the muck. Nothing looks promising until he sees a smooth stretch of what he knows without knowing is green bone, just above the waterline. He looks closer: a skull, an eye socket. The mule. He plucks a boot from the muck and steps into deeper water. It is sharply cold, for being ever out of the sun, and it fills his boot and comes up to his knees, then his thighs. He wades three steps through the water. It is still and black and somehow denser than normal water, like a soup.

'Have you found it?' John calls.

'Is it there?' Jack shouts again. 'Is it?'

Thomas bends over the skull and estimates where the bags — if they are here — might be. There is a thick scum gathered at the water's edge around the bones, and the smell is cold and rich at the same time. He rolls up his sleeve and dips in his hand. He feels slime-covered things that part before his fingertips. He does not want to think what it might be. Flesh? Or rotten leather? Odd how one would be foul, while the other fine, when they are one and the same, only treated differently after death. He feels nothing more until he scrapes against something hard. A series of bars. The animal's ribs. At least he knows where he is now. The mule must have broken its neck in the fall. He feels carefully. His hands begin to numb to the wrists. The smell has changed, and the surface of the water is muddier where he has stirred things up. He takes his hands out and shakes the warmth back into them.

'What've you found? What's down there?'

He does not answer. He puts his hands back and starts sweeping forward. What is he feeling for? He doesn't quite know. How are coins carried? In small bags? A large bag? Loose? He feels something soft. A pile of matter. Do not think about it. He trawls his fingers

353

through. He is sure he can taste rotten mule in the air. Everything down here is in the process of breaking down, of being temporary, of returning to the earth.

And then, there, is the first feeling he has of something that is not natural, something that is solid and heavy, something that is not returning to the earth. His fingertips brush unyielding rough edges. He stops. Goes back. Picks at the thing. Isolates a seam and then tweaks it with his thumbnail and plucks it and it is—He holds it in his palm. Black. Diseased, somehow. Black and round as an old bloodstain, but heavy.

He rinses it in the dirty water. Scratches it with his thumb. His heart is thundering. It is a coin. He cannot tell from where it comes – if it is French or English – but when he runs his thumbnail over the black, it leaves a scrape of burnished gold.

'Ha!' he yells.

'What is it? What is it?' they all shout back. 'What've you found?'

'A coin,' he calls up. 'I've found a coin.'

There is a moment's pause.

'Only one?' comes Jack's disappointed voice.

'No,' Thomas says, more to himself. 'No. My God. There are hundreds of them. Hundreds and hundreds.'

24

It is just before noon on a day during the week after Christmas, and Katherine Everingham, with a new woollen cloak and a scarf at her throat, stands in the yard with her hand placed on her turbulent belly and watches Thomas and Rufus walking back up the road from the butts in the village. They are carrying their unnocked bows over their shoulders, a bag of arrows apiece, and two grey lurchers are trotting ahead with their noses pressed to the track.

She is wondering what her husband and son are talking about until she sees Thomas pointing at something in an oak tree before making a curious motion with his hands that she recognises as being the grinding of a pestle in its mortar. They are talking about oak galls and ink-making, she thinks, which pleases her: Rufus has not the makings of a bowman, even Thomas acknowledges that, so it is good to see him enquiring of his father after more scholarly subjects, such as letters and illuminations, at which she fondly imagines he will prosper.

She tightens the scarf around her throat and settles the cloak over her shoulders, and while she waits, she cannot stop her gaze drifting over the sawn ends of the wood in the stack, still well over half-full despite it beyond the year's turn. Each piece is a testament to their labour since coming back from the Northern Parts, rich beyond the dreams of avarice with all that gold.

To begin with none of them could believe it, since these things did not happen to people such as them. On that first day, after they'd found it, Thomas had climbed out of the mine shaft in the ground and – after some argument – they'd decided to leave the coins where they were, undisturbed under the blanket of murk, and they'd spent the night – once more – in the hut in which they'd once sheltered after the battle of Hexham. The next morning she and Jack had ridden back to the town and, with that single coin Thomas had brought up, bought all they needed and more besides: bags, rope, a new saddle, an extra mule. They returned to the forest to find the others gathered around the rim of the mine, and the next day Thomas and Jack went back down into the hole, and they began hauling up the crusted piles of filthy black coins and piling them in the leaves by its side. At first they danced with joy. Then, as the piles mounted, they stared at them with incredulity, and eventually they became uncomfortable as a subtle, deep fear took hold of each of them.

'Someone will rob us,' John said.

But no one did. They spent two days there while Thomas and Jack raked their fingers through the rich black waters to get every last coin, and then when at last they were bagged up and the mules were loaded, they rode south, cagey as cats, careful to appear not worth robbing. They travelled with pilgrims wherever possible, down through the Vale of Mowbray again where the Duke of Gloucester's men were busy, to York and then on to Gainsborough where they crossed the river, and thence finally to Marton.

Isabella had been waiting for them, having received Thomas's message, with her new husband at her side, and a patch over one blind eye. Katherine had thrown herself on her knees before Isabella and begged forgiveness for what she had done, but Isabella had lifted her up and kissed her and told her there was nothing to forgive.

'The sight in this eye comes from you, and from God,' she said, pointing to it, but despite the success of the cutting, she had become determined not to ask Katherine to cut the other eye, for just as the sight in the first was sent by God, so the blindness in the second was likewise His gift. She repeated that it was a penance for some sin of which she did not wish to speak, and she was certain that suffering blindness now would only shorten her time in purgatory, and so hasten her progress to a seat at the Lord's right hand. Katherine was grateful.

'I do not think I could do it again,' she later told Thomas. 'Or not successfully.'

It had always struck her that taking the pale disc of the cataract from the ball of the eye would have left a space within which any manner of humour might take residence and lead to permanent blindness. She was lucky, she thinks, that a good humour must have filled Isabella's, though she still has problems seeing clearly, she says.

When it came to dealing with Isabella's estate, Sir John Ffytche had been naturally suspicious at first, as of course anyone would be when a man such as Thomas produces such an amount of money, but William Hastings had vouched for him, and that – along with the lure of taking the money for himself – was reassurance enough for Ffytche. Before the lawyers' seals were dry, the coins had vanished into his own coffers to be transported south by a troop of heavily armed men in his livery.

With Isabella packed and gone, Marton Hall and its remaining estate was theirs at last. Jack and Nettie took over the old house that Thomas and Katherine had built, while John stayed in the hall with them and three servant girls that came up from the village, and it still comes as a shock to Katherine to wake every morning to find that she has the help of three women at her command. And they have needed their help. The work needed to restore the estate to what it once was has been hard and long, and it is yet unfinished. Dykes have had to be repaired, and furlongs have had to be drained again, and left to dry before they can be ploughed; woods have been coppiced for firewood, and for the poles they need to make the pens for the geese and the seven pigs they've bought and are keeping through the winter, and for the hovels they've started rebuilding with mud and straw dredged from the wet fields. Sheep have been bought in – the sort with forelocks and long wool – and the cow and two oxen and a donkey to lead them, as well as two ponies. They have restored the malt house and the dairy, and they have planted the garden with everything they will need for the year ahead.

Katherine has bought bolts of bright-dyed cloth from Lincoln, and clothes are made: jackets for Thomas and Rufus, a curious half-sleeved pourpoint for John, who complains that his stumps get cold, even in the mildest of weather, and dresses for the girls. She has made shoes, stitching the leather with a curved needle as well as any cord-wainer, and her family and servants now stand like soldiers, and all memories of the time when they walked with only the skin-thin soles of their boots between them and the bare earth are banished.

And in all that time they have heard nothing of King Edward, or of Lord Hastings, or, more crucially still, despite every great fear, the Earl of Warwick himself. It is as if she and Thomas have been for-gotten, or have slipped off the end of the world into the Lincolnshire mud, taking with them all rumour of the ledger. With each day the silence lasts, the more hopeful she becomes that it will last forever: that the days will become weeks, will become months, then years, and that she and Thomas will be permitted to live this life. That they'll be permitted to plan in advance, battling only the seasons and acts of God, rather than the random whims of madmen who will send them to fight again, in one guise or another.

It came as a shock to find herself here at last, with Thomas and Rufus, with a home of their own, of which no man may legally deprive them, on land of their own, from which no man may legally drive them. Every morning she is surprised to wake with the pros-pect of a day ahead furthering her own interests, rather than of seven, eight, nine, ten hours spent grinding for another man's profit, with the only reward at the end of it enough food to survive to do it all again the next day.

On top of all that, she is now with child again. An extra blessing from God.

And now Thomas and Rufus are in the yard, their faces pink with exercise and the cold, but they are well wrapped against it, and happy.

'Come in,' she tells them. 'You must be frozen through.'

Thomas asks how she is feeling and she rolls her eyes and pulls a face.

'Nettie is cooking,' she says, for she is unable to stand the smell of stewing meat, and has for the last two weeks lived on nothing but rye bread and ale. She lets them past, and turns and watches with an almost overwhelming sense of fraudulence — as if she does not deserve this happiness — her husband and her son hang up their coats and jackets, and unwrap the scarves, and hurry to crouch by the fire, shoulder to shoulder, to extend their palms to the flames. Thomas asks Nettie how Kate her baby is and Nettie groans and gives the contents of the pot a firm stab with the long stick. It is stewed rabbit they are served, with good fresh bread and ale, and more of the apples with withered skins they gathered in the autumn, and soon there will even be medlars.

After they have eaten Thomas and Katherine and Rufus go out into the yard where Jack has pulled down the tangles of pea haulm from the stables' rafters and they sit there on the logs, just where Sir John used to sit, and despite the cold they are content, all three of them in the low sunlight, going through the dried stalks, pulling out the peas for spring planting. When that batch is done, they walk with the dogs to the field under the poplars, carrying armfuls of the discard for the two ponies and the conker-brown cow. The animals come over to eat from Rufus's hands through the fence; he likes them very much, and he talks to them in his own language, and Katherine feels her heart overgrown in her chest, and she thinks that perhaps he has forgotten all the things he has seen in the last year, and that he will miraculously be left undamaged.

When they have fed the ponies and the cow, they walk along to find the sheep where they are nuzzling the new furze of grass in one of the higher fields. Thomas tells her he will have to get Jack to help him trim their nails, for they need that, this breed, but he says they are handsome sheep, and that their wool should fetch a decent sum at market, and so it will be worth it. And they stand awhile, the three of them, close enough to touch one another, their shadows very long on the mud beneath their boots, and she lifts her head to look around at what they have done, what they have made for themselves, and she feels solid, undentable, undimmable contentment.

But then Rufus cocks his head and looks over the heads of the sheep.

'Who's that?' he asks.

He points to the trees, and there, in among the trunks, two hundred paces hence, is a man on a horse, very still, just watching them, and when he sees they have seen him, he turns and slowly rides away.

And in an instant that contentment vanishes like mist under the sun, just as if it had never been.

A Note from the Author

Divided Souls is set in 1469, one of the more complex and peculiar years in English history, during which an Earl simultaneously had two Kings under lock and key, but about which such chronicles as survive are patchy and, even by the usual standards, comically confusing. So, to make any sense of the events, I've had to make a couple of bold assertions that may have struck you as improbable, or even ludicrous, and which I should explain.

The first real oddity occurs in the run up to the battle of Edgecote, in July, when Robin of Redesdale came surging down from the North. Why did King Edward dawdle so? No one really knows the answer to this, but though it is possible that he was led astray and given reports that underestimated the threat Robin of Redesdale posed, he seems to me to have been the sort of man who might be prey – up to that point at least – to overconfidence. And so I have imagined him not really bothering to send out scouts, and not really taking too much interest, always sure that when push came to shove – literally – he could beat any rebel army in battle. After all, was he not the victor of Towton?

The second inexplicable oddity occurs the night before the battle itself, when the Earls of Pembroke and Devon argued. It is known they did, but not precisely why. Some chroniclers suggest it was over a woman, and others that it was over accommodation. Now, since this is not what my novel is about, I have gone for the simplest explanation. As a keen camper I know how prized a flat pitch is, and so that is what I went for, since it made me smile. If at some point in the future we discover either of the Earls' diaries, though, and their explanation is wholly other, then I apologise in advance.

In my defence, the chroniclers at the time were far from certain of events themselves: 'Hearne's Fragment' in *Chronicles of the White Rose of York* suggests that Edward himself sent the army that defeated the Earl of Pembroke, while Polydore Vergil doesn't mention the Earl of Devon at all, but has two battles – one between Pembroke and Redesdale, and then another between Pembroke and the joint forces of Warwick and Clarence. Waurin places the battle in Tewkesbury.

Another unknown is under what constraints the Earl of Warwick held King Edward in Middleham in the summer of 1469, and, subsequently to that, under what conditions he let him go. I've imagined it as I have, since he was certainly not held as old King Henry VI was – in the Tower – and nor was there any sense that King Edward was not still the King, so he must have been treated as such and held in pretty good condition in what was, by the standards of the day, an extremely luxurious castle. Was it then just understood that he had to stay in Middleham? But that he could not summon his lords – men such as Lord Hastings, and his youngest brother the Duke of Gloucester – until the Earl of Warwick permitted him to do so? Again, my character Thomas would not have been privy to – or necessarily interested in – the arrangements, and since this book is about Thomas, not Edward, then I have simply gone for a largely unspoken understanding between King and Earl.

And as for King Edward's release, that too is speculation. Some say the Earl of Warwick needed King Edward's authority to help to suppress the rebellion of Humphrey Neville of Brancepeth, but can that really be true? The Earl of Northumberland could easily have crushed it, I am certain. Indeed, what was the Earl of Northumberland doing at the time? Keeping out of it? No one is quite sure of that either.

I have had to devise likely scenarios for the above so as not to hinder the flow of the novel, since these events are the backdrop – albeit an extraordinarily colourful one – to Thomas and Katherine's continuing adventures. However, I have not tweaked known fact (as far as I know) and my suggestions are at least possible, if not – now that I really think about the camping site argument – probable.

What I have glossed over is the debate about exactly who Robin of Redesdale really was, since his identity is unknown. I chose to do this for clarity's sake, and because to most men fighting, and to all the camp followers, and again, to Thomas and Katherine, I am sure it would not have made much practical difference. For what it is worth, most chroniclers think he was either John Conyers of Hornby, or his son, also, inevitably, John, or his brother, William, of Marske.

I also ought to explain the presence in *Divided Souls* of no-armed John Stumps, a character who might be presumed to cause more narrative problems than he solves, but who is an homage to a man called Tom Stumps, a faithful servant of the Paston family in their hour of crisis in 1469 when the Duke of Norfolk was besieging Caister Castle, and who claimed, despite his disability, to still be able to use a crossbow. How? Very well, thank you very much.

Another thing that might raise eyebrows is the idea of the Trent being tidal all the way to Nottingham. Sadly I have misplaced the reference to this, but it was, apparently, so. With fewer bridges the tide came all that way. Amazing.

Divided Souls leaves Thomas and Katherine in a moment of calm, though one that cannot last, and I imagine this is what England must have been like at the time. Having the Earl of Warwick as an enemy cannot have been a comfortable position for anyone. And on top of this, King Edward had troubles with his restive brother George, Duke of Clarence, as well as, across the sea, with his old enemy Margaret of Anjou and her son – the warlike Edward of Westminster – who were waiting, constantly nagging anyone with any money to finance an invasion of England.

Throughout the country it must have been an extraordinarily precarious time, with the old chains of feudal loyalty in broken pieces, with nothing much except military might yet to replace them, and so perhaps it was always going to kick off again, as inevitably it does, in book four of this series, in which Thomas and Katherine are to be dragged centre stage once more . . .

Toby Clements
June, 2016

Acknowledgements

Divided Souls has been easier to write than *Broken Faith*, but it has not been without its attendant frights, and I'd like to thank and name a few people who helped me out and on my way.

First, a leftover thank you to Ingo Hippisley, who took his red pencil to *Broken Faith* with such shaming acuity that I blotted the whole episode from my mind. Thanks Ingo. Second, as usual I owe a huge debt to the great professor David Allison who has been unstinting in his constructive criticisms, not only of the medical procedures that Katherine has to perform – and on which he is an expert – but on more or less everything else too – about which he also seems to be expert. Thank you so much David. I owe you a huge pint.

I should also like to thank my agent, Jim Gill, who has been fierce and funny, and, again, I would like to thank my editor Selina Walker who has performed another terrific feat of literary chiropractic to get my twisted narrative to stand on its own two feet. I must also thank Richenda Todd for her astonishing attention to detail and amazing ability to spot temporal infelicities. I'd like to thank Darren Bennett for his beautiful maps, and Beth Kruszynskyj for her tireless organisational skills.

More generally I'd like to thank those who are still awaiting their cheques-in-the-post (whom I will have to thank individually and in person so that they never learn the True Horror of the length of the list of my creditors) but whose day will come, I promise . . . and of course I'd especially like to those who have borne with me over the last year – particularly Kazza, Martha, Tom and Max. Thank you all.

'Magnificent. An historical tour de force, revealing Clements to be a novelist every bit as good as Cornwell, Gregory or Iggulden.'
Ben Kane

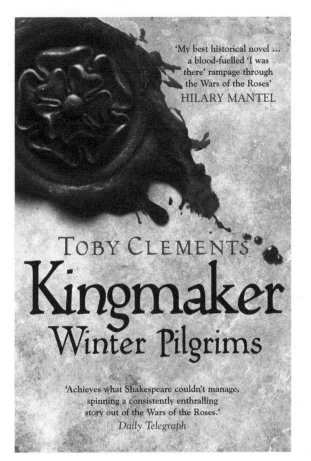

Book one of the
Kingmaker series

OUT NOW

'This is history in the raw: powerful, potent stuff, always real, but always gloriously unpredictable.'
Manda Scott

'An enthralling, honest and powerful re-imagining of the Wars of the Roses.'
HILARY MANTEL

Kingmaker
Broken Faith
TOBY CLEMENTS

Book two of the
Kingmaker series

OUT NOW

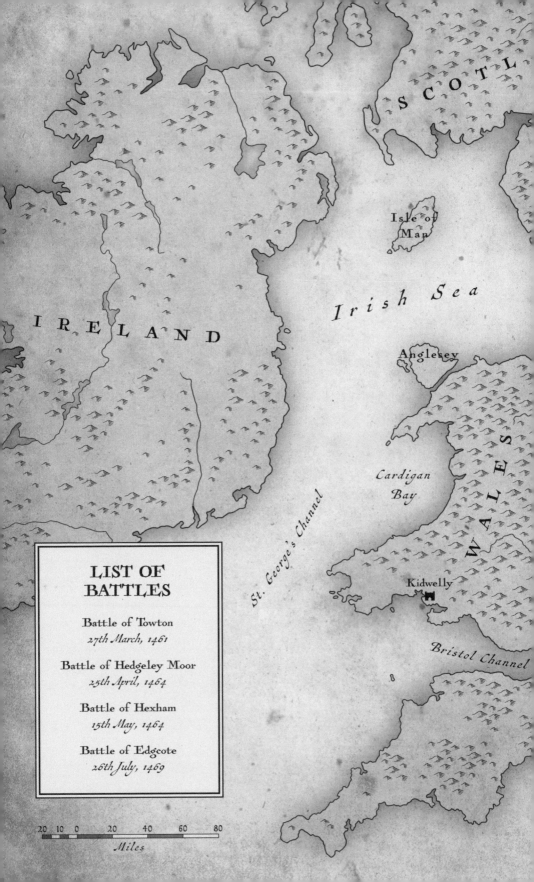

SCOTL

Isle of
Man

Irish Sea

Anglesey

I R E L A N D

Cardigan
Bay

W
A
L
E
S

St. George's Channel

Kidwelly

Bristol Channel

LIST OF BATTLES

Battle of Towton
27th March, 1461

Battle of Hedgeley Moor
25th April, 1464

Battle of Hexham
15th May, 1464

Battle of Edgcote
26th July, 1469

20 10 0   20   40   60   80

Miles